To Lou Costa —
Navyman and friend
Jim Bo[..]

The Real Thing and Other Tales

ISBN: 1-4505-5374-5
ISBN-13:978-1-4505-5374-2

LCCN: 2010915171

The Real Thing and Other Tales

James Baar

2011

Dedication

To Beverly, as always

Contents

I. Tales of Fog and Spin — 1

Alchemists of the New Age — 3
The Real Thing — 15
Making Mistakes — 37
The Smoothers — 53
Believe Me! — 65
Reality TV — 79
Bad News on the Turnpike — 97

II. Tales of Icy Water and Cold Turkey — 101

Criminal Poop — 103
The King and the Journalist — 115
Amazing Events — 129
Low Expectations — 143
Last Chance — 155
In the Gulf — 171

III. Tales of Signs and Portents — 185

Adventure in Archeology — 187
Email — 195
Walking the Labyrinth — 207
Exodus Revisited — 213
Angelic Tip-Off — 219
City of the Plain — 225
Art Search — 231
The Candidate — 243
Have a Look! — 255

IV. <u>Tales of Epiphanies</u>   **271**

Variations on a Theme   *273*
Downward Facing Dog   *287*
Teachable Moment Redux   *303*
Somewhere on the Elbe   *305*
Miracle at the Bridge   *329*
Cleansing the Sepulchre   *355*

Other Books by James Baar

<u>Fiction</u>

<u>Ultimate Severance</u>

<u>The Great Free Enterprise Gambit</u>

<u>Non-Fiction</u>

<u>Spinspeak II: The Dictionary of Language Pollution</u>

<u>The Careful Voter's Dictionary of Language Pollution</u>
<u>(Understanding</u>
<u>Willietalk and Other Spinspeak)</u>

<u>But Wait! There's More! (maybe)</u>
[coauthor: Donald E. Creamer]

<u>Polaris!</u> [coauthor: William E. Howard]

<u>Combat Missileman</u> [coauthor: William E. Howard]

<u>Spacecraft and Missiles of the World</u> [coauthor: William E. Howard]

All of the players in this mosaic of tales are creatures of imagination. Any resemblance to persons living or dead is coincidental although certainly is to be expected. The challenges they confront, of course, are painfully real.

Beyond the purple veil,
Behind the carmined screen,
Immersed in yellow fog,
God's Plan is clearly seen.

Beware! This is no jape.
The Word is plain to see.
But keener sight is needed
For the likes of you and me.

I.
Fog and Spin

Alchemists of the New Age

"It is very dangerous to play with reality.
       —John LeCarre, *The Secret Pilgrim*

THE GOOD GUYS

"You understand that I specialize in a very special brand of public relations: There are literally hundreds of people in this town who can make relatively acceptable silk purses out of sows' ears. But I'm the only one who knows how to convince people that manufacturing purses out of sows ears is the way to go.'

The voice belonged to G. Cameron Lightower, famously defrocked White House spinmeister and now one of Washington's pricier independent consultants. Cameron, his flabby expensively draped body and pasty face exuding his famed ersatz self-confidence, was finishing his standard stump speech for prospective clients. In this case, he was delivering it over mounds of iced shrimp at an intimate, rococo restaurant two blocks from the Capitol. His sole listener was a representative of the Republic of Greater Buhara.

"I understand perfectly," the representative, Ali Towanda, said, helping himself to another shrimp. "But, if I may suggest, do not use that example of the sow should you meet our Protector-for-Life, Marshal Mumdando. I, myself, take no offense because I am a graduate of the Harvard Business School. But, despite the teachings of Mohammed, Allah be praised, the Marshal and the people of Buhara regard the Great Pig of the Old Religion as a divine being. Unfortunately, those who take her name in vain often die disgustingly."

'Of course, of course" Cameron said. "I will keep that in mind when ordering dinner. But you do understand that what you are asking me to do, this critical project, is something that is almost impossible? The fees could be very high."

Ali smiled. He allowed that money was not a concern to the Marshall as long as the program succeeded; only performance was a concern.

"After all," he said, "we understand that most Americans know of Greater Buhara only through the specialized pages of the National Geographic Magazine. That is a difficulty. We are seeking $20 billion in aid to build factories and infrastructure. How would you propose that we sell the Administration and Congress on our true capabilities?"

Now Cameron smiled.

"You cant," he said. "That is why you need me. Selling the capabilities of Greater Buhara, no matter how skillfully packaged, would fail. Although I assure you that there are many who will tell you that they could pull it off. They are nothing but flacks and mountebanks. Guys hungry for a buck."

Cameron shrugged and his mastiff eyes saddened more than usual at the thought that such people could exist.

"And what would you do?" Ali asked.

"I assume that you, as a man of honor, will protect the proprietary nature of what I am about to disclose to you and you will protect my right to compensation," Cameron said.

"Of course," Ali said and sniffed.

"Of course,' Cameron said and sighed. "I always regret discussing money when dealing with matters of such international importance to us all. But it has to be mentioned, doesn't it? Well, I have given this great challenge of yours considerable study already and I find that you have three possibilities: national famine, newly-found oil reserves, or strategic military bases."

"None of those would seem to apply to Greater Buhara," Ali said. "Naturally, we have many poor but few really go hungry. We have no oil. And we have no sites for military bases that any sane person would call strategic. This is the problem today in Greater Buhara. We have so little. That is probably why the French gave it back to us so readily.'

Cameron winked and nodded mysteriously. 'You could have all of these things," he said, pronouncing each word as if the sentence were a mantra. "Famine is easy. There is no problem in producing for the TV crews on a nightly basis a few starving children covered with flies. It just might work, but frankly I think it has been overdone. I could produce two retired generals tomorrow who would leak reports on the strategic value of Buhara to certain Muslim Fundamentalist groups in the pay of certain Middle Eastern countries. That has real possibilities. But I don't like it as much as our third option. Think what will happen when we have two Japanese geologists discover evidence of huge unsuspected oil reserves in an extremely remote part of Buhara. Properly handled, that will be our best chance of success."

"But, Lightower, there is no oil."

"How do you know?' Cameron said, shaking his head as if in wonderment at such naiveté and chewing slowly the last of the shrimps. 'No one knows. Technical proving of great oil discoveries such as the ones we are sure to find in the all but inaccessible Buharan back country take time. Much will have to be done just to do that. And it will be in the strategic interest of the United States not to leave this for the Japanese so that those unfortunately tricky people can establish themselves in Central Africa. No, no, my friend, long before the oil question is settled, your aid will be there. Billions in aid. We can do no less. We must make sure that the good guys win."

Cameron sat back with a swaggering wriggle. Ali leaned forward: his brown eyes widening from sleepy slits for the first time, his voice confident.

"Lightower, normally I live by the ancient Code of Greater Buhara which forbids all alcoholic beverages except for fermented milk of the ibex, but I think a little wine is in order. We will drink to the good guys."

FRIDAY

Arthur Ballentine, Executive Vice President of Marketing, put into his attaché case the remaining few items in the top drawer of his desk and looked around the denuded office. The movers had already packed and taken away 14 crates of papers, books, pictures and useless memorabilia.

Also, this week, he had starred at three early retirement luncheons, two late afternoon parties and a farewell breakfast. Now it was truly time to leave.

Until today he still told himself it was all a great idea. He was 56. He was healthy. He had three grown children: two talking to him. He had a beautiful trophy third wife who was in her late 30's. He was in reasonable shape financially: Well, almost reasonable. And now it was time to play, as his wife, Gail, had said repeatedly since he told her that the Company was suggesting that he could best further its latest reengineering plans by leaving.

Arthur was very realistic in assessing the situation. The Company, like so many others, had had major problems for several years: its markets were being eaten by foreign and domestic competitors; its expenses, much too high; its R&D, slow and off target; it's shrinking profitability maintained only by financial legerdemain. This was the third cycle in five years of reassessment, reengineering and wholesale severing of heads. But why his head? Any fair observer would agree that a dozen other even more expensive and far less capable heads would have served as well if not better.

He had repeatedly dismissed that thought. This was a gift. He would be free to do many exciting things. As Gail said, he was free to play. He had earned it. However, so far, he couldn't think of anything he really wanted to do; certainly nothing that he thought would be very exciting. And, although he was told that he would get over it, he felt empty and betrayed.

Also, he knew what had to be done to fix the Company's current problems. Once the Company had been great. And he had been there. You were proud to be a part of it. You felt good coming to work. The shimmering idea of what the Company was and did was no myth: it was based on a world of magnificent accomplishment and the idea of that world made magnificent accomplishment possible. But, as always, mediocrity was the enemy of that world and growing, festering mediocrity had destroyed it. Surely that world needed to be restored, Its absence led to chaos

Maybe it still wasn't too late for him. He could talk to some of his friends on the Board. He could talk to the Chairman. He could talk to some of the top customers; some of the top institutional money managers. He knew that the Vice Chairman to whom he reported had done him in to save himself. And Arthur knew that that little jumped-up twerp could never save the Company. That was really what Arthur would like to do. That would be really exciting. And he would be perfect for the job.

Looking out the window, Arthur could see the Chairman's car parked in front of the building. If he walked down the hall, he probably could see the Chairman now: Lay out his ideas; talk candidly; change the universe forever. Isn't that the way great generals won battles in the last minutes of the last day?

Sweep the enemy from the board! Next scene: salute cannon booming; bells ringing; flags everywhere: Victory after all!

The phone in the middle of his naked desk rang.

"Arthur, tootsie, you're still there!" It was Gail's voice. "Arthur, we're going out to dinner."

"I was just leaving," Arthur said. "See you in a half hour."

He closed his briefcase and left. He could always make phone calls on Monday.

DAILY LOG

6:20 A.M.   Mark Juliani, 29-year old master of cyberspace and virtual reality, orders cranberry juice, English muffins lightly toasted, and coffee at Breakfast-Is-Us off Route 110 two miles from his Los Angeles office at Hypersoft.com, Inc., this year's NASDAQ honneypot.

6:40 AM.   After two requests, the waitress, a scabrous girl with unwashed hair and five rings in her nose, returns with his order: the English muffins are heavily charred. Mark asks to have the order redone. The waitress says: "This way they come, you know. Hey, you gotta problem?"

7:20 AM.   Mark parks his new racing green BMW in the Hypersoft.com Annex parking lot after being aced out of a closer parking space in a near collision by a programmer from Healthyland.com, last year's NASDAQ honeypot.

9:30 A.M.   Mark is working on his computer. Many layers into cyberspace, he hews the shape of Organa, a wonderful virtual world that he is designing for a new party game website, www.rapine.com. Organa is protected by infinite walls, a dragon and multiple multi-lingual codes. The rules are absolute. But security still needs work. Nearby at Redondo Beach an explosion that police later will say was of mysterious origin cuts off all power in southern Los Angeles. Mark's computer screen flashes and turns black.

10:45 A.M.   Mark comes out of a particularly bad meeting with customers and asks an administrative assistant wearing a skin-tight blue leather jump suit to bring the group fresh coffee, more doughnuts. "Kiss my Blackberry," she says. He makes the coffee and skips the doughnuts.

12:35 P.M.   Mark and a black colleague go to the company cafeteria for lunch. As he reaches for plastic silverware, a black accountant named Dennis cuts into the line and Mark says: "Like, there is a line here, you know." Dennis laughs and says with a wink: "What you got against us blacks?" And he stays in the line.

2:30 P.M.   Mark gets a call from an IRS agent who is auditing his taxes. "You're going to have to pull together your backup for the last three years," she says. "We have a lot of problems here with all of this income."

4:00 P.M.   An email letter tells Mark that he must call Human Resources regarding his health care insurance. When he does, someone named Juanita tells him that his Form 5432 covering his last three medical claims has been returned with a "rejected" stamp. He asks Juanita what he did that was incorrect. "How do I know this?" Juanita says.

5:15 P.M.   Electric power returns minutes before a cleaning crew made up of three Mexican cleaners and much equipment rushes into Mark's office and begins to vacuum and dust furiously but ineffectually. He tells the cleaners that he is trying to complete some important programming and asks them to come back, "You crazy," one of the cleaners says. "We gotta finish up to get outta here."

7:25 P.M.   Mark, replaying in his mind his most recent foray in cyberspace and the disappearance of 22 lines of code, edges his BMW into an inside lane at a stoplight and prepares to turn right on to the Freeway. Before he can start to turn, the BMW is rear-ended by a white six door Lincoln limousine. Mark whines an obscenity, gets out of his car in the almost viscous traffic and walks back to the Lincoln.

7:27 P.M.   "What the hell's the matter with you," he shouts at the driver through the closed purple-tinted window. "Are you stupid? I signaled. I was stopped." The window rolls down slowly and the driver, a man with a wispy beard and outsize silvered goggles, fires a large handgun twice into Mark's chest. As Mark sags to the street, he reaches out and grabs a heavy gold chain hanging around the driver's neck and the chain breaks. "The mother dissed me," the driver says to a fat bald dwarf sitting next to him and pulls away into the traffic. "And the creep busted my fuckin' chain."

CRUISE STOP

Normally, the Sovereign Queen didn't stop at St. Croix, but there had been a dockworkers strike at St. Maarten. St. Croix was the alternate port of call.

Most of the passengers signed up for a tour of St. George's Botanical Gardens and lunch at a large resort hotel not far from the cruise pier in Fredicksted. But Diana, on an impulse, took a taxi across the island to the town of Christiansted, the island's old Danish capital. She had been there ten years ago on a honeymoon trip in February with Jack Minott, her second husband. They had stayed at the Club Comanche, a romantically faded jumble of buildings and palm trees scattered on the harbor.

It had been an idyllic week: The tropical weather was perfect; they were an attractive couple; they visited decaying historic sugar plantations; they sat for hours drinking jumbo daiquiris at the Comanche bar in the shadow of a huge outrigger canoe; they mingled with the well-healed, well-oiled regulars and the charming island conmen; they talked seriously about never leaving. But they did. And they never returned. Instead, they were divorced two years later.

As such things go, the divorce was mutually cordial. Diana had just made vice president at one of the country's largest fast food companies. She was very bright; well liked by her bosses; worked 65 hour weeks; and always looked around for more to do. Jack Minott's career to a great extent had matched hers, but he was unlucky in his job choices: his last two companies went bankrupt. And, when he and Diana married, he found himself increasingly bored with his latest job and increasingly irritated by her passion for the fast food business. She found herself increasingly irritated by Jack.

In the final difficult months, Jack suggested several times that they both quit their jobs and move to the Caribbean. She laughed and demurred. He finally went anyway. She felt relieved.

Now she sat for a moment at 11:30 on a pleasantly warm tropical morning in a battered island taxi in the narrow street outside the Comanche deciding whether she wanted to go in after all. Normally she had no patience with such indecision and she quickly pushed it aside and got out of the car.

Nothing appeared to have changed as she walked up the outside stairs to the bar. So much so that she thought she would not be surprised to see Jack sitting there on one of the rickety stools. Therefore, when she did see him sitting there looking little changed in white shorts, a scruffy blue sports shirt and sandals, she felt and acted as if the meeting were a totally ordinary event.

"How about a daiquiri?" he said by way of greeting.

"Seems like a wonderful idea," she said. And they sat at the bar and talked as if they were picking up on a conversation that had ended a few hours earlier at breakfast on the Comanche porch. They had a second daiquiri and lunch.

Jack told her that when he returned to the island after their divorce he had taught business courses at the local university, but he had found that too frustrating: too many of the students had never learned much about writing and adding.

'So I got into a little real estate peddling for awhile like a lot of others around here," he said. 'But for the last few years I really have something going: You'll love it."

Jack dug a card out of his pocket and put it on the bar. It said: ORIGINAL CARIBBEAN ART, LTD. and there was a postoffice box number, a fax number, a website and a picture of a small voodoo statuette.

"Instant antiquities," Jack said. 'Very hard to get these days. We have to make them all here over in the rain forest. We use strictly aged local wood and shells. I have three great guys turning out the stuff. They're the real thing: direct from Port au Prince. Came here in an open boat. Illegals, of course."

He was living only ten minutes from the Comanche in a 150-year old rundown Danish plantation house: stone walls, stone floors, indifferent wiring, a sometime view of the sea when you cut down a little of the encroaching jungle. No new wife; just two big island dogs, Mandrake and Merlin. He wanted her to see the place if she had time.

When she left, they shook hands and he held her hand an extra moment.

"I wish you had time to see the house," he said. "You might come for a visit. You'd like the dogs and I could show you the instant antiques factory."

"Maybe," Diana said. "Maybe on another trip. I've always liked really good Haitian art."

BREAKFAST IN WASHINGTON

President Gomes liked the Green Room best. Many mornings before he dressed he would go down to the Green Room, ring the butler's bell and eat breakfast there; just as if, he always thought, the Mansion were his old family house.

No matter how bad things continued to get, the Green Room gave him a sense of well-being. The royal green silk wall covering, the ante-bellum furniture, the portrait of Benjamin Franklin, the bucolic landscapes: all fit his self-created history enshrined at the center of his being: the way things would have been back home if only God had paid more attention.

"Just the fresh fruit, poached eggs and wheat toast, Jonah," he said. "Dry."

He adjusted his Gucci dressing gown. It was an undeclared gift from either a prominent Vegas entertainer or the President of Yemen. He couldn't recall. Warily, he opened a newspaper. Very disturbing headlines again: Twisted! Biased!. If this continued, he knew what would happen. So many hated him now, Congress would vote. He could lose. He would go down. He couldn't bear that. He would resign first. Maybe he should now: Today.

He reminded himself once more that this was the best job he had ever had. Dumb, just plain dumb, to give up so good a deal. Never get another this good. If he could just be reassured that he was still "most liked" the way it had always been, he knew he would feel better. And then he heard them coming.

"Hey, there he is," a fat aged woman in shorts and a Burger King T-shirt shouted. She waved her knitting bag enigmatically over the velvet rope as she passed amid a group of touring citizens of the Republic.

"Hey, hello there," he said, smiling a big class presidential smile and waving back. "I'm Beau Gomes. Great- to-see-ya, y'heah."

He felt better immediately. The people loved him, after all.

"I'll never cut tail and run on them,' he told himself and pulled back his shoulders. "Why, I guess they'll just have to shoot me first."

The Real Thing

I paint things as they are. I don't comment.
—Henri Toulouse-Lautrec

We can evade reality, but we cannot evade the consequences of evading reality.
—Ayn Rand

The painting had been part of Jake Drayton's life as long as he could remember.

The first time that he recalled seeing it was in the early 50's when he was about four or five. He was hiding in the library of his grandfather's cavernous, darkened apartment in one of the better old buildings on Sutton Place in New York. It was only a few hours after his grandfather's funeral. Jake vaguely remembered the funeral Mass and a long trip in a limousine with his mother and father to a cemetery in Brooklyn. But he clearly remembered the painting because his father and his Aunt Winkie, a beautiful tall woman who always smelled wonderfully, had a fight about it.

John Wolfgang Drayton Sr., an international investment banker and sometime diplomat, had lived in the apartment for 50 years and filled it with objets d'art, books and scores of pictures purchased during his European business travels, particularly in Bavaria, where his mother was born. Two years ago his wife, Antonia, had died. Now he was dead. His sole heirs were his daughter, Wilhelmina, and his son, John W. Drayton Jr. The art collection was generally a mixed bag. But the painting in the library was always thought to have been a great find.

"I suppose you want that damned picture," Aunt Winkie said. "That's perfectly all right with me. I've always thought it was creepy. It was you and Daddy who went in for that kind of stuff. I'll be happy to take my share in cash."

They were standing in front of the painting: an alarmingly exaggerated, realistic depiction of Christ being crowned with thorns. Purportedly it was 15th Century German, one of the panels from an altar screen that once stood in the Great Chapel of the famous Benedictine Monastery in Melk. Jake had escaped the reception for funeral guests going on endlessly in the livingroom and diningroom to sprawl inconspicuously on the library floor and peruse lithographs in his grandfather's first edition in the original German of Kottenkamp's *The History of Chivalry and Armour*

"I certainly want it but I don't know if I can afford it," his father said. "It's supposed to be worth a lot. Maybe we could share it."

"The hell with that," Aunt Winkie said. "If you can't afford it, we sell it. I need the money."

"You don't really."

"John, dear, you know I always need money. And I assure you I don't want that weird, depressing picture in my home even on a part time basis and I won't pay for the insurance."

Much later Jake learned that his father after much haggling and some bitter words gave Aunt Winkle $100,000 for her share of the painting. Based on its appraised value at that time, it was a bargain. While Jake was growing up in their big house in Rye overlooking Long Island Sound, the painting was always prominently displayed. His father delighted in talking about it to guests.

"It was painted by Jorg Breu of Augsburg or possibly by someone in his atelier. It was one of the panels in Breu's great altar screen in the abbey church at Melk," his father would begin. "Some say the best of the panels. Look at those faces! The three evil hoodlums holding the crown of thorns on Christ's head with long poles while another varlet pounds the poles with a stool. They love what they are doing. And look at how much fun that fat moronic peasant is having making faces and sticking out his tongue. And Christ, with all the power of the universe at his command, just sits there looking pained and takes it. He's playing with them!"

Later, even after his father suffered major financial reverses, he refused to sell the painting despite several handsome offers including a very private one from a dealer representing a Saudi prince who collected scenes of Christian martyrdom. The painting continued to have a place of honor in his father's more modest residences, each progressively closer to town. It was in the last of these, an apartment in Larchmont, that he suffered what may have been a mortal reverse.

He was entertaining mostly old friends at a small cocktail party and, as usual, he lectured briefly on the painting.

"You know the entire abbey was neglected after the Reformation and many of the monks left the monastery," he said. "Then, in the Counter Reformation, when the abbey church was totally redecorated in that magnificent baroque style, the altar screen was taken down, stored, forgotten. It was during this period that the experts believe some of the panels were dispersed."

"Possible, but unlikely," a paunchy man with ferret eyes and a goatee mumbled and sniffed. He had been introduced to John earlier as Dr. Wilmot Richter, a curator at a major Chicago gallery and a weekend house guest brought along to the party.

"You question that they were not dispersed at that time?" John asked.

"Not at all. Some may have been," the sniffer said agreeably. "I question that this panel ever was one of them. I think more likely that this is a copy. A very good one, yes, but still a copy.'

"Ridiculous!" John said. "I have its unquestioned provenance. My father purchased the painting in Munich between the wars. He paid a sizeable price for it and I assure you it has been highly appraised ever since."

"These things happen," Dr. Richter said and shrugged. "But at least my eye tells me that it just isn't quite the real thing. I think our advanced technical tests would prove me correct. Not that that scientific mumbo-jumbo is everything, of course. Nothing beats the professional eye. If you ever want to pursue it, please feel free to contact me."

"I think I would rather drink a cup of hemlock," John said with a forced laugh in which he was joined by the group around him. "In fact, I suggest we could all use another drink. Not hemlock, of course. But maybe a stiff Scotch."

There were no further art lectures or discussions about the painting that evening, but when Dr. Richter departed he thanked John for his hospitality and, despite John's polite but cool response, presented him with his card.

"If ever I can be of service," Dr. Richter said. And he sniffed. .

"Thank you so much," John responded in a tone that clearly told him to go to the devil,

No one would ever know how deeply Dr. Richter's supercilious comments had wounded John: he was practiced at burying mental pain under a stoic quip. But it was only a month later that his physician told him that he was dying of a rare form of cancer. Possibly, he could expect to live another year, possibly he would not live much beyond his 75th birthday the following spring. And within another month the physical pain began, a pain that would surprise him and that he found increasingly difficult to hide.

When he discussed the devastating prognosis with his lawyer and reviewed his will, they determined that his estate with the exception of the altar painting would not exceed a half million dollars. Only five years previously the painting was appraised for just over two million dollars. If that appraisal held or, as was more than likely, increased, it would mean that the painting would have to be sold to pay more than one million dollars in death taxes. Jake Drayton, John's sole heir, was a 46-year old college professor who lived very comfortably by adopting the convenient habit of his class and generation: he always spent beyond his means.

Despite some success in the souks of academe, Jake had generally been a disappointment to his father. The problem was that for the most part John Wolfgang Drayton III, who fervently called himself Jake to his father's annoyance, adopted the accepted wisdom of so many in the inappropriately-named Boomer Generation: the protected children of well-to-do parents had determined to give them what was called the good life which was viewed by the ungrateful recipients as a natural birthright.

Armed with more comforts than any Renaissance princeling, Jake became a card-carrying player in the 60's youth revolution against everything that made it possible for his generation to participate in it. He consistently made all of the relevant bad choices. However, some lucky bit of genetic code always caused him to hedge sufficiently to save himself from total destruction. Therefore, he had the thoroughly enjoyable experience of marching in protest of the Viet Nam War, capitalism, his hopelessly retrograde parents and America; but he perpetrated little serious damage to persons or property and, accordingly, stayed out of jail. He smoked marijuana and engaged in some sordid sexual exploits, but he avoided the rot of chemical substances, cocaine and numerous nasty social diseases. He dodged military service by attending graduate school and obtaining a doctorate in history, but he avoided the ignominy and illegality of hiding in Canada. His first year as a young instructor he lived openly off campus with one of his students, a pretty, dark-haired young woman named Delores Sanchez. She was devoted to smoking pot and leading protest marches; talked romantically of revolutionary cells back home in the San Francisco Bay Area; and boasted to her classmates about her abortion plans when she became pregnant. But, when that biological event predictably occurred because of boredom with precautions, Jake stubbornly opposed an abortion and insisted on marriage. The wedding ceremony, which his parents avoided by taking an important business trip to Cap d'Antibes, was conducted in a meadow.

As his father often put it later, Jake enjoyed the safety and comforts of campus life so much that he decided to remain there forever rather than sally forth into the wicked and risky world that financed the campuses. There Jake continued to criticize that world and carp cynically about its habitués through writing much flawed, deconstructionist history. Naturally, in day-to-day conversation, he joined his chosen companions and associates in dismissing as pabulum for peasants all established religion; always voicing support for Democratic liberals who verbally bled for the preferably distant downtrodden, and strongly favoring freedom of speech solely for his circle and those who agreed with its wisdom.

But, for all that, he was John W. Drayton's only son and the eventual progenitor of two beautiful granddaughters. Also, John, as religiously faithful as his father had been, believed deeply in forgiveness of sin and redemption. With age, he found increasingly irrelevant Jake's chosen lifestyle, tattered political ideas and self-justifying grudges. Accordingly, John wanted in his remaining time on earth to do something very important for his son. He wanted to make a final effort to free him of secular mortal error and evil. The instrument for accomplishing this would be to pass to him as a powerful living fingerpost the "Crown of Thorns" masterpiece that he had received from his father. To do this successfully, the painting had to be unencumbered of government taxes.

John had dismissed as academic idiocy the contention of Dr. Richter that the "Crown of Thorns" was probably nothing more than a good copy. But now John cunningly chose to use Dr. Richter to achieve different ends. Therefore, he wrote to ask if Dr. Richter still had a negative judgment of the validity of the painting and what might be involved in testing that judgment further. John expressed an interest in putting the painting on the market.

Dr. Richter replied every bit as arrogantly as John had expected:

Drayton:

Based on my long experience and expertise in the study of medieval and Renaissance art, I have little if any doubt that the painting is not authentic.

To cite just one problem, Breu almost always used recognizable figures from Dürer. I can recall none that match the figures in your picture. Also, I would question some of the blue pigment as too modern. And, if memory serves, the crackle from aging is suspicious.

Most important, although admittedly the subjective opinion of a scholar, the feel of the picture is simply wrong. It is too much of a cartoon and lacks the humanity of Breu. My assumption is that this is a copy of the original which is still somewhere at the abbey or has been lost

Obviously, to confirm my opinion and obtain the absolute judgment needed for sales purposes these days, there is an array of technical tests that would have to be made. As I am sure you are aware, these would not be without significant cost—possibly more than $10,000. I suggest that would be an unnecessary expenditure in view of my initial judgment since the cost would far exceed the actual yield of the picture as a copy on the market. However, if you should wish to proceed, I am at your service.

Most sincerely,

Wilmot Richter, PhD

John took the letter immediately to his lawyer and his accountant. They, in turn, used it to establish an appraised value of eight to ten thousand dollars for the 'Crown of Thorns." When John W. Drayton Jr. died four months later the painting was included among his household furnishings along with his books and some rather good late 19th Century Gorham silver. The entire estate was valued at approximately 475 thousand dollars—well below the tax line. Except for some small charitable donations and a bronze double-headed Hapsburg eagle that John Jr. purchased for cigarettes and rations in Salzburg after helping to liberate the city in 1945, everything went to Jake and Jake's daughters. The eagle went to John's confessor who had much admired it. There also was a personal letter.

My dear John,

By the time you receive this letter, I am confident that I will already be well on the way to marvelous adventures beyond the world.

You and I have not, as the saying goes, always sung from the same sheet of music. I must say with candor, and I know that I must be candid at this time, I often loathed and felt deeply wounded and ashamed, at things that you said and did. I longed for you to achieve merit and honor But that longing ache did not spring from ego, as you might say; rather from love. For I know that the chaff of this world will be gathered and burned. And I fear for you.

It is that love and fear that has driven me to make certain that I can put safely and totally unencumbered into your hands my most valuable possession: the "Crown of Thorns" painting. It goes to you with hope. You will be told that its authenticity has been seriously questioned, that it is not the real thing but at best a reasonably good fake. That may indeed be true. But, whether painted in the early 1500's by Jorg Breu or in the late 19th Century by a skilled copyist, one look at the painting tells you that it is very much the real thing. Only an artist whose brush was informed by the hand of God could have painted it.

Your grandfather and then I myself have had our faith strengthened throughout much of our lives by this painting and the truth that it imparts. Many others have told me the same thing. Now that the painting is yours, I urge you to keep it close to you. It will continually refresh you and renew you. It will bring you close to God who always is ready to heal the contrite. No sin that you may have committed, no honorable act that you may have failed to perform, cannot be remitted if you have faith. Therefore, I commit the painting to your care as a perpetual benefice.

We shall not see each other again in the life of the world, but I look forward to seeing you in the future on the roads and in the many mansions where I am sure I will travel.

      Your loving father,

      John Wolfgang Drayton, Jr.

"So it isn't even worth a decent goddam Picasso sketch!"

The comment came from Jake's wife, Dolores, as they sat in the open beamed living area of their suburban row house eight blocks from the University. Jake and Dolores along with their two teenage daughters were eating take-out vitello parmigiano accompanied by a medium priced California Pinot Grigio. Jake had been giving his wife an edited version of his meeting that afternoon with his father's lawyer.

"Not exactly," Jake said. "It could be worth that much."

"And I suppose there are plenty of strings on the rest of the estate," Dolores said, finishing her third glass of wine.

"Not really," Jake said. "Most of it goes to set up college trusts for the girls. I get all of his household furnishings and a lump sum of $50,000

"I just don't understand it," Dolores said for about the tenth time although there was little that she did not understand about money and its absence. "What happened to all the goddam money?"

"He lived on it," Jake said, disgustedly. "What did you expect?"

When the painting arrived, they had a fight over where to hang it. Dolores hated its religiosity, regarded it as a public embarrassment and opposed hanging it at all. Jake, still feeling a mixture of righteous annoyance and some twinges of unrest from his father's last letter, a document he had not shared with Dolores, suggested hanging the painting in the hail outside of his cramped second floor study. In the end, no decision was made. Instead, they left it wrapped and put it in a small attic storeroom reached by a pull-down ladder.

Jake became totally absorbed in the following weeks in the publishing of his new book, *The Raping of Mexico: A Biography of President James K. Polk.* This was Jake's third major book. His first, *Origin of the Cold War: The Victimization of the Soviet Union,* was a critical success, particularly among hard-core left-leaning reviewers. His second major book, *War Criminals in Washington,* was also a critical success among liberal reviewers who support Third World governments regardless of their nature. But neither of these books sold well. Jake's publisher, Realbooks, Inc., an American subsidiary of a large French house, believed that *The Raping of Mexico* could become at least a minor best-seller.

"We have a lot running our way," Mildred Fitzbauer, PR director of Realbooks, told Jake. "Our timing is perfect with the illegal immigration issue coming to a boil. The Hispanic market should love it. And, if right wing rednecks attack you, and I certainly hope they do, we should get plenty of broadcast talk-time and ink.'

"I'm in hopes that the book will be seen as an important building block for my special viewpoint and scholarship,' Jake said.

"Sure, that, too," Mildred said. "That's automatic."

During the next six months, Jake toured the country, speaking at colleges and universities, appearing at university-town bookstores, occasionally appearing on local talk shows. Generally, it worked: boomer liberals praised the book; Mildred scored some positive reviews in the national media; sales were much better than in the past. Jake's biggest success came the day he told a talk show host in Minneapolis that "no Mexican was really an illegal immigrant because they were merely returning to Occupied Mexico." AP picked up the soundbite and a number of cable news networks carried the story that evening: three approvingly, one scathingly.

By the time that Jake returned home to resume his full-time teaching schedule, he clearly had advanced into that faculty tier where the happily tenured spent more time on committees, outside speaking engagements and international conferences than on instruction of the young. Graduate students and other lesser beings handled such scut work. It was all very fulfilling. But it also called for improvement in their lifestyle as Delores told him on numerous occasions: a larger house, a new car, more clothes for her and the girls, possibly a vacation home in Tuscany, nothing really out of line, Dolores insisted, for someone of Jake's enhanced stature.

Clearly, the sale of five or even ten thousand more books and some outside speaking engagements would not do it. Jake needed a new source of money.

As Jake's economic frustration mounted, Dolores, who now applied the same ingenious logic to her present objectives that she once applied to radical causes, took to stating that Jake's father had cheated him of his rightful inheritance and that possibly they should invade their daughters' educational trust. Jake did not like the suggestion. But, as a peace gesture, he agreed to discuss what options he might have if any with his father's lawyer, Talcott Goodman.

"You have no grounds to invade," Talcott told him disapprovingly when they met. "You could only do it in case of dire medical need or a similar emergency."

"How about borrowing against it?' Jake asked. "Just a little."

"Not even a little," Talcott said. But..."

Talcott paused and stared at his desk. Although he had not read it, he was aware of the general content of John W. Drayton's last letter to his son.

"But, what," Jake said rather petulantly. He hated all lawyers and their evasions and euphemisms and meaningful pauses.

"Well, you might possibly have another major asset, you know. The "Crown of Thorns" painting could be worth a lot of money and, even if you didn't wish to part with it, as I assume you do not. you might borrow against that."

"I thought it was a fake. That's what my father said.

"Not exactly. An art expert from Chicago said it was a fake and he thought so highly of his professional opinion that he put it in writing. Your father, who was an astute but unlucky financier and who castigated the government for high taxes, waste and corruption his entire life, merely accepted the judgment. As a result, there were no death taxes—taxes which he considered confiscatory anyway. I am sure avoiding them gave him some small pleasure in his final days."

"You really think that painting may be an original then, not a copy?" Jake asked.

"Who knows?" Talcott said. "Art experts have been proven wrong. Very wrong. And I know that your father under the circumstances of his illness never had any forensic tests made on the painting or obtained a second opinion. Or, I should say, of course, he never had time to do so."

Jake had the time and the motive. He immediately contacted Waterstone's International, Ltd., a premier auction house and art dealer. He personally drove to New York and placed the painting in their hands without comment other than to give them Dr. Rector's letter and the written provenance that his grandfather had obtained in Germany when he purchased the painting. For the last 80 years, the painting had been in the possession of the Drayton family.

Waterstone's placed the painting in the hands of Palmer-Hutton, one of the world's leading art research and conservation laboratories. Two months later Palmer-Hutton held a confidential conversation with Waterstone's followed by the submission of a forty-page report. Waterstone's, in turn, contacted Jake and proposed a meeting in New York about what it called "a matter of great importance."

The meeting took place in the Waterstone's Customer Room, an elaborate two-story Renaissance chamber. Old Masters and tapestries covered the walls. A heavy oak table with high-backed, golden velvet-covered chairs filled the center of the room. Livy Waterstone, himself, a tall elegant man with white hair neatly parted in the middle, sat at one end of the table. His chief curator, Dr. Morris Hummel, a cadaverous gnome with a thin white mustache and half-glasses, sat at his left. Waterstone invited Jake to sit at his right. The "Crown of Thorns" rested on an easel at the opposite end of the table. A baby spot in the ceiling lighted the painting so that it glowed.

"We have excellent news," Waterstone began and patted a bound report in front of him. "Excellent, excellent news."

Dr. Hummel allowed himself a small, smug smile. Then, Waterstone asked Dr. Hummel to read highlights from the report.

"Comparative microscopy tests show that the panel on which the painting was created is made of wood common to one of the royal forests where the Babbennbergs hunted wild boar," Hummel mumbled rapidly without inflection. "The forest was destroyed in the 16th Century during the Wars of Religion and never replanted. Carbon dating tests show the wood is at least 500 years old. Other tests with our electronic nondispersive analyzer show that the paint is unquestionably of the period. No zinc in the browns; no cadmium in the red. The crackle is absolutely authentic—no late cuttings into the varnish, no newly applied grime. Except for a small touch-up of one of the torturer's hands clearly dating before the 17th Century, there is no overpainting. Numerous comparative X-rays show the underpainting to be most certainly the brush work of Breu. The conclusion of the technical research: there are no facts casting doubt on the painting's authenticity; there are numerous facts supporting it."

Dr. Hummel looked up at Jake and offered another small, smug smile.

"We began, of course, with the most important technical instrument: the professional eye. Based on my own extensive study of Breu and the Danubian School, this painting unquestionably gave me that feel of authenticity for which there is no substitute. Now, in view of that judgment, combined with the overwhelming forensic research before us today, our team of independent scholars has come to the obvious conclusion: this painting indeed is an original Breu."

Jake was happily stunned. At best, he had hoped to be able to fudge the question of authenticity and thereby make the painting saleable to the art world's risk takers or less exacting dealers. But this seemed to be a complete reversal.

"What about the opinion of Dr. Rector?" he asked, feeling that he had to try to test what he had heard. "How does that fit."

"It doesn't,' Dr. Hummel said. "He was obviously in error."

Waterstone assumed command of the meeting and cut off further discussion.

"You are to be congratulated, Mr. Drayton, on your immense good fortune," he said. "Be assured Waterstone's will handle everything for you in the most discreet fashion. We shall quietly explore the possibility of private sale and weigh with you the advantages of auction. The matter will have my personal attention."

"Yes, of course, I shall want to move forward," Jake said. "Have you any idea at this time as to what the painting might sell for?"

"Very hard to be definitive until we have tested the waters now that we are assured that this is the real thing," Waterstone said. "A Breu of this quality has not come on the market in some time. But prices of the 16th Century Germans have been rising sharply, I am happy to report. I can at least say that we are quite optimistic, aren't we, Morris."

"Yes, yes indeed" Dr. Hummel said and allowed himself another small, smug smile.

As the sale turned out, Livy Waterstone's optimism was well founded. When the painting was offered privately and very discreetly, buyers were not turned away at the mention of sums ranging upward to nearly two million dollars. At that point, Waterstone recommend that rather than engage in "Byzantine haggling for limited reward," the final price could be "handsomely enhanced" by offering the painting rather less discreetly at auction. And the enhancement was handsome: The "Crown of Thorns" was knocked down to an anonymous bidder for three and a half million dollars.

Jake was overjoyed. Dolores was overjoyed. Waterstone was, of course, pleased to have been of service. The *Times* noted the sale in a small article that featured several American school non-representational works that sold for much more. Dr. Richter wrote a venomous letter to *Art News,* but the editors declined to run it on advice of libel counsel.

In the next few months, the Draytons found many ways to utilize their new riches: They moved to one of the large, older Victorian houses close to the original campus quadrangle; Jake purchased a Volvo racing green convertible; Dolores purchased a light blue Volvo station wagon; they became patrons of the Civic Chorale for Ancient Music, and they purchased and began modernization in Fiesole of a crumbling 16th Century stone house, much overpriced because of its distant view of Florence.

It was shortly after this period that Jake met the Collonna brothers, early dropouts from the university's Turing School of Computer Sciences and cyberspace entrepreneurs who had founded a company called earlsgeneralstore.com. Earl Collonna, who was 28, served as president and CEO. His 26-year-old brother, Tucker, was Chief Technologist. The earlsgeneralstore.com website featured Earl, himself, wearing granny glasses, a straw boater, and garters on the sleeves of a candy-striped shirt. He personally offered millions of Internet shoppers knock-off designer clothes, knock-off designer leather and sporting goods, knock-off gourmet groceries and low-cost generic drugs from Mexico. Earlsgeneralstore.com had yet to earn a dime, but Wall Street loved the Collonnas: stock in earlsgeneralstore.com had gone from 20 cents to 70 dollars before it split and doubled again. The tide was rising rapidly. Very big money flowed.

Jake was introduced to the Collonna brothers by an investment banker, H. Mitchell Butterworth, a member of the University Board of Trustees and famous for favoring select University officers and tenured faculty members with inside market tips. Initially, the meeting was not totally reassuring. The Collonnas were wearing torn warm-up suits.

Their high-rise offices were furnished with computers, mazes of tangled wire, used dirty take-out food cartons and apparently repossessed metal desks. But later Butterworth suggested to Jake that the Collonna brothers were about to announce a supplementary issue of earlsgeneralstore.com stock and that it was not too late to "climb aboard" by buying into Butterworth's latest technology investment fund, DotTech IV. That way, Butterworth explained, Jake would not only become a major investor in earlsgeneralstore.com but would spread any risk across a number of other high performance technology companies in the Butterworth portfolio: Cheapseats.com, for example.

Jake agreed. And, during the next year as the bull stock market continued upward, he continued to invest larger sums in DotTech IV; an even newer technology investment fund, DotTechV, and directly in the ever soaring stock of earlsgeneralstore.com. Jake was made euphoric by his financial success. Everything he touched went up. How he wished he could show his father his dazzling triumphs in the financial world: far greater than his father achieved in his best days; far greater even than his grandfather if one ignored inflation. In less than two years, he had turned a few million real dollars into an enormous fortune on paper. Jake's confidence in his financial prowess was so complete that when the Technology Bubble suffered an initial 26 percent downdraft in April that year, he never wavered.

"Perfectly normal correction," bulls insisted. "This is a buying opportunity."

Jake agreed and invested on margin. That positioned him nicely to be swamped in the final collapse that began in October. By the end of the following February, earlsgeneralstore.com had filed for bankruptcy and was under investigation for what the Securities & Exchange Commission called "wishful accounting." All Butterworth funds also were under water. Jake found himself with a portfolio of single digit stocks, large mortgages on two houses and two leased Volvos. The mortgages and the leases had been taken out to leverage his mounting profits as the market neared its most intoxicating highs.

Nor was that the only dispiriting news in the ensuing weeks. He broke his car leases, but because of high penalties he could not afford to buy back the Volvo convertible and could only refinance Dolores' station wagon. He renewed his contract with his speech agency, but he was advised that, because he had allowed an hiatus in engagements, it would take at least six months to refill a schedule for him and that honorariums because of the bad economy would be lower. He discussed as quietly as possible with real estate agents selling his new house as a way of reducing large monthly mortgage payments, but he was told that because of a lackluster housing market he could not hope to break even on repayment of his outstanding loan. Finally, when he reluctantly wrote to Dolores in Tuscany where she and their daughters were spending a lengthy spring vacation and told her that she would have to stop modernization of the Fiesole house at least for the present, her response pushed him into excessive drinking and a state of depression that lasted a week.

Dear Jake:

What a wonderful time the girls and I are having in Fiesole!

Last week we just chucked everything and went into Firenze to do museums. We were so lucky to have Enrico, our architect, join us as our personal guide. Of course, we had been to the Uffizi twice before, but when Enrico took us around the galleries it was as if we had never seen anything. He really is a genius.

On Monday Francesca put up a beautiful picnic for us in two big wicker baskets and we visited the Roman ruins here. Luckily, Enrico again was able to get away from superintending the workmen at our wonderful little house and join us. The girls were enchanted. Enrico was so knowledgeable about the Etruscans and the Romans and he explains things so well.

Last night I was invited to dinner at Count Bobolis. I am sure you remember him from last summer. He certainly remembers you and hopes to see you soon. Dinner was delightful and the cucina, of course, was meravigliosa! So was the conversazione! There were just six of us: Il conte and la contessa, Professore Giacomo Marti (such a brilliant man, I know you will like him) and his wife (something of a drag) and Enrico, who turns out to be the Count's nephew.

I was so sad to hear about your financial problems, but surely they can't be so awful that you can't turn them around. Jake, I have great confidence in you when it comes to money matters. We could, of course, move more slowly for awhile on the house, but Enrico says that will just cost us a lot more in the end.

The house already looks so beautiful and it is only half done. I am sure you will be very pleased.

The girls join in sending molti kisses,

Dolores

Jake stayed at home with curtains and shades drawn. When Fatima, the cleaning woman, arrived, he told her to take an unpaid vacation for a few days. Alone for the rest of the week he began drinking a lot of wine, then he switched to a case of half-gallon plastic bottles of bargain vodka. Occasionally he opened a can of SpaghettiOs; then he began to go through a six-pack of canned cream of asparagus soup.

He tried to read but failed. He couldn't write. Most of the time, he sat in his darkened study, a commodious room on the first floor of the new house in which he now took no pleasure. He sat staring at his messy desk, feeling numb and empty, trying to figure out what kind of demons seemed to be feasting on him. Or, he would prowl the house, opening drawers and going through bits and pieces of the accumulated artifacts of his life. One afternoon his random searching led him into the attic where he spent hours looking through cartons of books and papers and a mélange of decaying memorabilia. In one carton, he found a worn leather double frame with two automobile pictures. One was a picture of an elegant Packard Twin Six sedan parked on a summer day in front of his grandfather's Sutton Place apartment house. His grandfather was standing at the rear door which was being held open by the chauffeur. The picture was dated 1916, the year before America entered World War I. The other picture was of a white La Salle convertible at the front door of the Westchester Country Club. The top was down and his father in a tennis sweater was at the wheel. It was dated 1940, a year before the Japanese attacked Pearl Harbor and his father enlisted in the Army the day after Christmas.

Jake went back to his study and set the leather frame on his desk next to the remains of a half-gallon plastic bottle of vodka. He was at a fingerpost. There in the miasmic gloom of late afternoon, he thought he heard both of those men in the pictures saying to him: *Remember the painting! Look at the expression on Christ's face. Pray, Jake, pray! Miserere mei peccatoris. Orémus!* But he didn't. He couldn't. The picture was gone. And no prayers came. Instead he finished the vodka and fell asleep in his clothes on the study couch.

Jake was awakened Monday morning by Fatima. She was cleaning the house. He felt too ill to tell her to go away again. Instead, he took a shower, shaved away a four-day beard and allowed Fatima at her suggestion to make some dry toast and tea for him. By midafternoon, when he returned to his now orderly and cleaned study, his saving resilience had taken command. He was hungry. He ordered the delivery of an enormous pizza with double cheese and, after eating all of it, collapsed on his bed before sunset.

The following morning, after a night of deep sleep, Jake began telling himself that his bad turn of fortune was only what he should have expected from what astute history scholars such as him had long ago recognized as the flawed underpinning of American society. In the end, it had ruined his father. It was continuing to hollow out the futile lives of millions of Americans. However, it would not destroy him. He and other intellectuals like him would continue to fight what they knew was the good fight. They would continue to point out where America had gone wrong and continued to go wrong. They would point the way to a better future.

He spent the entire morning in his study reviewing the outline for his new book which he had put aside for more than a year. The working title had been: *America: the Crippled Crusade*. Now he changed it to *America: Land of Perfidy*. Shortly before noon he looked out of the window at a flood of early April sunshine: a marvelous day. He decided to walk over to the Faculty Club for lunch in the Club Lounge, a handsome Edwardian hall where only senior faculty ate from a menu heavily endowed by long dead alumni. The daily special was always a particular bargain and much favored.

Jake felt better than he had in months as he cut across the University quadrangle. Huge financial losses, importunate greedy creditors, the half-finished house in Tuscany, Dolores and her genius Italian architect—all seemed to vaporize into that unsatisfactory world that he understood so well; a terrible, superficial world that he would now in his books and lectures resume full time dissecting and criticizing for its own good.

Even the disastrous futility of the sale of the "Crown of Thorns" painting did not bother him: in fact, he saw how he could put it to some helpful use. Waterstone's clipping service earlier in the year had sent him an article and photo of the painting, reporting in the caption that an unidentified benefactor had returned it as a gift to its original home among the friars at the Benedictine Abbey at Melk. Jake had noticed the blurry black and white newspaper photo still in a pile of papers on his desk that morning and he formed a tentative plan to provide material to various art historians to ensure mention of his family and himself in future art histories of the period.

Contentedly he began thinking again about his new book as he turned from the quadrangle into the University Green, a large sweep of grass and geometric beds of new plantings that as he watched were being trampled into a muddy wasteland by a mob of more than a hundred shouting students. The protestors, many with silver rings and studs implanted in their lips, tongues and eyebrows, carried a potpourri of homemade signs that said:

LOVE CARIBOU NOT OIL

STAMP OUT GLOBALISM

FEED THE HOMELESS

WOMYN CHOOSE

WAGE PEACE

MUSLEMS ARE OUR BROTHERS

CURE AIDS NOW

MISSILE DEFENSE SUCKS

Student leaders with bullhorns and lacrosse sticks held high urged the screaming mob onward toward the Administration Building.

Jake joined several colleagues who were watching from the safety of the columned porch in front of the classical revival doors at the top of the Faculty Club steps.

"Great to see this kind of spirit," said Professor T. Lester Hobart, a short, fat sociologist with blonde tufts of hair sprouting randomly from his balding scalp. "These kids are really listening to us. Gives you faith in the future."

"Makes you wish you were a student again," said Dr. Rudy Rose, a tweedy, body-builder Egyptologist wearing a designer leather vest, heavy boots and a two-pound gold chronograph.

"It's the real world," said Dr. Haji Zahir, a tall, saturnine-looking professor of Eastern Civilization Studies.

"It's the real thing," Jake said. "Let's grab a table before the special is all gone."

Making Mistakes

The chessboard is the world. The player on the other side is hidden from us-—he never overlooks a mistake or makes the smallest allowance for ignorance.
          —T.H. Huxley, English scientist

When I make a mistake, it's a beaut.
          —Fiorello H. LaGuardia, Mayor of New York

No one has accused us of any wrongdoing. Mistakes were made.
          —William J. Clinton, U.S. President

That Saturday night in the City three bad things happened.

First, Cincinnatus Irving, chief pathologist at St. Benedict's Hospital and discoverer of a cure for Egbert's Syndrome, fell down a flight of service stairs at the World Center Hotel. He was looking for a guest lavatory after a dinner party.

Second, three young hoodlums, while joyriding in a stolen red SUV, picked up at gunpoint two students, Tony and Babs, on their way home from a high school dance. The hoodlums drove Tony and Babs to a closed miniature golf course called the Happy Pirate. There they stole 32 dollars from them, took their gold class rings and shot them both in the back of their heads as they knelt in the Happy Pirate desert island sand trap.

Third, Dorothy Schneider, a sophomore at the University, shared a full fifth of gin with her roommate while they watched an MTV movie in their dorm. Then Dorothy went to look for her boyfriend at the nearby Chi Sigma fraternity house. She failed to find him but did find more gin and another young man whom she knew only as Martin the Lacrosse Player. The following morning about 5 o'clock she awoke in Martin the Lacrosse Player's bed along with Martin, dressed while he continued to sleep and returned to her dorm. She remembered nothing about the last 12 hours after having one more final drink and throwing up while Martin gently held her quite pretty blonde head over a wastebasket.

Dr. Cincinnatus Irving lay sprawled upside down on his back on the bottom steps of the stairwell for more than a half hour before he was discovered by Bartolomeo, a dishwasher on a smoke break. Bartolomeo, determining that Dr. Irving was unconscious, removed the doctor's wallet from his open suit coat. After his smoke break, Bartolomeo, who spoke almost no English, told his supervisor a confused story about finding *un chardo borracho* (drunk nigger) sleeping at the bottom of a stairwell and identified the wrong stairwell.

A half-hearted search was made. When no one was found, it was assumed that the drunk had recovered sufficiently to go home. The dishwashing crew left for the night.

The early morning cleaning crew found Dr. Irving still at the foot of the stairwell. This time an ambulance was called and the unconscious, still unidentified man was taken to St. Benedict's Emergency Center. There a medical team composed primarily of young foreign interns worked on him along with the victims of two shootings, a woman much axed by her boyfriend, four children with third degree burns from an oil burner explosion and the usual half dozen or so cases of heart attack or stroke. When Dr. Irving was finally recognized by a nurse as the hospital's chief pathologist, a number of the City's leading neurologists and the hospital's chief surgeon were called. They worked on him for several more hours. But nothing helped. It was too late. Dr. Irving died shortly before breakfast of internal brain hemorrhaging, severe neural damage and related complications.

Francis "Juicy" Pelletier, Pietro "Petey' Gaucho and Douglas "Loverboy" Jukes had a night of fun and thrills after leaving the Happy Pirate miniature golf course. They bought a case of beer which they consumed while playing dodge 'em on the Interstate. They drove to the town park where they harassed several couples parked there on a secluded byway. They drove downtown to the all-night King's Feast Diner where they noisily ate chili dogs and ducked out without paying. And, as they cruised empty streets, they spotted two nurses in a convertible heading home from work. With Juicy at the wheel and Petey and Loverboy hanging out of the SUV's windows shouting obscenities, they followed the nurses at close range with such dedication that they failed to notice where they were going until the convertible stopped in front of police headquarters.

Juicy gunned the SUV around the convertible, raced down the avenue and swerved at high speed around a corner. The top-heavy SUV skidded wildly to the left and crashed into the multi-color flashing show window of Blume's Video-CD Bazaar. All three hoodlums, bleeding from multiple cuts, crawled from the store window and ran in different directions. Police easily followed the trails of splattered blood. Within an hour, Juicy, Petey and Loverboy were in a holding cell.

Dorothy had a terrible hangover. Despite taking a lengthy shower and being able to keep down her breakfast, she still felt brain dead and moved automatically and numbly through the early morning hours. Only later that morning, just after her women's studies course called "Exploring the 21st Century Womb" and before her deconstructionist history course called "Myths of the American Revolution," did she remember a smattering of details of the previous night. The most significant: a round of rather ineffectual sexual foreplay before she totally passed out.

This foggy memory during the next several days increasingly troubled her. She didn't like the idea that she could not remember specifically what had transpired. She didn't like the idea that Martin Whatever-his-name had not contacted her. She didn't like the very likely possibility that Martin regarded the entire incident as an hilarious anecdote to be related to his buddies and undoubtedly improved upon with each telling.

It was this last highly irritating thought that drove Dorothy by midweek to a decision: she concluded that she clearly had been raped. Moreover, to protect herself from being the butt of vicious male jokes, she had to report the incident to the University Counseling Office. This was a serious step. But, when she reviewed it with her roommate and three other female friends, they all told her firmly and enthusiastically that she had no choice. That afternoon she went to the Women's Issues Counseling Office and had a long understanding chat with Ms. Joanna Tobias, chief counselor.

Representatives of the medical world could unquestionably be expected to mourn the passing of Dr. Cincinnatus Irving. But, because Dr. Irving was a divorced man of 62 who lived with an ill and aging sister and did not speak to his ne'er-do-well son and only child, Wilmot, there was no knowledgeable relation readily available to make funeral arrangements and properly inform the media and the medical world.

The task, therefore, was undertaken by an assistant hospital administrator, a clerk with little or no sense of how to handle the news media in so delicate a matter as Dr. Irving's demise. Accordingly, routine funeral arrangements were made; a handful of medical leaders in the City were notified; cremation was planned as requested by the deceased according to his attorney, and a three-paragraph death notice was sent late to local newspapers.

It was this last bit of routine procedure that created unforeseen consequences. Dr. Irving's death, under the best of circumstances, was surely of some news value. Here was a prominent black physician who had discovered a cure for an obscure but nasty disease. He had made substantive if peripheral contributions in other areas of medical research in mankind's long fight against various maladies. That should—and could—have been the story. But when the hospital sent along its brief notification referring vaguely to an "unfortunate accident" the media immediately assumed that something was being covered up and proceeded accordingly. In response to many questions, a hospital spokesman said Dr. Irving died as the result of an accidental fall despite the best efforts of his fellow physicians who presumably were the City's most proficient. But, how come they failed? And what kind of a fall? Where? Who found him? How quickly was Dr. Irving treated? And, of course, the leitmotif running through all questions and subsequent news reports was Dr. Irving was black.

No one at Police Headquarters was particularly interested in Juicy, Petey and Loverboy until just before lunchtime. That was the moment that some pre-lunch golf enthusiasts found the bodies at the Happy Pirate sand trap.

That morning the three hoodlums had been booked on a substantial list of charges including car theft, driving to endanger, driving under the influence, wanton destruction of property and sexual harassment. It also had been discovered that all three had past records and that Juicy was a parole violator. The police also routinely questioned Juicy, Petey and Loverboy along with a number of usual suspects after the discovery of the bodies at the Happy Pirate. But then it was discovered that Loverboy was wearing the school ring of one of the murdered teenagers. Under more intensive questioning that included some pointed references to the death penalty, Lover-boy confessed that he did, after all, have some knowledge of the kill-ings: he had reluctantly witnessed them; he was only along for the ride; Petey fired the gun; Juicy was the ringleader; he, Loverboy, told those two guys that what they were doing was a bad idea.

By the end of the day, the other school ring was located in the wrecked SUV and the murder weapon was found at the bottom of the Ben Gunn water hazard at the Happy Pirate.

Robert Schneider, one of the biggest Ford dealers in Milwau-kee, was a man of economic substance, practicality and generally sound judgment. None of this was particularly helpful to him in un-derstanding the strange phone call that he received from his eldest daughter, Dorothy. No, she was not in trouble. No, there was nothing to worry about. But, yes, there was going to be, like, an important meeting with her Counselor, a Ms. Tobias, regarding some infrac-tions of college rules about which she was to be a sort of witness and, you know, the University thought it best if at least one of her parents were present because after all, like, she was still a few weeks shy of her 18th birthday.

Schneider arrived by plane the next day and ate lunch with his daughter before their appointment with Ms. Tobias. But nothing that he heard at lunch made a great deal of sense. Apparently Dorothy had attended a party at a fraternity house and some young man whom she kept snidely referring to as "Mr. Lacrosse" had tried to take ad-vantage of her. Or maybe it was more than tried. Dorothy's replay of events was a little sketchy. In any case, the University frowned on that sort of thing and was contemplating some disciplinary action against "Mr. Lacrosse."

"Dorothy," Schneider told her again. 'Please don't misunder-stand me. I'm on your side. But I know these things can happen. It wasn't that long ago that I went to college. Unless there is something you're not telling me, maybe you should just forget the whole thing."

Right," she said disgustedly. "You really are a typical male. Of course, you defend 'Mr. Lacrosse.' Your daughter is like raped and you, Mr. One-of-the-Boys, think I should forget it."

"Rape?" Schneider said, both shocked and stung. "No one said anything about rape."

"Well, Daddy, why do you think, you know, you're here?"

Major, sensationalized news coverage of the death of Dr. Cincinnatus Irving had one positive result that would have pleased the deceased. Many of his medical peers throughout the country as well as several in Europe learned of his death in time to join the mourners at the Second Lutheran Church. On the other hand, he would not have been as pleased that among those who crowded into the church were the Governor, three congressmen, the Mayor and two high-ranking officials representing the National Association for the Advancement of Colored People and the American Civil Liberties Union.

The latter non-medical mourners may, as some cynics whispered, have been attracted to the obsequies by news reports implying that Dr. Irving's death was the result of second class medical treatment and neglect caused by racist bias. But there could be no other explanation for the presence of Bobby Pangborn, known to the legal community and millions of TV viewers as Counselor Race Card. Nor were Pangborn's immediate future plans hard to determine when he sat in the front row between Dr. Irving's only living relatives, his ancient sister and his son, Wilmot.

To Dr. Irving's friends, the appearance of Wilmot was an even bigger surprise than the appearance of Pangborn. All of them knew that Cincinnatus had not talked to his son in 20 years. Wilmot, an unusually attractive young looking man, had shown a strong preference early in life for rock stars, dumb teenage girls, and controlled substances. Despite numerous arrests in drug crackdowns and two years in a federal prison, his preferences remained constant as did his periodic pleas to his father for cash. When his father finally refused one of the more outrageous of these supplications, Wilmot angrily did his father the favor of swearing that he would never talk to him again and for once kept his word.

But now, there he sat, staring emptily from a worn but still handsome face toward the altar; his emaciated body clothed in a shiny black suit, heavily starched white shirt and probably his only tie. Just yesterday he had been sitting in a lunchroom in Miami wondering how to pay the rent on his sleazy room. Then someone from Pangborn's law firm had located him and told him his father was dead.

The organ began playing "Rock of Ages." The funeral had begun.

Yang, as so often is the case, followed ying in the misinformed media hysteria about what was now being called the Happy Pirate murders. In the process, the two slain high school students, Tony Littlejohn and Babs Johnson, were converted from unfortunate but rather ordinary teenagers into tragic around-the-clock cable TV victims.

Details provided by Loverboy to the police were subsequently made public and endlessly worked over and massaged in TV and tabloid heavy-breathing reports and on radio and TV talk shows: Juicy was furious that the couple only had 32 dollars; they were forced to kneel and plead for their lives; they prayed while Juicy sneered; Petey suggested that "maybe we should have a little fun with Babsy," but Juicy said he 'didn't go for fat girls'; Loverboy repeatedly said they should "get out of here"; Juicy finally agreed, but he didn't "need these two whining to the cops" and told Petey to shoot them and "make it look just like a Mafia job on TV"; Loverboy protested; Petey fired one bullet into the back of each of the victims' heads.

The media ably stereotyped the lives of the murdered couple: both came from "modest, loving homes"; Babs—"a shy, serious young woman"—was studying to be a social worker in minority communities; Tony, "quiet and dutiful" was a "straight A student" who wanted to be a zoologist dedicated to saving obscure endangered species; their parents were "hardworking" and "church-going." Tearful parents, sorrowful fellow students, grief counselors and local politicians were interviewed endlessly by the media and talk show hosts and provided a plethora of clichés on cue. The District Attorney vowed "justice will be done." Repeatedly, the crime was quite accurately called "horrible," "evil," "unspeakable" and "beyond belief."

Meantime, the accused trio obtained legal counsel which immediately began its constitutional task of sowing doubt despite the facts and all common sense; several civil liberties groups raised questions about possible unconstitutional and brutal police procedure in the case; the troublesome issue emerged that "little Pietro" a.k.a. Petey had lied about his age and was only 17 and that Loverboy had turned 18 only two months ago; several neighbors of the Pelletiers and the Jukes families told reporters that Francis and Douglas were "really good, quiet boys who couldn't possible have done this terrible thing;" two civil rights groups felt it important to point out that Pietro was an Hispanic, and the City's leading newspaper published an editorial saying that "society had to look beyond 'just kids' for the real root cause of this monstrous crime: the growing gap between rich and poor in America."

Ms. Tobias met Robert Schneider and Dorothy in the lobby of historic University Hall and led them to her small severe office overlooking the somewhat littered greensward of the University Common. As they walked through the corridor lined with antiques donated by long-dead alumni, Schneider noted with dismay Ms. Tobias' blue patterned polyester dress and jacket, her fat legs, her glasses hanging on a woven ribbon from her neck, her stressed visage. He felt certain that he was not about to have a happy experience.

"I am sure Dorothy has given you the unpleasant details of this most unfortunate incident," Ms.; Tobias began. "It involved the type of shocking male behavior for which the University has zero, absolutely zero, tolerance. And poor Dorothy is to be commended, of course, for her courage in bringing the matter to our attention and her determination that an example be made to help stamp out this kind of Neanderthal conduct."

Dorothy, looking scrubbed and wholesome in a white linen blouse and green kilt, sat silently gazing out the window. Schneider looked momentarily with raised eyebrows at this attractive young woman who refused to look at him. He tried to keep foremost in his mind that this was his little girl whom he and his wife had raised with loving care.

"Dorothy and I have discussed this, of course," he said. "But it might be helpful if you told me your understanding of what happened."

Ms. Tobias' expression became even more stressed than usual and she shrugged with resignation.

"This is not a pleasant subject to discuss with a father," she said, employing the same tone as she would have used had she substituted the appellation 'Martian' for 'father.' "The simple facts are that this very young woman who is not used to drinking at all was plied with alcohol at a fraternity party; tricked when ill into the bedroom of an older male student and raped. Even if Dorothy had not been ill, she could hardly have resisted. She can't weigh more than 110 pounds. Her hulking assailant was a 160-pound lacrosse player."

If Schneider was supposed to demonstrate parental shock and indignation, he disappointed Ms. Tobias. Alcoholic beverages were not unknown in the Schneider household. By the time each of his children reached college age, he thought that he had instructed them on how to drink properly and all of them had successfully engaged in social drinking. Furthermore, although distanced from college by a quarter century, Schneider recalled his own undergraduate days as a two-fisted drinker and his own experiences involving the party-time conduct of college-age males and females. Certainly, Ms. Tobias' version of events could be correct, but more likely there was another version of the story.

"I assume." Schneider said, eyeing his daughter who was still studying some distant trees, "that you have verified all of the facts. I mean, we do have the right man and, in all fairness, do the sordid details all check out?"

"Bob, I can call you Bob, can't I?" Ms. Tobias said, her tone becoming tutorial. "I know how hard this is on a parent, particularly a father. Naturally, you want to help your daughter. But, of course, you also think like a male. I assure you that everything that Dorothy has told us has been verified as well as one can verify such matters. We have talked to more than a dozen students, some who were at her dorm or at the party, some whom Dorothy talked to the next day. We have talked to her assailant and those who know him well. He, of course, falls back on the usual myth: it was all consensual. But those who saw him that night and who know him well, let me say: they clearly make us believe otherwise."

"Well," Schneider said. "What happens now? Is this a police matter?"

"No, no, no, the University has no interest in involving the police; no need. We handle these things quietly ourselves for the good of everyone involved. The purpose of this meeting, Bob, is for Dorothy to sign a statement of facts which, because she is a minor, we need you as her parent to witness. Then Dorothy can go back to pursuing, as best she can under the circumstances, her normal university life."

"What about this guy? What happens to him?"

"He is already on temporary probation and has been sent home," Ms. Tobias said with great satisfaction. "However, once we have Dorothy's signed statement, the Dean has determined that under the University's rules he will be expelled."

Less than ten minutes after the burial of the sparse post-cremation remains of Dr. Irving in the family plot, Wilmot Irving and Bobby Pangborn held an impromptu news conference in the rain at the cemetery gates. Wilmot said very little. His aunt, who had told him she wanted no part in his plans and otherwise had barely spoken to him, was on her way home to meet with old friends. Pangborn did most of the talking.

"You will hear more details later about the outrageous racist neglect and malpractice that caused the death of this great physician and medical scientist," he said indignantly to the TV cameras. "Today the family is mourning. Next week the family will seek justice."

Pangborn, wearing his usual custom-made blue wide pinstripe suit, had positioned himself so that the cemetery was his background. Wilmot stood silently at his right. Pangborn had the light tan complexion a man might obtain by spending much time on tennis courts and the decks of racing yachts. However, his complexion was not quite as light as Wilmot's.

"We blacks cannot permit the powerful forces of racism to cover up the kind of treatment that Dr. Irving clearly received only because of the color of his skin," Pangborn said. "We will show in court how both the World Center Hotels Corporation and St. Benedict's Hospital are clearly responsible for his death. And that they have tried to cover up the tragic, needless death of this great man by saying that this series of events and bumbling responses were only human error, that merely mistakes were made. But why, we ask, were those mistakes made? Why? We will show they were made because of the underlying racist attitudes that poison our society."

"Bobby, have you put a number on this suit yet?" a reporter asked. Pangborn grinned and shrugged.

"How can you put a price on one of our greatest medical scientists? Who knows what cures the world has lost because he was taken from us prematurely? We may seek as much as 200 million. That would enable us to use a portion to endow future medical research. That's what Wilmot here really wants. He wants to carry on the great work of his father."

Considering the senseless brutality of the murders, it was no surprise that the death penalty was openly on the table. The District Attorney formally announced that he would seek it. Later he said he would seek it despite the age of the alleged murderers. Still later, he said he would seek it for two of the alleged murderers but Douglas Juke a.k.a. Loverboy should be given clemency for becoming a state witness.

Then the case began to unravel.

The usual protests were raised by civil rights groups favoring delicate handling of obvious barbarians and by opponents of the death penalty for crimes no matter how foul. Originally, these protests were dismissed as the part of the groups' annual fund raising campaign. But as both defense and prosecution dug into the excellent police work that had solved the case in a matter of hours, they found some possibly embarrassing flaws in routine procedure; possibly embarrassing flaws that could result, as the organized cacophony for clemency grew, in a judge throwing out the case or in a hung jury.

Matters became further confused when Francis Pelletier a.k.a. Juicy, the ex-con parole violator and the only defendant over 21, offered to plead guilty to a charge of accessory to manslaughter—a charge that could result in a maximum of 20 years in prison, but with good behavior much less.

The District Attorney reconsidered his options. After deep consultation with his legal and political advisers, he announced acceptance of Juicy's plea; the turning over of young Pietro a.k.a. Petey to the juvenile court system; and the reduction of all charges against Loverboy because of his cooperation to a minimal sentence of one year of public service.

The District Attorney said: "In this difficult case, it is clear that these socially impaired young men made mistakes. However, society can only benefit in the rehabilitation of these youths through the justice system."

Schneider felt that he had to sign Dorothy's statement, but he was uncomfortable doing it. That discomfort increased a week later when Dorothy came home for Thanksgiving weekend: while brushing his teeth, he heard her in the next room laughingly advise one of her younger sisters never to drink a half bottle of gin at one sitting.

Schneider reported this comment to his wife. She, in turn, had a long, teary conversation with Dorothy. And Dorothy confided to her mother that it was all so horrible and, although it doesn't really make any difference because of the principle involved, she really didn't remember much of anything that happened. And, you know, why can't everyone just leave her alone.

On learning this, Schneider immediately wrote a letter to Ms. Tobias describing Dorothy's consumption of gin and suggesting that under the circumstances the subsequent events were not very clear cut. He also suggested that the "poor guy," whom he had made it his business to check out, was an honors physics major as well as a star athlete and "in all fairness" should receive a much lesser penalty than expulsion.

Ms. Tobias responded with a prompt, short note:

Dear Bob:

We thank you for your continued concern and your wish to make certain that no injustice is done in Dorothy's case. I assure you none has been.

We find that it is not uncommon for young, unsophisticated women to exaggerate in order to impress friends and especially siblings. But, even if Dorothy made the naive mistake of drinking somewhat too much and that led to other very human mistakes, the fact remains that her more experienced assailant acted in a totally irresponsible and boorish manner that violates all women's rights as incorporated in our University rules.

Your compassion for poor Dorothy's assailant as a fellow male is fully understandable. But, Bob, know in your heart, the University and Dorothy will be better off because of his permanent removal from campus.

Sincerely,

Joanna Tobias

Director, Office of Women's Issues Counseling

The Smoothers

I know you believe you understand what you think I said, but I am not sure you realize that what you heard is not what I meant.
—Fallaciously attributed to Alan Greenspan, US Federal Reserve Chairman and famous obscurantist

Kenny Comstock could recall precisely the moment that the proverbial lights first flickered for him at World Tech. He was sitting in front of his computer screen deleting the overnight crop of "adult" junk mail:

Fiona...Horny girls are waiting inside for you...

Tx435...Pill to increase your ejaculation 581 percent...

Sunny...Animals in action!!!!!...

The CEO direct phone line rang.

"Meeting of the Executive Staff Group at 8 o'clock in Mr. Rotchglove's office." It was the mellifluous voice of Myrna, Mr. Rotchglove's personal assistant known in World Tech executive ranks around the globe as the Velvet Virgin and Keeper of the Holy Secrets.

Kenny sighed. He liked to cleanse his email of the daily dump of smut and other spam, then it was easier to sort by importance and read overnight messages from the media and financial analysts along with critical internal mail before becoming embroiled in whatever the new day presented. Lately, this objective was increasingly difficult to achieve. As Chief Communications Officer, his daily dose of electronic mail was sizeable and growing. And, despite new software screens and advanced fire walls, the daily wave of smut and spam was rising much faster.

When Myrna smilingly waived Kenny into the CEO's office at the top of World Tech Tower One, although the time was only 8:25, Kenny found that he apparently was last to arrive. Gathered about a round antique table in one of the multi-windowed side chapels of the sprawling two-story office were four fairly standard issue corporate executives: Dieter Pine, Chief Financial Officer; Holmes Thornbrook, Chief Counsel, and Desmond "Steve" Downing, Chief Marketing Officer. Leonard Rotchglove, his full lips turned downward, stood as commandingly as possible for a man just over five feet tall at the table beside his chair and looked impatient as Kenny sat in the only other vacant seat. Outside the huge windows Kenny watched spring sunlight play off World Tech Towers Two and Three and the long reflecting pool below in the courtyard.

"We have a new challenge," Rotchglove began. "You are all familiar with our joint investment in Punjab Broadband with the Indian Government and the increasing problems with devaluation of currencies in Central Asia. Now we are faced with further uncertainties because of the economic downturn on the Indian subcontinent. As a result, we could be looking at some will call major losses."

"What's major?" asked Holmes Thornbrook, a lawyer keen on semantic niceties.

"It could be a billion dollars," Dieter Pine said, squinting with distaste at the top sheet of some green printouts.

"Possibly 15 cents a share drop in earnings this quarter," Rotchglove added. "Some analysts have been talking until now about another 20 cents gain."

There was a difficult silence before Steve Downing seized what he saw as an irresistible career opportunity.

"We may be able to help," he said quietly. "As Dieter I am sure would agree, we have been much too conservative in recognizing our router and other component sales in the U.S. market. Currently, we are forecasting 1.9 billion this quarter. I see no reason that we can't with a little aggressive accounting take some sales we know we have in the drawer in the next few months and make that three billion, maybe a shade more for this quarter."

"I would call that very aggressive," Dieter said.

"But not unrealistic," Rotchglove interjected. "I trust Steve's judgment on this. All we would be doing here is a little smoothing of earnings."

"Common practice," Thornbrook said, putting a figurative finger in the corporate breeze. "Just has to be managed properly."

Kenny, who had learned early on that Leonard took umbrage when offered public relations counsel that suggested any significant change in what Leonard had already decided to do, took extensive notes but refrained from comment.

The following Tuesday, as investors around the world waited with high hopes for World Tech to announce its quarterly earnings, Kenny devoted more than a half hour to cleansing his email file.

Nudge   ...20 clips of college girls on spring break...

Galpal   ...Brothers and Sisters have fun in sun...

Heidi   ...Animal farm...

Freaky   ...Hi...

The smut tide was definitely rising and the waters around him appeared to be viscous, roiling, dark. But he had no more time to deal with it. He had to complete the final draft of the quarterly earnings release.

He worried the release for more than an hour. Kenny was a craftsman. Each word, each phrase had significance, nuance, layered meanings, euphemisms of euphemisms: messages that worked. He chose them with enormous care, using his more than twenty years of experience to create a professional product that he felt gave substance to his days. And when he succeeded, he could not have been more content had his patron been Sixtus IV and the assignment the rising cost of the Sistine Chapel.

> Newark, NJ, April 12—World Tech, Inc., international leader in technology service, announced today a 12-cents a share jump in first quarter earnings, well within market expectations.
>
> Leonard Rotchglove, Chairman and Chief Executive Officer, said first-quarter results were "highly gratifying" because they confirm World Tech's strategy of balance in its international portfolio of enterprises.

(more)

Somewhere toward the last paragraphs the release mentioned "projected losses" from Punjab Broadband that were "more than offset" by "gratifyingly high revenues" from component sales.

Kenny reread the release on his monitor screen for the fourth time and made some incidental adjustments and corrections. He felt particularly pleased with the phrase "strategy of balance." He knew Leonard would like that when he saw it.

Unfortunately for World Tech neither economic conditions nor acceptance of its products and services improved during the next six months. More smoothing of earnings was required in order to avoid reporting large losses in the second and third quarters. Steve Downing remained buoyant and, with Leonard Rotchglove's support, confidently advanced the argument that dangerously mounting receivables would be paid in the "next quarter" for sure. Kenny artfully reinforced World Tech financial credibility during this period by the use of such phrases as "shift in buying patterns" and "new customer mix." Leonard emphasized management's "strategy of balance" when talking to financial analyst groups.

But two weeks before the end of the last quarter of the year as a huge, designer decorated Christmas tree was erected in the lobby of Tower One and troubled financial reports arrived from World Tech operations throughout the world, it became clear to Dieter Pine that that the situation had worsened considerably. He forced this unseasonably bad news on Leonard and Leonard, in turn, called a meeting of what had now come to be called internally the Challenge Management Committee: the Executive Staff Group plus Fritz Hofmeister, Chief International Officer, and Paul Fluk, president of Tankron, Ltd., a wholly-owned subsidiary which in the present crisis was now contributing 40 percent of World Tech's earnings.

"Dieter and I have now seen enough numbers to know that this quarter will be very disappointing. The word disaster comes to mind," Leonard told the group. "We have to take some strong steps immediately and all of our options are damned unpleasant. Dieter and I have put together a tentative action plan."

"The economy has certainly not been helpful," Steve said. "But let's not throw out the baby."

"We will if that saves our ass," Leonard said. "Dieter, summarize the plan."

"Our various options are listed in the Challenge Plan which I'll pass out in a few minutes," Dieter said. "All of them, as Leonard indicated, are unpleasant. Those that look like our best bets are four:

one, dumping Punjab and the rest of the broadband business; two, cut back our research budget by about half; three, sell off, if we can, some of the component businesses; and four, cut payroll across the board by 10,000. We do all of that in the next two quarters, we can pack a lot of our roll-over losses in with the costs as non-recurring expenses."

He paused and looked around the table at his silent associates. "Questions? Comments?" he asked.

Paul Fluk, a North Country Englishman in a Savile Row suit, cleared his throat. "One question, Dieter. Is this going to do the job? Will we have done enough?"

"No notes," Dieter said meaningfully and several pens were pocketed. "Paul's question is on target. This is not enough if we expect to continue to show profits and maintain Wall Street support. Fortunately, in the last few months four of our special purpose vehicle partnerships—specifically Orkney III, Canary.com, HiLo and Sunnydays—have raised sizeable amounts of capital from outside investors. These SPV's now will pay a significant portion of what they raised to World Tech as earnings. And the SPV's, of course, can carry this as a debt or a loss without any of that appearing on our books."

"What do our independent accountants at Dancer Humas say to that?," Thornbrook asked as casually as he could.

"They essentially approve, "Dieter said. "They see it as somewhat aggressive but normal. In fact. their independent consulting arm suggested it."

"Other comments?" Leonard asked in a tone that reflected a low tolerance for further commentary.

Fluk, the current earnings hero, thought the plan "right on the target." Hofmeister, the original negotiator of the Punjab deal, and

Steve, the astute early recognizer of sales, muttered general approval. Thornbrook promised to "thoroughly review" the written plan and "get back promptly with any legal wrinkles" but he thought it sounded "quite buttoned down." Kenny had no comment as usual and promised an early draft of the release.

As they left Leonard's office, Myrna smiled beatifically and wished everybody "happy holidays."

Dawn. Kenny had been working since 4:30 on the much rewritten final draft of the quarterly release. He refilled his bronze and blue World Tech "Big Team" coffee mug for the third time and switched from working on the release to his email.

Glenda   ...Cute Guys! Hot Girls! Private Rooms!

$$834#   ...Animal Love!!!!

Doctor   ...Amazing cream: Enlarge your breasts...

Sabrina   ...Hi, I'm waiting inside for you, Baby

The rising smut tide never abated. After the first dozen porn emails, he still had three windows-worth scrambled with offers of cheap mortgages, hot stocks, low cost printer ink and bargain airline tickets packaged with tacky hotels. He also had about three score media and analyst questions and an equal number of internal memos.

Kenny made a sour face and returned to the release:

Newark, NJ, Jan. 14—World Tech, Inc., international leader in technology service, announced today a 5-cents a share gain in fourth quarter earnings before non-recurring costs for company-wide reengineering.

Leonard Rotchglove, Chairman and Chief Executive Officer, said the reengineering program involving non-recurring costs of $1.25 cents a share is designed to maintain the company's long-term profitability and growth in the new fiscal year.

"World Tech has been hailed as an engine of profitability for the last five years," Mr. Rotchglove said. "Our top international management team is now fine tuning that engine for the next five years of exemplary, innovative performance."

(more)

Mid-way the release disclosed the sales of Punjab Broadband and various other assets; a $1.4 billion reduction in "non-essential" research and "early retirement packages" for 10,000 employees. It also reported "management gratification" over earnings growth of 60 cents a share for the full year before non-recurring costs. The SPV transactions were not mentioned because they were too complex to explain in a press release and Dieter felt that they could be disclosed sufficiently in the footnotes in the formal report to the Securities Exchange Commission.

Kenny took one final look and made one last minor edit. He hoped Leonard liked "engine of profitability" as much as he did.

Dieter hated all independent accountants. They were either worthless or trouble or both. For enormous fees, they counted your money and told you whether you counted it correctly. If they said that you did, you thanked them by giving them enormous fees for additional consulting. If they said you didn't, they charged you enormous fees to tell you how to correct the problem which you thought you had buried. More important: they also promised never to mention this to anyone unless, of course, they were subpoenaed.

In the month following the fourth quarter announcement, Dancer Humas had been all over World Tech in preparation to giving their annual blessing to World Tech's books. Alas, they had found some problems. Dieter was surprised to learn from the accountants that apparently some underlings had been engaged in channel stuffing: the shipment by bookkeeping only of goods to customers and the recognition of those shipments as sales. Furthermore, there seemed to be a deplorable lack of public disclosure regarding major losses. And, in general, the accountants felt on second thought that World Tech had engaged in "very aggressive accounting" not in accordance with accepted principles.

Ordinarily, this might not have been too bad, only temporarily embarrassing. World Tech could easily choose this moment when it was talking about "reengineering" to clear its legal decks with a restatement of earnings and put all the bad news behind it. But there also was the matter of what the accountants referred to as "the appearance of insider trading." In the last three months, World Tech stock had dropped from 75 to 30. During this sharp decline, all members of the Executive Staff Group except Kenny, who had pledged whatever he had for college loans for his children, sold large quantities of the stock. Leonard alone had sold three million shares; Dieter, one million.

Therefore, the accountants were nervous about giving approval to the firm's annual audit without adding some kind of qualification. Leonard and Dieter were incensed and suggested to the accountants that they could be fired. While the accountants were pondering this distasteful idea and how such a financially unpleasant event might be avoided, there was an alarming turn of events which might have been anticipated.

Kenny had never thought of himself as a prime mover. Rather, he saw himself as an observant player at court where from time to time he moved the action along with some clever lines. But early one morning toward the end of January he made an important discovery in the midst of his email.

Dottie   ...Hard core, gangbang action!!!

Adam   ...Natural penis enlargement

Sweetsue...Funny accounting

Tina   ...Nude celebs

Kenny had already clicked deletes through "Tina" when he backtracked to "Sweetsue" and did what he rarely did with spam and smut email: he opened it.

From: Sweetsue

To: Bob Grove—SEC Enforcement Division

Cc: Kenneth Comstock
Subject: Funny accounting and many games

Bobby: You will find big pay dirt if you look into the way the books are being cooked at World Tech.

Ex-bean counter

Kenny thought Sweetsue's message was hotter than anything "Tina" or "Dottie" had to say; smiled at his little joke; and suddenly felt nauseated. He had an ailing wife; two children in college; a big mortgage; a beach house. He just followed orders. Why did the whistle blower copy him? Everyone would think he was involved. Spinspeak immediately gushed and bubbled through his mind: No one was cooking the books. They were just keeping things on an even keel until problems could be solved. Sweetsue must be some disgruntled loser who didn't get a raise. Maybe a serial voyeur. Maybe someone fired for sexual harassment. The cloying genie of euphoria called from its bottle by his own words began to soothe him, but his common sense also told him a deeper truth: these guys were neither smart enough or morally strong enough to manage this corporate elephant. To cover himself, he better warn Leonard immediately of Sweetsue. No, maybe he better go to Dieter first. And he did.

In the ensuing Gotterdamerung, Lawrence and Dieter accepted generous early retirement packages at the urgent request of the Board; Steve, who had just returned from a celebratory sales meeting in Acapulco, was fired for violating company policy; Hofmeister accepted a job with the Indian government; Dancer Humas was discharged; World Tech restated its earnings for the last three years showing two and a half billion dollars in losses; and shareholders filed 38 class action suits with claims totaling four billion dollars against the company, the accountants and all directors. Naturally, a noisy and righteous search for additional miscreants would continue until the media and politicians lost interest. So far, Thornbrook, who spent much time doing public hand-washing, and Kenny survived. Fluk, of course, was golden.

Kenny watched from the window of his office as the early March light spread across the reflecting pool in World Tech Plaza. As he always did, he had come in early to take a last look at an important press release. But beforehand, as always, he was cleansing and reading his email.

23$@@1   ...Hi, I am Wilma and I have a dream

cissy   ...54 shots of Carmen doing the bull

Ruben   ...Old McDonald's farm

Mona   ...Satisfy with low cost Viagara from Mexico

As the World Tech crisis abated, Kenny's mail from the media and analysts had declined markedly, but not the rolling waves of smut. That continued to rise despite his continuing efforts to delete it and stop it. In his mind, he saw it not as just a dark tide anymore but as a great sea roaring through cyberspace, choking communications channels with its sick slime, pouring through millions of computer monitors and finally engulfing 21st Century mankind. He thought that image was so exact, so iconographic, that he scratched a sticky pad note to write it down later because he had to put final touches on an important release in the next five minutes.

> Newark, NJ, March 20—H. Paul Fluk, 42-year old president of Tankron, Ltd., today was appointed Chairman and Chief Executive Officer of World Tech, Inc., by the World Tech Board of Directors.
>
> In making the announcement, Marshall Bamberger, Chairman of the Board's Audit and Nominating Committees, said: "After an international search, Paul was far and away the obvious choice. We have tremendous confidence in his ability as a true corporate captain of corporate captains World Tech back to new heights."
>
> Tankron, an international wholly-owned World Tech subsidiary headquartered in London, has doubled its size to $1.2 billion and tripled its earnings in the last five years under Mr. Fluk's leadership.
>
> (more)

There were four more paragraphs about Fluk before the release mentioned his predecessor or referenced what the release called "troubled finances now corrected." There was no mention of law suits.

Kenny read over each word with even more than his usual care. After all, this was a new era at World Tech. He hoped that Paul liked the phrase "corporate captain of corporate captains."

Believe Me!

The American people don't expect much out of us anymore and we seldom disappoint them.
         —U.S. Sen. Fred Thompson (R-Tennessee)

As Congressman Millard Shortcuff remembered it later, he was completing a speech at a campaign fund raising breakfast at Windows on the World at the moment that Muslim terrorists flew the first aircraft into the World Trade Center.

The breakfast meeting was in one of the private dining rooms off the main restaurant on the 108th floor of the North Tower. When the plane hit only 20 floors below them, the building swayed back and forth and the lights went out. But then they came back on and everyone around him crowded and pushed to get out through the doors into the hall. An aide led Millard into a small office, said something about checking the exits and left him alone. He said he would be back shortly.

Millard sat behind the desk in the office and tried to use the phone. It was dead. Smoke and bits of debris choked the view from a large window so that he could not see the street or look out at the Statue of Liberty in New York harbor. But a TV set on the desk still worked. On the screen he saw pictures of the North Tower where he was sitting; also pictures of the smoking hole where the plane had crashed into the building; pictures of panic in the downtown streets; pictures of police and firemen. The handsome face of a network anchor safely ensconced uptown said people still alive on the upper floors of the tower were trapped and probably could not be reached. He said some were jumping out of windows. Then the lights went out again and the screen went blank.

Millard looked at his watch. He had been there in that office fifteen minutes. The aide obviously was never coming back. Just another disloyal bastard. Millard audibly sighed and prepared for the worst. He, a man who seldom entered a church except for photo ops at political funerals and on Easter and Christmas, decided to pray; to confess his sins; to put himself in the best state possible to face whatever was to come.

Throughout his adult life Millard knew that he had lived most sinfully, clutched to himself, fattened on numerous great lies, lies that over the years had grown and metastasized until they had evolved into a totally new, rebuilt Millard Fillmore Shortcuff; this rebuilt Millard Fillmore Shortcuff, through increasingly easy reelection in a run-down one-party district, had become, primarily based on seniority alone, a congressman of great power, a party leader, a dispenser of many favors, an inside player, a man sought out by captains and kings; and this rebuilt Millard Fillmore Shortcuff had through a life of covering lies and half-truths with ever greater ones fooled many but no one so much as years went by as the original Millard.

According to the congressman's official biography:

Rep. Millard Fillmore Shortcuff was born in poverty in Cabotburg, Massachusetts; the grandson of a Polish war refugee named Stanislaus Shorkoffski but renamed Shortcuff by an immigration agent in Boston. Stanislaus, who fled Poland before its conquest by the Nazis and the Soviets in 1939, sold vegetables from a pushcart in Boston's North End.

All but one of Stanislaus' five children died of disease or malnutrition before they were 10. The sole survivor, Stanley, a large, handsome young man, worked on a railroad repair crew that drifted to Cabotburg in eastern Massachusetts. There he wooed and married an even younger schoolteacher from Buffalo, N.Y., named Catherine O'Bryan. Three years later, Stanley was killed tragically when he was trapped in a faulty railroad switch and was run down by the Flying Yankee enroute to Portland, Maine, and Bar Harbor. He left two baby boys, Grover and Millard, to be brought up by his young widow alone.

Catherine, who loved history and had named her sons after Buffalo's two U.S. presidents, taught fourth grade in a public school in one of the city's poorest neighborhoods. She also took in laundry to help support herself and the two boys, after the eldest, Grover, contracted polio. From the time little Millard was seven, he helped out by delivering newspapers, doing yard work and shoveling snow. Later Catherine's finances improved somewhat after she played a major role in organizing the local teachers union and long overdue pay raises were won. Unfortunately, by then young Grover had died. However, Catherine was able to enroll Millard in one of the city's best parochial schools.

Recalling the truth, understandably, caused Millard pain as he sat in the darkened office and smelled traces of rancid smoke.

In the early 30's, Stanislaus, Millard's grandfather, and an infant son fled Poland where Stanislaus was wanted for stealing chickens and poaching small game from an old czarist estate. Previously, he had lost his wife and two other children in a typhoid epidemic that swept their farm village. He did sell vegetables from a pushcart in Boston, but not for long. Within a few years, Stosh, as he was known to his customers, owned a small fruit and vegetable market. By the time he retired to Florida a few years after the end of World War II, he owned a chain of six markets in the Boston Area. When Stosh died, his only son, Stanley, was much disappointed to find that his father had left almost all of his money to Polish War Relief.

Stosh had deeply disapproved of Stanley, who preferred alcoholic beverages to work. When Stanley married Catherine, Stosh came to the wedding and gave the couple a check for 1,000 dollars. Stanley assured Catherine that this was only the beginning. But Stosh died two months later; his generosity to Polish War Relief was disclosed; and Stanley had to look for a job. He was rejected for military service in World War II for medical reasons associated with early alcoholism. He had difficulty holding jobs as a door-to-door salesman for the same association. He failed to sell low cost insurance; then, vacuum cleaners; then, "the world's finest" cutlery. In his last job, he sold sets of the Encyclopedia Britannica, and it was sudden success in this endeavor that led to his premature death. One Friday afternoon, he sold three sets of the Britannica and he celebrated this triumph in one of his favorite bars near the Cabotburg Railroad Station. Late that night as he was returning home he tripped while cutting across the mainline railroad tracks and was run over by a slow-moving freight train hauling fractional horsepower motors.

Catherine supported herself and her two children on her earnings as a public school fourth grade teacher and the returns on a small insurance policy left her by her father, a Buffalo paint contractor. She lost her job when she refused to join a newly-formed teachers union, but she was hired by a local Catholic school which later enabled her to send Millard to St. Ignatius Prep on full scholarship.

According to the official biography:

Millard was an outstanding student at St. Ignatius. He excelled in all of his courses. And, as he studied and matured under the guidance of the Jesuit Fathers, he became increasingly interested in Catholicism and seriously thought that he might have a vocation. He was increasingly encouraged to consider joining the Society of Jesus itself.

But, the more this brilliant scholar explored the many philosophies and religions of the world, the more he moved away from what he came to see was a narrow sectarianism and the more he appreciated the meaning of diversity and non-judgementalism. He had been born a Roman Catholic and would always be one at heart. But, when he left St. Ignatius Prep, he shared with millions of his fellow Americans a world view dedicated to understanding and helping people regardless of their faith or gender or ethnicity.

Of all the faculty at St. Ignatius, Millard remembered Father Linus the best. Father Linus, who was christened Buel but when he took his vows chose the name of the second Pope, was from New Orleans. He was very bright; very subtle, and, in the end, very devious. He spoke with a low, aristocratic drawl. He also possessed great style and, although Millard longed to be like him and admired by him, he feared that neither was possible.

"Shortcuff, my boy," Father Linus would always say when he was about to be most cutting, "you just aren't smart enough for us. It would be wrong to encourage you."

"But, Father, I feel more at home here than I ever have anywhere else."

"The Society of Jesus is not a shelter or comfort station for the homeless, Shortcuff. We play a great role in the universal Plan as much as we can know that Plan. We must be about our Father's business."

"I am ready to dedicate my life..."

"Shortcuff, my boy, you think you are but you are not. You would tire of us soon enough and what then? Stay in the world, Shortcuff. That will be difficult enough for you."

When Millard was graduated from St. Ignatius, the Viet Nam War was at its height and competition for scholarships that would delay being drafted was keen. With only average grades, he failed to obtain a scholarship. Desperate to avoid the Army draft and an early introduction to the dangers of jungle warfare, he enlisted in the Air Force.

According to the official biography:

Congressman Shortcuff served as a twice decorated enlisted man in Viet Nam. He enlisted in the U.S. Air Force immediately after graduating from St. Ignatius Prep and saw combat during the Tet Offensive and subsequent missions.

Following his return to the United States, he enrolled as a student at the University of Massachusetts where he was an active leader in the student anti-war movement.

Millard felt increasingly uneasy when he thought about this period of his life. He had, of course, done everything that he possibly could to avoid serving in Viet Nam. After he was rejected by the Jesuits and subsequently failed to gain entry on scholarship into a college, any college, he discovered two wonderful things about the Air Force: the promise of a college education in the future in exchange for immediate enlistment and the comforting rumor that non-pilots would not be sent overseas. He signed up.

As things turned out, he was sent overseas, but his luck held: he was stationed as a clerk at a bomber base on Okinawa. While there, he put himself in for and received a Combat Readiness Medal for working round the clock at his desk during the Tet Offensive. He also received an Overseas Service Medal for serving in excess of 30 days in the Pacific Theater. Just before he was to be shipped back home and mustered out of the Air Force, he wangled a one week leave with some of his service pals in Saigon.

Upon his return to the United States, he was admitted to the University of Massachusetts where he majored in something called business science; achieved only moderate grades despite increasing grade inflation; and became involved on its fringes with the anti-war movement. Here was an association that he found it useful to recall in an enlarged way during his early political campaigns; later he further enhanced the objectivity of his anti-war credentials by describing himself as a twice-decorated Pacific veteran.

As for the more colorful final version of his wartime and post-war activity, this was a matter of normal image creep generated by his media consultants, his handlers and his own off-the-cuff remarks. After all, he well remembered being in Saigon: the intense heat, the smells, the drugged bar girls, the endless drinks, the many stories of danger lurking in the jungle.

According to the official biography:

Upon graduation from college, Millard began a highly successful business career at Softone Technologies, an early leader in the development of cheap cell phones and pagers. Rapidly rising in management during the next few years, he was named Deputy Vice President for Human Resources shortly before he became one of the high tech industry's first "whistle blowers" regarding sexual harassment in the workplace. Millard, always compassionate when he saw abuse to fellow workers, was the author of what became known as the "Softone Hostile Environment Report" exposing the corrosiveness of sexually explicit jokes. Initially, he loyally circulated the confidential report to Softone top management. Only when it was ignored, did he feel compelled to make it public.

The report resulted in major reforms at Softone and many other corporations. It also helped launch Millard's public service career. Within six months, he was elected for the first time to Congress.

Millard looked back warmly on this period of his life. He had been hired originally at Softone as a sales trainee, but after more than a year, he had demonstrated little talent for selling technical products that were supposed to do what the salesman said they could do. Millard's sales continually backfired because of the fanciful expectations that he often raised among customers who were mostly number-oriented engineers. As a result, he was transferred to the Human Relations Department where his style seemed more suited.

For several years in Human Relations his career stalled. Then, he had a lucky break. His boss, the Deputy Director and Vice President, announced that he had terminal cancer and was retiring immediately. Millard was promoted to Deputy Director without the title of Vice President. And there he remained for four more years with no prospect of advancement until the current director, a Senior Vice President named T. Norman Priddle, either left or retired, neither event being probable soon: Priddle had never worked anywhere else, was a very healthy 53 and had numerous children to put through college.

Again, Millard was lucky. A rather unpleasant, plain young woman who worked as a secretary in the Marketing Department filed a complaint that she was being sexually harassed. Millard was routinely told to investigate the complaint. He found that the young woman, Melinda Boll, worked at a desk outside the office of the Northeast Regional Sales Manager, a voluble career salesman named Dennis Monahan, a man convinced that telephones worked only if you shouted into them, an irrepressible teller of bawdy tales to his large, loyal band of customers.

"Melinda is very upset," Millard told Priddle. "She demands that Monahan be disciplined. She says no woman should have to put up with what she calls Monahan's disgusting sexual abuse."

"Did he make advances? Did he touch her? I remember her working here temporarily last fall. Hardly a sex object, Millard."

"It's all verbal," Millard said. "Monahan is famous for off-color stories. She said he repeated a particularly objectionable one last week at least a dozen times during loud phone calls. Something about an Arab prince, a gay Englishman and an oversexed camel."

"There is no way that I am going to the mat with one of our most successful sales executives because some secretary is eavesdropping on his phone calls," Priddle said. "Just transfer the woman; give her a promotion, give her a damn raise if necessary. We can always fire her later. I'm sure we can find a reason. Handle it, Millard. Handle it. You know what to do."

Millard certainly did. This woman could cause a lot of trouble and he was not going to be the fall guy if Priddle's solution proved inadequate as he suspected it would. Moreover, he sensed a career opportunity. Two days later he sent a lengthy report to Priddle outlining his concerns about the rights of women and recommending a major 21st Century Behavioral Educational Program for all executives. He took the liberty of sending a copy to the Corporate Counsel and felt that he was well on the way to being made a Vice President. Possibly, the case might also begin to edge Priddle toward early retirement.

None of that was to be. The Corporate Counsel talked to the President; both met with Priddle; the three agreed that Millard lacked judgment and should seek new employment. Millard, in turn, leaked his original report to several female investigative reporters. The resulting series of very nasty, major news stories on sexual harassment at Softone won a Pulitzer Prize; made Melinda and several lawyers quite rich; pushed Softone down the road to being acquired and eventually dismembered; and propelled Millard into the hands of local politicians desperate that year for a hero to help them hold on to power in Cabotburg and the once prosperous but now rotting old textile towns around it.

According to the official biography:

On arriving in Congress, Shortcuff immediately began to strive to improve conditions for working Americans—particularly women and members of minority groups. His activism attracted congressional leadership who saw him as a major asset in advancing the well-being and rights of an increasingly diverse citizenry. He brought to Congress a unique mix of everyday experience: a man born in poverty that he had surmounted; a man who learned early in life the true nature of religion, war and business; a man of compassion who understood the struggles of the working family. This assessment of Congressman Shortcuff has been repeatedly tested and proven during his more than 25 years of service in the U.S. House of Representatives. Today he serves as a senior member of three of the House's most powerful committees: Rules, Ways & Means, and Armed Services.

Millard audibly sighed again. Sitting alone in the face of death, he saw himself and what he had perpetrated: a lifetime of mendacity was a lifetime of sin: lie had encrusted on lie like mollusks on a rock until the rock was completely encapsulated, hidden, gone from his recognition most of all. He saw that. But even now he had to struggle to generate some feeling of true contrition, some trace of longing that he wished he had done otherwise. Well, he felt some trace. Yes, he did. But to accomplish his objective maybe he should feel something more. Too bad he couldn't talk to his old mentor, Father Linus. Linus knew the drill; Linus knew how things worked. And then the miracle occurred: a young Hispanic waiter looked into the dark office where Millard sat and beckoned him.

"Come, hurry," he said. "I know a stairway. It is still maybe open."

Millard wrenched himself from his musings, took a last look at the swirling smoke outside the window and followed the waiter out the door, through the hall into a kitchen and through a red metal security door. Beyond the door was a smoke-filled metal stairway; hot air hit him the face; the smell of burning oil and flesh sickened him. But, ahead of him, the waiter with a wet towel over his head handed him a similar towel and urged him forward.

The heat became painful, searing, agonizing as they rushed down the stairs. The stairwell, designed as a fire escape route, was still whole even as it dropped past the floors where the plane had hit. Then, beyond the area of greatest destruction, the heat began to diminish and the smoke partially cleared. Big numerals on the walls told them that they had passed the 70th floor, the 60th, the 45th. Now, the air was only balmy; the smoke much abated. Five minutes later Millard and the waiter pushed open a fire door that gave way directly into the cacophony of a side street jammed with rescuers, injured and fleeing office workers, debris, and fire trucks. Millard pressed through the crowd toward the end of the block and then the next where another miracle occurred: his limousine with its congressional plates was at the curb. Toussaint, whose first and only job since illegally entering the United States from Haiti 12 years earlier was to serve Millard as his driver, was sitting at the wheel. His mahogany face was all but hidden behind his chauffeur's cap and outsize silver-lensed aviator glasses. Millard opened the back door of the limousine and turned to let the waiter get in, but the waiter was gone.

"Ah, Monsieur Le Congressman, truly it is important that we are soon enroute," Toussaint said in his soupy Haitian franglaise.

Millard got in and the limousine started to inch forward through the crowd with the help of police who had spotted its congressional plate. An half hour later the limousine was on the F.D.R. Drive moving uptown along the East River.

Millard turned on the TV embedded in the back of the front seats of the limousine. Both World Trade Center Towers were burning. Another plane had crashed into the South Tower. As he watched and listened to the reports, he came to realize for the first time the full horror and international implications of what was occurring.

The limousine was supposed to have taken him to another fund raising breakfast at the Waldorf. Obviously that had been cancelled. He picked up the secure car phone and tried to reach his office in Washington. An operator told him that the Capitol Building was being evacuated. He talked to Lionel, his Assistant Administrator at his District Office in Cabotburg. They decided that for security reasons he would avoid the airports and would drive immediately in the limousine to Cabotburg, approximately a four hour run. He told Lionel to advise the media that he was safe; that he had escaped from the burning Tower; that he would hold a news conference soon after he arrived in Cabotburg that afternoon. Toussaint was already driving toward the highways north to New England.

But, of course, this was not exactly what happened.

Millard spoke that morning at 8:00 AM to a small group of tort lawyers in one of the private dining rooms of Windows on the World. Before he left a few minutes after 8:30 AM, the tort bench had pledged a comforting $300,000 for his next campaign and promised more. He left them drinking coffee and proceeded to an express elevator that took him to the street and his waiting limousine which was to take him uptown to a second fund raiser at the Waldorf.

The limousine was already moving on to the F.D.R. Drive when the Muslim terrorists flew the first plane into the North Tower. The limousine, slowed by increasingly heavy traffic, was moving off the Drive when the terrorists flew the second plane into the South Tower at 9:05. The limousine parked in front of the Waldorf on Park Avenue less than ten minutes later, but Millard never got out. He had been watching the evolving disaster on the limousine's TV; had failed to reach his office in Washington but had talked to Lionel in Cabotburg. Security had already contacted the office. He was advised not to return to Washington, but to proceed to Cabotburg by limousine, not by plane.

"We're skipping the second breakfast," Millard said, speaking to the back of Toussaint's thick, black neck. "We're driving to Cabotburg right now. Time to go."

"C'est vrai," Toussaint said and moved the limousine out into the Park Avenue traffic.

The limousine was on the highway passing Greenwich, Connecticut, at 9:50 AM when Millard watched the South Tower collapse. He was approaching New Haven when he watched the North Tower where he had eaten breakfast crumble in a cloud of smoke into the financial district. A police lieutenant told a TV correspondent on the street that he doubted anyone on the top 20 floors of the North Tower could have escaped. Only two hours earlier Millard had been sitting in that very dining room with all those supporters. Now they were gone. Fortunately, he had the pledge cards, but what a human loss, what a tragedy, what a wipe-out of well-healed supporters.

Somewhere between New Haven and New London, Millard sank into a deep melancholy. Had he delayed his departure from the breakfast at Windows on the World a half hour, he would have been trapped with the others and he began to imagine vividly what it would have been like.

In his mind, he saw himself being guided into a small office. He sat behind a desk and, as his peril became evident, he went back over his entire life, opening all of those old drawers full of half-truths and fantasies and mendacities. He was sincerely confessing as best his could to prepare himself for whatever was to come. He was truly trying to feel some contrition. Now, as he sped by the rich Connecticut towns, he saw only the smoke and debris swirling outside the office window in the doomed North Tower. He could have been still sitting there when the steel frame finally melted and the whole great structure with everyone who was trapped there imploded and 120 floors disintegrated one after another and cascaded into downtown Manhattan.

But he got out! How? It was certainly conceivable that some young Hispanic waiter who knew the way saw him; recognized him as an important man; led him down a fire stairway to the street; disappeared in the crowd; no doubt went on to help others; an angel of salvation, fighting through the smoke until he more than likely fell and smothered under the ruins. What was his name? He never said. But Millard knew this: there would be few greater heroes that morning.

It was a great story. And it was his story to tell without contradiction. No one at Windows on the World that morning could be asked precisely when he had left the breakfast. Toussaint, an illegal alien and loyal obligated servitor, would certainly concur with a somewhat later departure time if queried. Lionel, his Assistant Administrator, knew only that they talked on the phone sometime after the second plane had hit.

Millard sat up straight. There was no smoke outside the window anymore, only the highway through Rhode Island and southern Massachusetts. He was alive; he had survived; his inspiring life story stood intact and now was enriched. Soon they would be on Route 128 and headed north of Boston to the familiar industrially blighted mills and streets of Cabotburg. There the media and his constituents would be waiting to hear of his miraculous escape and how he would help defend them and the nation against future terrorist attack.

Millard reached for a yellow pad and began to make notes for his remarks to the media. Forgotten at least for now was his long, secret confession to himself. Cast aside was his difficult effort to generate some feelings of contrition for his acts. None of it was really a big deal, anyway. A little fudging here, a little shoving there; everyone did it. Now he had to concentrate on striking just the right tone, using just the right words. And surely he would make certain that no one would get a bigger build up than that little nameless Hispanic minority vote waiter. Millard already had his opening off-the-cuff line:

"Believe me! I'm lucky to be here."

Reality TV

The Grand Duchess Olga was not pleased. Her loving cousin, Alexander II, Czar of all the Russias, decided to include her in the small impressive assemblage that he was sending to America. It was a royal good will tour following the successful but unpopular sale of Alaska. The assemblage would be headed by another cousin, the Grand Duke Alexei, a womanizer and accomplished spendthrift whom Alexander mistakenly looked upon as a statesman. Alexei was also a widower. Olga would be a highly suitable hostess and companion. That assignment was easy. She also was to keep him free from scandalous behavior. That assignment was more difficult.

For Olga, the trip was an absurd idea. It was an inconvenient idea. It meant neglecting her many charities in St. Petersburg including the endless reconstruction of the cathedral. It meant neglecting her children of whom she saw little enough in her own palace. Worst of all, it meant ocean travel which she feared and hated.

For maximum comfort, it was determined that the royal party, twelve plus more than twenty servants, would not sail on the royal yacht but on one of Russia's newest ocean liners, the *Empress Catherine*. She would sail directly from St. Petersburg, docking only briefly at Southampton, before crossing the Atlantic to New York. When the royal party boarded, they occupied, along with 220 trunks and suitcases, most of first class. Some of the luggage was stored with the servants on lower decks. The royal jewels and certain state papers and financial documents were put in the ship captain's private safe. Olga insisted on keeping in her suite a small diamond tiara and her pearls. However, she reluctantly confined to the Captain's safe her other jewels including a more elaborate tiara and her most important possession, the 15th Century Cross of St. Sergius, a large pectoral gold cross that hung from a heavy gold chain. The cross was encrusted with diamonds, rubies, sapphires and emeralds. A rock crystal reliquary in its center encased a finger of Sergius, most beloved among Russia's saints and founder of Holy Trinity Monastery at Zagorsk. .

The *Empress Catherine* docked at Southampton on a cloudy Tuesday shortly before noon. Two royal Dukes and the British Foreign Minister were waiting and came aboard immediately. After a brief but impressive ceremonial greeting, the Russian and British royals along with the Foreign Minister and several Russian diplomats went ashore for a private lunch. During the afternoon, a few British steerage passengers and some cargo were taken aboard. Early that evening, only an hour after the Russian royal party returned, the *Empress Catherine* sailed with the tide.

Two days out of Southampton, the *Empress Catherine* was sailing through an unusually calm North Atlantic shortly after 2 A.M. when large explosions deep in her hull blew two cavernous holes below her waterline—the cause, possibly an engine fire, much more likely anarchist bombs. The liner sank in only twenty minutes. The acute angle of the deck prevented the lowering of any boats. Because of the time of the explosions, few passengers escaped from their cabins.

Irish fishermen arriving in the area just after dawn rescued two Russian sailors and an Orthodox priest, Olga's confessor, all clinging to wooden deck chairs. Only these three survived.

Professor Lincoln Quimby crunched his mouth to his nose as if he had detected a foul odor and put down the latest issue of *National*

Geographic Magazine. He had just reread an article by his supposed academic comrade in arms but actually his hated rival, Dr. Homer Alston of the Deep Water Institute of America. Dr. Alston's article once again recounted his heroic exploration of several men-o-war sunk at Trafalgar; the special techniques that he, Homer, had invented to overcome the enormous difficulties; and the important historic artifacts recovered. All true as Lincoln knew. After all, he had participated; in fact, he had participated significantly although few ever knew how significantly. Homer always saw to that.

Lincoln didn't really begrudge Homer his posturing and stardom too much. If he were Homer, he probably would act the same way. The problem was he was not Homer. And ocean archeology in the 21st Century was no longer what it was: a cozy academic affair sponsored by a university or two to satisfy the intellectual curiosity of its faculty members and, in the process, enhance their tenured careers. Big money was required. And Homer and his Deep Water Institute had a knack for acquiring it. Lincoln and his university were not so financially adroit.

However, Lincoln continued in his own small way to cast his professional net. Only this month, he too was published although not as conspicuously. Somewhere to the rear of *Archeology* he had a small piece that he called "Forgotten Treasures under the Sea." Lincoln listed half dozen ships that had sunk in the Atlantic in the last 200 years. All carried valuable artifacts to the bottom with scant hope of recovery because of the depth.

> *We know a great deal about these ships and the treasures that they had aboard. We know exactly where these ships lie. Because of the great depths marine archeologists cannot reach them with normal diving equipment. But now marine archeology has new technology—highly sophisticated ROV's (remotely operated vehicles) that we can control from the surface. The ROV's can dig a slit trench, open a suitcase or a porthole, pick up a Ming bowl.*

Lincoln sighed as he reread his words. What he had not mentioned was the enormous cost. You could hire an army of scuba divers for the cost of one ROV. This was the technology he had brought to Homer's latest expedition. Homer had provided what he always referred to as "noblemen with deep pockets." It was hard not to become discouraged.

That certainly was how Shelly Goodman felt that week. Sitting in his gymnasium-size office overlooking most of mid-town Manhattan, he felt very, very discouraged. He described his mental state to several of his associates in his usual colorful style: "If I could have eaten anything for lunch, I'd puke on my effing desk."

Shelly was reacting to the latest plunging numbers on his reality TV show "Gambling Gals." Two years ago it was Number One. Six women schemed and clawed and whored their way for a chance to play blackjack against the house for a huge jackpot in Vegas. Advertisers wrestled each other in Shelly's lobby for 30-second spots. Shelly's boss, the CEO of Großspiel, GmbH, a European entertainment and munitions conglomerate, shoved bonuses in his pocket every month. But that was then. This year, as Shelly graphically recognized, "Gambling Gals" was in the "le toilet."

"So I askyouagain," Shelly said, bugging out his eyes and gluing his words together as if they were German, "whatawegot?"

"You like nut-cake politics we could do that." This came from Mickey, the older and smarter of the two associates. "Billy Younie is peddling a show where four guys go at each other no effing holds barred to run for governor on a reform ticket. Maybe we goose it up with some cockfights"

"It's just a replay of lasnights news," Shelly said. "Whotheeffcares?"

"Pete Gunny who writes lots of comedy has a sock 'em, kiss 'em thing where teenage girls with lots of shape compete to sneak into a

Green Beret combat unit." This from Don, the better looking and sneakier of the associates.

"I never get a lot of chuckles out of Pete Gunny except when he's serious," Shelly said. "Gimmesomething new. Something that can be big. Ya knowwhatImean: BIG."

"Well," Mickey said, "I've got something here from the clowns over at Research that might be a real sleeper. They found it in some pointy-head magazine. What would you think about going after a safe full of royal jewels at the bottom of the Atlantic?"

Shelly slapped his desk with both his hands in a drum roll and his eyes bugged more than ever.

"I could love it," he said. "Tellmemore."

And so it came to pass that Prof. Lincoln Quimby, ME, PhD obtained "noblemen with deep pockets" for a major marine archeological expedition to the bottom of the Atlantic. The target: the *Empress Catherine*, lying 2800 feet beneath the surface. The deal: exclusive filming and live coverage of the expedition week by week on national TV with world rights including a final program at which the glittering findings would be revealed.

"We, of course, can't guarantee what we may find," Lincoln told Shelly and his associates while clearly enjoying a pre-lunch orange-flavored Martini and the view from Shelly's office. "Academic conservatism in these digs is always important. Maybe there will be a safe. Maybe it will have the royal jewels; maybe the Cross of St. Sergius; maybe other things of great interest. But who knows?"

"Exactly," Shelly shouted. "Whoknows? It's so beautiful. Think of the anticipation we pump up week after week as we talk about the jewels; as you get closer and closer; as you and your team overcome all obstacles of the deep water; as we disclose in detail the lives of those poor royals, a Grand Duke, a Grand Duchess, who wendownwiththeeffingship; of the arsonists, the terrorists, the bombs! It's gorgeous! It's BIG!"

The expedition and TV program rolled forward much as Shelly had planned. The battered skeletal remains of the *Empress Catherine* lay on her side no more than 300 yards from where Lincoln expected to find her. A large rubble field spread out partly under sand another 500 yards from her stern. Considering that she had been there for nearly 150 years, she seemed amazingly preserved when Lincoln first looked at her through his electronic viewers in the Command Cabin of *Grand Discovery,* the expedition's explorer ship.

Subsequently, his huge ROV and its two satellite ROVettes confirmed his initial impression. He and his team mates were overjoyed and, casting aside academic conservatism, felt increasingly optimistic and said so. The rubble field yielded a rich horde of artifacts: bottles, crockery, and fine porcelain bearing royal arms, silverware, and ship's brass. The ROVettes roamed the interior, photographing everything: some furnishings remarkably preserved under sand, a huge hole in the hull caused by the explosion, several staterooms long ago swept clear by the sea, the captain's bridge, an open purser's safe with coins and some gold bars, the captain's quarters empty except for a large, encrusted box .

"It's the captain's safe!" someone in the Command Cabin shouted at Lincoln. "We've found the captain's safe and it's still locked."

All of this action was also filmed by TV cameras: some of the video immediately flown to New York and edited for the show, *Treasure Trove,* which was well underway; some transmitted live to New York to meet the show's weekly prime time schedule. In either case, this caused continual disruption of Lincoln's program of archeological exploration that was trying to follow meticulous scientific procedures. The disruptions invariably began with daily phone calls from Mickey and Don usually quoting Shelly.

"Shelly says those shots of the stateroom were great but we need more," Mickey said. "Give us the staterooms occupied by the Grand Duke and the Grand Duchess."

"Let's get some shots of how the arsonists lived in steerage," Don said. "Shelly definitely wants to play up those bomb holes in the hull."

"Tell me again why we can't expect to find any human remains," Mickey said. "Shelly says there have to be some bones."

The show was built around two creamily attractive news anchors, Dirk Trump and Kitchie File. They knew little about either maritime archeology or Russian history, but they were masters at conducting superficial interviews with experts on both. In the first weeks, as the *Grand Discovery* crossed the Atlantic to the disaster site, Dirk and Kitchie skated through lighter-than-fluff interviews on the long assassin-ridden demise of the Romanovs, the dangers and horrors of mid-19th Century sea travel, the deep religious mysteries of St. Sergius' great walled monastery at Zagorsk, and the rivalries and technological triumphs of archeologists and assorted treasure hunters prowling the floors of the world's oceans.

All of this was smoothly interspersed with deliberately grainy black and white video showing or recreating the past along with live shots of Professor Lincoln and his team living through grubby days aboard the *Grand Discovery*, arguing with each other and nursemaiding their complex family of robots. Shelly also cynically introduced live interviews with Dr. Homer Alston and others. All were reverently referred to as giants of marine archeology and freebooting treasure hunts. All in one way or another said Lincoln would find nothing; if he did, it would have little scientific or historic value; and anything he did find of any value would have to be given back under maritime law to Russia or the Romonovs. On the other hand, big time lawyers produced by Shelly foretold of a fight to the Supreme Court.

Shelly lucked out on the day they found the captain's safe. It occurred the afternoon of a scheduled episode; plenty of time to transmit the video, edit it and rewrite it into the show that night. It was easy the following week to bring the safe to the surface live. To make sure there would be no slip up, Shelly insisted that Lincoln's team practice bringing the safe up on two test runs.

"There's a risk every time we do it," Lincoln complained. "Also we could end up compromising the scientific integrity of the whole venture."

"Prof, don't start that compromise integrity shit," Shelly, himself, came on to say during a videophone conference. "There's a risk you can't do it at all if you don't practice. This isn't cable; this is realty TV. Sogo practice."

Two days later, all TV cameras on, a special ROV with heavy grappling arms removed the captain's safe from the *Empress Catherine;* slowly, slowly brought it up through several thousand feet of water, and popped it up with much splashing into the sunlight. A huge crane hoisted the robot which still embraced the safe on to the *Grand Discovery's* deck. Everyone cheered. That afternoon they raised it again. The next day millions of TV viewers around the world watched a perfect third rising.

"Wait 'till those ratings are in," Shelly shouted at Don and Mickey, who were pounding his back and yelling obscene congratulations at each other and at him amid the crowd invited to watch in his triplex apartment. "We cleanedtheireffingclocks again!"

Prince Dmitry was not pleased.

"You know what they plan to do, of course," he said to his sister, Princess Marie. "They will bring the safe back here to New York and open it on that revolting show. Then they will parade our ancestor's jewels before the world like some gimcrack trophies at a cheap amusement arcade."

"Assuming they are there," Marie said.

The two were sitting in the library of the Prince's apartment on East 69th Street in Manhattan. The Prince, a short elegant man in his 40's, used his title only privately, very privately. Publicly he was a successful executive in an international investment bank. His older sister, who found her title useful, was the wife of an Austrian diplomat, a Hapsburg younger son. She was the mother of three boys all in distant line of succession to various thrones currently unused. The Prince and Princess had just watched to their enormous disgust the recovery of the captain's safe from the *Empress Catherine*.

"Let's assume they are there," Dmitry said. "What a circus for all of us in the family. But what can we do? Uncle Nikolai is talking about a lawsuit. I say no. The garbage press would love it. God, what a fiasco!"

"Just what do you think might be in the safe?" Marie asked, reaching for a long, perfumed cigarette.

"According to my grandfather, who certainly could have known personally the Grand Duchess Olga, his great grandmother, she had an enormous string of Oriental pearls that she always wore. She had any number of diamond rings and pins. She had several diamond coronets inherited from various czarinas. How much of this she had with her on the trip, how much she would have put in the safe, no one knows. But my grandfather always insisted that she always had with her an antique gold cross, the so-called Cross of St. Sergius. It was a favorite. However, again, who knows if she put it in the safe."

"What do you think it all might be worth?"

"Uncle Nikolai says 20 or 25 million at auction for the cross alone, but that's ridiculous. Really the cross is priceless. St. Sergius is still venerated by millions. The cross contains one of his fingers. People say it performs miracles. How could it be auctioned off like some dubious Picasso? It's a national treasure."

"Of what nation?" Marie asked quietly. "Maybe it would be hard to sell, but these people surely would try. I'm sure Uncle Nicolai would agree. I'm sure his position would be that if there is going to be a sale the family should get the money."

"I see only great expense, pain and a saturnalia in the press."

Subsequent conversations with lawyers fully confirmed what the Prince feared. Seeking an injunction to stop the broadcasting of *Treasure Trove* and prevent its subsequent highly valuable syndication throughout the world was folly. Suing under maritime law for rights to artifacts salvaged from the *Empress Catherine* had some chance of success. But the process would be lengthy and expensive, unwanted news coverage could be extensive, and eventually success in clearing myriad legal high jumps hung on the difficult challenge of proving original ownership and rights of inheritance.

As Lord Ferncroft, one of London's leading admiralty lawyers, put it at a secret family meeting: "The Grand Duchess Olga died almost 150 years ago. Since then, I am afraid that we have had a revolution and something of a dubious restoration, two world wars, widespread havoc and dislocations and enormous loss of documents. Ownership of the diamonds and pearls would be difficult enough, but as for the Cross of St. Sergius we would be tilting with the historic claims of the Russian Orthodox Church and the Russian State."

"Most discouraging," Dmitry told his sister. "Uncle Nicolai is ready to drop the whole business. The old boy is very depressed."

Ten days after recovering the captain's safe from the ocean, the *Grand Discovery* headed home in time for Lincoln and his team to participate along with the safe still locked in the final episode *of Treasure Trove*. Shelly decided that despite objections from the archeologists no attempt would be made to pick or blow the safe in advance of the show. It would be too risky to chance leakage of the safe's contents or face charges of fakery.

"Build interest," he told his PR squad. "Feed speculation: Is it full of diamonds? Gold bars? That crazy cross? Did the captain make a grab for it before he checked out? I wannaseeit all over the media. It's a made-to-order ratings builder."

Lists of the possible contents were fed to the media. Old pictures of royal jewelry and sketches of several versions of the Cross of St. Sergius appeared along with estimates of the jewels' great value. One expert from a leading auction house was interviewed on five talk shows on one Sunday alone. Several distant royal cousins were pictured dodging paparazzi in Paris and Rome. A London tabloid headline summed it up:

**ROYAL
JEWELS
JACKPOT??**

The night of the show Dirk and Kitchie were unusually antic even for them which some might say made them appear to be clearly committable. By contrast, Lincoln and several members of his team appeared weather-beaten and somber, a state brought on by having to wear makeup for the first time in their lives and Shelly's insistence that they appear in their oily, sea-battered work clothes.

Dirk set the tone for the momentous event by pontificating: "Tonight, when we open this safe for the first time in nearly 150 years, we are opening a door on a world that is no more."

Kitchie, one of TV-land's highest paid airheads, shook her Valentine's Day doll head in wonder and said: "Think of it. This is real history."

The climax of the show began with unveiling of the safe from beneath a large, filthy sail which Dirk absurdly suggested came from the wreck of the *Empress Catherine*. Baby spots picked out the safe on the dark stage. While everyone else stood back, two over-muscled workmen in hard hats and crisply pressed work clothes fired acetylene torches at the safe's door and slowly cut away the lock. Then Dirk and Kitchie, both maniacally grinning, ushered Lincoln forward from the shadows to the still smoking door of the safe. Using what looked like a backyard insulated cookout glove, Lincoln opened the door and immediately stepped back so that a bright spot and cameras could zoom in on the safe's interior.

The inside appeared dusty and dry. The green baize lining the shelves and walls looked almost new. There was an unscripted group gasp. The safe was empty.

The week before the final show Prince Dmitry and Princess Marie had found themselves involved separately in meetings that can only be described as being out of the ordinary.

The first took place on a sunny Tuesday afternoon at teatime. The Princess sat alone in a small sitting room on the second floor of her brownstone townhouse on East 66th Street, a few blocks from her brother's apartment. She was sipping tea and reading a magazine when the maid announced that a Father Vasili of St. Nicholas Cathedral was calling at the suggestion of the Metropolitan. The Princess did not know a Father Vasili, but she had been involved in a number of charitable projects at St. Nicholas, the Russian Orthodox Cathedral of the Russian Diaspora in New York, and she had dined with the Metropolitan. Accordingly, she told the maid to admit Father

Vasili who turned out to be a very nervous young priest with a full beard and enormous blue eyes. He was wearing a Russian monastic's traditional black inner cassock tightly fitted with a flaring skirt.

"I intrude," he said. "Forgive me."

"No, no, please sit down Father and have some tea," the Princess said, waving him toward a small gilded couch.

"No thank you. I must not stay," Father Vasili said, sitting down on the edge of the couch. "The Metropolitan sends his deep respects for being unable to come in person. He also says to tell you that he regrets the troubling stories in the press and that he prays for your family."

"The Metropolitan is very gracious. Please thank him for his prayers."

"I am to tell you that the Russian Orthodox Church Outside Russia wishes you all good things under heaven and that the Metropolitan has some information that may be helpful in this time of trouble."

"And the nature of this information?" the Princess asked, carefully putting down her teacup.

"I am told it is information passed down in the Order of the Holy Trinity for many years," Father Vasili said and removed an envelope with a wax seal from his cassock. "I am to give you this. The information is here."

Father Vasili rose and handed the Princess Marie the envelope, appeared relieved and smiled for the first time.

"I must go," he said abruptly and did, leaving the Princess alone holding the envelope in her hand. She broke the Metropolitan's wax seal, opened the envelope and removed a square yellowing piece of paper on which a series of numbers and letters was written in a firm European hand.

"Possibly it's the combination to the safe," Dmitry said, sitting alone with his sister an hour later in the same room to which she had excitedly summoned him.

"But how would the Metropolitan he get it?" she said. "And, even if it is what you say, what can we do with it."

"The priest told you. It was preserved by the monks. Olga or Alexei could have given it to Olga's confessor for security. As I recall the story, the confessor was one of the only three survivors."

"Even so what good is it? We don't have the safe,"

"You don't get to be a Metropolitan of the Russian Orthodox Church without some reasonable cunning. He has given us a possible bargaining chip. I'll talk to Uncle Nikolai and the lawyers tomorrow about the best way to use it."

But before Dmitry did that he experienced his own out of the ordinary meeting the following morning after an early routine business negotiation in an office tower near the United Nations. Dmitry and several of his associates sat across a table from several Russian executives and several Russian government officials to discuss participation in the risky and questionable financing of an oil pipeline. Afterwards, a friendly, rotund assistant to the Russian group asked Dmitry if he would join him at a coffee shop in the lobby and Dmitry agreed.

"Prince Dmitry," the man said as Dmitry recalled that the man had not been introduced at the earlier gathering where no one had addressed him as 'Prince,' "you are kind to take a few more minutes."

Dmitry nodded in cool agreement and said nothing.

"Let me introduce myself," the man said cheerily, speaking in short bursts. "My name, Yuri Chernikof. I am former KGB. It is no secret. Everyone knows. But now I am attached to our UN delegation and just do odd jobs. Like the oil negotiations. But also sometimes there are matters more delicate. Like this scandalous recovery of the safe on American television."

Dmitry nodded again. This man was a liar. He may no longer be KGB but as his subsequent remarks made manifest he was now FSB, the latest version of state security under the Russian Federation.

"My associates are very concerned about the safe: about its contents. Not so much the jewels although the cross has great meaning to many people in our country and the Orthodox Church. It is certain documents that might be there that are of concern."

"I don't think I follow you," Dmitry said. "What documents?"

"The royal group on the *Empress Catherine* was sent to America to solidify good relations with Russia after the sale of Alaska to Secretary of State Seward," Yuri said, barely moving his lips. "As you may recall the history, Russia proposed the sale to ease financial problems; but Seward's opponents in the Senate called it 'Seward's folly' and opposed it. The Russian ambassador had to encourage approval; several Senators were greatly enriched."

Yuri allowed himself a cynical smirk; drank some coffee; looked around to assure himself there were no unwanted auditors. Finally he continued:

"Despite the sale, Russia's financial difficulties persisted. We have reason to believe that the royal group aboard the *Empress Catherine* carried letters from the Czar to Seward and President Andrew Johnson. The Czar proposed a second round: the sale of more than a half million square miles of mostly empty tundra in eastern Siberia including the Kamchatka Peninsula."

"Truly ridiculous," Dmitry said. "Why would anyone take seriously the sale of part of Siberia to the United States?"

"With all due respect, your history is faulty. Seward, the imperialist, would have been very interested. The sale would have turned the Bering Sea into an American pond; the United States would dominate the northern Pacific Basin. You see: that is why it is felt that disclosure of these documents, if they exist, would be an unnecessary major embarrassment even now."

"Granting all this, I don't see why you come to me," Dmitry said. "The safe unfortunately is in the hands of American television and Hollywood."

Yuri again allowed himself a cynical smirk and spoke even lower.

"The television people are planning to open the safe during a live show. Meantime, the security is very poor. The safe could be forced open by burglars at any time; the contents removed. But that would be very public; there would be an investigation; the matter could become awkward. Surely, it would be much simpler to open the safe with the combination, remove the contents if there are any, and lock it again. A great surprise would await the world: there was nothing there after all."

"What would happen to the contents assuming they exist?"

"We would keep any documents. Any jewelry found would be returned to the rightful royal owners."

"And how would such a satisfactory result be accomplished?"

"Prince Dmitry, do not underrate your countrymen. We have good people here who are quite capable. But we do need the combination."

Two days after the sensational discovery on *Treasure Trove* that the captain's safe was empty a non-descript car double parked briefly on East 66th Street while a young boy delivered a Bloomingdale's shopping bag to the door of Princess Marie's brownstone. The delivery took less than one minute.

Inside the house, the Princess personally received the bag, carried it into the library and handed it to her brother, Dmitry. Their Uncle Nicolai, an ancient gentleman in English country tweeds, sat behind a curved French desk in front of a window with closed drapes. Dmitry put the shopping bag on a long table that he had cleared of objets d'art and silver-framed family pictures and began to unpack it.

Each item that he removed from the bag was neatly wrapped in yellowed linen. As he unwrapped each one, he examined it and handed it to his sister who handed it to their uncle who, in turn, returned it for placement on the table. When the shopping bag was finally empty, the display on the table included an elaborate tiara of brilliants and three central diamonds, an emerald necklace with large diamond droplets, four sizeable brooches with diamonds and other precious gems, and a half dozen diamond rings. The Grand Duchess' famous pearls and a small tiara that she seldom was seen to be without were missing; so was the gold pectoral cross and chain.

The Trinity Monastery of St. Sergius at Sergiyev Posad, formerly Zagorsk, sits behind white Renaissance walls that enclose a congeries of blue, white and gold cathedrals, palaces, churches and monastic buildings. St. Sergius founded the monastery in 1345 in a forest some 60 miles northeast of Moscow. Three saints and one of Russia's greatest czars, Boris Godunov, are buried there. The cathedrals, churches and other religious buildings house many relics and some of Russia's greatest art.

Pilgrims in great numbers have visited Holy Trinity for 600 years to pray and seek miraculous help. The Empress Elizabeth in the 18th Century made an annual pilgrimage on foot from Moscow. Numerous miracles and cures have been reported in every century. It is one of Russia's holiest shrines.

Possibly one of Holy Trinity's most miraculous events took place after the 1917 Revolution and the suppression of religion by the Communist Soviet regime. The Communists had turned Holy Trinity's churches into museums; silenced its great bells; destroyed and looted its religious treasures. But suddenly in the midst of World War II as German armies reached for Moscow, Joseph Stalin, ruthless tyrant, mass murderer and star seminary student, realigned himself with God. He declared that the "Motherland" was fighting a "holy war;" reopened 20,000 churches including Holy Trinity; recalled surviving priests from the gulags; ordered troops into battle shouting "God go with you;" and sent the wonder-working icon of Our Lady of Kazan in procession through the embattled streets of Leningrad, Moscow and Stalingrad

After obtaining victory, the ruthless tyrant, mass murderer and star seminary student reversed much of this. But Holy Trinity's decaying churches remained open. The flow of pilgrims which had decreased but never stopped persisted and grew. And, after the fall of the Soviet Communist regime, Holy Trinity was magnificently restored.

At Trinity Cathedral, where there are many relics of St. Sergius, pilgrims in recent years have reported that on Feast Days and other important occasions the monks display in procession a large gold pectoral cross of great age. Through the swirling clouds of incense, the faithful see and kneel before one of the most venerated relics of the saint. Pilgrims report that an increasing number of miraculous events have occurred.

Bad News on the Turnpike

The measure of man is what he does with power.
—Pittacus (650-570 BC), tyrant of Mytilene, one of the "Seven Wise Men" of Greece

The Senator habitually read his daily "A" File while traveling between campaign fund-raising stops and his commodious nest in the Russell Office Building. Today was no exception.

He had just come from a highly successful hotel breakfast in the suburbs with the Armenian Small Business League. He gave his standard pro-small businessman /anti-corporate fat cat talk laced for them with a solid shot of Turk bashing and Free Armenia Now. They loved it.

A gushing Vazgen Kocharian, chairman of the League, presented him with a framed certificate making him, the Hon. Maxwell Landfille Falkland, a High Knight of Armenia. Vazgen, a large swarthy man in a black silk suit, said: "We Armenians know when we have a friend and we do not forget." Tyrone, the Senator's campaign treasurer, told the new High Knight on the way out that the yield was better than $700 a head in campaign contributions. Beautiful!

The Senator's new diversity strategy was paying off handsomely. Let everyone else suck up to the blacks and the Hispanics and the Jews. Those gold fields were getting too crowded and too dicey. The Senator's new strategy was to target and stir up discontent and votes and cash among smaller groups like the Armenians, the Hindus, the Baluchs: this was win-win play, particularly if you could get there first.

As the Senator's limo moved slowly north on the Turnpike through late commuter traffic and the usual lines of monster trucks, he opened the sealed brown envelope that a young aide waiting in the hotel lobby had handed him. The label said:

STRICTLY CONFIDENTIAL

Senator Falkland—"A" File

Inside he found, along with succinct annotations from his top legislative assistant, a copy of his latest poll results ("not good, but improving"), an investigative report on his principal opponent's business partner ("even sleazier than suspected but probably not indictable"), an updated copy of the Senate floor schedule ("must attendance: OUR earmarks vote Thursday"), his teenage daughter's private school tuition bill ("overdue") and a sealed envelope addressed to him in a familiar handwriting. Opening the sealed envelope immediately, he read:

Maxy, you Big Shit—

Why are you treating me like this? Don't I always do the special things you like me to do? Now, just because of this stupid coming campaign, you want to pretend that I'm not around. Well, surprise, surprise, Maxy baby, I am!! If you won't take me to Bermuda next weekend like you know you promised, maybe I'll start seeing my old friend again at the Washington Post.

Tammy

Below her name, Tammy had drawn a sad face.

A strong feeling of nausea pervaded the Senator's normal well-being; he was glad he had eaten sparingly of the standard issue greasy sausages and cold eggs offered by the grateful Armenian small businessmen. The letter was an outrage, of course. What was the matter with the crazy girl? He had only known her for six months and she wasn't new to Washington. Before he slipped her into a job at Interior protecting birds and bears, she had worked part-time for some nutcake environmental newsletter. He first met her when she had asked him for an interview about saving swamps. She should understand what was going on: He was headed into a tough campaign for Chrisaskes!

The Senator picked up his cell phone and called his chief counsel, Hamilton Hootberg, on the supposedly private line but you never knew.

"Yes," Hamilton said curtly, sounding as always as if he were being interrupted while in a meeting with the Pope.

"Max," Max said unnecessarily. "I need to see you as soon as possible."

"I can be in your office by 11," Hootberg said. "The subject?"

"In my office," Max said. "We talk there."

"Oh, dear," Hootberg said and disconnected.

II.
Icy Water and Cold Turkey

Criminal Poop

Qui desiderat pacem praeparet bellum.
    —Flavius Vegetius Renatus, Roman military writer

Three events occurred each morning on Brattle Street.

At 6:30 AM. Dr. Gilbert Cumber opened the front door of his house to pick up the *Boston Globe*. By 6:35 he located the paper somewhere in his rhododendrons. As he turned to go inside his house, he saw come around the corner a huge mean-looking English Mastiff followed by a young man dressed expensively in what seemed to be the current stylish mode (neo-Renaissance Fop). And, as Gilbert shut his front door, he saw the Mastiff, his painfully worried eyes closed contentedly, squat and relieve himself in one of the long burgeoning beds of red and white New Guinea impatiens that bordered the sidewalk.

Each day for the last two weeks, Gilbert momentarily wanted to reopen the door and shout something about personal responsibility, but he restrained himself in the spirit of the non-confrontational, non-judgmental ethos of his world. Then, feeling righteous but increasingly frustrated, he joined his wife in the breakfast room.

On Brattle Street the houses are well-kept and costly in the Very Late Puritan manner and occupied for the most part by people who liked to think that they always think well of their fellowmen (and women). Or, at least, they think well of the less fortunate who do not live on Brattle Street. (Sometimes one's peers could be a trial.)

Certainly, Dr. Gilbert Cumber fully embraced that view of life. And why not? Gilbert was the distinguished discoverer of the elusive

D-particle, author of many barely readable but widely-praised books, celebrated in academic and political circles and, on occasion, a scientific expert on Sunday TV talk shows; he was safely and comfortably tenured in the J. George Husterman Chair of Nuclear Science; and even more comfortably invested. The value of Gilbert's house had increased by a factor of more than eight since he and his wife, Xenia, bought it when he moved to Cambridge as a young draft-exempt instructor during the Viet Nam War. By leveraging the house's growth in trendy value and his increasingly fat government consulting fees, Gilbert had been able to build a sizeable portfolio on which, as he always said modestly at Cambridge parties, he was happy to pay his fair share of taxes.

But Gilbert, his dramatic white hair more askew and his clothes more rumpled than usual, was clearly not happy this morning.

"It happened again," he told Xenia after trying without success to read a long, saccharine article in the *Globe* on the continuing discomforts and fully understandable biological transgressions of the homeless under the trees and on the walkways about Boston Common.

"Terrible for our flowers," Xenia said and nibbled a piece of toast purported to be made from 18 different grains, a mixture giving it the consistency of weathered slate. The toast was thinly spread with a new faux "butter spread" called *Cottswold Dew.* "Do you know the man?" she asked.

"Certainly not. But he must live in the area. Although obviously not for long. Obviously he doesn't know that you're supposed to pick up after your dog."

"Or doesn't want to," Xenia said. "I wouldn't. That's why we we've always had cats for the girls. You should speak to him. The impatiens will be ruined."

"I don't want to speak to him. I don't know him and I don't I want to. He looks like someone who sells polluted house lots or makes pornographic rental movies."

"Well, if you won't talk to him," Xenia said, "why not put up a small sign. And, if that doesn't work, you'll just have to say something to the police. After all, we do have laws."

Gilbert tried a sign the next day. In fact, he tried two. They said:

Please! Please!

No *Dogs!*

Help Keep Our Neighborhood

Beautiful!

Thank You!

The signs were placed neatly in the middle of two flowerbeds near the sidewalk. They were as decorous and unobtrusive as the indentured student labor at the university graphics office could make such a sign and still have it visible to the walker of any passing dog.

At 6:30 AM. Gilbert opened his front door and retrieved his newspaper from the nearby shrubbery. No dog walker. No dog. Gilbert went back inside and stood at a front window. Brattle Street was empty. An outsize red SUV cruised by piloted by a young woman with one hand as she chatted on a cell phone. The SUV missed by micromillimeters two other SUVs hulked along the curb and disappeared in the direction of Fresh Pond Parkway and the towered corporate souks of Boston. The street was empty again. Maybe the man and his beast had decided to walk somewhere else. Maybe the beast had run away or died. But, no: suddenly they appeared: the man and his Mastiff strolling languidly around the corner. The man wore a tightly tailored fawn linen suit (long five-button jacket, white double-breasted vest) and carried a short unattached Gucci dog leash. Unattached! The Mastiff wore an ominously heavy black leather collar and was snuffling the ground with much passion. They arrived in front of Gilbert's house and stopped. As Gilbert watched, the man read the first sign and walked on. The Mastiff snuffled loudly into the impatiens, squatted, excreted an impressive mound of ordure, kicked his hind feet in the flowers scattering dirt on one of the signs and trotted happily after his master.

'Well?" said Xenia when Gilbert, his face flushed like a dangerously rare roast, sat down at the breakfast table.

"Neither the man or his dog can read,' Gilbert snarled.

"Oh, dear" Xenia said. "So many of our young people today suffer from being behaviorally challenged. It's got a name: the Behaviorally Challenged Youth Syndrome, BCY. If you won't at least talk to him, you'll just have to call the authorities as I told you yesterday."

"Without fail," Gilbert said and angrily spread *Cottswold Dew* on his 18-grain toast with such emphasis that the square shingle crumbled. "My pleasure, thank you very much."

But, because Gilbert had had very little opportunity day to day to deal with the police, he overestimated how much pleasure might be derived from the experience. In fact, when he made the phone call, he found himself immediately undergoing what he later described as acute cognitive pain.

"This is Dr. Gilbert Cumber," he told a woman who identified herself as Corporal Santini-Flynn. "I live on Brattle Street and I want to report a man who is allowing his dog to defecate in my flowers."

"How da ya spell Cumber?" Corporal Santini-Flynn said. "You go with a C or a K?"

"With a C. I am Dr. Gilbert Cumber."

"Right. And you're living on Brattle. Now: Ya live in an apartment or a house, Gilbert?"

"It's a house. My house."

"Right. Ya rent or own?"

"I own. Officer, can we..."

"Right. So, Gilbert, what's the complaint?"

"As I told you, a man is allowing his large dog to defecate in my flowers."

"Sorry, Gilbert, I missed that. What's this dog doing in the flowers?"

"The dog is using my flowerbeds as a public toilet"

'Oh. I get ya. You got dog poop in your flowers. So what's the complaint you want to file with us?"

"I told you. And I want this stopped. I want this man fined. I want this dog off my property."

"Like did you talk to him, Gilbert? The man, I mean. You know, tell him to get a pooper-scooper, maybe? Whadhesay?"

"Nothing. I didn't talk to him. I don't want to talk to him. That's what you people are supposed to do. That's why we have police. That's why I pay taxes. I want something done."

"Now listen, Gilbert: you want like action on this you got the wrong department. We don't do dogs here. Or rather we don't do dogs unless, you know, they're killing or mauling little day care kids or bag ladies or something like that. Maybe what you want is to talk to the Dog Officer. Maybe he can help. Give you some advice on what to do. I'll try transferring you over there, but you can call him through the City Hall switchboard case we get disconnected. Now hang on, Gilbert, I'm transferring."

He hung on; there was a burst of music; an announcement about no trash pickup on Evacuation Day; another burst of music; then the line went dead. Gilbert called City Hall, asked for the Dog Officer and was put through immediately.

"You have reached the Office of the City Dog Officer," a recorded female voice said. "If your dog is missing, press 1; if you have found a dog, press 2; if you want to adopt a dog, press 3; if you have been bitten by a dog, press 4; if you are reporting an attack by a pit bull, press 5; if you are reporting an attack by a pit bull on a minority child, press 6; if you would like a copy of our popular brochure *Living in the City with a Person's Best Friend*, press 7; if you wish to talk to the City Dog Officer, press 8; press 9 to hear this menu again."

Gilbert chose "8." A very friendly male voice said: "Hi, I'm Larry Girandole, First Assistant City Dog Officer. The City Dog Officer and his entire team are out working on cases just now so we can't talk to you. But your call is very important to us. Please call back after 4 P.M. Eastern Daylight Time when we'll be back at your service." The line disconnected.

Gilbert could barely speak as he left the house. He could barely get through his lecture that morning on the *Three Missing Particles*. He brooded in his office. He brooded though a runny egg salad sandwich on organic nut loaf in the Faculty Club. He brooded through an early afternoon departmental meeting on recent additions to the list of student disadvantages about which he needed to be concerned. No amount of brooding changed the basic facts: He hated the man. He hated the dog. He hated the police. He increasingly hated whatever was in the air that made all this possible. Most of all, he hated being made to hate all of these people and he hated himself for feeling so helpless. Finally, by midafternoon he decided what he had to do.

He left his office and, after a discreet discussion with a university security guard, drove to a shopping mall over the nearby New Hampshire border where the right of a citizen to bear arms is better appreciated than in Massachusetts. Feeling like a recidivist alcoholic awash with shame over how some might regard his behavior but much relieved for the present at the blessed smell of gin, he walked into a chain store called Sporting Life and purchased a twin-barreled shotgun and a box of shells.

"This baby can stop anything up to 500 pounds," the salesman said. "You want to take it under your arm or you want me to wrap it up?"

"Please wrap it," Gilbert said. "I assume there's an owner's instruction manual."

That night Gilbert slept no more than an hour. At five o'clock, he was up. He dressed and ate an orange. He took up his post at the front window before six. The shotgun was in the hall closet. He had checked three times to see that it was properly loaded. At 6:15, a truck drove by and slowed as an apparently disembodied arm hurled a copy of the *Boston Globe* into the rhododendrons. Gilbert winced and for a moment saw himself rushing into Brattle Street with the shotgun and firing at the departing newspaper delivery truck.

"Don't let yourself be diverted," he told himself firmly. "You're a scientist. Focus. Focus. Stick to the plan, Gilbert."

He remained seated and unmoving. Five minutes...10 minutes. He checked the gun in the closet for the last time. He returned to the window. No one. Some sparrows. Two cardinals. Then Xenia's behaviorally challenged youth and his behaviorally challenged dog came along the sidewalk. Gilbert rose and walked almost casually passed the closed hall closet, out his front door and up his front walk. He would confront the enemy.

Gilbert saw before him a soft-faced young man with thinning blonde hair and an equally thin mouth. His costume this morning was tightly-tailored olive linen (long five-button jacket, red brocade vest with lapels, a broad gold tie featuring copulating green squirrels). The man's feet were encased in large black and white running shoes.

'Good morning,' Gilbert said in a faux friendly, strained voice. "Nice dog you have there."

"A sweetie," the BCY said. "Great watch dog, too. These guys used to take on bears and lions under the Romans."

Gilbert nodded with a small appreciative smile at this bit of history and saw that the unleashed killer of bears and lions was already snuffing the edge of an impatiens bed.

"We all love dogs around here," Gilbert said. "But we love them even more if they don't ruin our flowers."

"No problem," the BCY said. "All Benny ever does is drop a little extra fertilizer here and there to help you out." He barked a hearty laugh at his witticism.

"Well, I would really appreciate it if Benny didn't do that," Gilbert said.

"Can't really help you there" the BCY said, rolling his eyes and assuming an expression of helplessness. "Benny does pretty much what he wants. Anyway, Benny, you know, he has rights just like all of us. Like it's a free country, you know?"

"That's the way you see it?" Gilbert said and heard his voice suddenly rising in an alarming gargle. "You think you can trespass on private property?"

"Hey, let's not lose it now," the BCY said. "This is no big deal. Why don't you just go back inside and have a nice breakfast."

Gilbert stared in open hostility at the BCY's pudding face, saw that he was now smirking. He turned without saying more and strode back to the house. As he shut the front door, he saw the BCY watching him triumphantly while Benny squatted in the flowers. By the time Gilbert came back outside, this time carrying the shotgun, the BCY and Benny had started to walk away.

"Hold on there, please," Gilbert called out, striding back down the path. "Hold on!" The BCY stopped, turned and froze in place because by the time he saw the shotgun and the possible implications of its presence registered in his mind Gilbert was only about 10 feet away.

"Hold it yourself," the BCY screamed. "Stop right there! Are you some kind of nut cake? Put down that gun or I'll sic Benny on you."

"Put a leash on that beast immediately or I'll shoot him," Gilbert said, suddenly feeling a miraculously pleasant "High Noon" rush. "Leash him!"

"OK, Pop, OK. Just let's not get excited. Stop pointing that shotgun at me"

"Leash the damn dog," Gilbert ordered again. "Leash him!"

"OK, OK," the BCY said and warily walked over to Benny and snapped the leash on his collar. Benny emitted an ominous growl. "See. I warned you. This dog can be pretty mean."

"Not with his head blown off," Gilbert said.

"Now, let's not get crazy. Calm down. Let's talk."

"We did that," Gilbert said. "You told me about Benny's rights. But you forgot to mention mine. One of them is that people and their animals don't trespass on my property and use it as their personal latrine. Another is that if they do that by accident they make amends. So get busy."

"Oh, come on. Get real. What do you expect me to do?"

"Take away what your dog left in my flowerbed."

"And if I don't?"

"Then we'll test my aim. Maybe all you'll lose is the use of your legs for a bit because I had to protect myself from your vicious dog. But be aware that according to the manual this gun jumps when it shoots."

"Easy, easy," the BCY pleaded, changing to the tone he might use in trying to placate a village idiot. "Look, let me get a shovel. Yes, that's what I'll do, you know. I'll get a nice big shovel and a pail. And then I'll clean up the flowerbed. I really will. You'll like it."

"You'll clean it up now. I'm going to stand here with the gun pointed at your legs and you're going to pick up your dog's droppings. And since you forgot to bring along your nice big pail and shovel, you can use your hands and your pockets. Now do it quickly like a good responsible citizen and, as you say, let's not get crazy, because I'm beginning to enjoy the real possibility of having to defend myself with this gun."

The BCY closed his eyes briefly. Then he made a career decision, shrugged and tip-toed into the flowerbed while still holding

Benny tightly on the leash, knelt in the red impatiens and began carefully scooping up Benny's considerable morning evacuation. The man put his gatherings into his jacket pockets as delicately as possible, but large dank stains immediately permeated the olive linen. When he finished, he resignedly wiped his hands on his trousers and rose to find himself standing awkwardly in his mired suit again looking into the twin barrels of Gilbert's gun.

"Good job," Gilbert said encouragingly as if he were talking to an undergraduate lab assistant. "You and Benny can leave now. Have a nice day."

An hour later Xenia joined Gilbert at the breakfast table and she was pleased to see that he appeared exceedingly cheerful.

"You seem in very high spirits," she said. "Did you resolve the dog walker problem?"

"Absolutely," Gilbert said. "I talked to him."

"Wonderful. I knew that once you explained to him how we all want to beautify our neighborhood with flowers, he would want to cooperate. Anything special on your schedule today?"

'Not much," he said. "Lot of paperwork. Later I think I'll run over to Beverly Farms and see my old student, Josh Whipple. I want to find out what's involved in joining the North Shore Skeet Club."

The King and the Journalist

The best government is a benevolent tyranny tempered by an occasional assassination.
— Francois Voltaire, French philosophe

(The dialogue takes place in the ornate café of the Gloriette Garden House overlooking Schönbrunn Palace, the great palace park and the distant city of Vienna. The Gloriette is a glass-enclosed hall inside a triumphal arch; classical colonnades extend from both sides; a massive imperial eagle with spread wings crowns the roof. The Empress Maria Theresa built the Gloriette to celebrate the triumph of Austrian arms over the Prussians.)

Well, Dickie, or rather I should say, Ludwig Richard Frederick Louis Maximillian, Elector of Saxony-Rhingrave, Lord of the Eastern Marches, Margrave of the Ilk, Prince of the Kingdom of Jerusalem, etc., you're a king at last.

I fear that is true. How does the old saying go? Sometimes better never than late.

But not too late this time, Dickie, I think. Not for you.

We shall see and that very shortly.

I must stop calling you Dickie.

Certainly not. All of my old friends know me as Dickie. And considering your connections, not you of all people.

All right, but no longer in public; no longer in your official dealings. You must be addressed as Your Majesty. And those who choose to do otherwise should be reprimanded. It's all part of what you have called in your writings and speeches the magic of monarchy.

Yes, yes, I suppose. That's part of what being a king is. Certainly, that is what I have been told all my life. Act like a king, Dickie, think like a king: We kings can't help ourselves. We must be royal or we are nothing. Of course, we must never forget how to bend regally at the right times.

So, if Your Majesty pleases, may we proceed with the interview? As agreed, it is entirely off the record. Everything will be attributed to a "well informed source" and only a very few in the highest reaches of our organization are aware as you would expect of the identity of that source. To begin: Tell me first: how are you personally adjusting to your new status?

You probably are not aware of the details of how I was asked to take the job?

Not really. I assume there was some sort of visitation by an official delegation.

Exactly. I was in Milano attending a performance at La Scala and received a message in the ducal box at the end of only the second act. Could I meet immediately with a certain group at the palazzo of Prince Ottoboni on a matter of great importance? Very annoying, you must believe. I was attending a magnificent performance of Verdi's Don Carlo, a favorite. However, I abandoned Verdi and went to the meeting.

Did you have any idea what the matter of importance might be?

To some extent. I had heard that there had been conversations among members of a powerful cabal of generals and ministers of the highest rank. They desperately needed a figurehead and were thinking about offering a crown of some sort to my grand nephew, the Archduke Franz. I assumed that these people were looking for support with Franzy, who can be difficult. What surprised me was that they wanted me, not Franzy, and that the job had impressive significance.

And now, six weeks later, how do you feel about it?

Probably I should feed you the usual blather about being humbled by so great an honor and my constant prayers that I will be able to fulfill the hopes and expectations of so many millions throughout the West. But, surely, knowing me well, you would struggle politely not to guffaw. After all, I am 70 years old and I have lived all of my life with the knowledge that I am by noble lineage and, of course, Grace of God, one of the most royal of royals alive. I have 144 quarterings in my coat of arms. That knowledge does not encourage humility. However, unless one is a total knave, it does encourage duty and service—a subject about which I have much to say. As for my personal situation, you know I am not overwhelmed. I have lived my entire life as a stateless but rich royal vagabond: occupying one large residence or another in Europe and the United States; aimlessly circumnavigating the world on private yachts often hung with mysteriously missing old masters; sitting out wars and other assorted unpleasantries in grand hotels and resorts. Now I am ensconced here at Schönbrunn: somewhat more grandiose than what I am used to but not much. Clearly I am no unbathed Communist brigand slipping into the absent emperor's bed. Members of my family, I may remind you, have resided here in the past.

Would you call it a lifetime of training.

I never have thought of it that way. More a millennium of training and a lifetime of frustration. You know the king business hasn't been much of a winner for the last hundred years. Misunderstood and still damned unpopular in many quarters despite the disasters that have ensued without us. Think about what's involved: By birth, you are born to rule—not because you wanted to or were asked. The obverse of that gold coin is that you are absolutely obligated to serve. Well, a lot of people don't like that idea even if you're capable; they think that they can do it better even though most can't. On the other hand, a lot of people like the idea of having someone in charge without a lot of democratic bickering, someone who can represent the good and the best. Then again, human frailty being what it is, even royalists get to resent what I would call the well-deserved perks for undertaking a very dodgy lifetime job.

Would it be better if you were to take on more modest trappings?

There have been so-called citizen nobles and citizen kings: Philippe Égalité, for example, and his unfortunate son, Louis Philippe. Both of those mushy intellects born of the royal Orleans line come immediately to mind. One died on the guillotine; the other was quite rudely deposed by the usual mob and fled. All such are failures in the end. You can't poor mouth kingship. Kings have to be kings or they don't serve the function. A king who lives in a walk up and practices his magic mostly on homeless beggars won't make it.

There is a precedent.

His kingdom was not of this world as you from your experience in covering the election of Popes should know better than most.

What do you think are the prime qualities needed for success?

Above all, relentless dedication to overall duty. The truly great king—as opposed to the standard trimming politician—continually strives, not merely proclaims he is striving—for the best for the nation and its people. And he does this while adhering to the highest moral standards possible. I say "possible" because the great king knows two pivotal truths: One is that absolute good and absolute evil really do exist. Two is that most men exercise their free will to partake or not partake in both. Niccolo Machiavelli, you know, made that very clear in his *Discourses.*

Can not a freely-elected democratic leader demonstrate the same exemplary qualities and moral stature?

For the most part, a freely-elected democratic leader is an oxymoron. To be elected, he usually sells or at least leases his immortal soul. Then, to lead he must begin to acquire some semblance of the anointed attributes of an hereditary monarch—a leader by birth set apart by legitimacy, tradition and social magic high above the common man. Even the best democratic leader acquires the magic on loan. And, if the democratic leader starts to believe his borrowed magic is really his to employ any way he chooses rather than something to be used wisely and sparingly, we call such men dictators and, quite frequently in a fit of righteous revolutionary ecstasy, we butcher them. Often, of course, rightly so. A very messy process.

But we have had great elected leaders.

Of course, and we have had perfectly terrible kings. Both types of leadership—kings and elected leaders—can be very dicey. That is why the combination is better. Sovereign kings who can be a check on elected democratic leaders and elected democratic leaders who can be a check on sovereign kings. Keeps everyone on the up-and-up. Both alone have a dangerous tendency to change into tyranny or fecklessness.

You refer often to the magic of monarchy. Just what is that magic?

It is what makes men fight and die for king and country. It is what makes even enemies bend the knee in the royal presence. It is what makes a Charles I act in the magnificent, noble way that he did as stepped through the window of the Banqueting House and walked to the block.

Can you give me a little more specificity, perhaps?

Specificity is always the enemy of magic, but let me try to name the components. First of all there is legitimacy; second, there is long continuity; third, there is memory, history truly is present; and fourth, there is national apotheosis: all of the greatness, all of the honor, all of the glory of the nation in which every citizen wishes to partake and takes pride is bound up mysteriously in the majesty of the monarch. We all want to be part of something greater than ourselves, don't we? The monarch serves that need at least in this world: he is the living embodiment of the nation. That is why when the monarch fails in his duty it is cataclysmic. Going home on dark nights men take great comfort in seeing a light burning in the office of the King and know that he is working to keep them safe.

But it can always be said critically by free men that no one elected the king for the job?

Correct. That's the strength of it. As I said, he was legitimately born to it. For better or worse, he is anointed by God. He has no choice—only duty. On the other hand, deep down inside ourselves we know that the compelling force that thrusts forth someone to be elected chief of state is usually only that someone's massive ego. Ask any candidate for President of the United States by what right should he be President rather than a score of other obviously superior men or woman and you get a lot of self-serving platitudes. It is buncombe. Real legitimacy is something built up and proven over time, normally much time. The closest that the United States ever came to it was the Adams family as Henry Adams well knew in his own convoluted way. He understood the power of such magic. Look what he wrote about the Virgin. Of course, the American political psyche was not ready for the magic of monarchy. At least, not then.

Or never. Many millions of people seem to live very satisfactorily without what they regard as nothing but political hocus-pocus.

Not really. They use substitutes, many rather tacky, many very dangerous. And these really are political hocus-pocus of a very high octane. Fascism and Communism gave us the all-seeing, all-intrusive totalitarian state. The United States and France give their presidencies imperial trappings that are easily and often made threadbare by the wearers. The African kleptocracies give us Presidents-for-life who tend to leave office quite suddenly. Moreover, even the real magic does not last forever although I believe it lasts longer than some suggest. Otto von Hapsburg used to say legitimacy cannot survive more than one generation. I disagree with that. I think, in his heart, he did too.

Speaking of legitimacy and continuity, is it premature to ask in view of your age what arrangements you and your supporters have made for succession?

Assuming success of the reigning monarch and his regime, not a sure thing at all, your question is not premature but a critical factor. Happily there is no problem. My late wife, the Duchess of Kronberg-Gotha, and I produced three sons and two daughters—all properly educated and trained to their position and some of them with considerably more than pedestrian intelligence. First in line of succession would be our eldest, Crown Prince Max, currently an investment banker in Zurich. The Duchess, by the way, had 52 quarterings. Unfortunately, as you know, we lost her in a yachting accident off Cowes some ten years ago.

Ideally, what do you consider the best education for a king, an education that prepares him for this special role?

How does one teach godhead? The history of the education of princes is not all a triumphal story. Many times it has been quite awful. But in all fairness you have to ask what it is the king was supposed to do at some particular time. If personally leading an army into battle is the prime attribute sought as it was in the 12th Century, Richard I's education was excellent. He was a superb general and a superb warrior. Of course, like all kings who prove to be great, he had some natural attributes working for him. For one thing, he was unusually big and had very long arms. You would have been wise not to confront him when he wielded a broadsword while leading the charging chivalry of Europe. Today, although military education is important, we look for numerous other talents: some learned from tutors, some by sound regal apprenticeship, still others by absorption of the royal effluvia, always the source of special knowledge.

Would you say kingship is more like an art than a profession?

James I of England called it a craft. And James was a very canny Scot.

Then it is good apprenticeship and experience that we should look for?

Not necessarily. Because of the burden of my hereditary position, I have been relegated in our democratic times to be only peripheral to all of the great historical events of our times: the Cold War, the major hot wars, the Technological Revolution, the Global Economic Revolution, the rise of the United States, the failure of the Third World. Therefore, my hands-on apprenticeship and experience is small. But I have been a very good and very close observer. Queen Elizabeth I spoke six modern languages and two ancient ones. I was schooled in an equal number and I have had much time to read and converse in all of them with many very smart people and many slow ones, too. I studied at Heidelberg and MIT. I was an officer in the British Royal Navy. It has been a reasonably good education for a king.

However, until now you have never exercised power. Even as a constitutional monarch, you will have significant political influence for the first time. Or, at least for the first time openly.

Don't be so clever. I have assiduously avoided all my life the apparent exercise of whatever political influence I might have. It has been far too dangerous a roll of the dice for any royal with half a brain since the end of the Second World War.

I truly understand. But there have been stories. For instance, did you not privately advise Western governments that the Arab oil cartel with its massive oil embargo in the 70's was a paper tiger that would collapse if confronted with real military force?

I believe that is a story based on some idle comments that I made at a small dinner party in Paris. Certainly I was not even privately counseling governments. However, as things have turned out, my comments were not far off the mark.

Then there is the story of your secret meeting with President Reagan in his plane when he came to Europe and you are said to have disclosed to him that very few of the Soviet ICBMs were still in operating condition.

That would, indeed, have been useful information for him to have at his Cold War negotiations with the Soviet Union that month. But my meeting with the President of the United States was purely social, hardly secret. I believe we talked about thoroughbred horses. He was a fine horseman, you know.

And it has been said that you were the first to counsel the Queen of England and the Comte de Paris about the nuclear threat to their countries from Muslim terrorists operating out of Frankfurt.

I have always been close to the royal houses of both countries. We are related, of course. But surely they did not need me to pass along tittle-tattle about such plots.

Still I also have been told that you spent the last few years privately imploring governments throughout the West to prepare to defend themselves for a renewal of the 1500-year-old wars with a fanatically militant Islam.

I would not deny that I held that opinion and I have been proven correct. But what would you expect of someone whose ancestors helped turn back the high tide of the Muslims at Tours, and at Lepanto and on the walls of Vienna? Did you know the Muslims actually burned the old chateau here at Schönbrunn before we defeated them in 1683?

So, I gather, you wish me to believe that all these and other reports are only rumor and coincidence. Still it must be a great relief to you now that you can feel free to contribute in the open.

And I will. Nothing in me has changed. I have the strong sense of duty that I always have had regardless of whether I acted or did not act. For better or worse, I have been asked at this crucial time to exercise it.

How are you being accepted by the generals in the Western Alliance?

About what you would expect. Those in Europe and America who favored having me exercise my claim as constitutional monarch of the new United Kingdom of Europe are delighted and doing everything they can to ease and solidify my situation. Those who opposed the idea act as if they are adjusting to it. But, of course, there are some who only act: they wait for the opportunity to send me packing.

Such as Henri Rostand, the French intelligence director?

Well, he may be one of those less than resigned to wait. He, or at least those loyal to him, will, how shall I say it, seek to encourage adversity. Particularly the French, who favored naturally a Bourbon or Bonaparte monarch if any, and the Russians, who always like to play naughty games.

But why? Don't they understand what the words constitutional monarch mean?

That's their very point. They long ago have cynically come to believe that words mean anything one wants them to mean. And they firmly believe that in my mind the word constitutional really means in time "absolute." Meantime, listen to them: note well how they already are changing their own words: the twisting, the transmogrifying, the daily cosmeticizing has already begun.

Do they really think that you would want to abolish the elected parliaments and their elected leaders and rule without them?

Not exactly. They think I will want to take away their various powers for myself while leaving the parliaments and subsequently the American Congress in place but only as well-paid but empty symbols. All something like the Roman Senate under the Empire.

Ridiculous! Nothing in your history could lead them to think that.

You think it would be the wrong thing to do?

I certainly do.

I should say I agree. That is the only correct position. But, confidentially, for what you call deep background only, I am not so sure. The European parliaments and the American Congress are composed mostly of truly spineless scrubs. Give most of them a fine lunch, some trappings of power and the opportunity to remain in office, and I find most of these people will do anything to avoid inconveniencing themselves. Only when the enemy is on the walls do they become anxious. That is what has happened. The continuing threat of the Islamists armed with weapons of mass destruction; the recent take-over of the Saudi government by a terrorist junta; the explosion of a dirty nuclear bomb in the Paris Metro and the thwarting of several similar atrocities—such alarming developments have finally caused these born appeasers to unite for the moment: first under a few military leaders; now under me as a constitutional monarch, because they fear the military leaders. But the military allied with a monarch can be a very effective combination in a controlled combustion. And I may need such a combustion to defend the West from the Islamists.

Surely, not when the monarch is someone such as yourself: a life-long constitutionalist, a noble aristocrat of the highest moral character; a man of deep religious faith, education and taste; a man trained from birth to serve the public good.

You are too kind. But I must remind you that even if I bear even some modest resemblance to the paragon that you just described it means nothing if I do not prevail. It is also important to survive.

Do you really think you are in personal danger?

Not today, but I am told that will change very soon. We are taking appropriate security measures. At least, I hope we are. It is all very annoying.

You find it confining?

Certainly to the extent that I can't walk along the Ringstrasse and attend a concert without a big fuss, I do. But the most disturbing aspect is what the problem portends.

I am aghast. Here in this peaceful park, here in the delightful Gloriette where Maria Theresa once sat, I frankly find the suggestion that you are in personal danger so soon impossible to believe.

I assure you Maria Theresa would not have found it hard to believe and would have been the first to take the necessary steps. Survival of the regime is essential to accomplish anything. You and your masters know that well and would forgive me. Now, we must stay in deep background, yes? Here, if events unfold as I expect, is what I plan...

(At this point, the dialogue was broken off, a cessation caused by the arrival of Schwester Hannah in a burgeoning white and red habit and the simultaneous disappearance of the journalist from the small round table in the café. Remains of little pastries and coffee served in Herend porcelain decorated with golden bows and colorful spring flowers and butterflies are still on the table. A pianist is playing Mozart.)

Ah, there you are, Herr Dickie. I hope you have had a pleasant afternoon. It is the time now we should be going back to the hospital for a nice dinner, nicht wahr?

Yes, yes. I have been having a splendid and most stimulating afternoon. But is it really so late as you say? I was just thinking that perhaps it might not be.

Amazing Events

...be our defense against the wickedness and snares of the Devil
—Old Prayer

And so the evil days followed one after the other, and there were no good days, and, as so often can happen, the basically good, hard working people cast away their caution and their ingrained reluctance to act, and a series of amazing events occurred in the land.

The Art Critics (Boston)

TIC was having a particularly good evening: He had spray-painted his name on more than half a dozen mailboxes, spread a seascape of whirls on a main highway bridge, put an enormous 'TIC TOKK" in red, black and yellow on the State House wall, and now was just finishing a major meretricious opus on the base of the Arthur Fiedler Bandshell.

TIC was already a famous *writer*. He had gone *all-city* only last year, but he was already *known:* You could see him all over the center of Boston. His illiterate scrawls were on lots of buses. He was *up* on subway cars from Southie to Harvard Square. And this work of blazing multi-color faux writing on the Bandshell was going to be a career capper.

The work would remain unfinished. TIC stepped back to determine whether he had spelled his favorite all-purpose word with enough "K's." As he did so, two large men grabbed him by the arms and a third hit him in the face with a cold cloud of Mace.

By the time TIC could see again, he had been driven in a closed van to the old Frog Pond in Boston Common. A silent crowd of Americans long tempered and formed in the melting pot of the Nation stood around the Pond's dry concrete bed. On the Pond's edge, TIC recognized a tight group of writers: A black guy who signed his work "ROV"—a big name! Another who signed his work "YUS." Maybe a half dozen other blacks; three Latinos; a couple of whites from the suburbs. All were in street uniform: oversize unlaced athletic shoes, outsize baggy trousers hanging below the crotch and cascading over their feet, bulky padded jackets.

Some obsolescent National Guard field lights hung in the trees. The lights flickered and dimly lit the area. A long table that appeared to be a solid block of wood stood in the middle of the waterless Pond.

"Put him with the other artists," someone said to the two men tightly holding TIC. The men half duck-walked, half-shoved TIC around the Pond to where the other writers were standing. All of them had their arms bound to their sides with yellow sail yards.

Hey, YUS," TIC said. "What's going?"

YUS didn't answer. Before he could, he was pushed to the table in the center. While one man held YUS in place, a second pulled his right tattooed arm from the rope and stretched the arm with his hand palm up on the table top. In the dim light, blue and yellow florescent paint glowed on his palm. A third man wearing a ski mask stepped up to the table, raised a machete over his head and severed the open hand at the wrist. One of the men holding YUS tossed the severed hand into a nearby bushel basket.

They did ROVE next; then the Latinos; then TIC. They only took about fifteen minutes to do the whole group.

Cleansing Fire (New York)

Four homosexuals dressed as giant condoms were the first demonstrators to arrive outside the Cathedral where the new priests were being ordained. As on previous occasions, NYPD barricades stood in front of the Cathedral steps and a line of riot officers with shields, helmets with face protectors and clubs stood in front of the barricades.

Five minutes later, six yellow and black buses parked across the avenue in front of Rockefeller Center blocking traffic and several hundred members of the Lesbian and Gay Congress of Greater New York disembarked. Almost all were specially costumed for the demonstration: Many cross dressed as men or women according to their sexual propensities; there was a rainbow of walking phalluses; two androgynous women wore the red robes of cardinals followed by retinues of mock priests surrounded by youths whom they constantly fondled; a motley line of transvestites circled the great bronze of Atlas holding the world with crosses bearing crucified female figures with heads in the shape of Christ.

Homemade signs of many shapes were everywhere. All denigrated the Church in a cloud of obscenities. And a huge banner denounced the Pope as Anti-Christ and Adolf Hitler for his various statements regarding homosexuality and abortion. Only the barricades and the shoulder to shoulder line of police held the screaming crowd back from the front doors of the Cathedral.

The Cardinal, other members of the clergy and the novices had already entered the Cathedral before the arrival of the demonstrators. But, as guests and the families of the novices arrived, the demonstrators pelted them with condoms and shouted obscene comments and chants. Throughout the ancient Mass of Ordination the chants and songs of the demonstrators could be clearly heard inside the Cathedral. And, afterwards, when those inside the Cathedral departed, the gantlet of condom throwing and chants was repeated.

At approximately 10 o'clock that evening a group of thirty-five men met in the offices of a major law firm in the City's financial district. The corporate tower was only a few thousand yards from the tavern where exasperated conspirators of an earlier time met to plot the American Revolution. This group of plotters called itself the Société de Saint Michel, a name suggested by a member who had fought with a similarly named group of underground French maquis against the Nazi Army of Occupation of France in World War II.

"Gentlemen, we are agreed that these repeated outrages to civilization shall not continue," a well-known litigator said. "We will go forward. Everyone has his assignment. Please be sure to leave the building two or three at a time."

Five hours after the group dispersed, uncontrollable fires beginning with large fireballs and many explosions broke out almost simultaneously throughout the City at fourteen notorious gay bars and bathhouses. All had closed for the night only one or two hours earlier. Apparently no one was in any of the buildings, but the buildings were so completely burned that it was not possible to be certain.

In only one instance, was anyone who appeared suspicious reported in the area of the fires. A drunken street beggar sleeping near a bathhouse in Soho told police he thought he saw two men unloading what looked like a mortar from the trunk of a black Jaguar. He said the men had black and dark green spread on their faces and wore baggy clothes and ball caps turned backwards. The police did not regard the witness as highly reliable.

Dinner at Grandma's (Philadelphia)

Cynthia sat impatiently in her red Saab 900 convertible and waited for the traffic to move in Center City.

Even in the early evening dark on this rainy night you could see that she was unusually beautiful. Without question she could have been a fashion model: Tall, thin, high cheek bones, almond shaped eyes, tawny black skin. But early in her high school career she become fascinated with biology and the idea of becoming a surgeon.

Fortunately for Cynthia, she had avoided the bottomless quicksands of the Philadelphia public school system and had always attended reasonably good schools. Her father, a plumber's assistant, and her mother, a part-time supermarket check-out clerk, insisted that she enroll at St. Cecilia's in their neighborhood; then they sent her to St. Francis de Sales High School. She was one of the best students in her class and had no problem in obtaining scholarships that helped her work her way through college and medical school.

Now, at 35, she was one of the youngest surgeons on the staff at the largest teaching hospital in the city. She had been written up in a major news weekly as one of the most promising black female surgeons in the country. In a time of different news values, she would have been recognized more simply and more correctly as one of the more promising young surgeons around.

The traffic oozed forward about 50 yards enabling Cynthia to drive car length by car length around City Hall into Market Street. Cynthia looked at her two year old daughter who was asleep next to her in a child's car seat. She had picked up the child at a day care center on the way to have dinner and spend the night with Cynthia's mother and father. Cynthia's husband, Luther, was working at the hospital. He was an orthopod assigned to the Emergency Room.

A delay at the hospital had caused Cynthia to be a half hour late at the day care center. A discussion at the center about the need not to be late and her requisite humble apologies had used up another 20 minutes. And the viscous traffic so far had cost her another half hour.

They moved forward again on Market past a large darkened used car lot. Then inexplicably the traffic started to flow but a taxi immediately cut in front of Cynthia and raced through a traffic light changing from green to red. She swore and jammed her breaks. The child lurched forward into her restraining strap, bounced back and began to whimper. " Damn it," she said and, as she reached over to comfort the child, a man in a black leather car coat and silver-coated pilot glasses yanked open the car door on the driver's side.

"Ho, bitch," the man shouted. "Outta the car. Ah'm jacking it!"

"My child," Cynthia screamed at him. "I've got to unstrap her." And she reached across the seat, fumbled a moment and took the child in her arms.

"Le's go, le's go, pretty momma, get yo ass out," the man shouted. "Or maybe I takes yo along. We have some fun." And he pulled with both of his hands on her left arm. As he did so, she dropped the child back on the seat, swung around and with her right hand smoothly ran a long thin surgical knife up into the man's throat. Then, using her outstanding medical skill, she nimbly moved the scalpel in a neat X-pattern before the screeching man stumbled backward awash with his own blood and dropped to the glimmering wet street.

When the police arrived, filling the area with lights and yellow plastic tape, one of the half dozen cops asked Cynthia if she needed anything.

"Just call my mother," she said. "We're late. I don't want her to worry.'

Naughty and Nice (San Diego)

The media called it California's worst crime wave of the decade. That would make it very bad, indeed. The Mayor called for an immediate war on crime. That involved an immediate mayoral request for additional federal money. The Chairwoman of the National Committee for a Better Life called immediately for additional early education spending on society's victims. The police immediately questioned most of the usual suspects with the usual result.

In four weeks, there had been within the San Diego Area 535 burglaries of homes involving nineteen murders, thirty-seven brutal beatings and eleven rapes. Hundreds of millions of dollars worth of property was stolen or wrecked. Not even the TV and radio talk programs that normally managed to relay all titillating and horrifying details of such events could keep up with the constant flow of violence and thievery from Coronado and Point Loma to La Jolla. The sun-blessed City was saturated with blood, fear and bombast.

There were few arrests. And, when arrests were made, the charges were often dropped; or the accused, mostly decorated with tats, rings and studs displayed on a broad assortment of body parts, disappeared into the fastness of the juvenile justice system. There were the usual charges of racism and minority oppression; the usual pleas for improved understanding of the socially impaired; the usual litany of the sad plight of the hard-working illegal immigrants; the usual undefined calls from various activist groups for government action.

It was at this low point that Daniel Marshall Sturgiss II decided what he wanted this year for Christmas and how he wanted to spend the Christmas holidays. Marshall Sturgiss, direct descendent of a trapper who came west with Fremont, was very rich. He was born that way. And, after graduating from MIT and fighting up to and back from the Yalu River in the bloody chapter of the Cold War that some non-combatant academics still insisted on calling the Korean Conflict, he helped invent early computer memory chips; became a lot richer; sold his company; invested his money and became a dabbler in California politics.

Now, as the Christmas holidays approached and the bad news continued, he sent an invitation to a select group of six friends:

You are cordially invited to take part in a Christmas adventure of mercy. Please come Tuesday for lunch.

During lunch at the sprawling Sturgiss Hacienda in the foothills of the Laguna Mountains east of the City, the six men sat in a long, tiled diningroom looking out across winterized gardens and grazing horses. Present, besides Marshall, were the president of a national polling firm, a prominent political consultant, a Nobel prize physicist, a retired Rear Admiral and the senior partner of a prestigious law firm. The lawyer was black; all of the others were white. They ate excellent sautéed gray sole served with haricot verte and pomme vapeur and drank Meurseult. Over coffee, Marshall opened a small oblong box and showed them a new sawed-off shotgun.

"The barrel is exactly 18' inches long—two inches longer than the kind that are illegal," Marshall said. "Entire length: 26 inches. Anyone can own one without a license. It's very easy to load and fire. The effect is decidedly discouraging to boarders. And you can hardly miss at short range."

Then they went outside on the terrace and each fired the gun a few times. All targets were badly shredded or they disappeared.

Within the next week, pollsters surveyed residents on attitudes toward crime throughout the three-mile square center of the crime wave. Meantime, 5,000 short-barrel shotguns were unloaded at a Sturgiss barn and were gift wrapped in holly paper tied with red ribbon. Each package contained along with the gun a set of operating instructions, ammunition and a holly-bordered note that said:

Have a Safe Holiday Season!

The Secret Santa

Three days later, the boxes were delivered to 4,875 residents who qualified through the survey for the gift. The principal qualification was readiness to use the gift to defend oneself.

Within a week, a pregnant mother of two children blew apart a knife-carrying intruder in her kitchen; a young accountant seriously wounded a burglar bagging silver in the diningroom of the accountant's condo; an 82-year old woman blew the head off an intruder going through a dresser in the bedroom where she had been sleeping; a retired plumber blew a crack-crazed junkie back through the porch door that the junkie had broken open with an ax; and a subway conductor held illegal aliens at bay in his garage where they were trying to start his car with wires, then shot both dead when they tried to rush him.

The media covered nothing else: all front pages, all TV news shows, all TV and radio talk shows. They interviewed everyone. They exhausted themselves doing special reports. They maintained scoresheets. The Mayor called for calm. Anti-gun groups called for restraint. The Attorney General called for an investigation. Several congressmen introduced legislation banning 18-inch barrel shotguns. Latino United called for a new comprehensive immigration program. But, by the end of the week, the flow of shot gun stories ceased; so had reports of break-ins, rapes and murders.

"Peace to the world," Marshall said, lifting a glass of Chateau Margaux at another small Christmas lunch at his home. The six guests at the table raised their glasses.

Everyone on the Bus (Chicago)

He was known as 'the Arab" but he was really for the most part a
Black Hawk or possibly a Kickapoo. Every morning about 10 o'clock,
after he woke up in his alley of choice, he positioned himself outside
the Drake Hotel, an historic hostelry that claimed to be the favorite of celebrities and heads of state. He would sit cross-legged on the
sidewalk, a pile of dirty dark rags with a red face. In front of him, he
had an Au Bon Pain paper coffee cup and a cardboard sign that said:

HOMeLeSS! HeLP!

Hundreds who passed by saw him every day and had learned to
ignore him as they had learned to ignore the more than 300 regular
beggars who positioned themselves daily like obscene bedraggled pi-
geons outside the City's main shops, office buildings, museums and
churches. On this day, however, he was doing well. Within an hour he
had picked up more than three dollars. With luck by noon he could
be ready to buy himself a bottle of Thunderbird.

Down the block, he saw "The White Queen" sitting with her
many bags in front of a branch bank. "The White Queen," who saved
her money for gin, always had bags from the better shops: Nieman's,
Saks, Hermes. She normally looked reasonably well-groomed until
you got close: her once expensive but worn clothes were grimy and
her aged pale face was heavily caked and rouged. Her body exuded
a strong odor. She also seemed to be doing well today. "The Arab"
decided there must be a lot of rube tourists in town.

Just as he was mulling over that possibility and the cash flow
that such a development could bring, he saw The Bus, It was big; yellow with blue stripes; a banner on the side that said: HOMELESS
PICNIC TODAY. And, as he watched, The Bus moved slowly around
the corner and came to a stop in front of him. Two men in uniden-
tifiable but official looking light blue uniforms got off and walked
toward him.

"Today's the big homeless picnic," one said cheerfully. Lots of free food. Lots of free drinks. Let's go. Everybody on the bus."

"I don' know," the Arab mumbled and didn't move. "I'm busy today. You from some goddam shelter?"

You're kidding?" the second man said. "Didn't you hear my partner: This isn't some shelter deal. This is free booze time."

"I don' know," the Arab said again but, as the two men reached to pick him up by the arms, he was already rising and hesitated only to grab his Au Bon Pan cup and his sign. They hustled him on to The Bus and into one of the front seats and handed him a bottle of cold beer.

"Who these guys, Roach?" he said to a pile of rags sitting next to him and took a long pull on the bottle.

"Beatsa shit outta me," Roach said. "But da beer is OK, like that's for sure."

The Bus had already moved down the block where the uniformed men brought The White Queen aboard. Then it started up again, moved along Michigan Avenue: stopped, started, stopped, started. Each time one, two or three of the regulars came aboard.

They picked up Raymond the Cat at the Ritz where he was waiting for the better shops to open. They picked up Miss Mo, a woman of great girth found shouting obscenities at niggardly office workers near the corner of Wacker and Michigan. They picked up Mr. Bogee at Grant Park where he always relieved himself in the cultivated shrubs before going to his post near the Fairmont Hotel with his sign that said: *I'm Homeless. I'm Hungry. Give me Money. No Personal Questions.* And, doubling back to the Loop, they picked up Gino the Dwarf, a psychotic who was screaming "Faggot" and "Slut" at people who resisted his whimpering pleas for cash.

And so forth.

Finally, forty-five minutes later, The Bus, all seats full, headed south on Lake Shore Drive toward the I-90. An hour later The Bus was rolling northeast through suburban Michigan; many beers and eight hours later, The Bus had traversed the Upper Peninsula; moved slowly through the little town of Raco; entered the Hiawatha National Forest and stopped.

By the time all of the passengers left under their own power or were removed from The Bus, it was late afternoon. A pile of boxes stood near an historic marker informing readers that warriors of the Ottawa, the French and the British nations had preceded them in the area. A family of hostile raccoons watched hungrily from the deep wilderness. One of the uniformed guards leaned out the door and talked through a bullhorn.

'Good news!" he said. 'You're less than 10 miles from the border. It's just down the road at Sault Ste. Marie. No passports required. For those who care to rest awhile before getting on your way there are blankets and food in those boxes. There are also five cases of Old Melody wine. Lots more over the border."

The door of The Bus hissed and shut. Moments later, The Bus headed back along the road south through the walls of huge pines and disappeared. In the clear northern sky, the first stars of the Milky Way began to appear.

Lunch in the Grill (Boston)

They always ate in the Grill at Loch Ober's, a dark, masculine Edwardian room that used to be called the Men's Grill but now just 'the Grill" although most of the occupants were still men.

The judge, Ronald Pierce Townshand, a tall, well-fed man with a generous mustache, felt that he looked like a judge and was one. He appeared truly solid and wise, a tone he particularly liked to assume at meetings of groups urging more gun control, greater educational opportunities for the socially deprived and a ban on the death penalty.

Nicholas Partman IV, the judge's luncheon companion, was a head shorter than the judge and 40 pounds lighter. He wore the normal uniform of a successful money manager: a blue pinstripe suit and black Italian kiltie loafers.

The two men had little in common other than class. Intellectually and politically they disagreed completely. But they were both sons of old well-to-do families; they were both in the same year at St. Mark's; they grew up with the same people. That was enough to cause them to lunch together at least every couple of months and exchange gossip.

"Ronny is a terrible ass," Nicholas would say to his wife, Hopie. "Nicky thinks Eisenhower is still president," Ronald would say to his wife, Binks. But when they met, they enjoyed themselves.

On this particular day, they sat at a table in the middle of the Grill. Nicholas faced the door. Ronald sat next to him looking toward the windows that opened out on an ancient alley. Accordingly, Ronald did not see the terrorist in a maroon leather jacket and black wool hat and stocking mask come through the door with an Uzi and begin shooting diners and waiters.

As the judge turned to face the oncoming nightmare, bleeding men were falling to the floor; a waiter with a suddenly crimsoned apron was hurled backward against the carved, mahogany bar; other diners were crawling under tables. The judge saw bits of food and people in the air. He saw the shooter moving toward their table. He saw a green "C" on the shooters wool hat. He did not see Nicky reach into his attaché case, remove a Sturm Ruger automatic and fire it three times. He did see the green "C" disappear and the shooter's head blow apart as if it were a huge tomato.

"Nicky, for God's sake," the judge heard himself shout. "You're carrying a gun!"

"Ronny, Ronny," Nicky said. "Didn't they teach us at St. Mark's not to take the Lord's name in vain."

Low Expectations

We do not forget the Crusaders and the loss of Andalusia.
—Usama bin Laden, Muslim terrorist leader

Taji Khan the Dwarf made bombs. Or, to be more exact, he was in a bomb production line.

Each morning he would go to his postbox #6749 and look for letters from his cousin, Tiza aka Fatima. She lived in Kazakistan and wrote Taji long letters about terrible times there since the collapse of the Soviet Nirvana and the communist orthodoxy, both now replaced for them by the Muslim Nirvana and jihadist orthodoxy of militant Islam. She also often included in her letters a small gift: about one or two grams of plutonium in a plasticene envelope.

Tiza was one of the few remaining workers in a crumbling former Soviet facility that housed an old but active breeder reactor. Her job was to help secure spent nuclear fuel assemblies. In the process, she managed to steal small quantities of ivory grade plutonium in support of the great jihad against the United States, the Great Satan.

On days when the letters included "the gift," Taji would hide the plasticene envelope in a secret compartment in his wallet. Then he would go to his job as a bag packer at the Big Oscar Supermarket four blocks from his room in a rotting Boston cellar. It was buried beneath a condemned Victorian town house that overlooked what once was a fashionable street but now was an endless polluted river of cars flowing along the Mass Pike. When he got off work at 6 o'clock he would go the nearby Mosque of the Holy Sword where he would meet his friend, a large black man with a full beard and a New York accent. He knew him only as Mohamet Abdul.

He didn't know where Mohamet lived or worked. They always met at the mosque where they would pray. Afterwards they would go to a Jolly Ribs and have the special which Mohamet assured Taji it was OK to eat in America as part of their cover and always paid for from a big roll of bills. At some point during the meal, Taji would give Mohamet the plasticene envelope.

Homer Jones sat hunched over by the only window in his cookie-cutter cubicle in the William Jefferson Clinton Federal Building, a faux neo-colonial brick ziggurat that the irreverent said looked appropriately like an open zipper with columns. It was riskily located in the center of a decaying low-cost housing project in Roxbury, one of Boston's most dangerous neighborhoods, a ruined backwater much favored for political photo-ops by compassionate politicians. Homer was reviewing his notes on a meeting that he had just completed upstairs in the Regional Office of the Department of Energy, Nuclear Power Division, Investigations Unit #6. The only other participants at the meeting were two fully credentialed spooks named "Dick" and "Roger"

"We have good information that a terrorist cell in Chicago has been accumulating weapons grade plutonium for the last six months," Spook One ("Dick") said. "Not, we understand, what we would consider top drawer stuff; but good enough. So it's not being stolen from us, but more than likely it's from old Soviet stockpiles. Somehow it's coming into the country. We think maybe through Boston."

"It has to be a pretty savvy setup," Spook Two ("Roger") said. "Some slick artist you'd never suspect coming through Logan. Top executive type, maybe. You know: shirt, tie and jacket; not the usual slob getup. Or maybe some oil rich student spends his time here chasing women, lives in a condo on the harbor, drives a showy car, never attends class."

'Pretty sure the stuff is being handed off to one or more operatives probably using cut-outs as it's passed to Chicago," Spook One said. "To get there, we need to unravel the chain beginning here. Stop the flow."

"What makes you think it starts here?" Homer asked, already knowing the probable meaningless answer .

"That's what our source told us," Spook Two said.

"Right," Homer said.

"The one thing you can count on, they're smart," Spook One said. "Never underestimate this crowd. This game wasn't put together by a bunch of yak herders.'

"Why does everyone make everything rocket science?" Homer asked no one in particular that evening as his wife, Kathleen, put a second helping of beef stew on his plate. "Police work used to be so damn straightforward: most crime is done by bad guys who aren't smart enough to make an honest living. And generally we know where most of these dumb creeps hang out. Oh, sure, every once in awhile a few twisted masterminds pop up, but usually we know them, too; we just can't put them away most of the time because they're kept in circulation by their sleaze lawyers and mush-head judges."

Kathleen, who had heard this speech on numerous occasions, let him finish. Finally, when he did and she had put some chocolate cake on the table, she said what she also had said on numerous occasions.

"I think you underrate what you do," she said. "You don't chase common criminals anymore. I know what kind of people these are even if you never talk about it. These people are spies and traitors and terrorists. They're different."

"No, they're not," Homer insisted. "They're mostly the world's creeps and losers who instead of trying to earn a dishonest living like normal criminals they've been sucked in one way or another into thinking that they are fighting for some cockamamie holy cause. And that tells you how basically dumb they are.

"Sometimes, Homer, you worry me," Kathleen said. "You used to say when you were in the Marines never kid yourself about the enemy. These people are fanatics."

"Damn true and I don't kid myself. Dumb as some of these guys are, they can be very dedicated. But you know why? For a lot of these guys, it's the best job they ever had; even better than sticking up 24-hour stores here or robbing tourists back home among the ancient ruins. Back home after a couple thousand years they still haven't figured out how to arrange for electric lights or running water most of the time and the latrines are the nearest handy floor. So these guys will do anything to keep their jobs. But if they had any real smarts they would have figured out how to fix the lights and the toilets long ago."

As Homer expected, the next ten days were a waste of time, but the effort had to be made.

He spent four days checking flight manifests. In all, he came up with a list of a couple dozen frequent flyers who fit the profile: upscale, Middle Eastern or strong Middle Eastern and Paki associations, apparently legitimate cover, numerous flights to cities favored by known terrorists. All but two had checked out OK in the past. The remaining two checked out now. He also checked the Port: no frequent maritime arrivals of interest. Finally, he checked the elite bar scene: a world heavily supported by stylishly dressed young Arabs equipped with student visas, numerous credit cards, low or no classroom attendance, voracious sexual appetites. But conversations with excellent sources yielded no bored and disaffected revolutionists in expensive designer clothing.

"Lots of dry wells,' Homer told Spook One. "Not even a few bum leads. Maybe the chain broke down, game's over."

"Not on your uninsurable life" Spook One said. "We're told Chicago is nearing a critical supply. Keep looking."

Homer broadened his sights to include more mundane frequent travelers along with airport and dock workers, but he achieved no immediate improvement in results. He went back to his earlier line of thinking: He would wait for someone to do something dumb.

Taji had been packing groceries for the last six hours with only three short prayer breaks but no lunch break and his performance was worse than usual.

On his best days, Taji was not a world class grocery packer. The problem was not his size. Big Oscar Supermarkets management was delighted to have an immigrant dwarf Muslim packing groceries: He was a living advertisement for Big Oscar diversity, multiculturalism and compassion for the handicapped. Accordingly, Big Oscar had built a special platform for Taji to stand on at the end of a checkout counter and provided him with a small ladder to get there. All day he stood at the end of the counter in his custom-made Big Oscar apron waiting like a pinboy in a bowling alley for the cashier to roll the groceries at him. . But his short arms limited his catch rate and his aim was poor. He had to hop down often to retrieve misses. And he would pack groceries every which way: frozen and hot items usually were bagged together; heavy items were dropped on top of tomatoes and eggs; bags were either stuffed and lumpy or underfilled.

Generally disgruntled customers quickly checked out Taji's physiognomy, consulted their politically correct fears and grumbled only after they left the store. But not always. On this particular late afternoon, Vincent Borden had been called on his cell phone during a sales meeting by his nearly hysterical wife and asked to pick up a last minute list of items that she needed for a dinner party that evening. As Vincent, already much irritated, waited impatiently with a half-filled hand basket on Taji's check-out line, a heavily made-up and heavily overweight woman with two carts full of items was arguing incoherently with the cashier about her rights and American oppression of the poor. The woman was paying with food stamps and, for the third time, the cashier sought to explain to her that she could not accept food stamps in payment for cigarettes, a set of copper clad pots and an aluminum beach chair. The argument was further impeded because it was being conducted in English, a language with which neither participant was proficient. Furthermore, it had become unusually heated because the cashier had suggested that anyone using food stamps for payment should not be buying two pounds of smoked salmon.

After ten minutes, a wishy-washy conclusion to the argument was negotiated by an unfriendly-looking square man in a suit with a friendly HELLO badge. The badge identified him as Harold the store manager. Harold stated with some authority that regrettably the cops wouldn't let him sell cigarettes, kitchen implements and lawn furniture for food stamps because of unfeeling bureaucrats in Washington. Possibly, he said, the customer would like to write to her congressman and, meanwhile, delay the purchases until some future time if by some chance she didn't have enough money with her. The customer reluctantly agreed after the cashier, at the urging of Harold, apologized for her rude, insensitive comment about the smoked salmon.

Vincent had remained in place only because all other checkout lines were much longer. When, at last, he moved forward with his purchases he found himself behind another woman with a full cart from which she seemed to remove items to the moving check-out belt with infinite slowness and care, arranging cold items in one group, hot items in another, and packaged products in a third. When these were passed over the electronic checker and shoved toward Taji, he mixed them arbitrarily into various bags. When the woman complained, he angrily dumped all of her purchases back on the counter and, while mumbling ugly noises, proceeded with the help of the cashier to repack them in a more or less orderly manner. The cashier then totaled the bill and the woman spent what seemed to Vincent a new eternity looking through her pocketbook for her checkbook, making out what Vincent could not help but notice was a designer check depicting Mickey Mouse welcoming visitors to Disney Land, and carefully recording the amount and deducting it from her balance. Then, since she did not have a Big Oscar "Customer Courtesy Card" with her, the check had to be authorized and more time passed while the cashier summoned higher authority. Finally, HELLO Harold appeared, initialed the check, and Vincent, his stress level approaching a medically dangerous high, found himself at bat.

Vincent's purchases—several packages of pâté, a pint of heavy cream, a plate of mixed hot hors d'oeuvres, two pints of ice cream, and two large bottles of San Pellagrino soda water—were efficiently whisked over the electronic eye by the cashier and catapulted toward Taji. But he, in turn, already much rattled in this final hour of his work day, packed the hot and cold items together in several bags and dropped the soda bottles in last, causing one bag to bulge awkwardly and the other to rip.

'Goddamnit, you idiot," Vincent shouted. "Repack those things properly; repack them now"

"Don't talk not to me bad like that, no one don't talk bad to me," Taji shouted back in his high pitched Kazakh accent. "You pack yourself."

'Tell that screw-up midget to repack those bags," Vincent shouted at the cashier. 'Call the manager."

The last request was unnecessary. When the shouting started, HELLO Harold was only a few yards away authorizing another check. Now he was at Taji's side, telling him quietly but sternly to keep quiet and go home, holding his arm, firmly helping him down from his perch.

"You don't fire me! I have the big rights. You fire him,' Taji screamed. "Death to the infidels! You'll see! God is great!" And he stalked away, bumping into several customers before he hurled his small compact form through the fortunately automatic electronic glass doors.

Harold let him go and turned to deal as well as he could with Vincent whose still mottled face at least no longer gave the impression that he was about to have a stroke.

"He isn't a midget," Harold said primly and smiled weakly. "He's just a little vertically challenged. Here, let me repack your bags."

Taji was still shaking with fury when he met Mohamet at the mosque an hour later and told him somewhat disjointedly what had happened. He hated these people. He hated his job. He hated all Americans. He was mocked, disgraced, humiliated. Allah willing, these enemies will be destroyed. Destroyed! Allah is great!

Mohamet, himself, felt increasingly incensed. It was not right that a man like Taji Khan should be treated in this manner. Was it not taught that Islam and the people of Islam should not be defiled by infidels? Moreover, Mohamet knew that the continuing flow of Taji's little plasticene envelopes was significant to jihad. He had been told so many times. Therefore, it was important that he showed Taji that they were true brothers and keep him in camp.

"First we gets you some ribs," Mohamet said and put his big hands on his unhappy friend's shoulders. Then we go over and give Big Oscar and the infidels a taste who they dissing, God willing."

Big Oscar closed at nine o'clock, but Harold stayed on for awhile to take care of reports for the day. Therefore, he was alone in the offices at the rear of the store when he looked out his office window at the nearly empty parking lot and saw one very large black man with a beard and one very small man standing next to his car. The car, a new Cadillac CTS, was parked in a space clearly marked 'Manager" in an area overshadowed by a nearby building. As Harold watched, the small man held a hooded flashlight on the car and the large man pounded nails into the tires with a hammer.

Before the last nail was pounded home, Harold had called Big Oscar Security and 911. As he continued to watch, the two men began taking turns scratching the fenders and the trunk with a screwdriver, an activity halted abruptly by the arrival of three security guards with drawn guns. Shortly, thereafter, two police cars with many red lights blinking careened into the parking lot.

Both vandals were spread-eagled on the desecrated Cadillac; handcuffed; searched, and shoved into the rear of a police car. Minutes later a police sergeant with several Big Oscar security guards appeared in Harold's office.

"Yes," Harold said when asked if Taji worked at Big Oscar's.

"No," Harold said, when asked if he had ever before seen Mohamet.

'Why would these guys want to smash up your car? Any ideas?"

"Crazy stuff. Taji had a fight with a customer and I calmed everyone down and told him to go home. But I don't know why he would take it out on me."

"Was the dwarf ever involved with drugs?" the sergeant asked.

"Not that I know of," Harold said. "You think he was on something?"

"They scratched *"Allah is Great"* on your trunk."

At Police Headquarters, Taji and Mohamet were held in a tank with a half dozen unseemly-looking regulars swept up from the city streets that evening: Two well-known panhandlers accused of relieving themselves in an exclusive hotel side doorway; a drunken Chinese chef who allegedly hacked off a surly waiter's nose with a cleaver; a convicted small time burglar and his alleged partner; and a black transvestite known as "Miss Lil." When Taji and Mohamet arrived, Miss Lil raised a general laugh by asking "What kinda tricks do the little guy do?" But Mohamet quieted and cowed the group merely by bulking himself to his full size and baring his teeth in a deadly grin. After that he and Taji sat unmolested in a corner while Mohamet kept all at bay with a mean sneer.

Meantime, the Police Crime Lab was checking out some powder in a plasticene envelope that Taji had passed to Mohamet while they ate dinner at the Jolly Ribs. The arresting officers subsequently found it in Mohamet's shirt pocket. As soon as the Lab determined that the powder was not heroin but a substance that appeared to be plutonium, the police called Homer and, after talking to him, Taji and Mohamet were moved to individual cells for very intensive interrogation.

"So we rolled up the network in a week," Spook One said and took another bite of his salami sandwich. The Kazakh lady, the pipeline, the Chicago cell, the stockpile: gonzo, kaput."

"Everything was in the big guy's apartment in Cambridge," Spook Two said. "I couldn't believe it. Right there on his laptop: names, codes, places, all in Arabic. Only thing we had to do was a little translating."

Homer, who was sitting at the table with them in their office, was checking some papers.

"The two key players in Chicago that weren't there when your guys arrived: I don't call it a success until we nail them," Homer said

"Then we're golden," Spook One said. "Our people think both of them were in the SUV one of our choppers took out in the woods just before the Canadian border."

"Maybe," Homer said. "The reports don't confirm it."

"Picky, picky," Spook Two said, "don't be so damn picky. No one's going to confirm stuff like that. On the record, it was a drug bust. SUV refused to stop. Too bad. Perps turned to charcoal. Anyway, you wrap up a really brilliant operation like this, you can't always get everyone and we don't."

"From what I hear about that charcoal I think there's a pretty good chance that this time we did," Spook One said. "The only thing I can't get my mind around is how does an ex-New York three-card monte hustler like this Mohamet learn Arabic?"

"You're easy to impress," Spook Two said. "His Arabic wasn't all that great."

Last Chance

We do not what we ought;
What we ought not, we do;
And lean upon the thought
That chance will pull us through.
　　　　　—Matthew Arnold, *Empedocles on Etna*

Houghton Porter III lived in a condo on the best side of Louisburg Square in Boston along with his wife, Mandie, their two teenage daughters and a King Charles spaniel named Barton. They had lived there for the last ten years. It was a fine condo; a little crowded, but it had a library and a parking space. Until recently, it also was a major asset in his total net worth. Unfortunately, that was no longer the case.

The 2008 collapse of the stock market had left Houghton's portfolio in general and his 401K in particular in tatters. As for the condo, it had been appraised for a significant equity loan at the height of the real estate boom, now known as the housing bubble, at $2.1 million. The best appraisal that he could obtain today was half that; the best price would be less than that assuming he could find a buyer who could afford the undiminished taxes and monthly fees. Moreover, total debt on the condo which he had liberally used as market leverage put its asset value for him with the fish.

Houghton, an able quant at one of Boston's tonier investment banks, sat in his condo library in front of his three computer screens and ran his personal portfolio numbers and balance sheet for the fourth time this week. He was very clever at this kind of exercise. Here a "tuck." There a "tuck." Everywhere down the road an optimistic "tuck tuck." He could make his position appear almost solid. Many might be fooled. But not he. He knew. Blue cash flow was retreating on the screen at an alarming rate. Meantime, red debits marched onward and upward: taxes, interest, condo fees, the daughters' private schools, Houghton's private clubs, insurance, doctors, lawyers, dentists, undocumented household help, dog walking services...not to mention liquor, wines, designer clothes for Mandie, travel, restaurants, concerts, gifts, major charities...nor even to mention food, heat, light, phones, and environmentally friendly trash removal. Financial disaster lightning crackled and flashed.

He had been monitoring this dodgy situation as it ominously evolved for a number of months. But his normal cheery outlook was always sustained by two ideas: the bad times would turn as they always did. And, with a little prudence, his far from shabby compensation with plenty of leverage when needed would keep him afloat. Then the world ended. One week ago on his personal Black Wednesday his boss, J. Standish Lugar, advised him during a clubby chat that the firm found it regretfully necessary to cut 500 of its top people. That group included Houghton but fortunately not J. Standish.

"You're the lucky bastard," J. Standish said. "You escape to some new high flying yacht. I have to stay around here and bail this floundering tub."

It was the kind of thing you could always count on J. Standish to say as he tested the scaffolds for others while letting them know that he could put his trousers on two legs at a time. In happier times, J. Standish always exhibited the affability of the lord of the manor and in no way indicated that his father had been a modestly successful used car salesman in Woonsocket, Rhode Island.

In less than a week, it became very clear to Houghton that in the present economic crisis there were no high flying yachts waiting for him to climb aboard. He couldn't catch sight of even a fast tugboat in need of his special skills. Moreover, should one of the ships still afloat come by, the water was filled with Houghton clones cling-ing to bits of flotsam. Competition for any even temporary perch was deadly.

Self-confident and prideful as he was, Houghton did suffer mo-ments of midlife discouragement. He had enormous, quite justifiable faith in his computer skills, intelligence, breeding and social position. But this was not the first time he had missed what he thought of as "big success" and come out a loser while the J. Standishes of this un-fair world continued to sup at the High Table. Somehow there was a lack of luck, out-of-joint circumstance or a suppressed or missing gene that kept him out back in the kitchen preparing the great meals that J. Standish consumed but could never prepare himself.

But Houghton was still game. Every day he spammed much of the wired world with emails and voice messages. He had developed six job search configurations: did the contact know of any openings for a hot-shot third party; he himself was restless and wanted to move on; he wanted a career change; he was blocked by politics; he feared being promoted to a job he didn't want; he simply was immediately available.

He scanned his incoming email six times a day; he scanned his junk mail just as frequently. The incoming email was continually dis-appointing; so was the junk mail but at least it offered some amuse-ment. Houghton loved to read about the numerous sex-starved wom-en ready to meet him; the secret potions that would greatly enlarge his genital equipment in only a matter of weeks; the many opportuni-ties to take over small lucrative businesses from their cancer-ridden owners who wanted only a few bucks to spend their last months in the Florida Keys. Most of all, he relished the astoundingly big money opportunity letters from Nigeria and other centers of international high-level chicanery.

From Spain: Barrister Norbert Bruno's client, Mr. Millard John-son, an expatriate oil contractor, died three months ago leaving 12.5

million Euros in a fixed deposit account and mandated Norbert to present "any family heir" for claims. Unfortunately, Norbert cannot find any family member to make a claim. Therefore, he is prepared to make Houghton the heir as soon as they agree on how to share the funds and exchange bank account numbers for the transfer.

From England: Mrs. Sarah Frank, a deaf widow with breast cancer, lost her only son in an auto crash two years ago. She has but two months to live and needs help in withdrawing $8.3 million from a fixed deposit bank account. Sarah wants Houghton, "no matter the color of his skin or his religion," to help her withdraw the money and distribute it confidentially to charitable causes.

From Nigeria: Ahmed Sabonbirini, Director General of the Department of Petroleum Resources (DPR), has a whopping sum of $55 million that he wants to transfer to Houghton's personal account from the Apex Bank of Nigeria. Ahmed and the DPR Auditor General will give Houghton 25 percent to make this "no risk transaction." Ahmed says "please contact me immediately you receive this message through my direct email for more lively information."

From Hong Kong: Miss Ivy Tan of DBS Bank Hong Kong writes on behalf of her boss requesting for a partner who is "reliable and capable of handling a $160 million legal transaction." If Houghton is willing to assist, he can contact Miss Tan's boss, a certain Mr. Frawong mrfrawong@yahoo.com.uk for details.

Again from Nigeria: I AM PASTOR: JAMES Johnson the special adviser to vice president federal republic of nigeria. i AM DELIGHTED TO INFORM YOU THAT THE OFFICE OF THE PRESIDENCY AND THE DIRECTORS CENTRAL BANK OF NIGERIA HAVE CONCLUDED ARRANGEMENTS TO CALL BACK YOUR FUNDS FROM THE WORLD BANK AND HAVE ARRANGED TO SEND YOUR PART PAYMENT OF $7 MILLION TO YOU VIA OUR ACCREDITED SHIPPING COMPANY. THE MONEY IS COMING TO YOU IN

ONE SECURITY PROOF BOX SEALED WITH SYNTHETIC NYLON SEAL AND PADDED WITH MACHINE. PLEASE DON'T WORRY FOR ANYTHING as the TRANSACTION IS 100 PERCENT RISK FREE. THE DIPLOMAT TRAVELLING WITH IT DOES NOT KNOW THE CONTENTS OF BOX. I DECLARED THE CONTENTS IS SENSITIVE FILM. IF ANYONE ASKS THE CONTENTS, PLEASE TELL THEM SAME THING OK. I HOPE YOU UNDERSTAND ME.

As Houghton sat in his library late that afternoon idly savoring these opportunities, it occurred to him that despite the efforts of the FBI and squads of cybercops at home and abroad the volume of offers was increasing. This had to mean that whatever the risks and overkill the return must be attractive. Clearly there was a sizeable supply of suckers in the world willing to play. Sooner or later, each would gullibly email a personal bank account number to Norbert or Ahmed or Sarah and within minutes all funds in that account would be stripped away and deposited in a secret account in Zurich or Budapest, Mumbai or Guangzhou.

But it didn't have to happen that way. What, thought Houghton, if, when the money transferred, a virus went along with it, cleaned out the bandit account and sent the total bundle elsewhere? Yes, yes, why not? It was the kind of software challenge Houghton loved; the kind Houghton could accomplish. So why not? What was the downside? It was theft, of course. But he was stealing from cyberbandits. He might, he told himself with minimal conviction, even be able to restore some of the money to its owners. He could become a cyberobinhood although that might be difficult, might even be too risky. Best to just steal from the bandits and keep it. There was serious risk, of course, if they could find him. That could be unpleasant. But that risk appeared small if he did his work well.

Mandie, wearing a new Armani dress and Jimmy Choo shoes, opened the library door and interrupted Houghton's exploration of cyber criminality.

"Why are you sitting here in the dark?" she said. "Come on, Houghty. We're due over at the Stuart-Harmons for drinks in half an hour."

Houghton noticed that Mandie was wearing her two-carat diamond stud earrings and wondered what he might sell them for if his job search emails continued to go unanswered.

Nothing that happened that evening at the Stuart-Harmons improved his mood. Stuart-Harmon groused that his family trust had lost 42 percent of its value. His wife worried vaguely about paying for their two sons at St. Paul's. One of the guests had had his incentive bonus reduced to one dollar by the Treasury Department; another confided that he would be unemployed at the end of the week; another said he was selling his sailboat.

Houghton slept restlessly that night until 3 AM; rose, and went to his library. He had hardly thought about what he was about to do, but he had made a decision. He would do it. This might be his last chance at "big success." For the next four hours, he applied himself to writing software code. By 7:15 that morning he knew he had what he wanted: it needed smoothing, testing, tweaking; but he knew he had it.

He had developed two powerful viruses. One could clean out a bandit bank account in seconds. The second could whisk the account's contents across the world and secretly deposit it anywhere. He called the first, the *williesutton;* the second, the *jimfisk*

The library door opened. It was Mandie.

"Houghty, what on earth are you doing before breakfast?"

"Building a rainbow," he said.

Two weeks later Houghton was ready for his first major play. He had run three successful tests, cleaning out new test accounts that he had opened at Citicorp branches in Boston and New York and moving the contents to other new accounts that he had opened in local banks in Schenectady, New York, and Burlington, Vermont. The *williesutton* had worked perfectly from the start; the *jimfisk* at first because of its sophistication was dodgy but was perfectible.

All Houghton needed now was a target. He wanted one that provided sufficient challenge to the software. At the same time, he wanted to start with relatively modest sums. He found what he wanted in an email from a Mr. Luwis Kartson, a staff member of the Absa Bank of South Africa, Plc. Mr. Kartson reported that a certain Sam Kawasaki, a Japanese gold consultant with the South African Solid Gold Corporation, maintained a numbered time-deposit account totaling $14 million which had been unclaimed for several years. An eventual investigation disclosed "the surprise" that Mr. Kawasaki had died in an airplane crash; further investigation disclosed that he died "intestate and without locatable heirs." Mr. Kartson generously proposed that Houghton could be "certified as next of kin" in a matter of days; that they initiate a series of partial withdrawals quickly before the unclaimed money reverted by law to the South American government; and that Houghton keep 30 percent for his efforts.

Houghton had in his kitbag powerful spyware that he had developed to check on financial client activities. With only a few tweaks, he could redeploy it to determine in advance whether the Absa Bank existed; whether, if it did, a Lou Kawasaki had a bank account there; and, if he did, what was in it. He was delighted but not surprised to learn that nothing was true. He had what he now considered a legitimate target of opportunity: a fat, exploitable scam.

In preparation for his caper, Houghton had opened a new account at Bank of America in Boston and deposited $10,000 as bait. He also had opened a numbered overseas account at a bank in Amsterdam with an initial deposit of 1000 Euros. Accordingly, when he received an email from Kartson the following Monday, he was ready to move:

> *All approved. As Kawasaki only heir, you are entitled to begin withdrawals. As soon as we receive your dedicated account number, we will send withdrawal authorization stating amounts beginning at $250,000 and account number at Absa.*
>
> *L. Kartson*
> *kartson@absa.net.sa*

At 0700 hours Boston time (1300 in Cape Town) Houghton emailed Kartson the account number in which he had embedded both the *williesutton* and the *jimfisk*, Opening the email would activate them immediately.

He had an early breakfast job interview with a banker at the Taj Hotel, aka the "old Ritz." As expected, it went nowhere and he hurried back to Louisburg Square. At 0930 he queried his account at Bank of America. It was empty. At 0935 he queried his numbered account in Amsterdam. He was stunned. The balance was 1,008,578 Euros—Houghton's 8578 Euros plus 1 million Euros of cyberbandit money.

The cyberbandits, wherever they were holed up, had cleaned out the Bank of America account and deposited it in their account at some unknown location. The *williesutton* had cleaned out that account and the *jimfisk* had dispatched the combined balance to Amsterdam. Total elapsed time: less than 5 minutes. Cyberbandits punished! Houghton rewarded! Justice triumphant! God exists!

Houghton spent the next two days planning his future. He would be careful. Very careful. He would not be too greedy. He must minimize alarm. But surely word of what he was doing would spread among the cyberbandit fraternity. Dedicated work would start on an antidote to the *williesutton* and the *jimfisk*. And there was always the danger of a nasty visitation. He had to move swiftly. He had already gathered numerous targets of opportunity and from these he selected three:

Barrister Cristian Alberto in Madrid reported that his client, Norm Shapiro of Michigan, died in the crash of Egypt Air Flight 990 leaving behind $75 million in a bank account but "no clear next of kin." Houghton could easily be "designated" the heir.

William Colgate II of the Audit and Compensation Committee of ExxonMobil in London needed help in the "sensitive matter of reprofilling" $12.2 million into Houghton's bank account. As a partner in this "honest" transaction, Houghton would receive 20 percent.

Sgt. Perry Rice, US Engineering Corps in Ba'qubah, Iraq, was searching for a "trustworthy partner" to help him and his military associates transfer an undisclosed large amount of "legal oil money" to a safe account. The "trustworthy partner" would get to keep 30 percent.

Within the next week, Houghton's new business successfully swept a fortune from the three cyberbandit accounts into new accounts that he opened in Zurich, the Cayman Islands and Luxembourg. From Barrister Alberto he netted $2.3 million; from Bill Colgate II, $3.6 million; from Sgt. Perry & Friends, $1.8 million. Total (non-taxable) income to date: approximately $9 million.

After each score, Houghton was careful to fudge his tracks in a many ways. He adjusted codes; jumbled procedures; reformed his firewalls; changed Internet Protocol addresses; scrubbed digital fingerprints; scattered false pointers. He felt confident that he had avoided detection. However, he also knew that somewhere around the worldwide web in more than one unhygienic cubicle unwashed nerds eating junk food throughout the night were trying to develop *williesutton* and *jimfisk* killers and find him.

Houghton decided he would be safe enough for one more strike. He would round out the enterprise by topping off his gains at better than $10 million and chose as his final target Mr. Ryan Anderson of Lloyds of London. Mr. Anderson had emailed his "deep regrets" that an unnamed client, an executive of the London Institute of Mining and Metallurgy, had died along with his wife and two sons in a terrorist-inflicted Tube explosion between King's Cross and Russell Square. The client left behind a bank account totaling 12.2 million British Pounds Sterling. Now Mr. Anderson had to find an heir or "face the consequences of the abandoned property decree." Mr. Anderson was ready to be overly generous: only 55 percent for him, 40 percent for Houghton, 5 percent for expenses.

As it turned out, Mr. Anderson was more generous than advertised. The *jimfisk* brought home to the Cayman Island account $4.2 million.

Houghton was more than content and prepared to quit and disappear. He closed up shop; again changed all his Internet Protocol addresses; strengthened his computer firewalls; and announced to Mande that he had a great new career opportunity as a financial consultant in the Cayman Islands and that they were moving. He had already rented a villa with a private pool overlooking a great beach on Grand Cayman Island and would go there immediately to establish residence, set up his office, join the yacht club. Mande, initially stunned by the disruption in her life, was mildly mollified by the gift of a large canary diamond ring and agreed to remain in Boston to handle matters there before joining him.

Three days later Houghton packed two suitcases, kissed Mande and took a limo to Logan Airport. As he sat in Delta's first class lounge drinking a Black Label on the rocks, two largish men in dark suits approached him.

"Mr. Porter," Thug One said politely but firmly, "we're here to escort you to your plane now."

"I thought we weren't boarding for another hour," Houghton said "I would rather wait here."

"No. You're boarding now. Please come with us should you expect to leave here at all."

As Thug One spoke, Thug Two allowed his suit coat to slip open briefly exposing a shoulder holster. Houghton sighed and rose.

"Well, of course," he said, cheerily. "Let's go."

Houghton naturally hoped that he would have an opportunity to run as soon as they left the lounge, but the two men locked their big hands on his arms when they reached the corridor, moved him swiftly through the terminal and out a side door. Less than a hundred yards away a Bombardier Global 5000 jet sat with its lights on. Less than five minutes later they were aboard, the door slammed, Houghton and his two captors were seated in large comfortable executive chairs. The plane was moving.

"May I ask where we're going?" Houghton said.

"Take a nap," Thug One said. "We got a long flight."

"And when we get there?"

"You get to meet Le Grande Grenouille," Thug One told him. "He's waiting. And I warn you: he's pissed."

Thug Two laughed and poured himself a beer.

Since no further enlightenment was offered, Houghton reclined his seat, pondered how he might escape after they landed and finally tried putting himself to sleep by recalling Kings of England. He succeeded between Richard II and Henry IV and dreamed of using his hacker skills to win the Massachusetts lottery. He awoke when Thug One shook him and offered him a tray with orange juice, a large croissant and coffee. Much sunlight came through the plane's windows.

"Half an hour more, we get there" Thug Two said.

"Where?"

"Monte Carlo. Very nice."

As they came in over the harbor crammed with yachts, Thug One pointed out through a window at a particularly large one riding near the harbor entrance from where rapid departure would be possible in an emergency.

"That's her: Le Roy Soleil."

They were met at the airport by a short Indian pilot who looked like a Ghurka; escorted to a helicopter and flown to the yacht, landing on the fantail. At this point, Thugs One and Two disappeared. A uniformed French ship's officer who met the helicopter escorted Houghton across the deck and through a hatch into a large main cabin furnished with Napoleonic Empire antiques. Three paintings which Houghton oddly thought he recognized from somewhere hung on the bulkheads. One depicted a storm at sea; the second, a private concert in a Dutch interior; the third, a man in a black hat. Across the cabin was a long library table desk decorated with many brass bees. A middle aged Frenchmen with a thin sunburned face sat behind it. He wore white linen trousers, a wide stripped blue and white shirt open at the neck and a heavy 22-carat buttery gold chain. He stared grimly at Houghton.

"Monsieur Porter," he said. "I am Michel Montegard. Some call me Le Grand Grenouille. Did you bring back to me my four million dollars?"

"What four million dollars?" Houghton mumbled shakily.

"Don't be *impossible*! More correctly you should ask which. But I am speaking of your latest crime involving our decoy, the most generous Monsieur Anderson of Lloyds. You were very naughty to him."

"I was only protecting myself."

"And in doing so, you stole $4.2 million from one of my accounts. And, as I indicated, this is not the first time. When you ripped off another of our decoys, the magnanimous Bill Colgate II of Exxon-Mobil, that $3.2 million which you stole was the balance that we had accumulated with much trouble in another of my accounts. We have tracked your little viruses in both cases and traced them back to your computers without question. So do not lie to me or make silly alibis about protection. The fact is Houghton you are a thief and, under normal circumstances, I assure you we would have you quite quickly pleading back in Boston for an opportunity to return my money with interest. But fortunately for you I have something better in mind."

"You do?" Houghton said, all but collapsed with fear.

"Bien sur! Why else would I bother to bring you here? The fact is that we are impressed with your high technical skills. We salute you, Monsieur! You have had a triumph! And we are prepared to give you a chance to earn what you stole from us and possibly much more."

"What do you want me to do? I wouldn't want to do anything really criminal."

Montegard laughed.

"Houghton, I will call you Houghton now. I've already told you what you have been doing and what you are. You are one big thief. So am I. What I want you to do is help me be a bigger one and possibly strike a patriotic blow. With the kind of software you can develop, we can improve our bottom line 200 percent and at the same time you can ease your conscience should you have one. Do you agree?"

"Well, I suppose..."

"Ah, then it is settled. Here is my proposition. You keep my money: call it an advance tax-free. You go to the Cayman Islands as you apparently planned. And from time to time, I'll give you a little project, oui? In fact, I'll give you an interesting assignment immediately."

Montegard for a moment studied a printout on his desk.

'Your little viruses sweep and redirect only one account at a time. Think what we would have if we had viruses that could sweep clean whole banks around the world. I specifically have in mind the banks harboring the accounts of Hamas and Hezbollah and al- Qaeda in Beirut and Damascus and other financial centers. Think of it: The whole sea of money that finances radical Islam continually disappearing. While quite properly rewarding ourselves, we would be doing more to save Western Civilization than all the trimmers and cookie pushers in Europe and Washington. Vive la France! Vive Les Etats Unis! We could call our lead virus the *lepanto*."

"You would empty the entire bank?"

"Teach the greedy bastards not to give aid and comfort to the enemy."

"It won't be easy," Houghton protested weakly. "It will attract much attention. Security will go crazy."

"But you can handle that, I know. You're so very clever. Just make them go looking for unwashed clowns in Bulgaria and Bangladesh. Any other questions? I believe my chef has prepared a nice lunch. We can talk while we dine."

"I do have one question," Houghton said as they rose to go out on the deck where waiters were setting a luncheon table under a large green awning. "Those three paintings on the cabin walls. I think I remember where I last saw them. Aren't they one of the Rembrandts, the Vermeer and the Manet that have been missing since the famous 90's heist at the Gardner Museum on the Fenway in Boston?"

"*Non, non,* Houghton, *non, non, non.* Your eye is not good. *Malheureusement*, they are of dubious provenance. I bought them online from a dealer in Dubrovnik."

In the Gulf

An infallible method of conciliating a tiger is to allow oneself to be devoured.

—Konard Adenauer, first Chancellor of Cold War West Germany

Admiral "Shark" Thayer Arnold sat in a canvas-backed chair in his quarters aboard his flagship, one of the U.S. Navy's newest nuclear-powered carriers, and said to the Commander sitting in a nearby chair: "Father, forgive me for I have sinned."

The Commander, David Towne, OP, chaplain of Carrier Battle Group 5 and the Admiral's boyhood friend, listened with his head lowered and his eyes partly shuttered as the Admiral went on to confess to struggling with arrogance, pride and general impatience with "sloth and simpletons" in high office.

Later, absolved of his sins, the Admiral and the Commander ate dinner in the Admiral's quarters, a 30 foot square cabin that served as sitting room, bedroom and office. Unlike the rest of the 1000-foot, 20-story high warship, the cabin's gray steel bulkheads were covered with dark wood paneling. There were three pictures on the walls: a lithograph of the Battle of Leyte Gulf, a portrait of Lord Nelson and a framed copy of a Venetian naval pennant with the golden Lion of St. Mark from the Battle of Lepanto.

"Davey, you give me no credit for the garbage that I have been putting up with from Washington," the Admiral said. "These last two months have been pure hell."

"You get full credit for patience," the Commander said. "But you get no credit for some of your private thoughts which you privately share with me, your hapless confessor."

"Do you realize that since the beginning of the year the crazy Iranians have committed no less than five international offenses that were essentially acts of war? Moreover, they have threatened repeatedly not only to nuke the Jews out of existence but they have threatened half of Europe as well as the United States. During all of this, I have been ordered twice to conduct saber-rattling war games and twice the Iranians quieted down. But nothing has really changed. We sit here with a battle fleet of four carrier strike groups—squadrons of planes, cruisers, frigates, submarines. From 35,000 feet over the Gulf and the Arabian Sea, it looks like a U.S. Navy parking lot. But the Persians are still encouraging the blowing up and beheading of Iraqis and Afghans and any of our Marines they can snatch. And the minute they really get some nukes, I know we're in for it."

"How do you know?"

"Davey, I know. In my gut. In my head. I know."

"I thought I just absolved you for being arrogant."

"I'm not being arrogant. I know."

The Commander carefully cut a piece of roast chicken. Then, he asked with equal care:

"What would you do that you are not already doing?"

"We have to go for them before they go for us. Maybe, just maybe, we have six months. We should do it now."

"As your friend, I urge you not to say things like that. As your priest, I can't agree."

"I'm not saying anything that I haven't already said repeatedly to Washington. They all know where I stand. And I don't understand your theological position."

"Of course, you understand it. How can a Christian believer, how can God, approve of arbitrarily destroying millions of Iranians?"

"Why would God prefer killing millions of Iranians only after they wipe out the Chosen People and a few million Europeans and Americans? That's what would happen,"

"Thayer, who knows what God would prefer; who knows His Plan? If Iran did what you suggest, there would be, as you say, a terrible response. Presumably that would be called a "just war," but, while there is any chance that there be no war at all, doesn't that best meet the Moral Law?"

"What if while we dither, they wipe out Israel and then hold a wimpy world at bay with nuclear missiles? Or, they take out just one of our major cities and then say let's talk. Would we chicken out? Could that possibly be God's Plan? The Iranians, the mullahs, insist that it is."

"Evil men in Tehran may say that, but I don't believe the majority of Muslims buy it for a minute."

"Davey, you Dominicans are always better on Thomistic logic than I am, but I can't agree with that kind of holy whistling in the dark. If Tehran can get away with blowing up Israel and dominating the Middle East, the Muslims everywhere will love it and those who don't will pretend that they do. The bad guys in Tehran are playing international bully and you and I learned early on, as I recall, that bullies do what they say they are going to do unless they're stopped."

Thayer Arnold grew up in the 1950s in a large house in the old Manor section of Larchmont, NY. Davey Towne grew up in an even bigger house across the street. Their fathers commuted to New York daily where they read the *New York Herald Tribune* on the way into town and played bridge and drank on the way home. Mr. Arnold, much decorated a few years earlier at the Battle of Leyte Gulf which effectively ended the Japanese Imperial Navy, now sold bonds. Mr. Towne, much decorated at the Battle of the Bulge which effectively ended the Nazi German Wehrmacht, now wrote a nationally syndicated news column on politics. The boys were the same age, but Thayer, always sizeable and athletic, looked older; Davey was always slight and bookish. Despite those differences, they were best friends. Each in his own way looked after the other: Thayer playing bodyguard and Davey keeping Thayer out of trouble. Also, they were allied for years in a secret game that they called "New Atlantis."

Davey had read about the Lost Continent of Atlantis when he was only six. That year he founded New Atlantis on the ancient site of the original; peopled it; gave it a current history; and told his best friend about it and insisted on lifelong secrecy. Thayer more than willingly took the dark pledge and made himself Emperor of North Atlantis. Davey became Emperor of the South. The game was on.

For the next five years hardly a day or two passed without some development in New Atlantis: wars, epidemics, panics, other disasters and triumphs, plans, plots and perfidies. Each was wilder, more complex, more sophisticated, more exciting. Characters were invented; maps were drawn; dispatches written, statements issued. Everything was always still secret: there were only two people in the world who knew what was happening on the Lost Continent.

The growing bond between those two was enormously strengthened by an incident the summer that they turned eight. During July and August, they spent almost every sunny day about six blocks away from their homes at the Larchmont Beach Club, a relatively modest WASP enclave on Long Island Sound separated along the shore from the Larchmont Yacht Club by several of the last Victorian summer hotels, huge white elephants with wide porches where the better city people still came to escape the heat. The Beach Club was a little boy's paradise. Watchers on that beach in 1937 saw the Hindenburg Graf Zeppelin arriving from Europe on its final fatal voyage. Two months later a Pan Am clipper passed over the Sound on the first commercial hip-hop flight to Ireland by way of Newfoundland. By the 1950's they could watch on early afternoons a parade of the world's biggest aircraft pass far out on direct flights to continental Europe.

On one of these afternoons, both Thayer and Davey hand paddled through the water in their alternate roles as Admirals leading the fleets of New Atlantis North and New Atlantis South against each other from their floating rubber tubes. In a surprise maneuver, Thayer cut in back of a float in preparation for a flank attack. Accordingly, he did not see Buster Stein, the beach bully, a large boy more fat than muscle, dive from the float under Davey's tube, upset it and pull Davey beneath the surface. When Thayer came around the float for his flank attack, he saw Davey's tube floating free; Davey, spouting water, his eyes bugging, arms flailing; Buster ducking Davey back under water and holding him there. Thayer rolled from his tube, plunged underwater to where Buster was holding Davey and broke Buster's hold, enabling Davey to escape. As the three boys popped to the roiled surface, Buster tried to kick Thayer in the groin but only hit his thigh; Thayer swirled and drove his fist into Buster's face; much blood spread immediately in the water. Before Thayer could hit Buster again, two teenage lifeguards reached the melee, broke it up and brought Davey, still gasping for air, and Buster, still bleeding profusely, to the beach followed by the unblemished Thayer.

While the lifeguards gave Buster first aid and calmed Davey with a Good Humor ice cream bar, kids crowded around Thayer celebrating the beating of the hated beach bully. However, when it became clear that Buster's nose was broken, the bleeding continued, and an ambulance arrived, the general hilarity trailed off into arguments about what really happened. Buster told the lifeguards before being taken away in the ambulance that Davey and Thayer trapped him and that Davey had gone under water in the ensuing fight. Most of the kids on the beach much preferred the story told by Thayer and Davey. But the lifeguards and an aging nanny who had watched from the shore with her charges agreed that both sides of the story were equally possible. And Buster was the obvious victim.

That night at home the situation took a further turn downward. Buster's father telephoned Mr. Arnold. Buster was still in the hospital where his mother would spend the night with him. His condition was serious. His nose was broken in two places. He would need surgery. Mrs. Stein was distraught. Mr. Stein, a prominent lawyer, had not decided whether to seek damages. It was clear to Mr. Stein that the two boys viciously attacked Buster and Mr. Stein also gave voice to the possibility that the attack would not have occurred if Buster's last name were not Stein but something more acceptable.

Mr. Arnold immediately phoned Mr. Towne who expressed exasperation. Mr. Towne knew the Steins well. Lenny Stein was really a good fellow. He and Lenny had been in the same class at Dartmouth before the attack on Pearl Harbor and everyone went off to war. The problem was his wife, Marjorie, a spoiled bitch who gave Lenny a very hard time and, when anything went wrong, always thought she was being put down socially. Buster was indeed a rotten overweight sociopath who picked on younger kids. He had almost drowned Davey. However, Mr. Towne said he would overlook those facts. Best to bury the whole business. Mr. Arnold need not worry. It so happened that Mr. Stein, a confidant of Tammany Hall Boss Carmine DeSapio, had called on Mr. Towne only last week asking him to hold off at least temporarily on an unusually nasty political column that Mr. Towne was working on and Mr. Towne had agreed. In the morning, he would call Lenny. Everything would be all right.

"You do remember Buster Stein?" the Admiral said.

"Of course, I do," the Commander said. "I haven't thought about him for years. I think I finally forgave him during my novitiate."

"I'll bet he never forgave me. In fact, if he's still alive somewhere, I hope he remembers me well every time he looks in the mirror. And he should. I've been thinking about that incident lately. You know when I hit him that day in the water, I wasn't just trying to hold him off. I think it was the first time that I ever recognized that there is absolute evil in the world and I wanted to destroy it."

"We are expected to forgive those who trespass against us. I must say, Thayer, you do not sound particularly forgiving even 50 years after the transgression."

"As I understand forgiveness, it benefits the trespassed by removing hate. At the same time, it does not make them stupid. They know that the forgiven trespassers benefit only if they are contrite and do penance. But it is a logical impossibility for absolute evil to be contrite about anything. And forget about penance."

"Under any circumstance, it is truly a hard thing truly to forgive."

"I'll buy that. With a world full of evil creatures, sometimes it's impossible."

"That's not quite what I taught my students."

"I'm only a simple sailor. Show me the logical fallacy."

The Commander laughed. "Thayer, you're beautiful. I don't suppose you received the nickname "Shark" because of your simplicity. In fact, as I recall when we were at school together at Rye Country Day, you were always a logic chopping genius. I'm sure those skills were further honed at Annapolis and the Naval War College."

"I would suggest that my education pales next to what you received over the years from the Dominicans and you've been perfecting that ever since. While I've been out flying airplanes and rowing boats, you've been writing books on history and philosophy. I stand before you, Father Towne, humbly seeking wisdom."

"Thayer, the day you do anything humbly they'll make me Pope."

They both laughed. This was their private put-down joke. Whenever Davey questioned Thayer's veracity, he suggested that if whatever Thayer was saying were true he, Davey, was certain to be the next Bishop of Rome. Thayer raised the same kind of doubt by suggesting that if something Davey said were true he, Thayer, would soon be elected Holy Roman Emperor.

The joke went back to when they were in school together. After graduation, they seldom saw much of each other but they always stayed in contact. Thayer went to Annapolis; Davey to Georgetown, then, abandoning the Jesuits for the Dominicans, he spent a year as a novitiate and six more at the Dominican House of Studies in Washington. Thayer went to flight school where he acquired the nickname "Shark"; then began serving on carriers. He flew fighter bombers in Viet Nam; served in several sensitive posts in the Pentagon; returned to sea and commanded a carrier task force in the First Gulf War. Davey obtained doctorates in moral philosophy and history; taught at three Dominican colleges; wrote scholarly books. All during these years, Thayer and Davey corresponded. They wrote long letters about their experiences and what was happening in the world. Then two years ago Davey took early retirement at the Dominican School of Philosophy and Theology at Berkeley and volunteered to become a Navy chaplain. With some political help from Thayer, Father David Towne, OP was accepted; given the rank of full Commander; and after indoctrination at the Navy Chaplain School at Newport and a brief assignment at the Naval War College there, was appointed chaplain to Carrier Battle Group 5 in the Gulf.

"Regardless of the state of my humility," the Admiral said over coffee served in Navy porcelain bearing a four star flag, "Buster Stein has always been to me an icon for bullies of all sorts. Early on they learn that they get their way by pushing around the weak. When they get their way they try pushing around the stronger and they keep doing it until they're stopped. That was Buster. That was Hitler. That was the Soviets. And that, my old friend, is the Persians."

"Surely, you can't put Iran in the same league as Hitler or Stalin?"

"Not quite yet. But the Persians are working on it. And it would be best if we stopped them before they get there—not after. Unfortunately, many of our wimpy masters have a problem with that approach."

The steward reentered the cabin and the Commander nodded that he would like more coffee and waited before speaking until the steward left.

"Thayer, you keep suggesting the killing of possibly several million people in a preemptive war. How do you personally face God after that? Do you think you have some special assignment from Heaven?"

"Maybe. Sometimes I do wonder why I'm here at this time rather than someone else, but I haven't received any divine messages of late. You'll be the first to know. I think much more likely my attitude is based simply on my evolutionary drive for survival. Davey, they threaten to nuke us; they kill our people; they negotiate only to stay our hand until they're ready. Tell me, did you ever teach your students about the defense of Malta by the Knights of St. John, the Hospitallers, against the Ottoman Empire? Possibly you don't recall that while the rest of Europe stuttered and stalled the Muslims surrounded the Hospitallers and the Sultan, Suleiman the Magnificent, sent them a message. He had all the Knights who had been taken prisoner decapitated, nailed to wooden crosses and floated past the defenders on the fortress walls. But the Knights did not say: 'Ah, poor

Sultan, he just feels put down by us Christians. He really wants to talk and make peace.' No, they took the Sultan's true measure. So from their battlements beneath their red banners with white crosses they jammed the heads of their Muslim prisoners into cannons and fired them into the Muslim lines. Then they withstood the siege."

"Thayer, that was in 1565!"

"Sometimes when I watch Muslims behead our people on TV it seems to have been only yesterday. What is our alternative to what surely would be a just war? Or do we wait for the repeatedly promised murder of millions in Tel Aviv, London and New York to motivate us?

"The only rationale that the Church recognizes for a just war is when all other means have been exhausted."

"That's fine. But how long do you wait when you're dealing with absolute evil—evil I might remind you that goes back 1500 years, a fact which many find it comfortable not to recognize. Davey, you ask what do I say to God after a preemptive strike. Let me ask you: What do our leaders say to God if they let us be attacked when they could have prevented it? What would I say? Davey, tell me: has God removed suicide from the list of mortal sins?"

During the next two days, the latest attempts to resolve the on-again, off-again international crisis stalled. Israeli, British and American intelligence insisted that the Iranian Revolutionary Guards had obtained nuclear warheads from their own government and was arming missiles with them. As usual, the Iranian government denied it. The world crisis rumbled forward.

That evening Commander Towne was reading in his bunk when he heard the repetitive boom of the carrier's four catapults launching jets. Then he was called to the hanger deck which he found crowded with pilots and crewmen readying more aircraft, checking their ordnance, guiding them into the elevators. As soon as the Admiral saw him, the Admiral and his executive officer climbed on to a platform, summoned Davey to follow and loudspeakers ordered the pilots to assemble. The Admiral spoke briefly:

"As you and planes already launched fly tonight, the fate of your country, the fate of Western Civilization, flies with you. I know you will do your duty. As one of our greatest writers said about another war long ago, when you are old and still honored for your deeds this day, 'gentlemen now abed shall think themselves accursed they were not here and hold their manhoods cheap.' Go with God! I have asked Commander Towne to pray.

"St. Michael, Archangel, defend us in battle," Davey started over the bowed heads and kneeling men among the planes. "Be our defense against the wickedness and snares of the Devil..."

Thirty minutes later in the Admiral's cabin, Thayer sat at a conference table along with a half dozen officers, looking at charts. Commander Towne stood nearby with several other officers drinking coffee. The last of the carrier's planes had been launched 10 minutes ago. Coded reports from the attack fleet's other three carriers in the Gulf and the Arabian Sea said their squadrons had been in the air for 15 minutes. Meantime, crews on surface ships and submarines throughout the fleet were standing ready to launch missiles. At this point, an aid handed the Admiral a decoded top secret message from Washington. Diplomatic back channels were reporting that the Iranians might be willing to resume talks. The order to attack was temporarily suspended.

"How much time before missile launch against our first targets?" the Admiral asked.

"Two minutes, sir."

The Admiral pursed his lips and looked across the cabin at the picture of blazing ships at Leyte Gulf; then at Lord Nelson, who, when flashed a similar cease operations order at the Battle of Copenhagen, put a telescope to his blind eye and said he couldn't see the signal. Thayer asked an aid to bring him his reading glasses from the desk at the end of the cabin.

Before the aid found them, the entire carrier vibrated from the shock of multiple-warhead Triton IIs breaking the surface of the sea and rising on tongues of flame after being launched from nearby Fleet Ballistic Missile submarines. The sound was like the thunderous howl of a great hurricane-force wind. The missiles in minutes would take out Iran's deeply buried command bunkers and nuclear facilities. Meantime, hundreds of Tomahawk precision missiles were also flaming from launch tubes on warships and subs across hundreds of miles of open water to blind and destroy Iranian air defenses and its command and control network. A moment later it was Davey who returned with the eye glasses.

"They were on your bed table," he said, dryly.

"Yes, thank you. I really need them to read the incoming messages."

The Admiral watched along with other officers from the bridge as the last first strike jets returned safely to the flagship carrier. Only six had been shot down by missiles, two were missing. Early reports were positive for almost all targets. A mop-up strike was already underway.

On the bridge, as the Admiral moved his finger across a chart, he left behind a scarlet streak.

"Your hand, sir!" an officer said. "You're bleeding,"

"Just a paper cut," the Admiral said and wrapped a handkerchief around his right palm, causing a scarlet spot on the outside of the white cloth.

Commander Towne, who was watching, whispered: "My God, Thayer, it's the stigmata."

"Very unlikely," the Admiral said. "Don't be dramatic."

Several returning pilots reported another very unlikely sight on their final approaches. They said they saw a large red pennant with a white cross and another long pennant with a golden lion flying in the semi-darkness from the carrier mast.

III.
Signs and Portents

Adventure in Archeology

If only God would give me some clear sign! Like making a large deposit in my name in a Swiss bank.
— Woody Allen, Hollywood movie actor and director

Schmidt did an evil thing.

He had spent much of the day in the library of the Monastery of St. Honoré reading the Codex of Brother Justin: dusty; convoluted; boring; nothing new. Then, just before the bell struck for nones, he came upon an entry concerning what was referred to as "the removal' and a 'casket."

Schmidt immediately recognized the reference. It was to a highly debatable event: the disposition of the Ark of the Covenant. He knew the story well.

The Ark into which the Jews placed the Tablets on which the finger of God wrote out the Ten Commandments for Moses was believed to have been last seen at the time of the destruction of the First Temple or possibly the construction of the Second. Certainly, it was missing from the Temple when Pompey the Great conquered Jerusalem in 63 BC. At that time, The Great One, Gnaeus Pompeius, personally searched the Holy of Holies, the small sacred inner room of the Temple where the golden Ark sat. It was not there. Nor was the Ark there when Titus captured Jerusalem again in 70 AD. Units of two Roman Legions literally waded through the blood of thousands of fanatic Jewish defenders to reach the Holy of Holies only to find it empty and convert the ruins into a Roman Temple of Jupiter. And assuredly the Ark was not there when the Crusaders in 1099 recaptured Jerusalem from Islam and seized the Dome of the Rock, that magnificent, Christ-bashing Muslim shrine built on the site of the Temple and what was still thought to be the center of the world at the apex of Temple Mount. The Ark was gone. Or was it?

The Poor Fellow Soldiers of Jesus Christ, known as the Knights of the Temple, spent their first years in the Holy Land digging tunnels throughout Temple Mount. Many believed this resulted in finding one or more secret rooms containing great treasures: the Holy Grail, the gold crown of the kings of Judah. Some said the Templars also found the Ark. Much of this treasure—particularly the Ark—is believed to have been moved to Europe, most likely France.

"The casket said to be of setim wood," Schmidt read, "is two and a half cubits long by one and a half cubits wide. It is overlaid with gold and has affixed to it on each side two gold rings through which the golden carrying poles can be thrust. On the cover two cherubim of beaten gold face each other with outstretched wings."

As, of course, he knew: this was the exact description of the Ark given in Exodus. "The Master had brothers of the Temple bury it at Chartres under the center of the Great Labyrinth," the Codex said. "All of the Poor Fellow Soldiers who knew about it died in the Suppression. But later, at the time of the Terror when the Labyrinth was desecrated, Gregory the Sextant found the casket and hid it with us. We, in turn, sent it to the New World for safety with the Martyrs."

Schmidt's stomach churned happily with the rich juices of academic covetousness. He looked up from the page and surveyed the bare stone walls of the medieval chamber. No one. In the heavy silence, he was alone, unobserved. Certainly only he knew of Brother Justin's notation. None of his group of medievalists had joined him that day at the Monastery. All of them were at Cluny where they felt more important finds were to be made. Schmidt, you waste your time on trifles, they said, and, Schmidt knew they meant: what, after all, could you expect of some under-published dullard like you, Schmidt?

Surely, St. Honoré was of minor importance and had little to offer: just suited for him, small beer. But Schmidt had not been so sure of that judgment and now his scholarly contrariness had been rewarded. He could not wait to tell of his discovery. And, of course, Science required him to share new knowledge with his fellows.

But then, Schmidt, so often put down by his peers, thought: why should he share? At least, why should he share so quickly? Who would know if he didn't? This was only the beginning: possibly a far greater discovery was at hand: The 3,200-year old Ark itself, the throne of Yahweh on Earth. Inside, possibly he would find the stone Tablets bearing the Ten Commandments, the Tables of Testimony that Moses carried down from Mount Sinai to the Chosen People. Inside, possibly he would find the Staff of Aaron. Inside, possibly he would find the Golden Pot of Manna. He, Schmidt, would be greater than Schliemann after Troy, greater than Carter after Tutankhamen. He would tell no one about the codex; at least not for awhile.

Looking around to assure himself again that no one was watching, Schmidt took his 24-tool Swiss Army knife from his canvas briefcase. Normally he used one of the knife's specialized tools when he was in the field to chivvy small bits of bone or baked clay or dry seeds from cracks in ancient floors. Today he selected the sharpest blade; cut the key page from the Codex, and quickly slipped it into his briefcase. There was no rumble of thunder; no flash of lightning. Silence enveloped him. He was still alone. And alone he would follow the trail.

That trail after a week of intensive research led Schmidt directly to the still forested shrine of three martyred French Jesuit saints in Upstate New York. All were missionaries to New France in the 17th Century. The shrine was located in what was once deep wilderness beyond the Dutch settlements in Albany and Schenectady. It was on the site of a Mohawk Indian village originally called Ossernenon and later Auriesville after the last Mohawk living in the area. All three missionaries—St. René Goupil, St Isaac Jogues and St. Jean Lalande—were brutally killed there by the Mohawks in the 1640's. If

Brother Justin were correct, the Ark would have been buried there in secret some 150 years later in the woodlands "with the Martyrs" above the Mohawk River.

Schmidt's research showed that canonically the plan was exquisitely consistent: The Ark had moved from the repeatedly failed Old World to the New, from the center of the world to the ends of the earth; there it was guarded by the three Martyrs until the time came at God's choosing for it to be revealed again to the nations.

The Jesuit Superior of the National Shrine of North American Martyrs at Auriesville received a cheery but somewhat vague phone call from Schmidt during the second week of Lent requesting a meeting. Schmidt wished to discuss an archeological matter of possibly great importance. The Superior said that Auriesville was not unfamiliar with archeological research; that it had been the site of numerous digs; and that many important Iroquois artifacts had been found. However, any new archeological exploration would have to be approved by the Father General in Rome. What might Schmidt be trying to find? Schmidt preferred not to say on the phone.

The Superior then pointed out that the shrine was crowded with many pilgrims during Lent. The shrine was conducting special masses at its log coliseum for the Blessed Kateri Tekakwitha, a Mohawk chief's converted daughter born at Ossernenon only 10 years after the martyrdoms. The pilgrims were praying for her canonization. The Superior suggested a meeting after Easter. Schmidt said the matter was too urgent, too sensitive, too important. The Superior would understand when they met. The Superior then reluctantly relented and agreed to see Schmidt briefly the following Monday.

Schmidt flew to Albany and rented a car for the 40-mile drive to Auriesville. Following his university's niggardly guidelines for Archeology Department travel, he rented the cheapest car available, a two-door Japanese sub-compact with a glowing tinny exterior and modest power. As a result, he made poor time on the New York

Thruway and resigned himself to the awkwardness of beginning his visit with a late arrival. But the delay did give him an opportunity for a final review of his strategy.

He would not initially disclose his real objective. The Ark was too big a discovery, too tremendous a prize. Think of it: the Ark was created at least 1200 years before the birth of Christ. As an artistic work alone, it was of enormous value. As a religious artifact, it was priceless.

The Ark indeed was believed to be the dwelling place of Yahweh. It was a palladium of enormous power, preceding with trumpet blasts the armies of the Israelites into battle and destroying their enemies. As such, it made Schmidt wary despite long attenuation of his religious beliefs. The Ark always protected itself: when the Philistines captured it in battle, they were horribly destroyed by plague; when the Israelites ignored the Covenant, they were relinquished to captivity in Babylon; when sacrilegious invaders looked for the Ark in the Temple, it had always been absent.

Moreover, the Ark involved mysteries and holy matters that went back to the beginnings of the world; studying it exposed the ribs of the universe. In the Temple at Jerusalem, the High Priest had approached the Ark only once a year with his eyes averted. The Ark was dangerous. It apparently had absolute free will. It could disappear and reappear anywhere as Yahweh chose.

Schmidt was crudely jerked from his thoughts by the blasting horns of an 18-wheel container truck speeding by him in the next lane at close to 80 miles an hour. The leviathan truck, hauling an outsize trailer filled with Ben & Jerry ice cream, sliced by Schmidt so narrowly that his small car rocked and yawed and for a moment he almost lost control. Shaken with fright, he numbly watched the truck roar ahead up the Thruway and disappear around the curve of a wooded hill. For the next few minutes, he concentrated on traffic passing him, steering his car at the edge of the breakdown lane, intensely gripping the steering wheel. But then, as the danger faded, he gave himself over again to the pleasure of reviewing and savoring his plans and the future.

Schmidt recognized, of course, that the Jesuits at the end of the 18th Century could have buried the Ark anywhere on the several hundreds of acres that now comprised the shrine. But he had studied old maps and he had a professional hunch that he should look in a remote section called The Glen. There in the deep, primeval woods a Mohawk tomahawked St. René for making the Sign of the Cross over an Indian child. St. Isaac Jogues found the half-eaten remains of St. René and buried them.

Later St. Isaac Jogues and St. Jean Lalande escaped. But two years later they returned. This time the Mohawks tortured and beheaded them. Schmidt needed to find out where the heads were buried. That, too, could be a rewarding area to explore if The Glen proved to be a false lead. His research failed to disclose the site of the buried heads, but surely the Superior could tell him.

However, Schmidt knew he must be careful how he asked questions and what he asked. The Jesuits were astute. If they guessed his objective, they would thwart him. They would probably try to keep the prize for some religious purpose. Science and Schmidt would be denied. Therefore, at first, he would tell them that he was doing field work for a new book on 17th Century exploration; the religious roots of New France; the conversion of the Indians; the spread of French culture and, of course, the critical role of the Jesuits. He would say that he had evidence that St. Isaac Jogues had buried a chest with important documents at the Mohawk village. What a surprise, he would tell the Superior later, that his careful excavations had uncovered the Ark instead.

By now, Schmidt had turned off the New York State Thruway and was driving along a narrow secondary road bordered by the Mohawk River and overgrown remains of the original Erie Canal on his right and rising farmland on his left. The river glinted; the farmland appeared lush with spring crops. Schmidt felt buoyed, optimistic, academically smug and content.

He already was able to picture the great day to come: A cool afternoon in the shrine's woods; open trenches with their neat webs of string and carefully placed markers in various colors; grubby graduate students in L.L. Bean boots sifting sandy dirt under a warm sun. Suddenly there would be a shout. "Dr. Schmidt! Over here!" And there at the bottom of a deep trench sticking up through the dirt he would see the head of a gold cherubim and the tip of a gold enfolding wing.

The happy dream was crassly and abruptly interrupted by a great billboard:

AURIESVILLE SHRINE
TURN LEFT

And then there was the immediate appearance to his left of a narrow road rising up a steep hill. Schmidt swerved precipitously to make the turn. As he did, a huge purple blur, a rapidly moving bus from Quebec packed with pilgrims, appeared like a fully rigged warship coming down the hill, jammed its brakes, hissed loudly and slid irresistibly into the side of Schmidt's car.

The car, spewing gas from its smashed fuel tank, overturned repeatedly across the road, down a bank and into a deep grove of aged Chestnut trees. Screaming pilgrims on the bus saw the car lay there looking like a battered toy for only a few frozen seconds; then a fireball engulfed it.

There was little left of Schmidt. There was nothing left of his canvass briefcase in which he carried the stolen page from the Codex of Brother Justin. The Fort Hunter Volunteer Pumper No. 2 sprayed the surrounding woods and fields with foam for several hours to prevent a forest fire.

Later, at the usual mid-afternoon Mass celebrated in the shrine's log coliseum, the First Lesson from *Deuteronomy* said: "The secret things belong unto the Lord our God." The Superior, who was the celebrant, did not mention the automobile accident in his homily. But he included Schmidt among the dead for whom the faithful were asked to pray.

Email

Surprise! Dr. Huck Franklin, Nobel laureate and explorer of abstruse molecular behavior, did not answer his email. Nary a snide comment. Nary a sick joke. Worse: he seemed to have disappeared.

At precisely 8 PM EST in the East a lot of snow was falling. In New Mexico it was 6 PM where, outside of Succoro, the Huck had a century-old ranch house without any ranch. The sweep of sky behind the mountains was undoubtedly impressive as always, red highlighting black clouds. I sat at my desktop computer watching the snow blow against my windows as I wrote what at least I believed to be witty commentary on the day's events and emailed it.

Within minutes, I had a negative response:

Delivery failed!
Server reports no such address as
huck@mesa.com.
Try again?

Of course, try again. Same answer.

Try again. Long pause. Then a totally black screen. Then three scary blinks. Then a red flash; a purple flash; a gold flash. Then the same answer but expanded.

Delivery failed!
Server reports no such address as
huck@mesa.com.
Sysop Alpha suggests try
huck@styx.station2.org.

The somewhat unusual email header on the message said:

*Received: from styx.stations.spqr.org (styx.stations.spqr.org)
[145.200.87.55]) by arcturus.net (8.5.4/8.Epsilon 12) with horub.org
by grail.ephesus.net for <gudbuddy@mesaeast.com>; Tue, 8 Jan. 2002
21:15:41 -0500.*

I tried the suggested address. Nearly an hour passed. Then I received the first of the following series of messages that probably I should suppress. Based on what I have learned, I would not want to do anything to hurt the Huck in his progress:

Message 1:

Sorry for screwup. Seems I died this morning just after breakfast. Computer down at the house ever since as you might expect. Meantime, I'm involved in some typical bureaucracy here. Regular people on holiday. No one can find the right papers. Schedules for popular river crossings apparently filled for months. Fortunately, they let me borrow a laptop. Cool chip, as you would say. Lots of toys. You can reach me here for the next few weeks anyway at the address that you used. I'll advise you of any change if I can.

You'll be interested to know that I am feeling pretty good all things considered. Unfortunately, I missed out next Sunday on leading the semi-annual tour to Trinity Site. Freddy Manytents, you probably remember him from Cal Tech and Los Alamos, will just have to take over. Always a great trip. Glass on the desert floor never changes, but always good to see old colleagues.

Time at this place seems to have stopped permanently at early summer evening. The sun is down but the sky is still light. I'm sitting cross-legged under a rock shelf on a hill overlooking this big river. Down on the shore there is an old boat house, a couple of LSTs from World War II and what looks like a wrecked Venetian galley out of some Italian opera. But I haven't seen anyone around there since I checked in this morning. You won't believe this: the guy who checked me in at the Camp was a Roman centurion.

I understand that even if they find all my papers that I may be here for some time anyway. As you might expect, it's a question of indoctrination, right attitude and generally getting with the program.

The Centurion, who says he doesn't "know shit about what's going on," also says that from what he can see I probably can pass the early screens, but he says there are a lot of troubling things, too. When I asked 'such as?" he said "if you have to ask that question that's what's troubling."

Please confirm that you have received this message. We may have opened a communications channel that could be important. Maybe illegal.

Huck

Message 2:

Glad that I'm getting through. I'll try to answer your questions, but as you know I am new here and I don't think they're telling me everything. Frankly, IMHO, there is plenty going on that I may or may not learn about depending on how things go. For example, the Centurion has already advised me that I need to watch myself using acronyms like IMHO. "Sort of a putdown code, isn't it?' he said. "I mean, I know it's just shorthand for 'in my humble opinion,' but what it really means is: 'I'm special. I talk in code.' Just not done here, you know. Let me give you a tip: Speak English like God intended." (Joke?)

As for my situation, it is really unchanged. I'm still sitting on my hilltop waiting for news. The Centurion introduced me to one of his associates, a Persian Gentleman, who asked me a couple of stupid questions about my goals in life.

Apparently they have more of my papers than they let on. For instance, from what the Persian Gentleman says, they appear to know all about my early electronics work at Huntsville with the Krauts and my part on the Mach 4 stealth gunships that no one wanted us to use in Nam. And they know about the missile defense stuff that we did under the table in the 70s. Their interest in all of that appears to be finding out why it wasn't used to better effect and they seem to put part of the onus on me.

Another puzzler: they seem to think that one of the reasons I retired to Succoro is because of my interest in Trinity Site and eschatological matters and they seem to approve of that. I keep trying to get the Persian Gentleman to explain, but he just laughs and says 'you'll see."

"Who are 'they?'" you might ask. I am not sure but I think I get to learn that tomorrow. -H

Message 3:

Fascinating day. The Centurion called me up to the Camp. He said "they" were ready for me. I walked into a big tent built like a 15th Century military pavilion with a purple and gold gonfalon floating out from the top. Inside three men and two women sat around a conference table in canvas director's chairs. There was an empty canvas chair at one end with my name on it and I was told to sit in it.

A short round-faced man with bulging eyes stared at me for a few moments. His expression was a combination of weary amusement and extraordinary disdain.

"All right," he said. "Let's get to it. Dr. Franklin, you see before you what we quite correctly call a Mediocrity Investigating Panel. Not that that necessarily describes my associates although certainly some in their lives showed a great aptitude for it and all assuredly have experienced a lot of it in others. In fact, that is why they were chosen for this particular panel. As, indeed, even possibly myself."

At this point, he led a round of soft, self-deprecatory laughter—something like the simultaneous rustling of a hundred old pages in a quiet reading room.

"But," he continued, "it is not any comfortable enrapturement of ours with Mediocrity that is under consideration here today, but rather the extent to which you embraced it during your brief time on Earth.

"Like most of humanity, you probably in one way or another have thought of Good and Evil as stark opposites: one difficult to pursue, the other regrettably easy for weak mortals. Not so! Certainly, God loves his saints (and we shall leave the definition of sainthood to another time), but equally God loves great sinners—a condition that, despite popular opinion, is most difficult to achieve.

"It is puling, crawling Mediocrity, unfortunately the true condition of much of mankind, that God disdains while, of course, offering opportunities for remission from sin. And let me lay bare Mediocrity for you in its revolting true form: It is nothing but the result of sloth. And sloth is the bubonic plague of the soul. Sloth, much promoted by the Devil, is sin. "

The Chairman of the Mediocrity Investigating Panel mouthed the word "sloth" several times for emphasis and his associates nodded mournfully in unison. The Chairman continued:

"All of us emerging from the Somewhere on our way to the Somewhere arrived on Earth with a mixed bag of talents. Some arrived with a better bag than others. Some with better chances. Some in better times. But all had the same challenge to strive, to excel: to be the best mathematician, the best discus thrower, the best postman or physician or weaver or swine herder, even the best publican or the best clerk at the Motor Vehicle Bureau. And, if not the best, to be at least one who sought valiantly to achieve that goal.

"Ironically, most do not fail. Most simply do not try very hard. They stupidly misread our mission on Earth. They wallow in sloth. And, as a result, they become part of the world's Great Mediocracy: The lumpen life material that must be reprocessed to try again."

He paused dramatically and winked at his associates who merely appeared bored. They obviously had heard the speech.

'So here we are, sir. An early review of your files shows that you have not escaped Mediocrity in your life. But, happily, you also have excelled on occasion. Your spotty record is not without merit. How do we weigh you up? Do you go back into the pot, so to speak, or are you ready to go on to higher things after some reorientation—an intellectual sauna that the Doctors of the Church and the Council of Lyon wittily called Purgatory. This is what we want to determine about you. This is what brings us to this table.

"Now, before we begin, let me introduce the Panel: General Arnold, late of Saratoga and London; Mrs. Longworth, late of Washington; Mr. Adams, late of Boston and Chartres; Mme. Plantagenet, late of Acquitaine, Paris, London and Antioch. My name is Mencken, late of Baltimore. All of us have come a long way from the other side of the River for this. It may even have been worth our while."

More later. -H

Message 4

Hell of an ordeal, my friend, and I am using the phrase with great precision. Here is how it went:

General Arnold: "This Mach 4 stealth gunship that you developed. If deployed in Nam, what effect would it have had on the war?"

Franklin: "Some felt that aggressive use of it in numbers would have resulted in total collapse of the Communists."

General Arnold: "As I suspected. Why wasn't it deployed, then?"

Franklin: "Funds were blocked in Congress."

Mrs. Longworth: "After your congressional testimony, dear boy, which I believe was never declassified."

Franklin: "Congress knew very well what that weapon could do."

Mrs. Longworth: "But the public did not and the public had turned against the war. Of course, even then, if we could have been victorious that would have been different. Nothing like victory to make the public love a war. Henry, did I steal that line from you?"

Adams: (ignoring her): "We have read your testimony, Dr. Franklin. I fear it was dry, technically viscous, complex. No bonfires were lit."

Franklin: "I gave them the facts."

Mrs. Longworth: "Vitamin pills from the engineering elite when you should have served raw meat. And then when the decision went against the program, you retreated."

Mencken: "Surely you appreciated that all Congress was doing, as usual, was pandering to the booboisie."

Franklin: "Yes, but what else could I do? I couldn't fight Congress. What good would making myself a martyr have done?"

Mme. Plantagenet: "I would tell you this, M. Franklin. Although it has been said that I personally prefer kings to monks, martyrdom is a role highly thought of in these parts."

Adams: "Tell us why you feel your truly brilliant efforts on missile defense systems in the 70's never succeeded."

Franklin: "Possibly if they had really been truly brilliant, as you say, they would have."

Adams: "No exhibitions of foolish modesty, please. Our technical advisors here, who are the very best, I assure you, tell us your work was outstanding. That means it was. But, despite your accomplishment, it was brushed aside by the politicians and the usual time-servers. Can you say why?"

Franklin: "They were misguided."

Mrs. Longworth: I assure you that Henry and the rest of us would agree that that condition in Washington can generally be assumed."

General Arnold: "Dr. Franklin, *you* were not misguided. You knew what your work if pursued could do to the Soviet missiles. You would have changed the balance of power in the world, sir. The Soviet military would have been routed without a shot. The Cold War would have ended 20 years earlier.

Franklin: "Yes, of course. But what more could I do? I was not President of the United States."

Mrs. Longworth: "Lucky for you in the long run."

Mime. Plantagenet: "M. Franklin, both from very personal experience and long observation, I have learned that no one can tell any man or woman at the great moment how to reach beyond themselves. But M. Franklin, when the great moment comes, some do, some do."

—H

Message 5:

I am afraid that things are going very poorly.

The Persian Gentleman, who recorded the proceedings and provided me with a copy, squeezed my arm and nodded somewhat positively after the hearing was adjourned. But that could be merely the smile of the executioner.

Certainly, no one on that Panel looked reassuring. Both of the women seemed to be enjoying themselves greatly at my expense. And the men seemed in accord when the General complained about what he called "an increasing lack of divine spark in mankind's pitiful spawn." I regret having to assume that the comment was inspired by me.

The General obviously takes no prisoners. And I'm afraid I annoyed Adams when I innocently first addressed him as "Mr. President." He corrected me, saying he was "neither his grandfather nor his great grandfather," and Mrs. Longworth said "Henry's so modest."

From what I have gathered from the Centurion, even if all went well, the best I can hope for is an opportunity to perform some form of honorable expiation that may prove instructive. But I have no idea what form that would take. Or for how long. Although time seems increasingly to be of no concern.

So there it is. I remain here on my hillside in the half-light of early evening. It is very quiet. Down below one of the LSTs seems to be getting ready to make a crossing. This is the first time that I have seen that happen. There are two passengers standing on the deck and, although the light is very low, I think that one is General Arnold and the other shorter passenger has to be Mencken. Now Mrs. Longworth and Mme. Plantagenet are being escorted aboard by Adams and a sailor is hoisting a great purple and gold flag.

No one told me that they were leaving. I don't know if their departure is a good or bad sign. But possibly an answer is on the way.

A few minutes ago I received an email message suggesting that I visit a link with the following somewhat unusual address:

http://www.mandala.org/altbahn.html.

You might try it, too.—H

Naturally, I tried immediately.

There was a long pause. The gray screen was frozen. The screen went white. A few minutes passed. The screen went black. Then very slowly, very slowly, four silver buttons in the shape of circles surrounding octagons appeared with a menu of choices. The first item was *THE WORD;* the second, *PENANCE;* the third, *GOOD AND EVIL;* the fourth, *KNOWLEDGE*

I hesitantly clicked on the first button. The sound of a small gong came from my computer and a message appeared immediately. It said:

Password please: _____

Too bad. Huck had not given me the password.

I sat looking at the screen a long time. I tried to print it. The page came out blank. I tried the other buttons. I could do nothing with it. I copied it with a pencil on the back of an invoice and closed it down.

Nor have I ever been able to raise it again. Nor have I received any more email from the Huck.

Walking the Labyrinth

Prayer is not asking. It is a longing of the soul.
—Mohandas Gandhi

Palmer kept having the same dream.

He is 22. He is a first lieutenant in the US Army. World War II is lumbering possibly toward an end. He is in Chartres on his way east to Paris. He rides in a jeep with Thorncastle, the Catholic chaplain in his infantry unit which they are trying to find and rejoin. It is mid-afternoon, sunny, hot. They are parked in the empty square near the west porch of the cathedral. Ruins and scattered rubble from the recent three-day battle for the town are all around them

"Henry Adams' all-time favorite church," Thorncastle says. "Much favored by the Virgin. World's greatest glass. We absolutely must take a look inside."

"You want to get shot by some goddam sniper hiding in a pew," Palmer says.

"Oh, Palmer, you poor misguided Protestant. There aren't any pews in a proper cathedral. Besides, the Germans are long gone."

"So you say. You want to go in, you go first."

They enter with Thorncastle in the lead, Palmer covering with an Ml carbine. The cavernous cathedral is dark and full of shadows. The only light is from streaks of late August sunshine full of dust motes coming through broken boards on the enormous windows. All of the great glass is gone; buried for the duration of the war.

They walk down the nave to the crossing. There is a more light here from the clerestory and the choir. They can make out a maze of curved lines on the stone floor: a convoluted path of worn blue and white stones; it twists back and forth, back and forth within a huge circle leading finally to a large rosette in the center.

"It's the labyrinth," Thorncastle says. "The Road to Jerusalem. They laid it out here 700 years ago. You walk it to the center and back and say prayers. That gets you a bargain indulgence for your sins. It was for the busy pilgrim who didn't have time to go to Jerusalem on Crusade."

Who punched their tickets?"

"The priests, I suppose. But that isn't necessary. It's between you and God and He knows if you are just kidding around. Want to walk it? The war isn't over. Could be helpful to us."

"Thorncastle, we have to get to V Corps in Paris. Let's go. Anyway, I don't know the right prayers."

"You know the 'Pater Noster" surely. We can say it in English. Come on. As you officers say, follow me.'

And they walk the labyrinth. Or at least they start. It all depends when Palmer wakes up.

Last week Palmer had the dream three times. Then he had it again on the night flight from New York to Paris.

Palmer, a retired engineer and international expert on development of water resources, spent the next two days at the Quai d'Orsay at a Senior Executive Planners Work Summit of the new U.N. Middle East Peace Process Advancement Group. The new group involved more than a dozen nations of widely varying viability and consequence. It was created after the latest outbreak of rolling violence that left corpses of Jews and Moslems in bombed out buildings and streets from Antioch to Gaza.

Muslim Palestinians on Temple Mount hurled rocks and bottles filled with burning gasoline on Jews praying below at the West Wall of the Second Temple, real estate now occupied by the Dome of the Rock. Israeli troops dispersed the rioters on the Mount with tear gas and bullets. Some of the rioters died on the steps of the Al Aksa Mosque, sacred to Muslims, onetime military headquarters of the Templars. Within the hour, a Palestinian terrorist blew himself up in a Jerusalem pizza restaurant. The blast from the bomb packed with nails and ball bearings killed and wounded more than 100 people, many young children. Body parts mixed with pepperoni pizzas were scattered over the square. Then Israeli helicopter gunships took out a Palestinian terrorist headquarters. There was nothing left to scatter.

A bloody miasma of hate hung over Mt. Moriah. It spread; it thickened; it choked all Jerusalem. The Church of the Holy Sepulcher closed its doors to pilgrims as a "temporary' security measure. The Church of the Nativity, essentially behind the lines in the contested Arab West Bank, also closed.

At the Quai d'Orsay, two hours of acrimony and the usual feckless speeches opened the Senior Executive Planners Work Summit. It was obvious to Palmer and most of the other technical experts that there was no chance of processing any peace in Jerusalem for some time or even accomplishing much technical ground work. Certainly no one wanted to talk seriously about development of water resources in Samaria. But the political planners present could not go home until they jerry rigged some glimmering thing to announce. Therefore, the days wore on.

However, on the night of the second day as Palmer slept fit-fully in his suite at the Crillon, the dream came again. And, the next morning after eating breakfast in his elegant small sitting room, he watched discontentedly from his window the hustling cars in the Place de la Concorde and made a decision. He would absent himself that morning from what obviously would be another empty meeting of the peace planners. He ordered a car to take him to Chartres. He had to walk the labyrinth again.

Palmer felt like a schoolboy on holiday as he was driven out of Paris through mid-morning traffic. He thought regretfully of Thorn-castle, wishing Thorncastle could have joined him. But Thorncastle was long dead. He had been killed near Bastogne, hit by mortar shell fragments while giving last rites to the wounded in a farmyard. Palm-er would walk the labyrinth for both of them.

The limousine parked by the west porch of the cathedral ap-proximately where Palmer had parked his jeep fifty years ago. Flow-erbeds meticulously tended and neat signs in French and English warning dogs not to soil the walkways now replaced the debris of war. Two huge tourist buses parked nearby were loading their passengers: the first group, an orderly line of properly dressed, elderly Germans; the other, an ill-formed line of much younger Americans costumed expensively as Balkan refugees or members of urban street gangs.

Palmer looked upward for a moment at the cathedral's two mis-matched spires, triumphs of Gothic architecture that as he recalled he had little noted on his last visit. Although now he also recalled that Thorncastle had told him that the older and smaller of the two was the most perfect piece of architecture on earth. He walked across the porch and entered the cathedral. Immediately, he was stopped by the almost physical force of the light pouring through the stained glass windows. Bright sunlight was transmuted into ethereal blues and reds and greens, engulfing everything from a dozen angles, an exultation to the infinite glory of the Virgin and God. This was what

Thorncastle had longed to see, to stand in the center of the rosette and be washed with that light. .

"Pardon, Monsieur," a voice said to him from nearby. "C'est fermé dans cinq minutes."

Palmer looked in the direction of the voice and saw a short, bulky old woman all in black sitting in a chair with a large sheaf of lottery tickets.

"Ah, Madame," he said in his rocky French. "I come from a long way to walk the labyrinth."

"C'est impossible!" she said and rocked her head disapprovingly. Then, rocking her head with more vigor and holding up a definitive thumb, she said: 'Un. It is time for the dinner." Holding up her thumb and one finger, she added: Deux, It is not possible to walk the labyrinth anyway today because the labyrinth is covered with the chairs."

"Madame, possibly I could move the chairs?" Palmer said.

'Non, non, c'est impossible. The chairs, they must stay."

Palmer reached in his jacket for his billfold.

"Possibly, a donation, Madame? To help make up for the difficulty of moving the chairs."

She paused for a moment. He thought he saw a flash of Gallic greed in her eyes, but, if so, it disappeared as the cathedral's great bells began to toll noon.

"Non, non," she said with finality. "Now it is time for the dinner. La cathedrale, c'est fermé. C'est fermé." And she rose agitatedly from her chair and shooed him toward the doors.

In the limousine riding back to Paris and the certain dreariness of the afternoon session of his meeting that he could not escape attending, he remembered something that Thorncastle told him after they had walked the labyrinth and were driving along this same road.

"Walking the Road to Jerusalem isn't as easy as it looks, you know. It isn't for everyone."

Maybe, Palmer thought, he could try again later in the week, but he already knew that would not happen. The conference, his schedule, the insidious inertia of age, everything militated against it. However, maybe his intent had been enough. Too bad he couldn't ask Thorncastle. Palmer was sure Thorncastle would know.

Exodus Revisited

All thieves who could my fees afford
Relied on my orations,
And many a burglar I've restored
To his friends and his relations.
        —*W.S. Gilbert, English operetta lyricist*

Woe to those who call what is bad, good,
And what is good, bad,
Who substitute darkness for light
And light for darkness,
Who substitute bitter for sweet
And sweet for bitter
        —*Isaiah, prophet*

Malcolm Plumb's best memory, as the saying goes in clever legal circles, was that he had participated during the earlier part of the evening in a rather routine, generally boring dinner at his club with Michael Potemkin, a much indicted hedge fund operator.

Potemkin, as usual, needed a lawyer who could really keep him out of jail. Malcolm Plumb was precisely that kind of lawyer. He specialized in giving wealthy citizens the legal defense they had been guaranteed by the Founding Fathers regardless of perceived degree of guilt. When his elegant, delicately aged form appeared in a courtroom, experienced observers knew two things immediately: Malcolm's client was guilty beyond doubt and Malcolm would get him off entirely or for no more than a spot of public service reading to little children and a fine involving relative pocket change.

On this particular evening Malcolm happily ate venison chasseur and half listened to Potemkin describe the development of a giant financial suction machine that had relieved large sums from a greedy but unwitting public; the stupidity of one of his egomaniacal partners when questioned on a TV cable news show; and the inevitable attraction of the attention of several slippery, power-hungry congressmen. The latter, recognizing a winning campaign issue when they saw one, had expressed great outrage and demanded a criminal investigation and hearings.

As the client droned away, it occurred to Malcolm that here was a slimy miscreant, indeed; a sincere-looking weasel in a three thousand dollar suit; the latest in a long malodorous line of well-served clients devoted to enriching themselves by pillaging and destroying their fellowmen. But, for the protection of all Americans, even people such as Potemkin had rights that must not be violated. That was the life-long task to which Malcolm dedicated his great talents and, fortunately for Malcolm, such dedication was very well rewarded.

Although, now that Malcolm thought about it, his rewards were truly niggardly compared to the treasure that cascaded in recent years on his younger brothers at the bar for *their* dedication. Their professional labor was the finding and protecting of the multitude of newly discovered and often unaware victims and would-be victims of great corporations and governments; also the great rewards in cash and power that they garnered for defending celebrities and politicians clearly guilty of crimes, grossly unethical conduct or outrageous immorality—usually some combination of all three. Malcolm sighed. He was too old for all that drama. He would remain content with his more modest share of the legal profession's rewards.

Dinner had begun about 7:30. But, because of the many shady and arcane convolutions of the matter under discussion, dinner ran on. Malcolm and his client were almost the last to leave the club.

On reviewing the evening much later, Malcolm recalled that he had one large Scotch prior to the serving of some excellent petite marmite, two glasses of a rather nice Chateau Latour with his venison and one Scottish malt after coffee: Hardly enough to befuddle the mind of a trained imbiber. And that made what happened in the next hour all the more mysterious.

The spring night was warm. Potemkin's car and chauffeur were waiting at the curb outside the club's entrance. Malcolm declined Potemkin's invitation to drop him at his hotel apartment where since his wife had died he lived alone. The hotel was only a short distance from the club and he had had enough of his client. He warmly thanked Potemkin, said he preferred to walk and proceeded to do so.

Two blocks away Malcolm entered a small park and headed directly for the opposite side. Empty benches and unplanted flowerbeds bordered the path. The park was quiet. Malcolm was alone.

At the center of the park he came to a striking war memorial dedicated to the dead of the Wars of the 20th Century: a bronze soldier on one knee supporting himself with his weapon; his head bare; his expression defiant. The statue was surrounded by a three-foot high square of holly bushes. Malcolm walked briskly by; then he stopped and turned to look again at a most extraordinary sight. The entire holly bush at the eastern corner of the memorial was burning.

It was impossible, of course, but he had to be sure. He walked back a few steps toward the burning holly.

"Malcolm," a voice from the bush said. "You are walking on holy ground. Take off your shoes and come no closer or you will surely die.'

"This is a monstrous joke," Malcolm mumbled to himself, but no sooner did he say that than the flame became a fireball; an enormous wave of heat engulfed him; the ground beneath him shook and heaved. Malcolm fell to the ground and cowered as long familiar words that he first heard during his childhood days in Sunday school cascaded from the bush.

"Malcolm, I am the Lord your God. I am who I am. I am the God of your fathers. Malcolm! I am calling you."

And Malcolm wondrously heard himself saying: "Here I am, Lord."

And the Voice, now clearly identified and accordingly capitalized by Malcolm, said: "Malcolm the people of the nations have displeased me in many ways. But among those who displease be most in these terrible times are you and your professional associates, lawyers and judges, chosen people to whom I gave the divine gift of knowledge of good and evil by which blessings can be brought to all men. And what have most of you done with that gift? You tricksters wrap it in sophistries to defend and encourage the worst rather than the best. And you do it to what end? You do it solely to engorge yourselves and to fatten on the riches and power of this world?"

Malcolm began to protest: "No, no, no. We only seek to protect the innocent, to defend the rights..."

"Enough!" roared the Voice and the bush blazed up again into a blinding white fireball. Malcolm buried his head in his arms to ward off the light and the heat.

"You, Malcolm, must cleanse the world forever of such prevarications. Do not bring me to anger. For I am a compassionate and ever hopeful God. And I have chosen you, Malcolm, to be my instrument. You are to be a great prophet."

The fireball had receded again and Malcolm dared to look up.

"But what am I to do?" he asked. "What am I to say?'

"You are to go forth in the coming days and months to the stiff-necked magistrates in their legislative halls, go into the courts of the corrupt judges, go into the palatial offices of the tricksters and mountebanks of the law. Give them this message: Cease your wicked defense of evil. Cease saying that the bad is the good. Cease favoring the lesser thing. And remember, Malcolm: although I am a compassionate God, if these sinful people do not turn in their ways, I will not leave one stone upon a stone. Only then can we start again."

The Voice ceased. The flame slowly dimmed until it went out. Malcolm put his head in his arms and huddled on the ground for a long time. The night became cool. The park was dark. Finally, when Malcolm looked up, he saw before him the holly bush unburned. He saw his shoes nearby. There was no one but him in the park. He looked at his Cartier gold wristwatch that had double dials. The dial for Eastern North America showed past midnight. He figured that he had been crouched on the ground for more than an hour. He stood up, limped to a bench and put his custom made Italian shoes on his damp feet. The knees of his Armani bespoke trousers were soaked and stuck to his legs.

Walking home, he used his exquisitely sophisticated legal mind to examine minutely each element of his experience (the fire, the voice, the message); to develop a convincing explanation (alcohol, a heavy meal, a small stroke, a fit); to give credence to dismissing all that had occurred on the simple grounds that it was simply absurd. Finally, with great relief, Malcolm triumphed. He convinced himself that the combination of overwork, age and stress abetted certainly by alcohol and rich food had caused him to collapse in a faint during which he had bizarre dreams. He would see his doctor the next day. And he buoyed himself by thinking how in the coming weeks he would retell to convivial companions the evening's experience: a rather amusing anecdote along with witty commentary, a major addition to his repertoire.

The hotel lobby was empty except for a night clerk who greeted Malcolm with a curious expression while obviously failing in an attempt to ignore Malcolm's appearance. Malcolm, in turn, said goodnight, rode the elevator to his penthouse floor where the door opened directly on his apartment. It was only later as he stood in a dark blue silk robe in front of a sink and brushed his teeth that he noticed his face: It was deeply reddened as if he had been exposed for hours to a tropic sun; his eyebrows were bleached white; his eyes, bloodshot.

He went to bed but he could not sleep. He was deeply troubled. The highly rationalized explanation of his collapse in the park had dissolved into wisps of smoke. He, like one of his intellectual heroes, Pascal, understood wagers and odds and in Malcolm's mind the odds in this case had dwindled to almost a sure thing.

He knew precisely what he had to do. He had no time for sleep. He ached for morning. He had to plan a great campaign. He had to organize his resources. He had to prepare a basic speech. He had to begin talking and writing. The major editorial board meetings, the national conferences, the Sunday TV talk shows, all awaited. Many would try to ridicule him, shout him down, belittle him, defile him, destroy him.

But the calculation of his chance of success in his assignment was not for Malcolm to make. That was beyond him. Regardless of what happened, he would go on, as he knew all prophets of God must. He, Malcolm, would go on.

Angelic Tip-Off

El maktub maktub. (What is written is written.)
—Arabic proverb

Harrison, of course, told no one about the angel.

It was too much to explain. It was embarrassing. It was all in his head.

But it appeared that it was not.

Each morning when Harrison entered the chapel the angel was standing immediately inside the door. The angel was blonde and about six feet tall. He wore armor and carried a sword. Probably he was St. Michael. He didn't say; he didn't say anything; he just stood there.

Harrison first saw the angel on Tuesday during the first week in Lent. That was the day he determined to attend a second Mass each week to fulfill his Lenten vow. The Mass was conducted at 6:30 A.M. It was convenient for him to attend on the way to his law office in a nearby high-rise.

But now, for the last several weeks, Harrison stopped by every day to see if the angel was there. He was.

Oddly, none of the dozen or more other people attending the Mass appeared to notice the angel. There was the usual early morning mix: some business executives, a fireman, two scraggly panhandlers, an elderly woman totally in black with a young girl, a fast food cook wearing a square paper hat. Harrison saw them walk within a foot of the angel without looking. Only Harrison seemed to be aware of the angel's presence. And Harrison felt certain that the angel clearly was aware of him although the angel still said nothing.

On the following Monday, Harrison arrived earlier than usual. He found no one in the chapel except the angel. 'Good morning,' Harrison said. He had tried to sound casual and cheery as if he were addressing his secretary. But the voice he heard himself using sounded uncertain. The angel stared at him and seemed to smile. But he still said nothing. Harrison moved on to a pew. The angel was not there when he left.

Sitting in his office overlooking the Financial District, his mind drifted from records on the legal case of Grout vs. the United States to the much more interesting matter of the angel. He no longer questioned at all the reality of the visions. He felt certain that he was not suffering from some mental derangement. Nothing in his life, nothing in his daily routines had changed except for these sightings. He thought that perhaps he should at least discuss the matter with one of the friars at the chapel. But, no; what if the friar tried to put him off with some cant; worse, what if talking about it made the angel go away. He did not want that. He was convinced by now that the angel had some sort of message for him, possibly some dire warning.

So he said nothing to anyone and he continued to return to the chapel every morning and waited. And every morning the angel was there standing silently by the door. Harrison tried to ignore the angel by concentrating on the liturgy, on the words rather than the familiar formula. He put extra energy in saying the Lord's Prayer and tried to avoid his usual vindictive tone when he mentioned "those who trespass against us." But the presence of the angel haunted him. Each day after Mass as he walked to his office he looked for unusual warning signs. He imagined bizarre possibilities: begrimed gypsies begging alms, dead two-headed ravens, blind lepers in a red wagon, a reappearance in the sky of the doomed Hindenburg Graf Zeppelin. However, the city sidewalks appeared unthreateningly normal.

Then, on Monday of the third week of Lent, the angel was gone. He was not at the door. He was nowhere in the rear of the chapel. Harrison was alarmed. He felt frantic. What had happened? What had he done? He had been there every day to wait on the angel. What had he not done? What should he do to make amends?

Harrison knelt to pray for enlightenment and as he did so he saw the angel in the aisle beside a pew at the front of the chapel. He stood with his sword drawn, pointing it at two men sitting in the pew. They wore dark Red Sox windbreakers and baseball caps. One had an uneven beard. Both looked like furtive, unwashed Bedouins painted by Sergeant.

As Harrison on his knees watched from the rear, one of the men, the one with the beard, took from the other man what looked in the gloom like a parcel, put it under his windbreaker and walked out of the chapel. Harrison rose immediately, followed him out and saw him moving rapidly down the block. Harrison without hesitation pursued him. Four blocks away they entered a large plaza in front of the renamed 40-floor Barack Hussein Obama Federal Building. The man, commingled in a crowd of office workers, was heading for a bank of revolving doors. Harrison hurried to a policeman standing before a huge fountain in the middle of the plaza.

"That man," Harrison said and pointed. "The dark one with the beard. You have to stop him. I think he has a bomb.'

"How do you know?" asked the cop.

"I saw him take a package in St. John's Chapel from some other Arabic-looking guy. That guy with the beard hid it under his coat and rushed over here."

"Give me a break, will ya," the cop said. "That's just a lot of racial profiling. I go check out some raghead on a story like that, they'll have my ass."

"I saw him pass the package," Harrison said. "I saw his face, his eyes: they were crazy."

'Come on. You got somethin' against Arabs. You don't look Jewish. That package he's got, you know, probably his lunch."

"I tell you, I'm certain." Harrison said, raising his voice. "That son-of-a-bitch has a bomb."

"Easy, calm down, cool it. What makes you so certain.

Harrison paused. How could he explain? An angel? St. Michael with a raised sword? Divine messages?

"Officer," he said with staged patience. "I'm a lawyer. I got a very reliable tip. Grab that guy. He's dangerous. Trust me."

The cop breathed heavily.

"Look," he said. "Just forget it. You went to Mass. It's Lent. Your mother, she'd be proud. Now go and have a nice breakfast. Otherwise, you keep up this stuff, you and I are going to have to go to the precinct with this cockamamie story and we'll have to file at minimum a four page 811-B2. And then, on what you're telling me, we're going to be up to our butts in paperwork with this kind of story for a week, ya know. And, trust me, there are gonna be a half dozen human rights nutcakes crawlin' all over us by lunch. And in the end, we get lucky, you get to go home instead of being locked up for a hate crime and I don't get no permanent new duty on some detail checking sewers for drug addicts."

Harrison never had a chance to respond.

An enormous hot light filled the plaza; Harrison and the policeman were hurled into the fountain; and, in a cataclysmic roar, the façade of the Obama Federal Building exploded into the street.

City of the Plain

If I find within the city of Sodom fifty innocent ones, I will forgive the whole place for their sake...
—Yahweh to Abraham, *Genesis*

Forty-five satellite pictures and a stream of repeatedly updated electronic data fresh from space and from the constantly patrolling air and sea surveillance craft told the story on the huge blinking screens in the War Room.

Combat units of 12 corps with thousands of tanks and artillery pieces of the Army of North Korea before dawn were crossing the DMZ and moving into jump off positions along the border of South Korea. Scores of attack helicopters in forward positions were being stripped of their badly camouflaged huts. North Korean submarines, missile boats and torpedo boats were moving south in both the East and Yellow Seas. And North Korea's six known nuclear-armed Taep'odong-3 ICBMs were being prepared for launch.

The White House, where because of the time difference it was early evening, was still digesting the war alert information when it received a warning memo from Pyongyang. The memo said:

Unprincipled and intolerable provocations by gangster political elements in Seoul now force the Democratic People's Republic of Korea led by its Dear Leader to liberate our fellow Koreans in the South and bring about national reunification under the victorious banners of Communism.

Occupying military forces of the United States must stand aside and withdraw immediately. Any attempt by the military forces of the United States or the military forces of other brigandish imperialist nations to interfere with the Korean People's Revolutionary Army will be met with the severest measures. Our nuclear armed missiles are positioned for immediate launch and are targeted on Los Angeles and other imperialist urban centers.

The peace-loving Dear Leader of the Democratic People's Republic of Korea seeks only national reunification of our citizens and friendly relations with our neighbors and the rest of the world.

The President was presented with three main options by his security advisors: Call for a new peace process; pull out; or fight and assume either that the North Koreans were bluffing about launching ICBMs or that the limited U.S. missile defense system would intercept them. "Peace process" had strong support, particularly among those with ties to California. "Pull out" had strong support if "peace process" failed. There were few votes for "Fight." But, at that point, a new report arrived from the War Room: Two People's Army corps had crossed the border; blown away the American positions there using a surprise mix of chemical and traditional weapons, and were already five miles from Seoul.

"I fear we have a decision," the President said. "Let's hope the missile defense system works if we need it."

That same evening a few hours before the North Koreans began their reunification program that so disturbed the equanimity of official Washington, Dr. Abraham Maximillian Ludwig Hapsburg was eating an early dinner alone in the palatial diningroom of the Metropolitan Club in New York. Dr. Hapsburg was very old, very rich and very intelligent. He towered in scientific circles as a chemist and a biologist and his basic research in these disciplines had led to the development of a cornucopia of life-saving drugs. He was by blood a distant cousin of former emperors of the Holy Roman Empire. And he was recognized to be a man of strong religious faith and an outspoken exemplar of the highest moral and ethical conduct.

As Dr. Hapsburg sipped a cup of espresso, a tall, well-tailored man with very bright blue-green eyes approached the table.

"May I join you?" he said in a slightly Germanic accent.

Dr. Hapsburg looked puzzled. He was certain he had never seen the man before, but he no longer completely trusted his memory. Possibly he had. And then some primordial sense made him feel a recognition and awe that continued to grow.

"Join me, of course," Dr. Hapsburg said. "I am afraid these days names and faces sometimes elude me. May I offer you some coffee? Perhaps a sweet?"

"Do so as you say" the man said and sat down and smiled familiarly, but he still did not mention his name, a deliberate oversight that Dr. Hapsburg now recognized as necessary. A waiter brought the man some coffee and a tarte aux pomme and the man spoke again.

"You are familiar, of course, with the reputation of the outrageously misnamed City of Los Angeles," he began. "It is by far the most wicked, depraved city in America. Every day there all of the Commandments are grossly violated, laughed at, belittled. Every day the people of this city poison the minds of the nations with evil thinking. We have received so many complaints for so long. Seldom have such gifts been given to a people who are such sinners; such embracers and encouragers of so much evil. Los Angeles truly must be overturned. The nations need to be instructed."

The man seemed to exude power and light as he talked and Dr. Hapsburg did not find that strange.

"Why do you tell me this thing?" Dr. Hapsburg asked.

"Your conduct: how you have lived your life. You are a proven, faithful man. This will be a new fingerpost to all. You are the one chosen. It is appropriate that you understand."

"But this troubles me very deeply. Surely, the innocent should not be swept away with the guilty," Dr. Hapsburg said. "What if among the millions of people in Los Angeles there are even only 100 who are innocent? Should they be destroyed?"

"If there are 100 innocent in Los Angeles, I readily agree: For their sake, the city should not be overturned."

'I don't mean to be presumptuous, but what if there are but 50 innocent?"

The man chewed a piece of the tarte and swallowed contentedly

"I agree. If there are 50, for their sake the city should be saved," he said.

"What if 20? What even if only 10?"

The man smiled. "Good Dr. Hapsburg! Even if only 10, the city should not be destroyed."

"May I dare suggest five?"

The man smiled again and nodded. "Yes, yes, even if only five."

North Korean tanks rolled into Seoul but their advance to the center of the capital city was halted by waves of American helicopter gunships. Meantime, hundreds of sea-launched cruise missiles followed by squadron after squadron of manned fighter bombers obliterated North Korean air defenses and the North Korean Air Force.

Masses of American and South Korean armored units began encircling the invading forces.

The military battle plan to stop and defeat a new Communist invasion of South Korea from the north had been under development and constant refinement throughout the Cold War. This plan was now being successfully implemented. The only open question regarding the outcome soon became the North Korean threat to launch its nuclear-tipped ICBMs. That question was answered quickly by the Dear Leader as submarine-launched cruise missiles began surgical elimination of all North Korean command and control centers. Dear Leader personally shot his wavering chief of staff and ordered the launch of his ICBMs

Dr. Hapsburg and his wife, Sally, sat in the library of their Fifth Avenue apartment eating breakfast as they watched the continuing cable news reports.

Norman Boots and Cissy Down posed decoratively behind a slab-shaped table in their network's enormous Central News Room Set labeled "somewhere in Washington" and recited knowingly from the invisible teleprompters as views of Los Angeles appeared on a smaller split screen.

"There is panic in Los Angeles," Norman Boots said in his deepest baritone. "People in that beleaguered city learned only an hour ago the terrible, the unthinkable news: North Korea might really be preparing to launch ICBMs aimed at Los Angeles and possibly other West Coast cities and Hawaii. People have been urged to remain calm. to seek shelter in cellars, subways and other underground facilities to wait for further instructions. But all roads out of West Coast cities and Honolulu are already jammed with cars. Only a lucky few are getting away."

TV pictures at first light from Los Angeles showed thousands of cars, SUVs, motorcycles and 18-wheeler trucks snaking bumper-to-bumper for miles along Southern California's superhighways. Next came a shot of the airport filled with a writhing mob of desperate people while outside dozens of airliners stood on the flight line where operations were hopelessly snarled. Then the screen switched again to show a helicopter rising from the crowded roof of a white Hollywood mansion. Screaming men and women, some in bathing suits, some naked, were standing on the struts and trying to climb aboard while a man in the open door struck at them repeatedly with a golf club.

"Those alarming pictures are from our Los Angeles affiliate," Cissy Down said, fulfilling her role to provide fluff on cue. "That last one was the roof of Jerry Shumberg's really fabulous new house. I understand they were having a gala all-night pool party celebrating the opening of his new billion-dollar blockbuster "Midnight Hustler III.""

"Here is a bulletin from the White House," Norman Boots said sonorously. "The Missile Defense Command in Alaska reports successful interception and destruction of three North Korean Taep'o-dong-3 ICBMs over the Pacific. The Missile Defense Command also reports that two Taep'o-dong-3's failed to launch. And the Command reports a near miss on North Korea's one remaining ICBM which is currently pursuing a trajectory still vectored on the Los Angeles Area. Two Arleigh Burke Class destroyers equipped with advanced missile defense systems are in position off the West Coast and will attempt an intercept during the Taep'o-dong-3's descent phase."

"Turn off the television," Dr. Hapsburg said to his wife. "We'll know what happens soon enough. We shouldn't risk watching. For people our age, we already have too much salt in our diet."

Art Search

per quem omnia facta sunt...
— Credo

PODCAST #247 LIVING ART HISTORY SERIES

(**Editor's Note:** The following reproduces the original disc as provided by the speaker.)

My name is T. Frederick Maddox, senior editor of WORLD ART NEWS. I specialize in investigations in the burgeoning business of lost and stolen great art, art fraud and the more colorful manipulations of the international art market. I have had a number of notable triumphs in the past, but nothing compared to what I may be about to achieve. My associate, Adolph Wagner, forensic archeologist of the University of Bonn, and I have been engaged for more than four years in a search for what may have been Tintoretto's greatest painting known only as *Il uno perduto,* the lost one. Our goal may now be at hand.

As I will make clear, this search just possibly may not be without some personal risk. Accordingly, I have decided to keep a current verbal diary, always a useful reference and some insurance that in case of misadventure our findings will be preserved for future historians of Renaissance art. Arrangements have been made for the diary to be made available to scholars in both the United States and Europe.

According to several contemporary sources, Tintoretto sometime in the 1560s painted in Venice a large fresco that apparently disappeared shortly after it was completed and subsequently nicknamed

Il uno perduto. In the last half millennium, all of Tintoretto's other known frescoes have also disappeared, mostly victims of the Venetian climate, specifically the ever creeping damp and *aqua alto.* The ruins of some were over painted by later artists. But, because of the very swift disappearance of *Il uno perduto,* the loss has always been attributed to theft; or possibly rejection by its donor and over painting by Tintoretto himself, or possibly suppression by the Church.

Theft would have been difficult: an entire wall would have had to be dismantled and moved rapidly in secret, a truly improbable event. Suppression was always a possibility in 16th Century Venice but doubtful in view of the high regard for Tintoretto by the Doge, the Patriarch and many *nobili* enrolled in the *Libro d'Oro,* the Golden Book listing Venice's patrician families. Rejection by the donor and over painting for many years was considered the fresco's most likely fate. If so, a great mystery remains: no contemporary source reveals where the over painted fresco was created or the subject of the second painting.

Important questions were raised in the mid-1600s in an early edition of Ridolfi's *Life of Tintoretto (La Vita Giacopo Robusti.)* It suggests that the painting was suppressed by the Church, possibly because of a serious disagreement with Tintoretto over money. But this suggestion disappeared from later editions and, in any case, the disposition of the painting and its location were not disclosed.

The British Ambassador wrote in 1760 to his mother, the Duchess of Moorehead, that he was told the story of the missing fresco by a "member of the Golden Book" and that Tintoretto had hidden it behind a painting of St. Lawrence and the Virgin. But the Ambassador did not indicate its location or say whether he had ever seen it.

Military dispatches to Paris after Napoleon's occupation of Venice in 1797 mention that the lost painting was on the list of art treasures to be looted and taken to the Louvre. But apparently the fresco could not be located by Napoleon's scavengers. It does not appear on the final manifests.

In the late 19th and early 20th Centuries, the burgeoning market in America for Great Masters generated much activity among legitimate and less than legitimate art dealers to seek out fresh offerings. It was near the end of this period early in the First World War that Gregory Brightman, president of Brightman & Sons of New York, eminent art dealers, received a secret letter bearing information that a Tintoretto of great value might become available in Venice. When Brightman's representative in Rome contacted the source of the letter, an Italian who styled himself only as Dottore Angelo, the agent was told that the picture was believed to be *Il uno perduto*; that it was somehow in the possession of one of Venice's noblest families unfortunately much impoverished by the war, and that the family would only deal directly with Brightman himself. Brightman, suspicious but game, booked passage immediately on the *Lusitania* and drowned when the ship was sunk by a German submarine. The deal, according to memos in the company files, copies of which are in my possession, went down with the *Lusitania*.

Toward the end of the 1920s word of *Il uno perduto* again is heard. At that time, Sir Harold Kornberg, the international art dealer, cultural impresario, and multi-millionaire, was specializing in providing the rarest Great Masters to the world's richest men at enormous prices. Accordingly, Sir Harold was more than interested when he was approached in the lounge of the Hotel Grand in Rome by a dealer talking in a very low voice about a *"Tintoretto grande."* Sir Harold knew of the dealer only by reputation as a purveyor of rare objects d'art of occasionally questionable provenance. But his story, if true, was compelling. The dealer said he knew the exact whereabouts of what without doubt was *Il uno perduto* and how it might be obtained. He would disclose this information for two million dollars, half in advance.

Files at Kornberg Ltd. in London show that Sir Harold obtained from his research department a thin, unsatisfactory report on *Il uno perduto*; consulted his partners in London, New York and Berlin; and obtained from one of America's greatest collectors a tentative sales agreement for the fresco, assuming its authenticity, for a staggering 10 million dollars. An advance was passed in the form of bearer bonds to the dealer at a meeting at the Gritti Palace in Venice in September 1929. The dealer, in turn, introduced Sir Harold to Il Conte Arcini who, in turn, disclosed verbally to Sir Harold the name of a church in Venice where *Il uno perduto* could be found. Il Conte said the fresco was in his family's chapel and could be removed under certain circumstances. The circumstances apparently involved a substantial additional payment to cover undefined expenses.

Sir Harold probably visited the church to inspect the chapel, but there is no record that he did nor did record the name of the church in any report. Instead, two days after his meeting with Il Conte, he took the express train to London and began organizing a team of experts presumably to examine the fresco. That never happened. The disastrous stock market crash in New York occurred October 24. Black Monday and Black Tuesday followed. Sir Harold and his firm had enormous losses. Outstanding loans were called. All lines of credit disappeared. Sir Harold, who was 75, suffered a stroke during dinner at White's in London while seeking to convince several fellow club members that all would be well. He never recovered. The bearer bonds paid to the dealer in Venice were nearly worthless. The information regarding *Il uno perduto* given to Sir Harold died with him.

I first heard about *Il uno perduto* nearly 40 years later in January 1967 when as a graduate art student I joined a group of volunteers working to salvage Venice's treasures engulfed by the *aqua alto*. That November a six-foot wall of water from the lagoon poured through the canals, flooding most of the city and endangering and destroying one of the world's greatest collections of art and architecture.

We slaved for weeks manning pumps, sloshing through water-logged palazzos and museums, meticulously scraping muck from famous paintings and statuary. Much was saved; much was lost. Also much was found. Books, letters, pictures stuffed away in ancient cabinets, cases and trunks were spread out, dried and treated. All of it was of historic interest; some of it was of enormous value; some of it brought to life for the first time in centuries great events of the long moribund Venetian empire.

One of the more significant artifacts that I personally discovered was an iron box in the ruined basement of the Capuchin monastery on Giudecca next to *Il Redentore*, Palladio's 16th Century church built in gratitude for the lifting of a great plague. The box was crammed with a variety of documents: bills of sale, work sheets listing the duties of various friars; a report on conditions of Capuchin houses throughout the Veneto; personal correspondence. Fortunately, the box had protected its contents from the flood. But the paper was old and brittle, the Latin difficult, the ink faded. I photographed much of it along with hundreds of other remarkable things, planning to catalogue all of it back in the States. The sifting and cataloguing has taken years and much still remains to be done. I became distracted with other matters; then I returned to it. It was on my most recent return that I came upon a letter that proved to be far more important than all the rest. I reproduce a full translation here:

I, Carlo d'Montebelluna, son of a butcher, lover of plump women, sometime drunkard and street brawler, artisan in the workshop of Jacopo Robusti who is known to the world as Tintoretto, to my younger brother and monk, Giuseppe, Greetings.

Only you will understand what I am about to tell you because you know me so well. And you know, although I am a great liar, I do not lie to you, a true brother of Christ which I certainly have not been for a long time.

You are familiar as is all Venice with the Scuola Grande di San Rocco and the cycle of paintings that we, mere daubers with the great Jacopo, have created on its walls. First, we were engaged on one of our most ambitious works, the Crucifixion, in the Sala del' Albergo much of which Tintoretto has done himself although you will recognize perhaps my brushstrokes in the two crucified thieves. Then we began the Life of Our Lord in the Salone Maggiore. Dozens of us labored throughout the spring on a Last Supper, a Flight into Egypt and a Circumcision. It was in the midst of this tremendous activity that a representative of the Doge himself interrupted Jacopo and ordered him to complete an earlier commission in the first right chapel at Chiesa dell Madonna dell 'Orto, a church not far from his home in the Fondimenta di Mori in Cannaregio. Jacopo was furious. What was more important than what in my opinion was to become his greatest Last Supper: the dark, ominous scene with Christ, dramatically positioned on the left of the elongated table, driving events. I, myself, did the large dog in the foreground and St. Peter. Ordinarily Jacopo would have ignored even the Doge. But since Jacopo had already been paid for the chapel and, of course, had spent the money as always, he had to do something and so he sent me.

The first chapel on the right at Madonna dell'Orto had a fine, new wall directly behind the chapel's altar and over a noble family's crypt. Jacopo, himself, had prepared it for what would be a large San Lorenzo with San. Nicolai and the donor, a cousin of the Doge. Before abandoning the project more than a year ago to work at San Rocco, Jacopo had roughly sketched the outlines of the saints, but the wall was now stained and cracked. New plaster would have to be applied and fresh sketches drawn before I could paint the fresco "in the style" of Tintoretto.

In only two hours, I made a small cartoon of Jacopo's old outline for insurance although years in his workshop enabled me to copy his style exactly. Then with the help of a sexton I assembled scaffolding and went to work preparing the beautiful space with fresh plaster. I stopped before noon Mass and while the priests conducted the Mass I ate my mid-day meal behind a statue of Our Lady, the surely miraculous but rather dumpy looking statue after which the church is named. It was not much of a meal: some sausage, bread, some hard cheese and only one bottle of Veneto red. Within the hour the church was empty again and I was back on the scaffold. Then it happened.

Everyone knows of my great capacity for wine and I swear, dear brother, that I had only one bottle. But possibly because of my sparse lunch, it went to my head. In any case, I was on the scaffold only a few minutes when I reached for the final pot of new plaster, lost my balance and fell to the marble floor on my back. There was an enormous flash of light that momentarily blinded me and a great voice sounded throughout the church.

"Carlo, Carlo," the voice boomed. "You know that you are a great sinner! For your penance, you miserable man, look at me! Paint me!"

"I can't," I moaned. "If you are who I think you are and I look at you, I know I shall surely die."

"Look at me, Carlo! Paint me now! Obey and surely you will be blessed. I choose to provide a sign for the faithful."

Then I rose from the floor and, despite the great light, I could see again and as the light slowly faded I painted rapidly what I saw.

By nightfall, it was finished and, as I stood back and looked upon my work, I felt great fear and awe about what I had done. It was a miracle. Instead of San Laurenzo, certainly, I, Carlo d'Montebelluna had painted the glowing Face of God so realistically that I could not look at it without immediately shielding my eyes. What would the authorities say when it was discovered? What would Jacopo say? Who would believe me? I didn't know what to do. I panicked. I covered the fresco with canvas sheeting and fled from the church. I had to get away that night. Before midnight I had escaped in a small boat to Murano; at dawn I crossed the lagoon to terra firma.

Later I learned that the priests discovered the painting shortly after dawn, looked under the canvass and fell on their knees. Others reacted quite differently as I feared they would. The Patriarch of Venice quickly proclaimed the picture the work of the Devil, dispatched several alarming messages under his seal to Rome, ordered an investigation and temporarily closed Madonna dell 'Orto. The Doge's secret police summoned Jacopo for questioning at the palace by the dreaded Council of Ten.

According to various stories I have heard, here is what happened next. Jacopo at first denied everything. But the inquisitors insisted that anyone could recognize his style. Furthermore, he could not deny that a number of his pictures already hung in the church and he had been commissioned to paint a San Lorenzo in the chapel. Now, they charged, after long delay and under pressure from the Doge, instead of painting a San Lorenzo he had painted while clearly possessed by devils a blasphemous God the Father.

When Jacopo persisted even under threat of torture that he was innocent, he was permitted to look at a small portion of the painting still hidden under canvas sheeting to remind him of his guilt. He staggered back and fell to the floor. When he recovered his senses, he was told that because of his many contributions to Venice the Patriarch and the Doge most generously had agreed to give him 24 hours to do penance for his sinfulness by repainting the wall. Guards then locked the church. Jacopo was left alone with my paint pots and equipment.

Averting his eyes as much as possible, Jacopo slowly removed the canvass sheeting and for a long time looked with great trepidation and half-closed eyes at the glowing image. Most certainly he was looking at a magnificent painting. Most certainly it was YHWH. Most certainly he believed that I, Carlo, clever as I am, could not have made it without divine inspiration. Most certainly, to obliterate the fresco by painting over it would be a great sin.

No one knows exactly what happened next. But probably Jacopo used a secret tunnel that ran to his house and a nearby brickyard to bring hundreds of bricks into the church; build a new back wall in the chapel a few inches in front of my fresco, and cover the bricks with fresh plaster. Once that was completed it would take the Master only a few hours to paint a San Laurenzo talking to San Nicholai and add the Doge's cousin, clothed in the traditional nobili black toga, kneeling in prayer at their side. Beside the donor, I hear he painted a small gonfalon hanging from a wall. It bore the words: PATREM OMNIPOTEM. And, knowing Jacopo so well, I suspect that before putting the last bricks in place he added a few brush strokes to my fresco as was his habit so that it could legitimately be called a Tintoretto.

Jacopo was triumphant once again. The investigation was dropped. The Doge and the donor's family were pleased. Jacopo went back to working at San Rocco, telling anyone who might ask that I had deserted him for a fat woman in Padua and cursing me for my disloyalty. He also said I was of little talent and a small loss.

Dearest brother: Do not look for me in Padua but perhaps in heaven. I caught a terrible chill crossing the lagoon and now am very ill. The nicely plump woman who cares for me but whom I am too ill to enjoy says I soon will be dead. If so, pray that the painting I made at God's terrible bidding has bought this poor artisan some grace.

Adolph Wagner and I had been working on and off for four years in search of the missing Tintoretto. We studied the walls and art of more than a dozen Venetian churches, crumbling palazzos and ancient public buildings; researched libraries and interviewed Renaissance scholars and art dealers and collectors. It led to nothing. Now, if the Carlo Letter were to prove to be authentic, we had a roadmap in hand.

We, of course, knew that there would be great difficulties to overcome. The *Madonna dell 'Orto* is a famous 14th Century church dedicated to a miracle-working Madonna found in a nearby vegetable garden. The church is crowded with Renaissance masterpieces including many by Tintoretto who it is said was forced by the Doge to paint them. According to Venetian legend, Tintoretto had added the horns of a cuckold to a portrait of the Doge after the Doge rejected it; took refuge in the church; then had to decorate it as penance. Among the Tintorettos there are a *Last Judgment* and a *Presentation of the Virgin*. Other masterpieces include Cima da Conegliano's magnificent *St. John the Baptist*, and Giovanni Bellini's small exquisite *Madonna and Child* (stolen but represented by a photo). We would need both governmental and ecclesiastical cooperation, no small matter, particularly in Italy. To uncover the missing Tintoretto we would have to remove and preserve another Tintoretto masterpiece, the *San Lorenzo*, and the brick wall on which it had been painted. Moreover, if Carlo's letter were truthful, the underlying Tintoretto would have to be downgraded to being "from his workshop"—always an unwelcome act.

Our strategy was to avoid initially any discussion of removing the San Lorenzo. We felt the Carlo letter was proprietary, our secret, and we would not disclose it until the appropriate time. We presented ourselves as being merely interested in continuing our art research. We would do no harm. We would employ only the most advanced forensic electronic tools and software to determine whether the missing Tintoretto existed. Adolph's through-the-wall cameras would confirm that and possibly give us some idea of what the missing fresco looked like should we find it.

Certainly, the latter also could raise a more cosmic issue for the Vatican: Discovery of a *God the Father* by Tintoretto would be a monumental event; discovery of a portrait of God made under divine direction as Carlo claimed would be a monumental miracle. Obviously, as in all such matters, the Vatican would move with great caution. Meantime, although Adolph and I were cafeteria Catholics at best, we cannot totally dismiss that we might be in some danger.

Looking at a great portrait called *God the Father* is one thing. Actually looking at the Face of God is quite another. For thousands of years, the faithful have longed to be permitted to do it as ultimate proof of salvation. But even Moses could only look at God's back. And for unworthy unregenerate sinners, the penalty for looking at the Face of God is death. And there was the very real record of bad endings associated with the picture.

All hopeless superstition! We were not to be scared off. The following month we were back in Venice, eager and excited. After only minor bureaucratic frustrations, we found the authorities quite reasonable. They were impressed with our credentials. They were even more impressed with our TTW radar. And they welcomed a cash contribution to several charities that they controlled. Although all Venice was preparing for Carnivale, we were granted permission to proceed with our research only two weeks after our arrival, a breakthrough for any such project in Italy.

On the First Day of Carnavale we have made several trips with our forensic equipment through the narrow streets to the church. Passage from our hotel in San Marco to Cannaregio in the afternoon was most difficult. Hundreds of masked party goers, fire eaters, acrobats, mimes, jugglers and assorted thieves crowded Venice for Carnavale. In the chapel at last we found the San Lorenzo fresco. It was somewhat faded, but exactly as Carlo described it: the saints are talking to each other, the donor in black prays on his knees, a small gonfalon proclaims the power of God. Although it was late in the day, we still had time to set up and take an initial view through the wall. The image on the screen of our TTW radar was cloudy; adjustments would be needed; but a vague outline of a figure behind the wall flickered, glowed briefly and disappeared. We felt triumphant and wanted to proceed into the evening. But the needed technical adjustments could take hours. We postponed them until the morning...

(**Editor's Second Note:** The diary ends here. According to news reports and records on file at the Office of Venetian Police, T. Frederick Maddox and Adolph Wagner ate that evening, the First Night of Carnavale, what they told the maitre'd at the Hotel Danieli was a celebratory dinner. Afterwards, they were seen outside the hotel pushing through the great mob of masked merrymakers to the dock on the Basin where they hired a gondola. Presumably they were headed back to their hotel, the Bauer Grünwald in San Marco. They never arrived.

(Early the following morning, the Second Day of Carnavale, a workman found their bodies in a small canal behind *La Teatre da Fenice*. A report signed by a Comassario Contarini said they had been fatally stabbed in the back and robbed before being dumped into the water, not an unusual mishap during Carnavale. The sexton at *Madonna dell'Orto* told police there was no expensive camera equipment in the church when he arrived shortly before dawn. Police speculated that it was stolen. A thorough investigation was promised. When Maddox' personal effects were finally returned by the Venetian police to his sister in Chicago, she found his diary on a small disc overlooked by his robbers. She already had a letter from his lawyer with instructions for the disc's distribution.

(Italian authorities have forbidden any further attempts to search for *Il uno perduto* at *Madonna dell 'Orto* to protect the important master-pieces on its walls and to assure that Tintoretto's tomb in the chapel to the right of the choir remains undisturbed.)

END PODCAST # 247

The Candidate

Walk wide 'o the Widow at Windsor,
For 'alf of creation she owns:
We 'ave bought her the same with the sword an' the flame,
An' we've salted it down with our bones.
　　　　　—Rudyard Kipling, *Barrack Room Ballads*

Historic Note 1: Six weeks before the election, Millard Sergeant, would-be President of the United States, held the first of four private meetings with Ogden Hauptman, the former Secretary of State. They met in the Fifth Avenue apartment in New York of Maximillian Kronenberg, an investment banker, cadet member of the House of Würtemberg and author of several obscure books on paranormal phenomena.

Historic Note 2: Maximillian, who styled himself Baron Max, recorded the conversations but the discs have never been recovered.

Historic Note 3: Denny Maloney, an alcoholic newspaper reporter whom Baron Max denied ever meeting, claimed access to the discs and wrote an article based on them. At the time the article was suppressed by the intelligence community.

Historic Note 4: Maloney subsequently died in a car crash attributed to heavy drinking. No autopsy was performed. Subsequently a copy of Maloney's article on the Sergeant-Hauptman Conversations was found by his sister, Mary Catherine, a nun, university professor and popular author of detective novels. She published it in part in the *Catholic Journal of History and Political Science.*

Here, still somewhat redacted, are critical parts of the conversations as quoted in the Maloney article along with explanatory notes by Sister Mary Catherine:

(First meeting in Baron Max's library: Millard Sergeant, a tall weathered-looking man with much gray hair and an easy air of total command, sits erectly on an Empire couch in front of a large Guardi of the Grand Canal. Ogden Hampton, elegantly dressed but shrunken and dry with age, slouches nearby in a high backed red leather club chair. Baron Max, a small Germanic aristocrat with a short white beard, sits across the room by a bulky Renaissance table piled with magazines and books. There is also a marble bust of Louis XV. The Baron, known for his eccentric clothes, is wearing an Austrian huntsman's green wool and leather jacket.)

Sergeant: You understand the problem, of course. My opponent, Senator Goodglos, is heading a peace party. It's more than a party. It's a crusade. Peace: an enormously popular idea. And Goodglos stands on the mountaintop and proclaims it. Naturally, Goodglos says he would defend the nation if necessary. But he smoothly assures us all that it won't be necessary. With him in the White House, pursuing his policy of reason and smarmy logical accommodation with the Triple Powers, he contends that terrorists will convert their IEDs into pruning hooks and international understanding will prevail.

Hampton: A desirable state of affairs. Truly peace in our time, to borrow an unfortunate phrase from the last century.

Sergeant: Hogwash and you know it. But Goodglos is highly persuasive. The question before us is what strategy do I pursue. If I tell the terrible truth, I don't get elected. If I waffle, I still probably don't get elected. And, if I go along with the hogwash, why should I get elected? After all. my opponent is better looking and is offering a peace bonus and free health care in every pot.

Baron Max: May I ask: what is the latest information?

Hampton: They no longer tell me officially but I what I hear unofficially is bad.

Sergeant: Much worse. The consensus intelligence estimate which is always suspect implies possible room for maneuver. But there is hard intelligence from (redacted) that enemy nuclear capabilities are in place and increasing rapidly. The most likely scenario in a peace-in-our-time world is the first strike obliteration of Israel and the threat of nuclear strikes on a half dozen European capitals if the United States dare retaliate. There are variations on the theme including dirty nukes from North Korea.

Hampton (deep sigh): Coming to the defense of Israel always confuses matters. So trying this defending of the Jews. Possibly it would be more useful to raise the threat of nuclear proliferation on our southern flank in Latin America.

Sergeant: Medium term that is very real, but it is only medium term. Meantime it can be denied and pooh-poohed by Goodglos, his media sycophants and the self-serving intelligence bureaucracy.

Baron Max: Why don't you think the voters will accept the truth? I would think many would find it refreshing.

Sergeant: Let's see how that would go: My fellow Americans. It may surprise you to learn without a doubt that Western Civilization stands on the brink of disaster. Within the next 24 months, the Triple Powers and their terrorist agents will try to hold us hostage. While they threaten us with us with annihilation by nuclear-tipped missiles and dirty bombs hidden in our great cities, they will obliterate Israel, force partly Islamized Europe to disarm into impotence, bankrupt the Japanese and traumatize Latin America. Accordingly, I promise you that my first act as President will be to confront them while we still have the power to do it with certain total destruction unless they verifiably disarm immediately. How many votes do you think I would get? The voters like the idea of peace bonuses and happy times to come. They don't like being told they live in a rotten world that they need to risk their necks to fix.

Baron Max: If I may suggest, there seems to be something terribly out of joint here that is causing our inability to deal with the challenge. Our humanity is based on our ability to think rationally, logically and that has enabled us to confront successfully irrationality and illogicality and the evil that feeds on it.

Hampton: I find nothing unusual in an irrational, illogical world.

Sergeant: Then I would hope that you have something helpful to suggest.

Hampton: Possibly next week after I talk to some more people. I may meet with (redacted). We need to establish a clearer picture of things.

Baron Max: Then I propose that we meet again here where you can be private. Possibly I will also call in a useful guest. It won't be easy, but it is worthwhile trying.

Sergeant: Only if we can absolutely rely on his discretion.

Baron Max (laughs): Of course.

(The remaining conversation is comprised of current political anecdotes; also some amusing gossip about who attended and who was not invited to a recent royal wedding of the House of Hanover.)

(Second meeting takes place in the Baron's library a week later prior to a formal dinner and multi-million dollar campaign fund raiser at the Waldorf. Both Sergeant and Hampton are scheduled to attend. Both are wearing dinner jackets. Baron Max is dressed in one of his Edwardian outfits: fawn

trousers, a dark swallowtail coat, high black boots. He will dine afterwards in his apartment with an unidentified guest.).

Hampton: What are you planning to tell us tonight at the dinner?

Sergeant: Not to swallow whole what Goodglos said at his news conference last night about the deep longings in Moscow to reason together.

Baron Max: How far will you go?

Sergeant: Just far enough not to look unreasonable myself. What do you think Ogden?

Hampton: The Russians will pull the international rug out from under us the first chance they get. You know about the special shipments, of course?

Sergeant: Which ones?

Hampton: All of them? The medium range components to the Serbians and the Venezuelans. The anti-missile systems to the Persians. The information comes from (redacted). I give it high credibility.

Sergeant: So do I, but we have nothing to show in public. No recordings, no email, no satellite pictures. Anything we say, will be denied. Goodglos will call me a dangerous scaremonger. The peaceniks will be out on every campus. I'll lose the election.

Baron Max: If you keep the threat vague, you can confront it immediately after the election.

Sergeant: Not if I don't win. And, if I am sufficiently vague, I'll be called a spin artist. Meantime, Goodglos promises the ultimate box of chocolates: Peace.

Hampton: You must win. It would be the end of the West if you don't. What we need is a cosmic hat trick that gets you into the White House. As I promised, I talked to (redacted). His sources are the best. And he says the situation is desperate. Maybe we get lucky and suffer an incident.

Sergeant: Max, I regret we have to leave for the Waldorf.

Baron Max: Too bad. Just as we were putting matters in focus.

Hampton: I thought you were going to have someone else here who might prove helpful.

Baron Max: I hope to. He's joining me for dinner. If I can convince him to join us, I am sure he could be most useful. But as I said earlier there are special difficulties.

(Third meeting occurs three days later. Again they met in the Baron's library. It is Sunday shortly after noon. Sergeant and Hampton find the Baron has come directly from the 11 A.M Mass at St. Jean Baptiste where he is head usher and has not changed from his morning suit, a costume on which he always insists. They also find him with another guest, a cherubic, round-faced balding man with an elegant beard and Roman nose. The guest wears a light gray flannel suit, a shimmering white shirt and a wide scarlet silk tie dotted with blue fish . He carries a silver-handled sword cane. Baron Max introduces him as his "old friend, Paul, of whom I spoke."

Baron Max: Paul is terribly busy these days, but I convinced him the other night at dinner to join us. He has enormous knowledge of things, excellent judgment, the very best contacts and I can assure you he is totally discreet.

Sergeant: Maybe he would like to run for President. (*Much polite laughter.*)

Paul: Not really my line, but thank you.

Hampton: I assume that Max has given you a sufficient outline of what we are facing.

Paul: Oh, yes. I already knew most of it, the present situation and its long history, and Max has been most forthcoming in filling in some details.

Sergeant: As of today, as I see it, nothing less than our civilization is at stake and we, quite simply, are damned if we act and damned if we don't.

Paul: Unfortunately, from what I know, it appears that you are absolutely correct. But I don't think you should let that trouble you unduly. Really, it's nothing new: the downfall of the Jews, the downfall of the Greeks, the Romans, the Europeans, now the Americans... always the same pattern. The anointed fail to make good choices, the players are swept back into the big box, a new game is begun in hope of a better result.

Hampton: And you don't think that should trouble us unduly as you put it?

Paul: Absolutely not. May I suggest that it is all part of God's Plan: Original Sin and all that.

Sergeant: If you will forgive me, sir, that is psalm-singing rubbish. If one follows that train of thought, no one would do anything and the world would go to hell all the sooner.

Paul: I certainly forgive you: You understandably misunderstand. The world is already what you say for many, always has been.

Full of demons. That's how it was designed. Think about the parable of Christ and the blind beggar. Possibly you recall that Christ restored his sight. No small thing, eh? The Pharisees asked our Lord if the beggar was blind because his parents had sinned or because the beggar had sinned. Our Lord said neither was correct. He said God made the beggar blind to set up the miracle of the restoration of his sight as a sign to the people.

Hampton: Following that logic, one might say that the Triple Powers have been set up as a some sort of test and it is okey-dokey for the outcome to be a disaster because that will also be a sign.

Paul: You do have free will to choose.

Sergeant: And if the choice is a poor one.

Paul: Whatever it is, the consequences surely will be a sign and the game goes on. But , of course, that is not the greater game. The hope of things to come is wisely held. Think about the old fairy tale of Little Red Riding Hood. That foolish child encouraged the wolf in his totally evil ways. She told him she was going to see her dear old grandmother and practically invited him to stop by for tea. She was what you call today an enabler. So the wolf does stop by; eats Little Red Riding Hood's grandmother; pretends to be the dear old lady herself when Little Red Riding Hood arrives, and, when the girl unfortunately fails to be very perceptive, eats her, too. But there was a greater plan. Subsequently, a mysterious hunter arrives; he cuts open the wolf; Little Red Riding Hood and her grandmother miraculously spring free.

Hampton (smiling sarcastically): I am afraid that I miss your point. The wolf dies; Little Red Riding Hood and her grandmother live: but we can't always count on such a happy ending.

Paul: You do miss the point! The little girl and her grandmother live, but only to try again; to face more choices. And I assure you, the wolf survives: the wolf never dies; the wolf lives forever.

Sergeant: Not a totally unacceptable conclusion. It seems we are back to our current dilemma. How do we arrange for the hunter to arrive?

Baron Max: In the westerns, I believe it's called the Seventh Cavalry. You can always count on their arrival.

Paul: Nothing is inevitable. You choose.

Baron Max: But you, Paul, have excellent sources. What might they suggest? What might they foresee? Can you talk to them?

Paul: I can promise only to try.

(The text of the conclusion of the meeting has not been found.)

(Fourth and last meeting takes place at Baron Max's apartment four days before the election. When the butler escorts Sergeant and Hampton into the library, they find Baron Max and his friend, Paul, drinking brandy. The Baron is dressed in a heavy Shetland tweed suit as if he had just been taking a long walk on the moors with his dogs. Paul wears a blue blazer with what looks like arms bearing a tiered crown on the breast pocket. Hampton, appearing gloomier than usual, accepts a cognac and retires to a wing chair in a darkened corner of the room. Sergeant, his hatchet face a blank mask, declines a drink and sits upright in a straight oak chair near Paul.)

Baron Max: Gentlemen, what news?

Sergeant: All bad. The polls show Goodglos leading in most of the larger states and in enough of the smaller ones to carry the country. The odds against us are very high.

Paul: But it is not too late to reverse that.

Sergeant: Is that a statement or a question?

Paul: Both.

Hampton (deeply sarcastic grumble): Whichever, the hunter will have to appear pretty damn fast.

Baron Max: What are you planning to do?

Sergeant: Our strategy team will decide that tonight. We meet at 1900.

Baron Max: Paul, did your sources provide any guidance?

Paul: Absolutely. I was surprised that they would.

Baron Max (eagerly): And?

Paul: It is more of a reminder: America and the West, as always, have free will to choose.

Hampton: That's the kind of advice the Romans used to get from the Sybil. You call that guidance?

Paul: The very best. I am truly saddened if you are disappointed.

Hampton: Tonight...

Sergeant: (redacted)

Baron Max: Will all of you join me in another cognac before you go?

Paul: Thank you, but I must leave now. I fear that I am already late for a critical appointment.

(Denny Maloney's article ends abruptly here. But before his death, he is believed to have written a subsequent unpublished article based on an exclusive interview with President Millard Sergeant regarding the decisive fortuitous accident in the last days prior to the national election. That article, which has never been found, is said to have made much of the odds in poker against being dealt a royal flush: 649,739 to 1.)

Have a Look!

"...the past is the only thing that we know, because the past was not only real once but is real now, too."
  —*A Thread of Years*
  John Lukacs, American historian

"...what happened was inseparable not only from what people thought happened...but also from what could have happened. Now this is something that the best novelists knew better than do many historians."
  —*Ibid.*

"When...understanding stands suspended, then Instances of the Fingerpost shew the true and inviolable Way..."
  —*Novum Organum Scientarum*
  Francis Bacon, English philosopher

The Comte, Henri de Saverne, and his 12-year old American nephew, Peter Mott, walked up the gravel path to the castle gate. Peter and his mother, the Comte's sister, Alix, were visiting the Comte at the family chateau in Alsace, a small 17ᵗʰ Century architectural masterpiece by Louis Le Vau in a much reduced park. The Comte had agreed to take his young nephew sightseeing while Alix and his wife, the Comtesse Isabelle, went shopping in nearby Strasbourg.

Peter's father, Gilbert Mott, a prominent New York lawyer, was in Washington where he currently was serving a term as an advisor to the National Security Council. The Comte, who found his brother-in-law's political thinking naïve, a perfect reflection of what he sniffily called "the cowboy culture," was delighted not to have to put up with his presence. The Comte was close to the French Foreign

Ministry and fully believed in the Ministry's position that only the sophistication of the European mind, particularly the aristocratic French mind, could grasp the nuanced diplomacy needed to address the complexities of 21st Century power politics.

The balding five-foot, elegantly-dressed Comte and the five-foot two blonde schoolboy wearing a blue blazer and a Richard Plantagenet haircut contrasted markedly with the small group of grubby tourists in exercise clothes whom they joined after buying tickets at the castle gate and with whom they waited within the courtyard for the tour to begin.

The tourist guide, who arrived precisely as the castle chapel bells rang the hour, looked like a Caravaggio angel except that she was wearing tight fitting jeans and a red silk windbreaker. She was tall with unusually large blue green eyes and straight golden hair. Her jeans fit her long legs like gloves. And it was only when you were close that you noticed age lines around her eyes and mouth. Caravaggio certainly would have included them.

"My name is Betta, short for Elizabeth," she said in German-accented English and laughed as if she had made a joke.

"Welcome to der Zauberschloss," she said. "First built in 848, yes, but we have solid evidence that the Romans earlier built a fortification here on this mountain: a natural high place overlooking the Rhine. Before the Romans, the Celts apparently had one here, too. The castle was greatly expanded about 1115 by Henry V, by grace of God, Holy Roman Emperor; it was damaged but not conquered by the French in 1693; and it was restored as a royal palace by the Hohenzollerns in the mid-19th Century. Between the First and Second World Wars it was certainly closed and it is believed by some that it was during those years that it took on its present unusual character."

Then, without explaining what she meant by "unusual character," she led the group into a huge two-story chamber called the

King's Hall. Royal battle flags with two-headed black eagles hung from the galleries. Ancient, brutal weapons hung on the walls. Full suits of armor and tall, blue Chinese palace vases stood around. An enormous Renaissance bronze boar hunt filled the middle of an oak table that dominated much of the room. Early stained glass depicting many saints and nobles opened the outside wall to the river far below. Four great carved heavy doors ran along the opposite interior wall.

Betta turned the lock in the first of the doors bearing carvings of triumphal arches, marching legionnaires and Roman eagles. She tugged the great door open.

"Something different," she said, grinning. "Have a look!"

Inside, everything was indeed very different. Now they were standing in what appeared to be the atrium of a large Roman villa. Water sprang upward languidly from a fountain in the center. Delicate bronze chairs, tables and lamps stood on a mosaic floor depicting sea monsters and goddesses. Flowering plants filled the room with pleasantly sweet perfume. Several small trees grew in large ceramic pots.

A chunky man with short curly gray hair and a half smile stood near a table strewn with papers in front of a small, thin computer screen. He wore a toga with a broad purple stripe at its edge.

"Welcome to Lutece," he said. "I am Lucius Marcus Antonius, governor of Gaul, Angleterre and Germania or what we call the Province of Europa Occidens. Today, as for you also, the date is the first of Augustus. It is also, as for you, the Year 2700 AFR—After the Founding of Rome."

Lucius sat down on a particularly elegant small lounge and waved a hand at the chairs.

"Do sit down," he said. "The servants will bring some cooling drinks. In the meantime, let me bore you with a little alternative history."

He paused briefly to adjust his toga, smiled again thinly and continued.

"You, of course, have been taught by Mr. Gibbon and later so-called historians that the Roman Republic became the Empire, which by the way we never really admitted; that the Empire became corrupt and soft; that it was finally overrun at least in the West by barbarian immigrant tribes in your 5th and 6th Centuries; that the West descended into a Dark Age only to emerge in the Renaissance, and that set the stage for all that followed. But that didn't have to be what happened. And here today in this world that we are in that is absolutely not what happened."

He paused and nodded knowingly. A finch flew through the oval opening in the ceiling and perched in a tree. Lucius proceeded.

"The Republic did morph into the Imperium, but basically it did not change into immoral mush despite some unfortunate spates of tyranny. Contrary to later detractors, the great majority of Roman citizens remained true to Roman *gravitas,* Roman *pietas,* Roman *virtus.* And please understand the true meaning at the heart of those Latin words—dignity, duty and manliness. The Romans did not become soft. The ranks of the legions continued to be filled by Roman citizen warriors. Our legions in the end have always been unbeatable. Rome has continued to be the sole superpower; Rome has continued to organize and govern the known world.

"The great fingerpost, of course, was reached in the reign of Marcus Aurelius as your Mr. Gibbon has instructed you. But, according to Mr. Gibbon's scholarship, our Golden Age ended with the Antonines in your 2nd Century because Marcus Aurelius was soft hearted and died leaving Rome to be ruled by his spoiled, monstrous teenage son, Commodus. Not so! Marcus did indeed quite foolishly make Commodus his co-emperor and heir, but, when he saw how outrageously Commodus performed, how he used his position to create and enrich a personal court of corrupt and vicious sycophants from whom alone he accepted counsel, Marcus recognized the appalling danger to Rome. For nearly a century, chance had given Rome five good emperors. Many Romans may have been lulled by this into forgetting that a bad emperor could succeed at any time with all the returning evil that that could mean; but Marcus was not so lulled. He saw what a villainous tyrant Commodus would become. He could not allow it. At a fingerpost of history, he boldly took the right path.

"At this time, both he and Commodus were at the military camp of the VIII Legion, the Augusta. They were encamped at Vindobona, your Vienna. Marcus had been leading a successful war against incursions across the Danube frontier by the Marcomanni, a most nettlesome Germanic tribe. But now, because he was seriously ailing, he knew that he must act quickly. Marcus Aurelius Antoninus, Imperator and Stoic, summoned Commodus to the imperial tent. The interview was bitter, explosive, final. Commodus refused to step aside as co-emperor and threatened his father. Then he haughtily and, as he soon learned, unwisely broke off the meeting and strode away. That evening Marcus ordered two of his most trusted tribunes and six veteran centurions to interrupt a dinner party that Commodus and some of his more dissolute companions were attending, remove Commodus and execute him immediately for impiety and treason.

"The next morning before dawn, after assuring himself that Commodus had been separated from his head, Marcus departed with a third of the VIII Legion—4,000 men—on a forced march to Rome. There seven days later he and some advance units joined his III Legion, the Italica, which was camped outside the Aurelian Wall. He ordered the army to stand in full readiness if needed; entered the City in accordance with law and custom accompanied only by his 24 lictors, and met with a select group of senators, the "Council of Twenty," a mix of representatives of the oldest patrician families and the "new men." Two days later Marcus stood on the Rostra in the Forum and decreed the restoration of the Republic in a new, self-reinforcing form. Henceforth, the 600 members of the Senate were empowered to use a complex voting system involving various checks and balances to elect a permanent First Consul who would rule with the Senate."

Lucius paused while two servants served iced fruit juice and little cakes. Then he said:

"Marcus died two weeks later and was buried with full honors in Hadrian's Mausoleum. He left behind a *Pax Romana* that has been maintained to the present day. Rome was assured continuity of good leaders. The Legions assured order and peace. The old Roman virtues held. The barbarian immigrations never took place. Also, using Greek science and mathematics and Roman engineering, we achieved 1,000 years earlier all that your modern science and technology belatedly achieved and began surpassing it. Today we have all of our mineral mining industry on Mars; our manufacturing on the moon; only agriculture and animal husbandry is still earthbound; all our electricity is generated by nuclear power; our average longevity is 130.

"Much of our success derives from the fact that, while we are all born Romans under Roman law, our society, like all proper societies, fully recognizes differences in ability and accordingly is tiered. But even our lowest orders live better than your upper middle class does today. And generally, thanks to the legions, we have continuing peace. Disorder is such a bore.

"I do not wish to imply that we have not had our challenges. As you might expect, Rome recognized the truth of Christianity in Year 1000 AFR and replaced our older deities. We also fully concurred with our Lord Christ that there was a very practical division between Church and State if men and women were truly to exercise free will. Accordingly, any attempt by the Church to secularize itself by wielding temporal power had to be suppressed and it was. After some unpleasantness, there has always been total harmony between the First Consul and the Pope. . There have also been challenges to the Republic from time to time, particularly from Persia and China. All of these were resisted; then, finally, eliminated after the early introduction of atomic weapons into our arsenals.

"I should be happy to show you a quick photographic tour of Europa and what you call North America and we call Nova Roma, but I fear there is not enough time. Your excellent guide is signaling me that you must move on. Possibly on another visit."

Lucius rose and nodded slightly in dismissal.

"Thank you as always Lucius Marcus Antonious," Betta said. "As you know, we must not stay long. We are pressed to move on."

The group reassembled in the King's Hall and Betta led it to the next of the great doors. It bore carved galleys, cornish crowns, the lion of St. Mark.

"You have been to Venice, yes?" she said. "But this is not something you have seen there. No, I assure you. Have a look!"

When they walked through the door, they found themselves in a long, much gilded reception room with a row of high windows at the far end looking out on the Grand Canal. Renaissance carved chairs lined the walls and in the center before the windows was a high-backed gilded couch. Before it stood a square, dark man dressed in the traditional formal black of the *nobili*. He held a silver and jeweled baton under his arm and a piece of parchment in his right hand.

"Giovanni Dandalo, at your service," he said. "Admiral of Venice, descendant of Doges, 67th in the Golden Book. Welcome to my Palazzo and to Serrenissima, the Venetian Republic, the City of St. Mark, Guardian of the Sacred Relics, Lord of a Quarter and Half a Quarter of the Roman Empire.

"It will surprise you to learn that this is not the Venice of the Fodor Guides; it is not even the Venice of the Grand Tour. This is the alternate Venice that my ancestor, the great blind Doge, Enrico Dandolo, foresaw in his heart. Poor Enrico! You will recall how when old and sightless, he led a great army over the walls of Constantinople; conquered Byzantium; died, and was buried in the south gallery of Santa Sophia. So unfairly condemned in your fallacious histories! Nor, unlike what you have been told, did we fritter away our opportunity: Through our Navy we already controlled the Mediterranean; through our merchants we dominated world trade. Now we wisely linked arms with our Greek cousins rather than try to subjugate them; we successfully incorporated Byzantium into the Venetian Empire; we reestablished a new enlightened Roman Imperium, and we created a naval hegemony that has ordered the entire world.

"You understand, of course, what that means. Unlike you, we saw the Church reunited as One; the Muslim Caliphate, the Ottomans pushed back into the desert and destroyed; that opportunist realtor, Mohammed, reduced to being a minor prophet at best; the feudal kingdoms of the West absorbed; the New World discovered by our mariners and its inhabitants civilized in the great cities of New Venice. No need for the Battle of Lepanto. No 30-Years War. No French Revolution. No Napoleon. No Hitler. No Stalin. Instead, we have had centuries of peace, commerce, growth of science and technology and creation of enormous liberating wealth."

Giovanni Dandolo spread out his arms.

"Behind me is the Republic of Venice, Capital of the World. There you see what a wise government of the few can accomplish. Enjoy it!"

Betta shook her head. "We thank Your Eminence but we cannot see it now. We already have used up the short time allotted to us. We must be moving along."

Outside in the King's Hall, Betta led the group to the third door. This one was carved with ships of the line, crossed cannon, and the arms of England.

"Here we have a very special treat, particularly for any of you who are Americans," Betta said as she opened the third door. "Have a look!"

They found themselves in the Long Gallery at Hayes Hall in Kent. Dozens of large portraits of titled Englishmen from the 18th to the 20th Century hung on each of the main walls. Along the center dividing the Gallery in half were Chippendale chairs and tables bearing large Chinese Imari bowls. The group was still standing at one end when a tall man in a dark blue pin-striped suit appeared through a secret door in the inside wall.

"Lord Matthew Pitt," he said, bowing slightly. "Direct descendent by way of a younger son of the Earl of Chatham, William Pitt the Elder. This country house was the seat of both the Earl and his eldest son, William Pitt the Younger. You may have been told if you have ever visited the ancient village at Hayes that Hayes House was torn down in 1933 to make way for some nasty redevelopment, but as you can see you were misled. Here it is after all. King George IV and his niece, Queen Victoria, were guests here. Earlier, Benjamin Franklin and other fellow members of the Royal Society dined here with the First Earl.

"By that time in the 1770's, as you will recall, English arms were triumphant throughout much of the world: North America, India. Australia, South Africa, strategic islands, the great oceans. But all of it could have fallen apart. In fact, it almost did. Franklin, a famous scientist, one of America's richest men, a great English patriot and supporter of the Empire, represented to the Crown about a third of the American colonies. He wanted very much to find a solution when some of the colonials in America were stirring up revolution over taxes. But, instead of working with Franklin, stupid ministers close to the King insulted him. Then, Pitt, the man most responsible for creating the Empire, visited Franklin privately: they talked in great secret at Franklin's modest residence in Curzon Street. ("You will lose us," Franklin told Pitt. "You will lose an empire.") Pitt visited the King. ("The Council and I will not be dictated to by colonials," the King said. "These are Englishmen in arms," Pitt replied.) Finally Pitt rallied support among Ministers who were sensibly not interested in losing North America. The government fell.

"The King made Franklin Secretary for the Colonies. Everything flowed from that. Englishmen on both sides of the Atlantic became truly one nation. They controlled the world's oceans and eventually much of the world."

Lord Matthew paused for effect and shifted some papers on a small table.

"I know we have little time so I will summarize," he said, looking up. "Englishmen no matter where they lived were represented in Parliament and soon we had a Duke of Virginia, an Earl of Quebec, a Marques of Sydney. There was no American Revolution; we mediated unrest in France in exchange for Louisiana. (No French Revolution. No Napoleon.) We freed slaves everywhere and paid their owners for their property. (No American Civil War). We maintained peace among our second-rank, client states on the Continent: France, Germany, Italy, Austria and Russia. (No Franco-Prussian War. No World War I. Certainly no World War II.)

"In effect, the English speaking peoples became the sole world superpower, building and regulating a peaceful and prosperous world for the last two centuries.

He paused and smiled a microscopically thin, aristocratic British smile.

"Do we have time for questions?" he asked.

"No," Betta said, sharply. "You know the rules. We thank you as always,"

Regrouping again in the King's Hall, Betta promised the "most interesting moment" of the visit to the Zauberschloss. They stood before the fourth door emblazoned with American eagles, Roman fasces and Greek laurel wreaths.

"Ja, I assure you; most interesting," she said and opened the door. "Enter! Have a look!"

The group walked onto the patio of a small, one-story glass and steel house in the hills above San Diego. In the distance under a perfect blue sky, three enormous nuclear aircraft carriers lay in the harbor, two at piers, one apparently deploying toward the open Pacific.

A very elderly man of medium height with a full head of white hair sat in a lounge chair with his feet up on a hassock a few feet from a swimming pool. He waved hospitably at the group but did not rise. A pile of newspapers and a tall gin and tonic were on a table at his side.

"You'll forgive me for remaining seated," he said. "My bad knee is bothering me today. My name is Smedley Colfax Grant. None of you will recognize the name because you have a very different perception of events in the last 75 years. For better or worse, and my political enemies certainly say worse, I served as 45th President of the United States. And to the annoyance of some, I served four terms by Grace of God and Act of Congress. Before that, I was a Marine for 40 years, retiring as a lieutenant general. I won't bore you with all that except that I am happy to say I did see some action and, in fact, picked up a few of our better medals. What I have been asked to tell you about and shall do so is one of my more entertaining experiences which occurred when I was serving as an aide to President Harry Truman at Potsdam. That took place, you may recall, in late July 1945. Germany was defeated; Japan was reeling; Hitler and Mussolini were dead; Franklin Roosevelt was dead; Truman had been U.S. President only a few months."

The General, as he said he preferred to be called, shifted his legs and momentarily twisted his mouth in a mildly pained expression.

"Potsdam changed everything, but not the way you may think, " he continued. "Not that I did much, but I was there to see it. I was shoved into the job after being posted back to Walter Reed Hospital from Iwo Jima for some personal patch up and recuperation. The conference was in a huge oak-paneled reception hall in the Cecilienhof Palace, the former summer residence of Crown Prince Wilhelm of Prussia. But it was a scene out of the Old West. The room was full of high-ranking American and Brit and Soviet generals and diplomats. However, they didn't count for a dime's worth of spit. The only thing that mattered was Truman, a really tough little guy, sitting directly across a round table from that conniving Communist bastard, Joseph Stalin. And here, approximately, is what Truman said:

Generalissimo Stalin, as you know we will drop one or two atomic bombs on Japan next week and when that happens we expect to see the Empire of Japan run up the white flag. I told you last night about our successful test in Arizona and our plans; I suspect from your bored reaction that your agents had already told you a lot more. What I didn't mention is that we have at least another 25 of these atomic bombs in the barn and our factories are running full tilt. Surely, you understand that this new weapon makes a lot of the things you and Prime Minister Churchill and I have been arguing about here beside the point. Instead, I think you should start thinking now about how fast you can get the Red Army to skedaddle out of Germany and Austria and our ally Poland and the rest of Eastern Europe and move back to the borders you had in 1939 before you got in bed with Adolf Hitler. We don't want a war, but if we have to have one, now's the time. We're ready. So think about all the good things that going along with my suggestion can do for you. Your country is in ruins. You can put all of your resources into rebuilding it and your collapsed economy now instead of into your military. We'll even help you. But I promise you, if you refuse, we'll turn what's left of the Soviet Union into a glassy desert. So I suggest we have a final Potsdam Declaration simply about peace and your withdrawal before we quit here. Tomorrow would be good. Obviously, there is very little time.'

"Truman really didn't have four aces, but he had a better hand than Stalin. The Germans had cut the heart out of the Red Army when Stalin ordered General Zhukov to get to Berlin first regardless of the butcher bill. Maybe Truman didn't have 25 atomic bombs in the barn, but there were enough to take out most of what was left of the major Soviet cities assuming all our fuses worked. In any case, the U.S. Eighth Air Force would mop up anything left standing with 1000-plane bomber raids. And General Patton was in Vienna screaming to be let loose and cut his way to Moscow. Truman was a first class poker player and it was Stalin who folded."

Smedley Grant laughed and slapped his thigh.

"It was some show! Old Stalin just stared those squinty little yellow green eyes of his at Truman. Then he said the meeting should adjourn for consultations and the meeting broke up. But that afternoon the American and the Soviet Foreign Ministers met along with all of their people. By dinner time, General Zhukov, who hated Stalin, had moved his tanks around the royal guest house where Stalin was staying. The following morning it was announced that 'Comrade Stalin had suffered severe heart palpitations and was being flown back to Moscow for emergency treatment.' Meantime, Zhukov had ordered tanks to surrounded the Kremlin. That afternoon what was left of the Polituburo announced the arrest of Lavrenti Beria, head of the NKVD, for 'adventuristic plotting' and the appointment of General Zhukov as General Secretary 'with full powers.' That following morning the American and Soviet delegations initialed the Potsdam Declaration which Truman had outlined to Stalin. The Cold War was over before it began. American hegemony, as the French like to say, was a *fait accompli*."

The General took a long drink from his gin and tonic and smacked his lips.

"Best thing in the world for a tricky knee," he said, holding up his glass. . "I guess you all have to go now or I'd offer you one. Nice to see you."

Outside in the courtyard, Betta gathered her group together one last time.

"The rest of the Zauberschloss contains many fine treasures," she said. "Rare 18ᵗʰ Century furnishings, a large porcelain collection that belonged to the Catholic branch of the Hohenzollerns including a Swan Service and some good polychrome Sung. There also is an outstanding collection of paintings put together during the last war and stored here, but they now have been returned for the most part to their former owners. Unfortunately, none of this can be seen today because the castle is still under restoration by its new proprietors, Search History, Gmbh, a wholly-owned subsidiary of World Theme Parks, Inc. However, there are many posters, postcards and catalogues in the Castle Gift Shop showing these things. There were CD's available on what you have just heard but regrettably they have been withdrawn."

Henri, Alix and Isabelle had dressed for dinner and now, sitting around the chateau library, they voiced their many complaints about the day. Peter listened politely while studying a painting of the chateau dating back to when peacocks still walked on the lawn. Isabelle expressed great disappointment at finding "a wonderful Napoleonic box" for her collection of small antique boxes only to discover that it had been made recently in China. Alix was outraged at the price she had to pay for an Hermes scarf. Henri was contemptuous of the "Disneyland" exhibits at the Zauberschloss.

"Pure cowboy," Henri said. "It corrupts the rational mind."

"Really, Henri," Alix said. "You are so prejudiced."

"*Non, non*, not at all," Henri said. "It's the great American Legend that is the problem. Always the same: the bad men threaten to take over the town; the good people are afraid to resist; the mysterious man in *le chapeau blanc* rides in, shoots the bad men and rides off into the sunset. It is so pathetically *naif*."

"Peter," Alix said, turning to her silent son, "what did you think of the Zauberschloss?"

"Cool," Peter said. "I really liked that old Marine."

IV.
Epiphanies

Variations on a Theme

St. James the Moorslayer, one of the most valiant saints and knights the world ever had...has been given by God to Spain for its patron and protection.
—Miguel de Cervantes, *Don Quixote*

The game's afoot:
Follow your spirit; and, upon this charge
Cry God for Harry, England and St George!
—William Shakespeare, *Henry IV Part II*

They were half way through the Chopin mazurkas when Pardon made his decision to break away at the Intermission.

Outside the typical August mid-day heat was unbearable. But inside the rococo Music Room it was quite pleasant. Pardon was seated on the keyboard side of the musicians, the ornate doors to the dark, state dining room with its heavy coffered ceiling conveniently on his left. He could easily escape through those doors before the applause ended and half the audience rushed in the same direction and down a nearby stairway to the public rest rooms.

Pardon would go immediately to the Preservation Society desk inside the front door Reception Room and join a tour of the Mansion. He had not been there since his hard-drinking grandmother, Concordia Woolcott Mount, had taken him as a child nearly forty years ago. Then the place, one of the larger of the so-called Newport cottages erected to establish social status before the First World War, was still occupied by his great aunt, Concordia's older sister. The engraved calling cards that she and her chauffeur still left at certain houses in Manhattan identified her as HRH Iona, Duchess of Gartenberg-Salva. Her relatives called her Aunt Pinky.

All of Pardon's actions that morning were spur-of-the-moment. Originally, he had planned to attend an all-day seminar at the Naval War College. But as he sat in the Officers Club eating breakfast he noticed in the local newspaper a picture of a fashionable woman who was his second cousin and possibly his only living relative. She was identified in the paper as "Countess Elizabeth 'Sissie' Plakos-Hunter, the vivacious honorary vice chairperson of our annual Music Festival now underway at The Lawns."

Pardon recalled meeting her only once before about twenty-five years ago at a wedding in New York. He was returning to the United States after a tour of duty in Europe and the Middle East. She had just graduated from Vassar and was doing some vague kind of work for a small publisher. She had introduced him to her fiancé, a radio ad salesman from Chicago named Billy. Despite the family trait of a pinched look about her mouth, she was quite beautiful that day. In her current picture, she appeared miraculously unchanged. The newspaper said the next Festival concert would take place that morning. Pardon thought that possibly she might be there and he could run into her. It seemed to him important that he did. Pardon decided to skip his seminar and go to the concert.

Benjamin Woolcott, a 19th Century technological tycoon and great grandfather of Pardon and Sissie, built The Lawns, an enormous Italian Renaissance country seat fronting on Bellevue Avenue and surrounded on its other three sides by a park. But prior to Benjamin came Jacob Pardon on whose shoulders Benjamin stood. Jacob was born in 1838 in Ft. Edward, New York, near the upper reaches of the Hudson River. Jacob grew up on his father's farm, helped work it while picking up a basic education at the local school house and was apprenticed down the river to a wagon maker whose shop was on a part of the old Saratoga battlefield.

In 1861, Jacob joined a New York regiment that fought at Gettysburg and helped turn the Confederate right flank during General Picket's disastrous run at the Union guns ranged on top of Cemetery Ridge and centered on the Angle. During the fighting, Jacob and some other York Staters in his unit had shifted to the left, joined up with a fresh New York regiment and arrived at the Angle about the same time about 200 Virginians led by General Lewis Armistead carrying his cap over his head on his sword broke through two Pennsylvania regiments and reached the federal guns. In the ensuing bloody melee, Armistead was hit a number of times, fell mortally wounded beside a cannon and the surviving Virginians fell back in retreat. This was the high water mark of the Confederate States of America. Jacob always claimed to have had Armistead in his sites and Jacob was a very good shot.

After the Civil War, Jacob returned to Ft. Edward very briefly, married and moved 20 miles south to Troy, New York, where he used his military bonus and a loan to buy into a carriage-maker business. Later he bought out his senior partner who wanted to retire and brought in a new junior partner and extraordinary tinkerer, his son, Benjamin. During the next decade, Woolcott Carriages became one of the larger carriage makers in America; it also became the holder of a string of enormously-profitable patents on some advanced gears and various futuristic steering mechanisms and manufacturing tools, all invented by Benjamin Woolcott. After Jacob died, Woolcott Carriages and these patents, in turn, became the basis for Benjamin to become a major shareholder in several railroad car companies and the nascent automobile industry.

In the Reception Hall of The Lawns, two lady volunteers at the Preservation Society desk fitted Pardon with ear phones and a tape player. They suggested that he start the tour by going up the Great Staircase and joining a group and a guide in the Gallery on the second floor. One of the volunteers, apparently in recognition of Pardon's pained look and the number of stripes on the sleeve of his naval uniform, said helpfully: "You don't have to join the tour, Captain. It's only that you might have some questions."

Pardon thanked the ladies, pushed the button on his tape player and walked up the Great Stairs to the first landing and stood in front of the first of a series of large tapestries. The voice of a curator said plumily into his ears:

This series of three Belgian tapestries dating from the early 17th Century depict some of the great naval battles of the world encompassing 2000 years of history. The first is the Battle of Lepanto in which in 1571 the Holy Alliance of the Pope, the Venetians and the Spaniards under Don Juan of Austria decisively defeated the naval forces of the Ottoman Empire and ended the threat of Muslim dominance in the Mediterranean. The second tapestry, despite some water damage, is one of the best depictions we have of the Battle of Actium in 31 BC. Here we see the end of the battle with the defeated galleys of the East fleeing from the victorious galleys of the West. In the upper right, you see Cleopatra and Mark Antony in their retreating Egyptian flagship with its silken sails. In the center standing on the bridge of their far more war-ready galley you see the victors, Octavius Caesar and Marcus Agrippa. The third tapestry depicts the victory of the Athenians in 480 BC over the much larger fleet of the Persians. Xerxes, the Persian emperor, watches disconsolately from the shore.

None of these tapestries are original to The Lawns at the time of its construction by Benjamin Woolcott, a widower, who essentially built it as a summer residence and social stage for his two daughters, Iona and her younger sister, Concordia. The tapestries were hung later by Iona after her marriage in 1915 to the Duke of Gartenberg-Salva. They came from Schloss Gartenberg in southern Germany along with other valuable furnishings and porcelains.

Pardon always remembered his grandmother, Concordia, with fondness and awe. His mother and Concordia's only child, Louisa, died of influenza only a few months after his birth and he was brought up in Hollywood by his father, Rick Bond, a movie actor famous for playing second string romantic roles. Rick, whose blonde handsomeness and arch smile was the basis of his screen career, never remarried but devoted most of his time when not before cameras to courting progressively younger starlets whom he liked to entertain at private pool parties at his home. He delegated the care of Pardon to child nurses and housekeepers, a routine enhanced periodically by sending him on long visits to Concordia in New York.

Concordia was still a beautiful woman in her late 50's despite her increasingly strong thirst for vodka. Each of her four marriages had ended in divorce and disastrous diminution of the money she inherited from her father. When Pardon visited her as a boy, she was still living quite grandly in a large co-op apartment just off Fifth Avenue, although her finances were in a state of disarray, a situation that increased her drinking and careless behavior. But Pardon was cognizant of none of that until later. To him, Concordia, in contrast to his father and the changing occupants of the family swimming pool, was a wonderful, magical lady who represented the respectable Great World where the best people lived, excellence was recognized, heroes were rewarded and the good triumphed.

We now finish mounting the Grand Stairway and walk across the center Reception Hall to the Long Gallery. Pause briefly to admire the beautiful coffered ceiling with bosses bearing the Gartenbereg-Salva coat of arms: two ermines rampant and a golden mace on a green shield. The Gallery itself is the work of Antonio Savonni, a treasure of the school of Palladio. The Gallery originally was built to house Benjamin Woolcott's art collection which included several excellent Titians and many 18th Century French paintings by Boucher and Fragonard in the sensuous and sentimental style so popular at Versailles. All of these were given to various museums upon his death in 1917 and were replaced with the family portraits that you see today including several by Sargent and Eakins. Of particular interest, is the portrait on the left of the Duke and Duchess in their robes and regalia. It was painted at Schloss Gartenberg which, of course, is now a state museum. To the right is a painting of the royal couple's only son, Prince Karl, who was killed during the Second World War.

Pardon took particular interest at the portrait of his cousin, Karl. He was painted wearing English tweeds in a country setting, possibly the castle park at Gartenberg. Two black Giant Schnauzers sat beside him and he held a riding crop in one hand. His high forehead and aquiline nose were exactly like his father's in the nearby painting, but his pinched mouth was pure Woolcott. The date on a brass plaque below the picture was 1938. That would have made Karl about 22 at the time. There was nothing to indicate that the following year he later became a Luftwaffe pilot and was shot down over Hastings during the Blitz.

> *On the west wall is a 19*[th] *Century portrait of Benjamin Woolcott, the noted inventor and captain of industry who built The Lawns. You see him here in his study at his Fifth Avenue mansion in New York. He is seated at his desk which is purported to have been made in the French Empire style for Joseph Bonaparte when his brother, Napoleon I, made him King of Naples. The painting is believed to be by Sargent but it is not signed, possibly because our research shows Mr. Woolcott protested the bill.*

Pardon looked into the wide, glaring eyes of his great grandfather: a square, meticulously groomed man who seemed even now to exude the power and unrelenting drive that created the American empire. Pardon wondered what Benjamin would have made of him. What had he made of his son-in-law, the Duke, and all the others? And then Pardon realized the plumy voice in his ear was talking of the Duke, himself.

> *If you proceed to the left at the end of the Gallery, you come to the Chapel. The Woolcotts were always Episcopalians and quite low church, but the Duke of Gartenberg-Salva was a Roman Catholic and Iona became one. When Benjamin Woolcott died in 1917, he left The Lawns to Iona and a few years later she had the Chapel installed. As you will see, this lovely white, crimson and gold architectural treasure box is a perfect copy of one of the rococo chapels in the Church of St. John of Nipmunk in Munich. . Of particular note is the altar with its carved polychrome statues of Saints Hildegarde and Wolfgang. The ceiling with its crowds of flying angels and cherubim washed with supernatu-*

ral light from hidden windows was imported from Italy. It is of the School of Tiepolo.

Pardon knew that when Benjamin Woolcott died he left more than a third of his fortune to the Woolcott Foundation for the furtherance of scientific and engineering research. He left the bulk of the remainder including The Lawns to Iona; a smaller but still substantial share went to his younger daughter, Concordia, with whom he was greatly displeased. Unlike Iona's marriage into a small but very royal house, Concordia had settled for Nicky Ogelthorpe, the scapegrace son of one of their millionaire Newport neighbors. Nicky's contribution to his young wife's education was to teach her how to drink. He also sired her only child, Louisa, Pardon's mother. The marriage lasted barely two years and before her father died Concordia was able to distress her father further by marrying an English polo player and moving to Mayfair in London.

Benjamin clearly liked the idea that his daughter was married to royalty, but his not particularly religious but very Protestant heart never would have agreed to putting a Roman Catholic chapel in The Lawns. Yet here it was. And Pardon could only concur as he sat in one of the pews that it was indeed an esthetic marvel. After World War I, the Duchy of Gartenberg-Salva was incorporated into the Weimar Republic, most of its ducal properties were confiscated and the Duke was effectively deposed. But he retained his title. He lived on until the late 30's, spending much time in a comfortable leather chair in the library at the Metropolitan Club in New York and in a lounge chair at his cabana at Bailey's Beach in Newport. Pardon wondered if Iona or anyone else used the Chapel after that time. He would have lit a candle and said a prayer but the chapel was no longer consecrated.

At the end of the corridor leading from the Reception Hall and just beyond the Chapel is the Duchess's magnificent bedroom suite. Note the great 18th Century bed by André Boulle, the French watercolors by Watteau and delightful reception area furnished with Louis XV fauteuils, a superb settee by Reisener and the delicate tables with exquisite marquetry overlaid with ormolu.

The room was totally familiar to Pardon after nearly 40 years. This was where his grandmother, Concordia, brought him at the age of 10 to meet Iona, his "dear Aunt Pinky." It was late morning and she was sitting on the settee with her white Shih Tzu, Mah Jong, beside her. As Concordia and Pardon were led into the room by an aged butler named Otto, Mah Jong growled and stiffened but remained on the settee.

"Iona, dear," Concordia said, bending over her sister and kissing her. "You look so wonderful. Just like Mama, really. And it is so wonderful to see you. Here is Pardon, poor Louisa's boy, with me for the summer. I knew you would want to see him, and we're only in Newport for the weekend. We're house guests of Polly Vaughn at Newlands. She's having the loveliest party tonight. Pardon, give your dear Aunt Pinky a kiss."

Pardon stepped forward shyly and pecked the cheek of the lovely lady he had never seen before and again Mah Jong emitted a low growl. The sisters, both in their early 60's, could almost have been twins and, with much gratitude to the cosmetic and surgical arts, appeared remarkably youthful.

"A beautiful boy," Iona said to Concordia, ignoring Pardon who sat awkwardly on the edge of one of the fauteuils. "He looks like his father, I think. Always so handsome in his films."

"A little, perhaps," Concordia said. "I think he looks a lot more like his namesake, our grandfather. You know that wonderful old picture that Mr. Brady took at the Grand Review in Washington. Put a blue uniform on Pardon and you would have a hard time telling them apart."

"You really think so? I suppose." And Iona looked over at Pardon. "My grandfather, your great great grandfather, was a great hero in the Civil War. Did you know that?"

"Yes," Pardon said. "Grandma told me. It was at Gettysburg, I know. He was really hot stuff."

Iona laughed. "Really 'hot stuff.' What a terrible expression! Where do you go to school, Pardon?"

"I go to the Studio Stars School in Hollywood, but next year I'll go away. I don't know where though."

"It hasn't been decided," Concordia said a little stiffly. "His father wants to send him to one of the private schools out there that caters to the children of movie people, but I think he should come east."

"Well, I think you're absolutely right," Iona said. "And I can tell you exactly where to send him. It's near here; Portsmouth Priory; run by the Benedictines; it's one of the best boys' preparatory schools in America. I wanted to send my poor Karl there but the Duke insisted that he go to his old school in Bavaria. Karl never came home again except for a few holidays. One of the biggest errors of my life."

"I have always been so sorry about poor Karl," Concordia said. "You remember: Felicia was visiting me in New York when we heard and I told her it was her duty to go to you immediately."

"It was a sorry situation," Iona said and sat up straighter. "And I regret that despite your good intentions my daughter did not improve matters when she arrived. However, we were talking about the right school for Pardon. If you wish, I can make all the arrangements to enter him at the Priory in the fall."

Pardon always recalled his six years at Portsmouth Priory, now Abbey, as among the happier in his life. He relished the orderliness of his surroundings; he liked and admired the Benedictine brothers, even those who disciplined him; he enjoyed his studies and sports, particularly sailing; and he found great comfort in the Catholic liturgy and teachings in which he became absorbed.

He also became attracted to the Navy. From the Priory campus, he and his classmates often watched large naval task forces move in and out of Narragansett Bay and Newport as part of the great military chess game underway in the early years of the Cold War. Each spring one of their field trips included a visit to nearby Quonset Point, a major refitting port for aircraft carriers, and a visit to the destroyer base or Naval War College at Newport. He always went.

By the time he graduated, Pardon had achieved a commendable academic record; had become a convert to Roman Catholicism; had been severely disciplined only once for drinking and disorderly behavior; and had been admitted as a midshipman at the US Naval Academy at Annapolis. Pardon's father did not attend. As he explained in a letter, he was on location in Los Vegas shooting a new movie, *Royal Bonanza*. Concordia had planned to come, but the day before she checked herself into the Westport Spa, her favorite alcoholic rehabilitation hospital, for the last time. Two weeks later she suffered a fatal heart attack.

As you leave the Duchess' bedroom suite, note the photographs in elaborate silver frames on the table near the door. All of the frames are early Gorham. Most of the pictures are of members of the family of the Duke and Duchess. However, in the center are informal pictures taken in the 1920's of Grand Duke Alexander of Russia and King Zog of Bulgaria during visits to Newport. Both are autographed.

Pardon noticed that one of the pictures taken at Bailey's Beach about 1920 was of the Duke and Duchess along with two children who obviously were Karl and his sister, Felicia. All were in tennis clothes and held rackets. He knew that Felicia subsequently became an outstanding player; it was during a game of doubles at the Tennis Club that she had met "Petey" Placos, the Portuguese tennis champion; and she subsequently married him despite her parents vehement objections. Felicia and her parents had not spoken for a number of years when her brother was killed. They became more or less reconciled after Felicia presented Iona with an only grandchild, the Countess "Sissie."

Proceed now down the Grand Stairway to the Reception Hall. This is the official end of your tour. However, if there are rooms on the first floor that you have not visited, rewind the tape and proceed to them. It has been my pleasure to conduct you through The Lawns where very little has changed since the death of Iona, Duchess of Gartenberg-Salva in 1970 and the generous donation by her estate of this magnificent property to the Preservation Society.

Pardon had no interest in seeing any more of the house. He walked down the stairway past the tapestries and returned the tape to hall desk.

"Did you enjoy the tour, Captain?" one of the lady volunteers asked.

"Oh, yes," he said. "Most interesting."

"Do come back. Some say it is better every time. Like visiting old friends."

"Yes, I'm sure," Pardon said and turned to leave. When he did, he saw his cousin, Sissie, talking to some of the musicians from the morning concert. He was certain that it was she. She looked exactly like the picture that he had seen in the newspaper. In fact, she looked little changed from one of the other much earlier silver framed pictures that he had just seen in her grandmother's bedroom.

His first thought was to go over and introduce himself. His second thought was to run. After all, what would he say? "Hello, there, you may remember me: I'm Pardon Bond, your second cousin from the wrong side of the family."

"How nice to see you," she would say in a proper, little voice and give him a proper, little smile . "But, really, Pardon, what a surprise."

"Just happened to be in town and, in a fit of nostalgia, thought I would visit the old family home. I remember coming here once before when I was 10 to visit Aunt Pinky, your grandmother. All quite interesting. But, you know, coming here does raise a big question in my mind. Maybe you can help answer it."

"Really, and what is that?"

"Well I was just wondering: What the hell went wrong? Why did just about everyone and everything turn out so badly?"

He continued to stand there a few more seconds trying to decide what he really wanted to do and then the necessity of deciding was gone. It was removed by a worried-looking naval officer whom he saw twist through the crowd and come to attention in front of him. They exchanged salutes and Lieutenant Fred Livingston of the USS Iwo Jima, a guided missile cruiser that Pardon commanded, presented an envelope to Pardon and said in a low voice:

"The Admiral's compliments, sir. We have a Code Black Star. I have been ordered to return you immediately to the Iwo. She's already out in the stream. I have one of our birds parked at the bottom of the park."

As the helicopter rose over Newport and headed over water crowded with sailboats toward the outer harbor, Pardon opened his envelope and read his Top Secret orders. He already knew the general contents.

The United States, the Islamist jihadists' "Great Satan," had dithered too long. For weeks it had been only a matter of waiting for the spy satellites to report that the game was on. Now it was. An Islamist coalition led by Iran was preparing to launch a nuclear strike against Israel within hours. Israeli fighter bombers, secretly given an aerial right of way by Saudi Arabia, were already over the great deserts of the Empty Quarter. Among the many unknowns was whether the mullahs in a burst of suicidal fervor would initiate the Islamic End of Days by launching their half dozen nuclear-armed ICBMs against "the Great Satan" before the missiles could be destroyed on the ground. If that happened, the United States' only defense was its anti-missile task force in the Western Atlantic. The task force was headed by the Iwo Jima.

Pardon could already see the Iwo Jima sailing dead eastward. Far to the north and south he saw the two sister cruisers that made up the heart of his task force. Two minutes later the helicopter made its approach and landed. As Pardon walked directly to the Iwo's combat center, he saw with approval that his pennant indicating that he was aboard had been raised and the Iwo was increasing speed.

By early evening the Iwo and the rest of the task force which included frigates and nuclear attack submarines were on station off the Atlantic Shelf. Pardon was on the Iwo's bridge with his chief operations officer, Commander James Sewell.

"What do you think, sir?" Sewell said.

"I'm feeling lucky," Pardon said. "I just hope I'm as good a shot as my great great grandfather was at Gettysburg."

Downward Facing Dog

...the whirligig of time brings in his revenges.
—William Shakespeare, *Twelfth Night*

Georgie's yoga master would be pleased.

During the last ten minutes, Georgie did three perfect Warrior poses; dropped into Plank; shifted into an excellent Downward Facing Dog that he held for three minutes alone, and moved smoothly into the Child's Pose.

Georgie spent the rest of the morning to doing the *New York Times* crossword puzzle in ink, listening to a CD of old Broadway musicals and rereading three chapters of Gibbon. At lunchtime he walked the 10 blocks down Fifth Avenue from his apartment to the Metropolitan Club to meet his younger sister, Betsy, for lunch.

"It's not just exercise," Georgie told her over smoked salmon salads. "It's how well you do it. Take Downward Facing Dog: there you are with your toes and hands on the ground, your head angled down and your rear end in the air. You should be in a perfect triangle. It's not easy."

"Certainly not when you're over 80 and overweight," Betsy said.

"I am not overweight. In fact, I wore my old morning suit last week at a funeral and it fit as well as it fit when I had it made just after the war."

"Really? I am always impressed by your thrift. Who died?"

"Buddy Crawford. The funeral was at St. Boniface's. I was an usher."

"I thought you loathed him."

"All the more reason to enjoy burying him," Georgie said and smiled. "Besides, Buddy wasn't the worst person in the world, just not bright. I could never understand why anyone would ever use him as an investment counselor. Although he had good taste in choosing ushers."

"Speaking of investment counselors, that's why we are having lunch," Betsy said. "I want to invade my Trust."

"Whatever for? I should think that you have more than enough."

"My smile, Georgie: I want a new smile. My dentist, Dr. Granberg, will do the whole thing for $50,000. He's absolutely marvelous."

"And you expect me as executor to sign off on this nonsense? What's involved: a lot of tooth implants? I should think it would be very painful."

"It will greatly improve how I look. Bunny Rumsfeld had it done last year and she looks simply gorgeous."

"You already are simply gorgeous."

"Very flattering, but all that yoga is obviously affecting your eyesight. So that's settled. You'll sign off on release of the money."

Georgie sighed and opened his hands in a gesture of helplessness.

"I suppose so," he said. "We all have to find new ways to entertain ourselves as the years roll along."

"Other than yoga, Georgie, what new ways have you found lately?"

"Death notices of old associates," he said. "I like reading them at breakfast."

Autumn sunlight streamed into the American empire breakfast room. Across Fifth Avenue the trees in Central Park formed a wall of orange and yellow. Georgie, waited on by his aging factotum, Jerome, sat at a small round table covered with a white linen cloth and set with his grandmother's 18th Century Spode breakfast set. His morning toast stood in a Georgian silver toast rack. A small Regency coffeepot waited nearby. Georgie absently buttered the toast with butter curls taken from a delicate covered ice dish.

This had become a special hour for Georgie. As he ate, he scanned the obituaries in the *Times*. Seldom was he disappointed. This morning he was rewarded early. There was a good quarter column on the demise of Bradford Howard. The headline said:

R.B. Bradford Howard, Millionaire Art Collector, Dead

"Rotten bastard," Georgie said to himself and read the story with delight.

R. Bradford Howard, retired corporate executive and noted art collector, died yesterday at his summer home in Exeter, N.H., after a brief illness. He was 65.

Mr. Howard was president of IGT, an international utilities company recently acquired by Groupe Meduse of France, and a well-known collector of post-modernist art. Many of Mr. Howard's paintings in recent years were donated to the Whitney Museum of Art and the Guggenheim Museum.

Prior to joining IGT, Mr. Howard was Chief Financial Officer, of Garland Research Company of Montclair, New Jersey.

Mr. Howard was born in Revere, MA. He was graduated with an accounting degree from Babson College. He served as a lieutenant in the New Jersey National Guard during the Viet Nam War.

He is survived by his wife, Wendy, two children from earlier marriages and one grandchild. Surviving children are R. Bradford Howard III of San Diego, CA., and Ms. Kathleen Tollman Howard of Ravello, Italy.

The obituary, of course, left out a number of facts which Georgie recalled with relish. Brad Howard married four times and consorted with a considerable number of suitable and unsuitable other women. His son was a career surfing instructor at a California beach; his daughter, incongruously named after Brad's first wife, was a lesbian tourist guide. Brad retired from IGT six months ahead of the company's near collapse, an SEC investigation and acquisition of the company's remnants by the French. Brad obtained handsome tax write-offs from the donation of his paintings which Georgie, a connoisseur of the early Italian Renaissance, adjudged to be nothing but well-framed flimflam.

Georgie first met Brad Howard when Brad was working as a junior accountant at Garland Research. At the time, Georgie was a partner at a venture capital firm that had been spun out of Standish Palmer Littleton, the old white shoe investment banking house founded by Georgie's father, the late Walter Standish. Brad was assigned to Georgie to help put together a deal that would make Standish Montgomery a major partner in Garland in return for investing 50 million dollars to commercialize key Garland patents.

Georgie relied considerably on Brad after finding him to be a stand-out player in a small platoon of Garland people who demonstrably ran the gamut from mediocre to stupid. Brad was also handsome, ingratiating and amusing. Accordingly, it was a natural development for Georgie to invite Brad one evening after a full day of meetings to join him for a late dinner in town at Club 21. When they arrived, they found waiting for them another couple, Elliot and Muffie Wellington, and Elliot's much younger sister and Georgie's fiancé, Kathleen.

Georgie, who was 42 at the time, was a very well-groomed pudgy man of medium height with straight blonde hair and a somewhat vanilla but enormously well-bred face. People of any intelligence realized on meeting him and listening to his bright, sardonic comments that they were dealing with a mind of considerable power. At the same time, they found quickly that his patience and interest in small talk were limited. So far, he had never married. He had found none of the numerous women his age to whom his family, friends and associates had introduced him fascinating enough to want to marry and the feeling was generally reciprocated. But then he met Kathy Wellington the year before at a charity cocktail party; decided he was in love; and pursued her.

Kathy, who was 15 years younger than Georgie, was certainly worthy of pursuit: she was beautiful, bright, charming, well-mannered, proper. She worked for an advertising agency writing clever copy for Prince Orange soft-drinks and the Mighty Beef fast-food chain. She was very popular among men who were her contemporaries. She found Georgie very different: more mature, smarter, cynically witty, rich in the understated manner of those who have always been rich. But, when Georgie asked her to marry him, she thought about it for weeks. She consulted Elliot, her older brother and only living relative. He enthusiastically approved. She consulted her best friend at college. The best friend, who was in the middle of a divorce, told her cryptically that "marriage is a great adventure." Then Georgie, brooding on what to do, decided on a bold stroke. He took Kathy to London for a long weekend and on that Sunday morning at the Ritz Hotel, looking out at the placid Green Park while sitting at a room service breakfast table, she agreed to marry him.

The engagement continued somewhat uneventfully for six months. They planned to marry after Thanksgiving and spend their honeymoon traveling in Province and Northern Italy. Meantime, Kathy continued to write clever soft drink and fast food ads; Georgie worked on finishing the Garland deal and finished, killed or initiated a half dozen others. Kathy and Georgie ate dinner together at least once a week; spent several weekends at her brother's home outside Stamford and one very unpleasant weekend at the imposing dark Tudor home of Georgie's widowed mother in Greenwich.

Then, three weeks after the dinner at 21, Kathy told Georgie that she could not make a second weekend call on his mother because she had to be away on business. The agency was sending her to San Diego. Georgie certainly understood. He would just as soon not visit his mother and divided the weekend between office work in his apartment and attending a matinee performance of Tosca. What he found difficult to understand is that when he tried to reach Brad Howard regarding some Garland financial reports, he was told, when he finally ran down Brad's manager at home in New Jersey, that Brad was in San Diego on business. Georgie might catch him at the Del Coronado Hotel.

Georgie learned from Kathy herself the following Tuesday at breakfast when she returned her engagement ring that "this was something crazy that just happened." The very next morning after the dinner at 21 Brad had called and said he had to have lunch with her. She had refused. He showed up at her office at noon and to avoid a scene she went along with him. After lunch, they "walked all over New York." They had "so much to talk about." They had dinner. He walked her home and stayed the night. They had been inseparable for weeks. It was crazy, but real. Surely, someone as balanced and mature as Georgie could understand. She was so sorry if she had hurt him.

Kathy and Brad were married that summer at St. Mary the Virgin Episcopal Church in Stamford. After a long afternoon reception hosted by her brother at the Westchester Country Club, they left by car for a honeymoon at Hilton Head with a one-night stop in Washington. A few miles north of Trenton, a huge Kenworth trailer truck sideswiped their car and catapulted it into the traffic on the northbound lane. Brad was thrown from the car and suffered only minor injuries. Kathy's body was found in the wreckage. She had been killed instantly.

Georgie, who was invited to Kathy's wedding but did not attend, did attend her funeral four days later in the same church. He stood in the back and left immediately afterward. He spoke briefly to Elliot, offering the usual platitudes. Then, his eyes glazed for the briefest moment and he said: "You know it could have all been different." Georgie saw Brad start to walk toward them. Georgie turned abruptly and left.

The next day Standish Palmer at Georgie's insistence withdrew from the Garland deal. Georgie said the Garland people lacked integrity. He would not do business with them and was disappointed, though not surprised, when others did.

A week after reading of Brad Howard's demise Georgie again was greatly rewarded by his breakfast reading of the *Times*. There, above the fold, was a boxed obituary of Lawrence Lime. The headline:

Tech Wizard Dies of Rare Disease

"Slimy swine," Georgie said to himself, took a sip of coffee and happily read about the alleged tech wizard whom friends and enemies called "little Larry."

Lawrence Harold Lime, Chairman Emeritus of International Knowledge Corporation (IKC), died today after a lengthy bout with Utrecht disease, a rare incurable malady normally found in sub-Sahara Africa. He was 78.

Mr. Lime, who early in his career developed VIGGAR © software, founded IKC and grew it into a world giant from the merger of a half dozen small electronics firms on Route 128 outside Boston. VIGGAR today still provides electronic switches essential to all computer systems.

Born in Liverpool, England, in 1927, Mr. Lime emigrated as a child to the United States with his mother and father, an itinerant book salesman. He attended public schools in Lowell, MA, and obtained a scholarship to MIT. He had to leave for want of tuition money after two years and went to work at Moonstruck, a small electronics research company operating in a former bakery.

After developing VIGGAR, Mr. Lime was able to attract sufficient investment capital to lay the foundation for his software empire. Before his retirement as President and CEO of IKC, he was awarded the Americus Medal for national technical achievement and was listed among the 100 richest men in the United States.

Mr. Lime is believed to have contracted Utrecht's disease during a tour of Congo for the United Nations as part of an economic development program aimed at establishing telemarketing operations in Kinshasa.

He is survived by his widow, Gertrude.

Georgie buttered an extra piece of toast. Normally he restricted himself to two small slices, but this now was a special day. Little Larry was finally dead and he, Georgie, felt just fine. Wind blew rain against the window of the breakfast room, but Georgie felt certain he saw some sunlight beyond the trees.

Little Larry's obituary was clearly pure Potemkin Village for anyone who knew him from his earliest days and Georgie did. Lime and Georgie worked together when they were both in their twenties. Georgie, a few years older than Lime, spent the early part of World War II at Yale; failed the physical when he volunteered for the Officer's Training School; then was drafted into the Army as an enlisted man in time to participate as a corporal in the second wave of landings at Normandy Beach. He was the third man back from point when his lieutenant fell dead in the sand in front of him. When Georgie was mustered out in 1946, he returned to Yale for an accelerated year; spent two more years at Harvard Business School; and rather than initially join his father's New York firm, he looked for work around Boston. His first job was treasurer for a start-up company called Moonstruck. Total payroll when he joined the company: 15. Larry Lime was one of the technicians.

Larry was a skinny, nerdy young man just over five feet tall who looked at the world through cola bottle glasses; a beaver who kept strange hours, liked to work all night, lived on fast food. Georgie, who also liked to work late, would occasionally join Larry in early morning take-out orders of a combination of faux cheese, relish and mystery meat called a " Total Burger" with machine-formed fries and chemically- laced shakes. While dining, the two would share cynical comments about the high tech industry and their coworkers. Jerry Baum, president of Moonstruck, came in for particular scorn.

As Georgie viewed the situation, Jerry, who was only about two years his senior, might be a technical genius but he most assuredly was a business ignoramus. As Larry viewed the situation, Jerry might have some great technical ideas but he never knew what to do with them. Both agreed that Moonstruck with Jerry as captain of the ship was headed for the rocks. And they told each other for several months how they would do things better.

"Money," Larry said. "We need money."

"We can get that," Georgie said. "But what's our product?"

"We have that," Larry said. "Not to worry. Jerry will never miss it."

The product, of course, was software that came to be known as *VIGGAR*. At the time, it was called *Starlight II*, one of many experimental software packages dreamed up mostly by Jerry Baum and allowed to languish for lack of a specific application and professional marketing.

Larry felt certain that *Starlight II* could be used as a critical component of some of the new computer systems evolving at the time. To make it that, he wrote a little additional code, renamed the package *VIGGAR* and applied for new patents. Meantime, Georgie developed a business plan. Then, dressed in his best blue pin-striped suit, he trotted around "The Plan" in a model B-school slide presentation to venture capitalists in Boston. Little Larry in his best homeless boy genius costume came along as a stage prop.

They struck oil early in the unimpressive office of the Isaiah Fund. Marvin Grooms, president of Isaiah, functioned behind a rented metal desk surrounded by tables supporting piles of reports, magazines and newspapers. But, as Georgie knew, he had somehow put together a five million dollar investment fund and he was building a portfolio of promising startups.

Marvin, a street kid with a community college degree in computer systems and a former hedge fund operator, felt an immediate strong rapport with Larry and an immediate class discomfort with Georgie the longer Georgie talked with his teeth closed. Marvin also fell in love with *VIGGAR* and "The Plan." Therefore, he had no difficulty, as negotiations progressed during the ensuing weeks, in agreeing with a mumbled suggestion from Larry that Georgie really could be replaced. And so they did. Marvin hired Larry who had VIGGAR in his pocket. Georgie wasn't part of the deal.

VIGGAR was an immediate success, yielding an ever larger cash flow. Jerry Baum, egged on by Georgie, sued. But Larry and Grooms ended all patent challenges and suits by buying Moonstruck in the first of a long series of acquisitions of various other high tech startups along with their patents and technical talent. Within five years, IKC was organized as a steamroller New Era corporation with

400 million dollars in sales, 50 percent a year growth in earnings and a voracious appetite for more acquisitions.

Georgie left Moonstruck for obvious reasons when Baum sold out. He joined his father at Standish Palmer Littleton to help in the development of the firm's new venture capital department which eventually became Standish Montgomery. Although he never saw Little Larry or Grooms again, he always sold IKC stock short whenever an opportunity arose.

Much sunshine. Cool air. Georgie took a walk before breakfast. The world about him looked good. It smelled good. He felt good. When he sat down to breakfast and opened *The Times* he felt even better. A headline on the obituary page said:

Former Sen. Tyndall Dead at 75.

Next to the story there was an hilariously fraudulent picture of the late senator taken twenty years earlier when he had much hair and no mustache. "Pompous crook," Georgie said to himself and happily read on.

Yonkers, NY—Leroy Harding Tyndall, Democratic U.S. Senator from New York, died here today at the Alonzo Sweet Nursing Home after a long illness. He was 75.

Sen. Tyndall, who served 10 years in the Senate and two terms in the House of Representatives, stepped down from several powerful committee assignments and resigned from office in 1995 in connection with the Tepee Casino Investigations.

Sen. Tyndall, originally a Republican appointed to the Senate to fill a vacancy, changed his party affiliation when his party declined to re-nominate him for a full term. He won nomination in a Democratic primary.

During his years in the Senate, Sen. Tyndall was a leading supporter of free prescription drugs, major increases in social security payments and government pensions and one-time slavery reparation payments limited to direct descendents of blacks who were slaves prior to the Fugitive Slave Act of 1855.

At the time of his resignation, Sen. Tyndall denied "any wrong doing" in the unreported payment of 20 million dollars in contributions to various senatorial campaigns by Tepee Casino, Ltd., of Bermuda. The Tepee Casino Ring was an offshore investment group that established a national chain of gambling casinos in the names of more than a dozen defunct Indian tribes.

Sen. Tyndall is survived by his third wife, Shana Tone, the Hollywood hip-hop country fusion singer; one son, Leroy Tyndall IV of Buffalo, NY, and a daughter, Tiffany Tone Tyndall of Santa Monica, CA.

Georgie grimaced. Unappetizing as the facts stated might be, the truth was even more so. But this was probably the worst that he could expect.

Tyndall, regardless of what ticket he ran on, was a lifelong political brigand. Georgie had to deal with him directly only once when Tyndall was State Motor Vehicle Commissioner and a major party fund raiser. Standish Montgomery had become a principal investor in an automotive electronic parts company in Rochester, NY. When the company was engaged in a standoff with its union over contract provisions that would have crippled it for years, Tyndall sought to put pressure on the company by proposing impossible new "safety" regulations for electronic parts.

A resolution of the situation looked hopeless. But when Georgie met with Tyndall at a private dinner in Albany, Tyndall made clear that all would be well if Standish Montgomery would become a "generous supporter" of Tyndall's first campaign for Congress. He also suggested that for all concerned cash was the best form of support. Envelopes were indeed hand delivered to an obscure Tyndall functionary; the regulations proposal died; and the union, confronted with a threat to transfer company operations to a more salubrious climate, compromised.

From time to time, Georgie would hear or read about Tyndall's increasing prowess in raising campaign money. But it was only when Sen. Hobart Thackeray, the state's junior U.S. Senator, died, that Georgie learned the full magnetism of the campaign fund raising art.

Georgie was thinking of retiring and taking on something new: possibly some kind of government service, possibly an ambassadorship in some civilized European capital. Actually, the idea originated with his wife, Alice, whom he truly wanted to please. Alice, his second cousin, was only three years younger than he was; finely bred, profoundly intelligent, rather plain, an accomplished hostess. They were married after her first husband, whom Georgie regarded as an idiot, was killed in a boating accident off Australia. After 10 years of marriage, he increasingly found her the best of companions.

Accordingly, he found himself at lunch at the Hay-Adams across Lafayette Park from the White House talking to the Chairman of the Republican National Party about possibilities and his talents. He certainly could afford the expenses of an ambassadorship. He certainly was qualified for something at Treasury. Based on his loyalty and support and connections, he certainly was deserving. The Chairman agreed with all of this and floated to Georgie's total surprise an alternative suggestion: Would Georgie consider appointment to the vacancy in the Senate caused by the death of Hobart Thackeray?

Georgie rose to the idea like a trout spotting a freshly cast fly on the surface of a clear stream. Of course, he had to discuss it with his wife. Of course. But he made clear that he was ready to serve.

That was on Monday. On Wednesday he called the Chairman and told him "yes." The Chairman said he had already spoken to the President and the Governor and all were agreed. On Thursday the Governor called him and suggested a meeting the following week.

On Friday the Chairman called and reported "bad news." They would have to discuss other possibilities after all. The Governor was going to appoint his campaign finance chairman, Rep. Leroy Harding Tyndall, to the Senate.

Another beautiful autumn day. Georgie, up early as always, practiced yoga for half an hour. He did the Cobra, the Bridge and a Warrior II. He felt particularly pleased with himself for holding a Downward Facing Dog for a full five minutes. He felt so good that he indulged himself at breakfast . He had Jerome prepare for him two high-cholesterol coddled eggs, yolks only, in his silver-lidded English porcelain egg coddler. Alice, who would have counseled abstinence, was still asleep.

The Times disappointed, reporting no departures from the world that would interest him. But that did not depress his high spirits. He had had an unusually big month of such reports. Outside the window the trees were a magnificent yellow and red. His breakfast was delicious.

For years in the past he had viewed his long life as one of narrowly missed great opportunities—opportunities that he felt he most certainly could have managed much better than others. But no longer: Had he, for example, become a billionaire; had he become a Senator; had he married Kathleen, who could say what tricky misfortunes of fate might have battered him? Who could say that he would be happier? Had he been an officer leading troops across the beach in 1944 rather than following his lieutenant as best he could, he might still be in Normandy.

All in all, he was quite fortunate. He had always been, as he would put it, financially comfortable. He had conducted himself for the most part quite honorably despite numerous temptations. He had enjoyed many small pleasures. And he and Alice had finally had thirty semi-regal wonderful months in Europe when he served as Ambassador to Luxembourg.

Georgie felt certain that Dante and Virgil or their implacable surrogates had already installed such people as Brad Howard, Larry Lime and Leroy Tyndall in one or another of Hell's more unpleasant Lower Circles. On the other hand, he felt that he could hope with reasonable confidence for a far better fate for Alice and himself. And, in the meantime, he, Georgie Livingston Standish, was still alive in his 80's doing very respectable Downward Facing Dogs and at the present moment eating an excellent breakfast in a world that looked very beautiful. Yes, indeed!

Teachable Moment Redux

Hell is a city much like London.
—Percy Bysshe Shelley, English poet

Abe went back to his large tent, his terebinth tree and his flocks. Y and His two companions continued on toward the plain where the sinful Cities lay. Along the way, they talked:

Michael: If I may say so, Sir, You certainly played him like a harp.

Y: Why so? I simply agreed to his wishes.

Michael: Yes, but You made him feel that he was haggling You down so successfully.

Gabe: Starting at 50 and finally getting You to agree to 10 and You knowing all along that there probably aren't five innocent people in the entire City. I could barely keep a straight face.

Y: I have great confidence in Abe. Unfortunately, his excessive zeal for compassion and for justice that often has many unintended consequences sometimes beclouds his mind.

Michael: But Gabe is right, isn't he? At best, there are no more than five innocents in that whole rotten place.

Y: That's what we've been told.

Gabe: And, of course, You know the truth.

Y: All such things must be checked out. That's why I'm sending you into the City before I do anything final.

Michael: You want us to see this chap, Lot.

Y: He'll be waiting for you at the gate.

Gabe: And we can trust him?

Y: He may be the only person in the City you can trust.

Michael: So it's really just one, not even five?

Y: We don't know that yet. It's probably four, three for sure. Lot's wife is charming but undependable.

Gabe: And You, Sir, want us to lead them out?

Y: However many innocents you find. Possibly there is only one. So be it. Abe thought 50 maybe. Potentially, of course, there could be hundreds.

Michael: But You don't believe that.

Y: I believe in free will.

Gabe: Whatever happens still happens tomorrow?

Y: Yes. And, in the meantime, be most careful. You're both very attractive, you know.

Somewhere on the Elbe

It is not certain that everything is uncertain
—Blaise Pascal, 17th Century mathematician and philosopher

When you come to a fork in the road, take it.
—Lawrence "Yogi" Berra, 20th Century baseball player

Zachariah Steuben Prescott, retired investment banker and former U.S. Army lieutenant colonel, sat at the bar in the lobby of the Adlon Hotel and listened to the Englishman with the plummy accent talk.

"Haven't been here since the Wall came down," he said. "Last time I was here this place was just a ruin. Nothing left of the old grand hotel but rubble. There was a little restaurant called the Adlon Café. You could buy the most awful coffee and an atrocious stale bun filled with nasty jelly. Nothing but the best for the citizens of the German Democratic Republic."

The new Adlon, a copy of the majestic hotel built in the first years of the last century during the great days of the Imperial Reich, again dominated one side of the Pariser Platz. The refurbished Brandenburg Gate once again opened to the Tiergarten at the front of the square. Unter den Linden, a shabby sad ghost for 50 years, was again a great glittering parade route running from Brandenburger Tor through the reborn heart of the ancient Prussian capital.

"Wouldn't know the place," the Englishman said. "Here for a conference over on the Ku'dam but I told my masters, 'I'll only go if I can stay at the Adlon.' Earned it, you know."

The Englishman never said why when last in Berlin he was drinking bad coffee and eating stale buns on the wrong side of the Wall. Probably negotiating with the Stasi or the KGB. Prescott was certain that he was ex-MI5. Not just some shadowy spook, though. He was too obvious to be anything but someone with rank protected by the code: You don't kill our top chaps and we don't kill yours. Generally speaking, of course.

Prescott mentally smiled, finished his Scotch and left the bar. He had two hours for some private sightseeing before dinner. He walked out the hotel front door and around the corner into the Wilhelmstrasse.

Although Prescott was 80, he was quite fit and his high cheeks were still ruddy. His white hair was parted in the middle. His custom-made clothes hung well on his tall frame. As he walked up the Wilhelmstrasse he could have passed easily as an elegant German of another era. He looked as if he were home. But Prescott, who had traveled extensively on business during his financial career, had been in Germany only once before. That was in 1945. Business over the years had taken him to the Far East, Saudi Arabia and Mexico. When he traveled for pleasure, he and his wife, Sissy, had always gone to warmer parts of the world: Italy, the South of France, Arizona. Some of his ancestors were indeed German; others Scottish, English and French; but all living in America by the early 1800's. This trip to Germany was not a homecoming in search of ancestors. It was a whim. It was a lark. It was a nostalgic guilt trip.

Prescott had been sitting in the library of his apartment in Manhattan sorting his mail when he came upon a brochure promoting what it called "a grand luxury river cruise" up the Elbe. He threw it in the wastebasket; then retrieved it. He read the itinerary. The ship would sail from Potsdam near Berlin. It would stop at Dresden and end at Prague. What really interested him was that the ship would also stop at Magdeburg and at least cruise past Torgau.

"You are really getting eccentric," Sissy said. "I don't do river boats. If you want to revisit your fun times fighting the Nazis, I'll go out to Canyon Ranch and revisit the daily beauty treatments. They have a new one that I love: the hot thyme wrap."

The Wilhelmstrasse, bombed and wrecked during the war and abused during its long aftermath, was once again becoming a home for embassies, mansions and government ministries. As he walked along the newly restored avenue, Prescott was continually reminded of those former glories as well as the Germans' obsessive affinity for order and record keeping.

One block up the Wilhelmstrasse Prescott came to the new British Embassy, an overpowering modern fortress decorated with an enormous steel gate and a huge Union Jack. More than a dozen German and British security guards armed with automatic weapons stood on both sides of the street. German armored cars formed road blocks at the corners.

During the next few blocks, Prescott stopped repeatedly to read historic markers celebrating a wide variety of notable personages, buildings and sites dating from the high-water mark of the Empire in the 19th Century through the final days of the Third Reich and Nazi Germany.

But Prescott was not looking for a memorial; he had been told to look for a building. And on the next block he saw it: one of several large, shabby apartment houses, superficially redecorated examples of the cheaply-constructed warrens that the Communists had scattered throughout the Soviet Union and Eastern Europe to house the working classes. These particular apartments located at Wilhelmstrasse 90-92 had been built over the ruins of Hitler's grandiose Reichchancellery where the Marble Gallery, twice the size of the Hall of Mirrors at Versailles, led to Hitler's ballfield-size office.

Prescott cut through an autoport between the buildings leading to their rear. There he found a parking lot and a plot of land covered with scrubby grass and broken brick. Underneath these were buried the ruins of the Führerbunker from which Hitler commanded the last stand of the Third Reich. Prescott found no historic marker. Nearby Hitler's body had been cremated in a bomb crater after he shot himself. No marker there either.

Prescott returned to the Adlon for an excellent dinner. The next day he took a taxi to Potsdam, drove past Frederick the Great's magnificent palace and boarded the Motor Vessel Queen Sophia-Charlotta for the trip up the Elbe.

The Queen Sophia-Charlotta docked at Magdeburg the following morning, 60 miles southwest of Berlin. The river looked much as Prescott remembered it except the blown bridges spanning the Elbe had been replaced. A new dock was not far from where he and a dozen troops had crossed in rubber boats in April 1945.

The U.S. Ninth Army had raced across Germany from the Rhine covering more than 75 miles a day. An advance recon unit commanded by Lt. Col. Zachariah Steuben Prescott reached the west bank of the Elbe April 11. The bombed-out city of Magdeburg was on the east bank. The Elbe was the halt point where the Americans had previously agreed they would link up with the Russians. But the Red Army was still fighting desperate battles on the Oder more than 100 miles to the east. Unopposed by enemy fire, Prescott's unit crossed the Elbe in the early evening rain to explore establishing a beachhead in preparation for a possible dash to Berlin.

The weather was mild and sunny when, after a large buffet breakfast, Prescott and approximately 20 other passengers from the Queen Sophia-Charlotta boarded a bus at the dock to tour Magdeburg. As the bus turned out of the parking lot and headed in the direction of Magdeburg Cathedral's spires, Prescott reviewed the mini-history provided on the ship.

Magdeburg (pop. 225,000): ancient capital of Sachsen-Anhalt; founded by Holy Roman Emperor Otto I in 973; Cathedral of Sts. Catherine and Maurice, first Gothic cathedral in Germany, started in 1209 on site of earlier abbey; famous Monastery of Our Lady built 11th/12th Centuries; great religious, political, commercial center; switched from Catholic to Protestant (Lutheran) control several times; destroyed during wars of Reformation and Counter Reformation; rose again as great military fortress and capital of Prussian Saxony; became important manufacturing center; destroyed again in World War II by mass bomber raids; suppressed during partition of Germany under the dead hand of Communism for half-century; after reunification, slowly being restored and rebuilt.

The first half-hour of the tour was depressing. The buss drove past long rows of Soviet-style apartments fronted by small scrubby lawns and battered cars. Then came block after block of dreary, haphazardly-built store fronts. The few people on the streets moved slowly and ignored the bus. Despite sunshine, everything looked gray, faces looked sullen.

"Much of what you see, yes, was built under the GDR," Ilse, a German guide in a threadbare raincoat, said chirpily in heavily accented English. "But here on the next block is a special treat: our new superstore."

The bus turned the corner and paused briefly in front of .a block-long two story glass and steel building surrounding a central court. Seedy-looking goods only partly filled the windows. Despite the new construction, the building exuded an aura of failure, poverty and despair, all hallmarks left over from the GDR.

"Magdeburg was heavily bombed during the war," the guide said, speaking as if 'the war' had ended only last week. "Much good rebuilding is underway, yes, since reunification. But we still suffer from the high unemployment in the East."

The bus increased speed, drove into the Old City center and parked in the square in front of the towering dark Cathedral.

"We tour the Cathedral of Sts. Mauritius and Katharina," the guide said. "First Gothic cathedral in Germany. Damaged by bombs, yes, but completely restored. A great pleasure."

Prescott remained alone in the square for a few minutes while his fellow passengers entered the Cathedral. When he last saw it, the great tower was damaged and ghostly against a rainy night sky. The square was littered with rubble. Two German Tiger tanks apparently abandoned for lack of fuel stood near the ancient front portal. Craters in the street were filled with oily water.

Prescott crossed the square with considerably less caution than on his earlier visit. This time he paused to admire the 13th Century carvings around the great west door: Christ enthroned surrounded by Apostles and saints. When he finally entered the huge vault of the Cathedral, a different guide, a young man standing near the beginning of the nave, was lecturing Prescott's shipmates.

"The tower is the highest in the East, 104 meters, the interior length, 120," he said. "We were much damaged during the war but that is not the first time. During the Thirty Years War in the 17th Century we had the sacking of Magdeburg; during the Napoleonic wars the French used the Cathedral to stable horses; under GDR, the Communists wanted to close us up entirely. But, as sexton of this holy place, I assure you much now has been done and there is still much to see."

The sexton, who wore a tan worker's smock, a stained blue woolen cap and a carefully cut beard, paused and swept his arms outward.

"It is too bad," he said. "Your time here is short. You must be sure to see outside the south portal the cloister, at least 1,000 years old; outside the north portal, the famous Paradise Doorway, you must see the Five Wise and Five Foolish Virgins carved no later than 1250; in the nave, there is the magnificent alabaster pulpit where Martin Luther preached; and in the chancel you see the tomb of Otto I, Holy Roman Emperor and called Otto the Great. Also, there is the important sculpture of St. Mauritius. Can you guess what is so important? Of special interest to Americans, I think."

Prescott did not wait to find out what might be of special interest. He discreetly moved away from the group and headed toward the chancel and the oblong marble box in which Otto lay. That is where he had seen a light when he cautiously entered the Cathedral on his first visit.

Unlike today, the floor at that time was strewn with debris, broken glass and discarded ammunition boxes. As he and two non-coms carrying automatic weapons approached the sanctuary they saw that the light came from a large military lantern on the tomb and a portable cookstove beside it. A nun in a blue habit stood at the cookstove, stirring a pot. A large wooden pectoral cross hung from her neck on a rope. She was medium height, rather square; her highly wrinkled but still elegant face indicated that she was at least in her seventies, maybe older.

"Good evening," she said in only slightly accented English. "May I offer you some soup? Tonight we have turnip."

"Are you alone?" Colonel Prescott asked. "Where are the soldiers?"

"All gone," she said. "Most of the people, too. They go south to get away from the bombers and the Russians."

"And you?"

"I stay to watch the Cathedral with only the sexton, Brother Klaus, but he is useless," she said. "And to whom do I have the honor of speaking tonight?"

"I am US Army Lieutenant Colonel Zachariah Prescott and this is Sgt. Philip Costello and Cpl. Edward Mundt"

"I am very happy to see you," she said. "I am Mother Superior Katharina von Hohoenlohe of the Holy Sisters of St. Maurice. Our convent here was destroyed in the bombing raids and the few sisters still living there have left. Tell me, Colonel: are there many with you?"

"An army on the other side of the river," Prescott said. "They may cross tomorrow."

"Danken Sie Gott!," she said and crossed herself. "Then you can save us. You will go on now and capture Berlin ahead of the Russians."

"Perhaps. Do you know what the Wehrmacht has positioned between Magdeburg and Berlin?"

"I know very well. There is nothing. Hitler has sent everything east to the Oder to stop the Russians. The road to Berlin from here is open. I am sure."

"How sure?

"I talked to the general in command of the district only two days ago before he left. He went east. All of the army, too. The general came here directly from Berlin. He received his orders directly from Hitler. There was a conference in that terrible Bunker."

"Who else here might have information? Officials? Deserters hiding out in the ruins?"

"You have all you need to know. I beg you: go back across the Elbe and tell your countrymen to come quickly. You must take Berlin to save us."

"You think it that important that we rather than the Russians capture Hitler?

"Hitler is now irrelevant. Our best generals are already dead or disgraced. Without the generals, he is nothing. He always was. It is Berlin that is important. You must take it for Western Civilization."

Prescott promised to pass on what she said, thanked her and left.

"Don't fail us," she called after him and blessed him with the sign of the cross.

Prescott's wish for an additional source of information was fulfilled as soon as he and his men left the Cathedral. A scruffy tall man in a filthy German officer's coat that hung on him like a blanket was waiting on the steps.

"Mein Oberst," he said. "You have been talking to the Sister von Hohenlohe. Trust me, she lies."

"Who the hell are you?" Prescott asked menacingly.

"A friend of America. I'm Brother Klaus, the Sexton. I live in the cloister. I was coming into the Cathedral when I heard you talking, but I hid. That aristocratic schemer, the nun: she hates me. She knows I'm on to her tricks and false stories. You're not the first American she's helped to meet our Maker sooner than expected."

"And the truth?"

"She told you that she talked to the General. She did. It was General Wenck. I was there. But what he told her was that Hitler was leaving Berlin and going south to continue the war from Berchtesgaden and the Eagle Nest. In the mountains there they have built a great National Redoubt. Wenck is regrouping the 12th Army between here and Berlin to hold the city while Hitler and the bulk of the Wehrmacht escapes. If the Americans take the bait to beat the Russians to Berlin, they will be driving into a death trap. Is Berlin worth 100,000 dead Americans?"

"How do I know you're not the liar?" Prescott said.

Klaus rummaged in the pockets of his greatcoat and produced a much folded official bread ration card. Prescott recognized it immediately. It was one of the delicately forged cards issued by the Army intelligence as a bribe to its German double agents.

Two hours later, still not finding any German troops, Prescott rowed back across the Elbe and reported to Ninth Army headquarters. He said, although Magdeburg was open and a bridgehead could easily be established there on the east bank, that sizeable German forces appeared to be reforming across the Magdeburg-Berlin autobahn. General Wenck, regarded by Army intelligence as one of Hitler's few remaining smart commanders, was believed to be in the area taking command of the 12th Army Group. If true, the butcher bill could be very high.

Prescott, not having slept for more than 20 hours, signed off on a dictated summary of his report and collapsed on a cot in a nearby field tent. When he was awakened hours later by the grinding of tanks and trucks, he found the entire Army in motion. Returning to the headquarters hut, an harried lieutenant told him: "It's on. We're going to Berlin. We're crossing tonight."

"That's crazy," Prescott said. "What's happened?"

"Have no idea," the lieutenant said. "There was a big meeting and the Old Man came out of it hot to move as always. Report is that the road to Berlin is wide open and we can be at the Brandenburg Gate in two, three days, maybe less. The Germans apparently rather have us there than the Commies."

A staff sergeant packing maps nearby shouted over the noise: "Better get going Colonel. I hear they got 200,000 bottles of wine in the cellar of the Adlon Hotel. You don't want to be left out when we start popping that champagne."

Within 24 hours, units of the Ninth had established a bridge-head near Magdeburg. During the next two days, bridgeheads were building to the north and to the south. Then the 83rd Infantry Division threw a pontoon bridge across the Elbe south of Magdeburg and a steady stream of armor and trucks moved across to the east bank.

Meantime, on that day, military censors had submitted to them a wire service news story that began:

> Somewhere on the Elbe, April 14—Units of Lt. General William Simpson's Ninth Army today established major beach-heads on the east bank of the Elbe in preparation for a final dash to Berlin.

The Supreme High Allied Command was not pleased. The censor spiked the story. The intelligence reports from Prescott and other sources had indicated that an American advance on Berlin would be fiercely resisted resulting in enormous American casualties. Gen. Dwight Eisenhower, the Supreme Allied Commander, did not consider bombed-out Berlin to be a major military objective in the first place. On the other hand, preventing Hitler and the Wehrmacht from rallying at the National Redoubt around Berchtesgaden had high priority. So did restraining breakouts in order to maintain the security of a broad frontal advance.

General Simpson was ordered to report to Group Army Headquarters at Wiesbaden. General Omar Bradley, Army Group Commander, met him at the airfield and told him to halt his advance at the Elbe. There would be no race to Berlin.

The bus took Prescott and his fellow passengers back to the ship by way of the Old Market.

"Much damaged," Ilse the guide said. "But still we have for you two famous statues: Our noble Horseman. He has been here guarding us since 1240 although some say he doesn't always do such a good job. And on the opposite side of the square, you see the statue of Till Eulenspiegel with his pointed cap and bells. He is Magdeburg's famous trickster who has been with us for 600 years."

Prescott spent the next two days aboard ship reading in a corner of the lounge or playing bridge in the library with a retired archeologist professor, Henry Hoover, and his two widowed sisters, Antoinette and Gretchen. Prescott showed no enthusiasm for "following in the steps of Martin Luther" when the ship stopped at Wittenberg. However, the following evening he was disappointed to learn that not even a brief stop was planned for Torgau and its castle. If he wished to see it, he was told he should plan to be on deck at 8 o'clock.

Prescott ate early and proceeded alone to the deck. He had no interest in the castle as it came into view. His interest was in the nearby smashed bridge abutment. Here, 13 days after he had crossed the Elbe to Magdeburg, Red Army troops linked up with troops which had been turned south rather than north to Berlin where the Russians still had only fought their way into the suburbs.

Prescott had watched from the west bank as excited, filthy Russian soldiers stripped to their undershorts and swam the river to shake hands.

"Bravo Amerikanski," Russians shouted. "Bravo Komrades. We celebrate. Our brothers are taking Berlin."

The Motor Ship Queen Sophia-Charlotta's next stop on the Elbe was Meissen, but Prescott declined the opportunity to watch the manufacture of expensive reproductions of Augustus the Strong's 18th Century porcelain. Although, as an international banker, Prescott much admired how the King had cut his enormous expenses for Chinese porcelain by stealing the secret Chinese formula with the help of the Jesuits and setting up his own manufacturing monopoly in the Altberg Castle. Prior to that, Augustus' profligate expenses had included giving a regiment of dragoons to the King of Prussia in exchange for a set of 48 porcelain vases.

Prescott remained on board and sat in the lounge reading newspapers and glumly looking out the window at the Altberg oblivious to the daily servings of bullion, tea, cakes, small sandwiches and finally Scotch. He was still sitting there when the daily lecture began. So far, he had avoided these. But this day the lecture began before he could politely escape.

"This young girl is quite bright," Professor Hoover, his bridge companion, assured him from a nearby lounge chair. "I heard her yesterday. She's an historian, but she has a technical background in physics and biochemistry."

The "quite bright young girl" introduced herself as Dr. Emma Schmidt of the University of Heidelberg. She was an attractive woman dressed in tweeds. Prescott guessed she might be in her early 30's, a product of post-war Europe.

"Today we talk about reunification of Germany," she said. "I must be blunt. It has been a disaster. But not so big a disaster as partition. That was the first post-war mistake."

Dr. Schmidt paused to allow her statement to register.

"After partition , with much help from the democratic, capitalistic United States, we Germans in the West built a new and successful homeland. . Behold the great German economic miracle. After partition, with much help from the Communist Soviet Union, Germans in the East built an impoverished prison camp and cynically called it a people's democratic republic. Behold the great German economic sinkhole.

"By the time of reunification, we had in the West what you might expect: a democratic efficient nation of highly productive, aggressive, optimistic Germans. In the East, we had a battered, socialistic tyranny populated for the most part after two and a half generations by beaten-down Germans trained to expect little and to obtain that little from the State.

"Is it any wonder that we now have 18 percent unemployment in a reunited Germany? Is it any wonder that we hear Germans in the East longing for those wonderful good days under the German Democratic Republic and the Communists. Why work, yes?"

Dr. Schmidt spent the next twenty minutes telling economic horror stories about East German inefficiency, ingrained bureaucratic corruption, lack of the traditional Germanic work ethic and increasing West German impatience and arrogance. Then she took a few questions.

"How well do young people in the East and West—people born long after the end of World War II—get along," one of Professor Hoover's sisters asked.

"What do you think is the first thing one German asks another when they meet?" Dr. Schmidt countered.

"They used to ask 'Are you Jewish?'" an elderly man in the front row said, eliciting nervous titters.

"We never, never ask that question," Dr. Schmidt said coldly. "Never. What we ask is: 'Are you Eastie or Westie?'"

"From what you've been telling us, that is probably about the same kind of question.," the man said.

Prescott ate dinner that evening with Professor Hoover and his sisters. They agreed over the paté that Dr. Schmidt's comments were "troubling" and with the turtle soup began to discuss Professor Hoover's last archeological expedition before his retirement.

"One of the newest digs just north of Petra," Professor Hoover said. "Very hush-hush so far but early finds make it look enormously promising. I am very optimistic. I hope to continue being involved as a professor emeritus."

"Henry is always optimistic," Antoinette said. "Look at the way he keeps bidding no trump at the bridge table."

"The early finds at the site give us every reason to have high expectations," Professor Hoover went on enthusiastically. "We have some early Christian holy vessels that are quite remarkable. And even more remarkable are what we are calling the 'Archangel Scrolls.'"

"What on earth are they?" Prescott asked.

Professor Hoover leaned forward and looked at nearby tables apparently to assure himself that no one could overhear him.

"Only two have been translated so far," he said. "They are ancient treatises on the importance of archangels as messengers of God and implementers of God's intent. Specifically, the scrolls talk about the importance of the Archangels Michael and Uriel, but we suspect the activities of additional archangels will be described in the four scrolls that we have yet to unwrap."

"How many archangels are there?" Gretchen asked. "I can never think of more than two others: Raphael and Gabriel. What a great source for crossword puzzle questions."

"According to the Prophet Esdras there are nine," Professor Hoover said. "The other five are Gabuthelon, Aker, Arphugitonos, Beburos and Zebuleon. We don't know much about any of them, but, as I said, we think the unwrapped scrolls will provide us with new information."

"I have never been quite sure about their various roles," Prescott said. "Michael, of course, is the great warrior who leads the heavenly host against evil. But what, pray tell, is Uriel's specialty?"

"Uriel has multiple roles," Professor Hoover said. "He stood with a flaming sword at the Gate of the Garden of Eden to prevent the return of Mankind. At the End of Days, he will hold the Keys to the Pit. Meantime, as other archangels, he has been a messenger of God and an implementer of God's will from the earliest times. For example, Uriel warned Noah of the impending flood. Uriel along with Michael, Gabriel and Raphael are active interveners."

"Your interest as a scientist in the doings of angels is quite amazing," Prescott said.

"Archeology is interested in whatever has interested mankind and I assure you that scientific evidence shows that angels have been with us in one way or another from our earliest days. One of their most important attributes is that they represent overwhelming might and power. Recall Christ's words regarding the option he rejected when he was arrested in Gethsemane: 'Do you think that I cannot call upon my Father and he will not provide me at this moment with more than twelve legions of angels?' Talk about of a heavenly host! Twelve legions! That's 100,000 winged warriors swinging broadswords. Katy bar the door!"

"May I show you the dessert tray?" the waiter interrupted. "May I pour coffee?"

The following morning they arrived at Dresden.

Prescott was first in the diningroom for breakfast. He had had a terrible night: no sleep; then dreams. He was back more than a half century after the war in Magdeburg Cathedral with Sister Katharina.

"Why are you here in this Protestant cathedral? Isn't your order Catholic?" he asked.

"It doesn't matter. The Protestants long ago were right, but now they are wrong. There is only one true faith. This cathedral is God's House. The soup is ready."

As she handed him a chipped mug of watery soup, she said:

"You are Catholic, yes?" she said.

"Yes."

"Then why didn't you do what I asked you to do? What did you tell your superiors? Why didn't you tell your people they could take Berlin and save us? God would not have had it otherwise, I think so."

"I had to do the right thing," he said. "It was hard to know the truth."

"It always is," she said. "Always."

Then he was awake. He lay on his back in his dark cabin. First light outlined the pulled drapes.

Now, sitting alone at his assigned table, he watched Dresden come into view. Sunlight brought into sharp relief the newly restored great dome of the Lutheran Frauenkirche with its golden angel. Beyond it rose the spires of the Catholic Hofkirche and the Royal Palace.

He did not wait for the tour. Shortly after 8 o'clock, he went ashore and walked up from the river on newly-hosed sidewalks past rows of still-closed cafes into the center of the Old City. In the last months of the war, 800 RAF bombers in a single night of vengeance destroyed much of Dresden, the baroque Florence of the North. The U.S. Eighth Air Force destroyed much of what remained during the next three days. Under the Communists, ruins were left unrepaired as an aide memoir to the survivors. Now most of the famous buildings had been restored or were under restoration

Prescott walked past the Frauenkirche which was still surrounded by scaffolding. On the next block, he walked by the porcelain mural depicting the Dukes and Kings of Saxony. At the next plaza, he confronted the great Hofkirche, the royal cathedral adjacent to the palace and tomb of Saxony's ruling family. Inside, at the other end of the enormous nave, a Mass was underway for about 50 of the faithful gathered in front of the rococo white and gold sanctuary. On his right, stood a row of confessionals with signs: FRANÇAIS, ENGLISH, DEUTSCH, POLSKI.

He entered the English language confessional; knelt; heard the wooden slide open and the breathing of his confessor; announced his readiness to confess and requested forgiveness.

"Father, I realize after many years that I have committed a great sin," he began, reciting the speech he had rehearsed to himself that morning while lying on his back in bed. "I helped bring on the Cold War and I feel much guilt for the suffering and death of millions. Now I have come from America late in my life to visit the scenes of my sin and have come to realize its enormity."

A half-minute of silence. Then the priest said in perfect Oxbridge English with Germanic undertones: "Surely, you exaggerate your role, my son. The Cold War was a great curse caused by many things, I think so. But it is good, very good, that, whatever your role, you are contrite. Furthermore you have made manifest your intention by making this personal pilgrimage. You should pray for better understanding of what you have done. As a penance, say 10 Our Fathers and five Hail Marys and pray for wisdom."

Prescott said the words he had known since early childhood: "*Domine Iesu, Fili Dei, miserere mei peccatoris.*"

The priest then gave him absolution. Prescott rose and walked to the front of the cathedral where the Mass had now ended and spent almost an hour on his knees.

The Queen Sophia-Charlotta arrived in Prague shortly before noon. Prescott took a taxi to his hotel, ate a light lunch and hired a driver and car for the afternoon.

Prescott's destination was the Vladislav Council Chamber in Prague Castle. On his previous visit to the great 15th Century hall in 1945, he took part as an aide in a US-Soviet Two Power meeting to discuss military administration of Czechoslovakia after six years of being incorporated into the Third Reich. The meeting did not go well. For Prescott, the most memorable moment was a conversation that he overheard between two American generals as they were departing down the palace stairs.

"Georgie says we should go to Moscow now," the first general said. "Georgie says "the Third Army, alone, with very little other help and few casualties, could lick what's left of the Russians in 6 weeks."

"Don't let anyone hear you talk like that," the other warned. "No one in Washington wants to hear that stuff."

That day the Chamber was crowded with long conference tables and many large flags. Now it was empty except for several small tourist groups being told in several languages about the Second Defenestration of Prague: the pushing of two Catholic imperial governors out of a nearby window in 1618 by Protestant Bohemian assemblymen and the start of the Thirty Years War. Later the tourists would be shown the site of the Third Defenestration of Prague: the window through which Czech Foreign Minister Jan Masaryk, a leading anti-Communist patriot, was apparently pushed in 1948 by the Communists to usher in Soviet domination of Czechoslovakia for nearly the next half century.

Prescott wandered through the Chamber to the adjacent Royal Reception Room. At first it appeared empty. Benches covered in red plush marched from the door to the front of the room and a high gilded railing. On the other side of the railing, a large gilded chair with a red plush seat stood alone. It was the 15th Century throne of the Hapsburgs. Light streamed through the windows, momentarily blinding him. Then, as he turned, he saw that he was not alone. A tall blonde man of indeterminate age was standing in a corner, but now came forward and smiled the confiding smile of someone with a shared secret. He wore an elegant black suit and a red tie with small gold crowns. He carried under his arm a thin black leather case stamped with an obscure gold coat of arms.

"You're late, Oberst Prescott" he said. "I've been waiting. May we talk a bit? No one will bother us at this hour. Here, let us sit up front in the first row."

The man walked forward as he talked and led the way to the front of the room, sat on the bench in the front row and, still smiling, proffered a seat to Prescott.

"Have we met?" Prescott said, hesitatingly. "I don't recall..."

"Years ago," the man said. "At Magdeburg. We spoke briefly after you met with Sister Katharina. It was wartime, of course, and my clothes were not so well pressed nor was I so well barbered as I recall."

"Brother Klaus," Prescott whispered. "On the cathedral steps. You gave me some very bad advice."

The man laughed pleasantly.

"No, no," he said. "I gave you the very best advice if I were to accomplish my mission at that time. But, as you will remember, it almost didn't work because of your General Simpson. Free will can be such a problem. Your General so wanted the glory of taking Berlin. He would have been perfect, too. Better even than the great Georgie Patton, maybe; although maybe not so colorful. But clearly your General Simpson knew how much it would have meant to have the American flag flying over Brandenburger Tor instead of that bloody Hammer and Cycle. Fortunately, we managed things despite General Simpson."

Again he laughed pleasantly and patted Prescott's shoulder as if they were sharing an enormous joke.

"Eisenhower and Bradley were delighted with the story I gave you and others about Wenck and his fictitious 12th Army Group so ready to kill 100,00 Americans. That was icing on the last big propaganda cake that Dr. Goebbles baked: the phony National Redoubt. Let the Russians have Berlin! Let them have Prague! Just so long as the Americans could maintain their play-it-safe broad front and cut off the dreaded National Redoubt. And what was wrong with that anyway? They won the war, didn't they?"

Prescott started to speak, but Brother Klaus held up his hand.

"Let me make two more points," he said. "First, the Germans, of course, knew what was happening and longed for last minute salvation from you Americans. The Red Army horde had already pillaged, raped and murdered its way across Poland and much of Prussia. Millions of Germans were fleeing before those animals as they crossed the Oder and started for the Elbe. And that was only the beginning of the long, terrible night of peonage to come.

"Second, this was precisely the Plan. Seldom in the long sorry history of sinful mankind have I been given a clearer set of directions. There they were: The Russians already under a curse of heaven; the Germans recognizing only too late the depth of their truly satanic bargain. Achieving salvation must always be possible, but who would bet at that time on epiphany with such abysmally failed mortals as these."

Again, Prescott started to speak. Again, Brother Klaus held up his hand.

"It's over. That's the good news. We had them all writhing in this earthly hell for 50 years. Hitler and Stalin, those monsters of evil, have been exorcised; half of Europe ground to dust; once more, Sodom destroyed. And now we try anew as so many times before. Behold, as we are wont to say, I have told you!"

"Who are 'we,' may I ask?" Prescott said. "Who are you?"

"I think you know, Mein Oberst. You prayed for wisdom in Dresden. Your prayer is now answered."

"You appreciate that most people would simply call you mad and walk away," Prescott said.

"But you won't. At the end of your life, you are filled with guilt about what happened here and about your role in it. You think you failed. And the need for penance and forgiveness brings you back on this pilgrimage with a contrite heart. Therefore, you know that, whoever I might be, I tell you only as much of the truth as you need to hear and can bear at this time. But remember wisdom is progressive."

"I once asked you how I could know you weren't a liar. I ask you that again."

"I was sure you would. That is why I brought something to show you. I have it here in my briefcase. But this, unlike my old double agent ration card that so impressed you, is no minor thing. It is very old and very precious. Therefore, first I must warn you, Mien Oberst, it is never wise to put God to the test."

Prescott was silent for a moment; then he sighed resignedly.

"Of course," he said. "Nor will I."

Brother Klaus nodded and patted Prescott's shoulder a second time.

"Good," he said and stood up. "An interesting room where we meet. Holy Roman Emperors of the German Nation used to hold court here; some of them holy, some not so holy; they sat in that chair over there. Another story, of course."

Prescott turned and looked at the high gilded chair emblazoned with a carved Hapsburg double eagle. . When he turned back, Brother Klaus was gone, leaving him with the problem of deciding the identity of whom he had met assuming that a meeting took place at all.

The following morning Prescott flew home from Prague. When he entered his apartment that afternoon at about 4 o'clock New York time, Sissy, back from the Golden Door that morning, was sitting in the living room drinking tea. After a week of expert pummeling, exercise and beauty treatments, she appeared to glow.

"Zach, darling," she greeted him. "So wonderful to see you. Did you have a marvelous time?"

Miracle at the Bridge

Once the symbolism had been accepted, the unicorn became even more real than the ostrich or the pelican.
　　　　　—Umberto Eco, *Art and Beauty in the Middle Ages*

"No?"

"No!"

"Really?"

"Really!"

The two men sat almost hip to hip eating lunch at Harry's Bar. Outside the sky over Venice was nacreous. Misty drizzle hung in the air. The *aqua alta* filled much of the Piazza San Marco, sloshed through low-lying walkways, drowned five-star hotel lobbies, washed over steps and into doorways along the Grand Canal. Lines of tourists in lumpy clothes walked in tight single file on raised platforms.

"You can't be serious about this," the older of the two men persisted. As he talked, he ate the last of his tagliatelli verde and wiped his large lips and guardsman's mustache. "We have at least two candidates who need your kind of speechwriting. You can write your goddam travel book anytime."

The younger man, who normally had the sallow, pained look of a Byzantine icon, appeared even more sallow and pained than usual.

"It isn't a travel book," he said. "It's about the myths of Venice."

"Of course, it's about myths! Your specialty! And you're wasting it on this Italian swamp."

The older man, whom all viewers of TV expert panels knew as Bobby Spoon, the American political campaign wizard, sighed and contorted his mouth in exaggerated disgust as he turned his head out of habit toward a non-existent camera. Seeing a waiter instead, he signaled for the check.

"Gotta get out of here," he said. "My plane for London: leaves at 4 o'clock: have dinner there tonight with a couple of *Daily Mirror* editors; back to Washington tomorrow. So, Chucky, what do you want me to tell 'em at the shop?"

"Tell them what I told you," Chucky said. "Tell them that I have decided to stay on after the European Union conference here and finish leg work on my book. It won't take long: couple of months maybe at most. Call it an extension on the accumulated vacation time you owe me but always have a reason why I can't take it."

Bobby signed a credit card chit that would have covered a normal lunch for a family of ten and squeezed to his feet among the close-packed tables.

"You called it, my boy," he said. "I tried. The great world rolls on. It isn't easy to hold open the best seats for long. I hope we can find remunerative employment for you after you finish indulging your literary fantasies."

Chucky watched Bobby Spoon move majestically toward the door, a well-tailored dark blue giant with ruddy cheeks framed by his great blonde mustache and thinning, meticulously coiffed white hair. Spoon lingered a moment in mid-passage to enrich the grinning and bowing maitre'd, then slipped along the bar and into the misty afternoon.

Charles "Chucky" Francis Ziegler was no Robert "Bobby" Spoon. The latter, a champion at all times of the main chance, had developed a uniquely packaged product called "Bobby Spoon" into a Washington political legend. If you wanted to get elected to something; if you wanted to be appointed to something; if you wanted special self-serving legislation passed, killed, or stalled; if you merely wanted to hang out with the famous or at least appear in the same room; if you wanted any of these desirable so-called special K Street services, you called the consulting firm of Spoon & Munder. But don't ask for Munder who suffered from early executive demise. Just hope you can get to Spoon.

Not that Bobby was always successful. But he was successful considerably more times than not. And, when he was not, there always were insurmountable difficulties for which Bobby would convincingly blame the client. Instances of epidemic client stupidity and maladroit speech that had occurred despite all of Bobby's hard work. Or, Bobby often found that despite his repeated warnings the program had been grossly underfunded.

Nor were these wonders when they did occur accomplished most times through Bobby's talents. His talents were primarily sales and the recruitment of people with great genius and low business drive; people, all given chummy nicknames such as Chucky and Tommy and cosseted smotheringly by Bobby, who would labor in the back rooms of Spoon & Munder's luxurious offices located in a converted 19th Century abattoir on the bank of the Potomac in Alexandria, VA. There the great magic always packaged and labeled "Bobby Spoon" was produced.

Chucky was a super nova producer of such magic. He was perfect for the role. He was an introverted, generally uncertain, generally pessimistic crypto-scholar; a polymath; a speaker of a number of languages but with limited facility for small talk. He always apologized to clients for any attempt to sell them anything. He was painfully unassertive. But he had an amazing ability to boil up huge pots of common dross; artfully stir in ingenious strategies; add a pinch of venom, a dropper of tears or a bit of wolfbane according to taste and need. The result: the perfect soundbite; the most memorable, 50-word crusher; the win-the-day, tearful defense. And, when he blended a large number of his soundbites into a creamy literary stew, he could produce a winner- take- all speech complete with drum rolls, soaring strings and trumpets.

He had been doing this with increasing facility at Spoon & Munder for kings, captains and wealthy commoners for more than a decade. But recently three disturbing things had happened: he found himself celebrating his little noted 35th birthday at an antic farewell party for the Administrative Assistant of a congressman recently indicted for funding a vacation home with kickbacks from a housing for the homeless program; his live-in girlfriend, Didi, used that depressing landmark occasion to advise him that she was leaving to find happiness in the much larger condo of a lobbyist for the tort bench; and one week later he was again passed over for an open Senior Vice President slot at Spoon & Munder because, as Bobby told him, he clearly should not be wasted on a lot of marketing baloney and client hand-holding. Chucky could only concur; but he also knew that at Spoon & Munder the experts in marketing baloney and hand-holding ate much higher on the food chain than he did.

Chucky began pondering seriously for the first time in years about what life might be like beyond the Potomac's insulated teeming shore. After a month of ponder, he made a decision. He would try writing—on company time, of course—what he told himself and two potential but skeptical publishers in book cover blurb language would be a new kind of book shining fresh light on the past: not history, not journalism, not historic fiction, but what he thought of as slices of history which, in the tradition of Thucydides, would further enhance true understanding.

He would explore the mysterious connection between happenstance, myth and national greatness. And, based on his eclectic reading and early Catholic education, he had decided that Venice would be a perfect subject. He would take as slices across the city's 1,500-year history key miracles and myths that had powered the city's destiny. Much historic data had been published; much was buried in the city archives; and he would bring it all into a new, revealing new focus with fictional conversations and, where necessary, fictional characters—all true to the spirit of the historic data. His working title: "Six Miracles in Venice."

Chucky planned to do major initial research on the book when he visited Venice on a two week trip as an advance man for the European Union conference. His job was to prepare background comments for one of Spoon & Munder's clients, Leighton Sims, U.S. Deputy Secretary of the Treasury. That was not an easy assignment. Leighton Sims had joined the Administration after a successful career as a New York banker. He was considered to be brilliant. All Spoon & Munder releases said so. He also was deeply suspicious of all foreigners and had trouble disguising it.

Chucky was always a quick study. He spent less than a week talking to Italian editors and American correspondents in Rome, Milan and Venice; he spent two days on the Lido with the advance men setting up the conference at the Excelsior Hotel; then, having what he thought he needed, he devoted the rest of his time in Venice to research for his book. The research went well; so well, that he had decided to stay on to continue it.

This afternoon, as he sat finishing a double espresso at Harry's after Bobby's departure, Chucky again reviewed his plans. The Euro conference had only one more day to run. Leighton Sims, making liberal use of comments provided by Chucky but now fully adopted as his own invention, had survived reasonably unbattered by the media; he had been personally congratulated on his great success by Bobby Spoon who had flown in the night before solely for that purpose; and he would leave that afternoon for Washington.

Chucky, free to pursue his new interests, would move out of the Lido and move into a flat he had rented in Castello. The flat was only a brief walk to San Marco and the Marciana Library, keeper of the precious archives of the long defunct Republic of Venice. He rose from the table, nodded to the smiling maitre'd whom Bobby had all but ennobled and walked the few steps to the vaporetto landing. Five minutes later he had disappeared in the mist, crossing the Lagoon to the Lido to say farewell to the Hon. Leighton Sims and congratulate him on his brilliant handling of the press.

Father Pietro Mocenigo, a thin man with a dark complexion and a black goatee, had a modest, shadowy office on a back corridor of the Marciana Library. It belied his position. After 20 years as a curator primarily for the more than 1000 years of correspondence between the Vatican and the Serrenissima, he could find almost anything among the rarest books of the Marciana and the immense Archives of the Republic. Father Mocenigo was a Dominican, but on this particular day he had chosen to dress in elegant well-cut clericals rather than the white robe of his order.

Chucky sat across from Father Mocenigo at an oblong, Gothic table piled with many books and files of various colors and age. On one wall, hung a small Madonna and Child that could have been a Bellini. A large etching, a copy of Veronese's "Apotheosis of the Battle of Lepanto," covered much of the wall behind Father Mocenigo. A leaded glass window in the third wall looked out on a shaded inner courtyard decorated with broken marble antiquities.

"Your chosen topic is most interesting, Signor Ziegler," Father Mocenigo said. "Venice was indeed powered by what many today would call great myths. But you must understand that for us, the citizens of the Republic, these were not myths at all. People are not empowered by myths; they are empowered by history. And Venice with all its buildings and streets and art is a great memory bank where that history is stored ready for recall and use."

"Please call me Chucky, Father."

Father Mocenigo looked at him with displeasure and forbearance.

"Maybe later," he said. "Today I prefer Signor Ziegler. Where have you started in your research?"

"St. Mark and the stealing of his body."

"Ah," he said and smiled. "That is an error. The place you must start in the case of Venice is quite appropriately at the start: the founding of the City on the islands and the marshes. As documents in the archives clearly state, the City was founded in 421 A.D. on the Feast of the Annunciation. The first Venetians, of course, were Romans fleeing from the invading barbarian mongrels on the mainland to the protection of the islands and marshes that lie across the Lagoon. The Lagoon was always our protection until the end. "

"Very interesting, Father. But what proof can there really be of that date?"

"It is clearly stated many times in the archives. Moreover, what day could have been more appropriate? The Venetians repeatedly saw how they were protected and favored by Mary, the Mother of God. "

Father Mocenigo smiled a small, enigmatic smile. It was a smile that could have appeared on the face of a Venetian ambassador bowing perfectly before an Emperor or a Pope 1000 years ago.

During the next several days, Chucky, at the suggestion of Father Mocenigo, read various documents from the archives and visited a half dozen of Mary's churches in search of understanding the force that Father Mocenigo said she instilled in the Venetians. In the Church of St. Zaccara, Chucky stood for almost an hour before the altar looking at the magnificent purity of Bellini's Virgin and Child flanked by four saints: St. Jerome reads a book, St. Peter carries one, Saints Lucy and Catherine look on. All are flooded with light: the special light of Venice. He stood even longer in the enormous nave of the church of the Frari before Titian's altarpiece; there he saw a far more sophisticated Virgin looking down on an armed warrior holding a standard and on a captured Turk. In the Ca' d'Oro Galleria, he saw a sophisticated Mary in an elaborate Renaissance bedchamber appearing only mildly surprised at the arrival of a magnificent Archangel Gabriel. And at the *Accademia*, he saw a concerned Mary being implored by a committee of saints to intervene in behalf of Venice against the naval might of Islam at the Battle of Lepanto.

Each picture and its setting made clear that Mary in one way or another had special concern for the welfare of the Republic and its people. This message was enormously enhanced by the knowledge that Mary for the most part looked down at the viewer from the original sites where the Venetians had always seen and worshiped her. As Chucky pursued his visitations to these sites, he began to form an interesting parallel: the similarities between the early Venetians so favored by Mary and the Puritan Saints of Boston who first proclaimed that America was a city on a hill, a beacon for all mankind, a special place protected by God. And was not the truth of the Puritans' words there for all to see in the years to come? Was not America and its entire works a nation advancing under divine protection as had Venice?

The next day, as Father Mocenigo had also suggested, Chucky visited the Scuola San Rocco to view Tintoretto's quite different "Annunciation." Unlike so many sunlit, joyful scenes, Tintoretto's is dark and soaked with terrible but great purpose: the Archangel Gabriel rushes from the sky on his godly mission; Mary is dramatically startled but clearly knowing: the Mary who favors Venice is to be the Queen of Heaven.

"Why did they need St. Mark?"

Chucky was back in Father Mocenigo's office. Rain had been falling on the City for hours. Even in this inner chamber, they could hear the horns warning that *acqua alta* was expected. The Piazza San Marco would be flooded again.

"To lead them in battle," Father Mocenigo said. "To be their special saint. Mary made them a race apart, a special people. But even the Venetians understood that they could not expect to monopolize her time. St. Mark the Evangelist was also a mighty saint. But he could be theirs. And, of course, so he was."

"Some would say it was a body snatch. They smuggled him out in a basket of pork."

"Venetians have always been clever. But your description, Signor Ziegler, is superficial. St. Mark was buried in Alexandria: that was one of the five great patriarchies of the Early Church. However, Islam had captured Alexandria. St. Mark was a prisoner of the Infidel. We liberated him and brought him here where God had promised he would return forever. Read the signs that are still everywhere: *Pax Tibi Marce Evangelista Meus.* God said that to Mark when Mark came here during his earlier travels."

"Truly a myth, a story."

"No: It is truth. So many people have written it; so many people have believed it; so many people have acted on it; so many people have seen miracles and interventions because of it , all of that makes it true; a special kind of truth, but for millions over many years, a great truth, a sacred truth. Venice has always been driven by many such sacred truths. They are all there in our memory encapsulated in the City itself."

Chucky half closed his eyes. He felt momentarily as if he were sitting in a meeting with Bobby Spoon. What you saw, you didn't; what you didn't see, you saw. But that was mostly the pseudo-magic of opportunistic spin. This was different: If someone saw something even close to what they wanted to see and enough people heard something about it enough times and their memory continually recalled it, then it was real for them. And, because it was real, they acted that way and then it was as real as most things.

"Tell me about the miracles and interventions," he said.

"They are all documented here in the State Archives. The best known, perhaps, was St. Mark's miraculous reappearance after his very body was lost. He disappeared when his basilica here was destroyed by fire in 976. It was rebuilt at the time and then, in the second half of the 11th Century, a much larger one, a copy of the Basilica of the Holy Apostles in Constantinople, was completed on the same site and rededicated, of course, to St. Mark. But now there was no relic, no body. For three days, several thousand Venetians led by the Doge prayed for St. Mark's return. Suddenly, in the middle of a Mass, they heard a loud noise: a piece of a column near the high altar had fallen away and the saint's arm protruded. St. Mark was removed from the column and buried under the altar. You can see the column today. Go look at it."

"You believe this?"

"They did. Why shouldn't I? Why shouldn't you? Well, maybe not now, but later perhaps. May I offer you an aperitif? Considering the *acqua alta,* I suggest you join me here in the library for lunch. Our dining room is not without some merit. Note the word 'some.' I always favor precision."

They lunched in a small, much gilded refectory on minestra di funghi, piccata al Marsala, insalata verde and a bottle of Fruili. As they drank espressos, Father Mocenigo talked of interventions.

"There have been many," he said. "All of the major military victories, all of the great diplomatic gains, all of the elections of Doges and any subsequent successes that they might have had—these were certainly the direct work of St. Mark. And St. Mark was usually involved even when other saints who favored Venice came into play. The flag of St. Mark was always personally handed by the Doge to his captain general at the beginning of a war. Venetians charging into battle and leaping from the masts of galleys on to city walls cried 'Marco! Marco!' And paintings all over Venice commemorating great victories invariably depict the Doge and his commanders giving thanks to St. Mark."

"And the Virgin, of course. And sometimes St. Jerome and St. Nicholas. And other saints.

" But particularly St. Mark. I can see you are learning. More wine? I think from now on I shall start addressing you as Charles Francis."

Leaving the Marciano Library, Chucky walked across the Piazetta, looked up briefly at the grinning Lion of St. Mark and the statue of St. Theodore on the tops of the two great Roman columns there. Formerly the columns were used for public display of the bodies of traitors hanging by one foot from a rope stretched between them, but today only a ragged gaggle of tourists squatted in their shadow looking like a pile of human refuse. Chucky stood at the Logetta by the tower of the Campinile. From the top of the great tower, the Archangel Gabriel looked to the sea. Below, in the Logetta, Doge Bartolomeo Gradenigo had sat on a throne and received from a fisherman one of Venice's greatest treasures, a gold ring given to the fisherman by St. Mark.

"On a terrible night in 1341," Father Mocenigo had told him, "St. Mark awakened a fisherman and asked him for a ride across the Lagoon: first to the Church of San Georgio Maggiori where St. George was waiting for them, then to the Church of St. Nicholas on the Lido where St. Nicholas was waiting; then through the Lagoon and into the Adriatic. A huge storm was blowing and headed for Venice; at its center, a great boat filled with devils surged toward them. But the three saints stopped the devils and the storm; saved the city; and, before disappearing, St. Mark gave the fisherman the gold ring for the Doge. It was this symbolic ring that the Doge used every year on the Feast of the Ascension. That was the holy day when he sailed in the golden Bucintoro in great ceremony out beyond the Lido to marry Venice to the sea."

"Something of a stretch," Chucky said. "I suppose the gullible believed that he threw the same ring into the sea every year?"

"He used a gold replica, of course. The original ring from St. Mark was reverently preserved at the Scuola Grande di San Marco. I assure you, Charles Francis, that if you insist on being picky about these things you will never understand."

Chucky crossed the Piazetta to the Doges' Palace and entered by the Porta della Carta. Above the gateway, the Doge who commissioned it 600 years ago knelt attentively before still another of St. Mark's winged lions. Inside in the Palace courtyard, hundreds of tourists moved forward as a pullulating, buzzing mass. Most looked like refugees in a scratchy World War II newsfilm. Many wore exercise suits and clunky athletic shoes. Noticeable by exception were four young Japanese schoolboys in gray flannels and monogrammed blue blazers. Chucky rented an electronic guide, plugged a hearing device into his ear and moved slowly with a crowd of scruffy, overweight gawkers through the great courtyard, up the steps of the imposing Scala d'Oro and into the first of the Grand Chambers.

"Buongiorno!" The electronic guide said in his ear in pompous Italian. "You have entered the Sala della Quattro Porte. Here, in this most beautiful room and in the next, the Anticollegio, ambassadors, petitioners, great lords from throughout the world waited for an audience. Be sure the wait was deliberately long. That way they had time to view with awe and think about the many great paintings on the walls and ceilings. See how again and again these beautiful masterpieces show always ever so clearly the galleys of Venice crushing their enemies and always you see the special relationship of Venetians with the greatest of the saints."

Chucky found it hard because of the continually moving river of sightseers to remain in any one spot to study the paintings that covered the gilded walls and ceilings. He found it equally difficult to hear his electronic guide over the tutorials in a half-dozen languages being shouted around him by guides for various half-listening groups. He settled for steadily moving with the flow from room to room and straining to hear the voice in his ear.

"You have entered the Sala del Collegio. Here, in this *superbo* room what essentially was the Venetian Cabinet met to run the Venetian empire; to decide the fate of the Mediterranean, the center of the world. Particularly note Veronese's masterpiece, *Venice Enthroned*....You have entered the Sala del Senato. Here the Doge met with Venice's 200 senators to debate and decide on great policies of state. Particularly note Tintoretto's *Descent from the Cross* with two Doges....You have entered the Sala del Consiglio dei Dieci. Here the Council of Ten met to guard the Republic from treason and spies and to handle the most secret diplomacy. Particularly note on your left Veronese's *Juno Offering Gifts to Venice*....Here in the Saletta dei Tre met the dreaded three Inquisitors of State, the supreme protectors of state secrets Note, as appropriate, the austere paneling of this small room....Now we enter the greatest room of all, the Sala del Maggior Consiglio. Here, before the Doge on the high platform at the end of this enormous chamber, would sit more than 2000 nobles, all of the male patricians over 25 years of age whose families were in the Golden Book. Their most important function was the election of the Doge, himself. Above where the Doge sat you see Tintoretto's enormous masterpiece, *the Paradise,* the largest painting in the world."

"So sad," Father Mocenigo said. "Always difficult to scrape beneath the layers of our current commercial populism. Possibly what I have here will help and then you can make another visit."

They were seated again in his office at the Marciana. On the table was an ornate blue leather file box closed with old silk ribbons. Father Mocenigo, with great care, untied the ribbons, opened the box and spread a number of documents before him.

"These are 15th Century construction records from the *Arsenale*," he said. "Here is a letter in official Latin from a certain Senator ordering the building of a new galley. And here are the *Arsenale's* plans: See, the galley is to be a trireme, 160 oars in three banks, a powerful warship to be called the *Nicoló* in honor of St. Nicholas. Here is a work log showing that construction of the *Nicoló* began at the *Arsenale* factory on the 23rd of April, it was completed and outfitted on that marvelous assembly line in one day; on the following day it was manned by officers and 500 free Venetian rowers, and within the week joined four other new galleys in the Lagoon and sailed to meet a Venetian fleet off Cyprus. All work, of course, was at the Senator's personal expense as was the custom in financing all *nobili* personal services to the Republic."

Chucky returned to the Palace the next day before it opened to a large waiting crowd of sightseers. Father Mocenigo had written by hand for "Dottore Charles Francis Ziegler" a special library scholar's *permesso* that would allow him to wander about the empty Palace trailed only by a bored guardian in an ill-fitting fancy uniform.

In the courtyard, he was able in the early Venetian light to wander up and down the Scala dei Giganti, the grand ceremonial staircase; then stand between the colossal statues of Mars and Neptune, symbolizing Venetian power on land and sea. Here was the coronation site of Doges.

He walked slowly up the Golden Staircase and sat for a long time in the Salle della Quattro Porte. Without the rude crowds, without the grating noise, without the heat, he could transport himself backwards more than 500 years. He was an ambassador waiting to see the Most Serene Prince. And, as he waited, he looked at the dark paneled and gilded walls and ceiling, the great spread of Renaissance paintings, the huge carved marble doorways: the message was unmistakable: only a 21st Century elitist fool could miss the point and dismiss this place as some Italian Disneyland for obese trippers; this place had been the locus for centuries of enormous, controlling power and faith that even now was palpable, that even now hung in ghostly shreds in the corners and corridors and secret places of the palace.

As he strolled from grand chamber to grand chamber, seeing and feeling today much that he had missed on his previous visit, he was overwhelmed by one message: Venice was favored, Venice was great, Venice was unique, Venice was rich, Venice was unbeatable.

In the Great Council Chamber, his mind filled that enormous, magnificent hall with 2,000 patricians in their red robes. The Doge sat at the other end of the hall on the raised platform. He wore a golden robe and the *corno* on his head. Beside him sat his councilors in scarlet, the Three Inquisitors in purple, the *Savii Grandi*, the Sages of Law and War in blue. And over their heads across the entire wall was Tintoretto's panoramic *Paradise*.

Retracing his steps, Chucky, still trailed by his still bored guardian, came again to the Room of Four Doors. Here he looked closely for the first time at a painting depicting King Henry III of France arriving in Venice on a famous visit in 1574. Henry is being greeted by the Patriarch and a man dressed as a Doge wearing the *corno* and a golden robe but if he had been dressed in black clericals he could have been Father Mocenigo.

"Yes, yes," Father Mocenigo said later when asked about it. "That was Alvese I. Nothing special, of course, in that ancestry. All of our old families, or most of them, have at least a Doge or two. We happen to have seven. But only Pietro and the first Alvese were particularly important. All long ago. I don't expect that we shall have any more."

Father Mocenigo held up a warning finger and shook it.

"You must beware of romanticism," he said. "These Doges whom we called The Most Serene Princes were semi-divine prisoners of Venice, not the absolute monarchs whom Venetians always feared they might become. They were elected from the *nobili* by the *nobili* by an incredibly complicated process that began with sending a patrician into the Piazza to recruit the first young boy whom he saw to draw ballots from an urn. But, when the Doge was finally elected, he was bound by a mountain of red tape. It was the *nobili*, the patrician merchant princes, to whom the galleys ensured control of world trade...who never lost to the barbarians...who, buoyed by an unshakeable faith in God and the special role of Venice, were operating as a group in the sanctified name of the Doge, making him more powerful than the Basilius in Constantinople...the Holy Roman Emperors...the Popes. These Venetians, always buoyed by their sacred truths, were the true sovereign heirs to the Roman Republic."

Early morning on the Molo: At the water's edge, one gondolier in a red and white striped shirt. No tourists. A luminous Canaletto sky over San Georgio. Chucky walking slowly from the Piazetta.

Out in the Basin of the Lagoon no boats except in Chucky's head. He sees the way it was the day they left in 1104 on the Fourth Crusade. Forty galleys flying banners fill the Lagoon; the Doge's galley in the lead flying the huge gilded banner of St. Mark. The Doge, Enrico Dandollo, blind, 94, stands on the castle. Trumpets blare. More than 5000 oars move in unison. Cheering Venetians jam the Molo and the Riva. Only days before they had jammed the Basilica to hear plans for the Crusade and roared back: "We consent! We consent!"

The scene changes. It is late afternoon. One galley sails into view. Trumpets. Drums. It has news from the East. Blind Gondolo and the banner of St. Mark led the Crusaders over the walls of Constantinople. Byzantium has fallen. Venice is *Lord of a Quarter and a Half Quarter* of the Roman Empire.

Morning again. Almost 500 years later. The year is 1571. Same luminous light. The Molo, the Basin, the City are at the height of their magnificence. Again, a single galley, the *Angelo*. One hundred and thirty eight oars propel it into the Bacino of San Marco. The usual trumpets, drums. People on the Molo and the Riva do not have to wait to hear the news. The *Angelo* is dragging behind it in the water the shredded green banners of Islam. The Venetians, Don Juan of Austria, the Holy League, a cross on every mast, have won the greatest naval battle in the world since Actium 1500 years earlier. They have destroyed the Ottoman Navy at Lepanto.

"For the half millennium between the overthrow of the Byzantines and the sinking of the Ottoman fleet at Lepanto," Father Mocenigo said, "the Venetian empire waxed and prospered. It was the leading naval power of the West; feared and hated of course, but highly effective. It's great governing secret was that no one trusted anyone too long with power; the Council of Ten watched the nobili and the nobili watched each other; no one stayed in office more than a matter of weeks or months except the Doge and he was the most closely watched of all."

They were standing by one of the great windows of the Library, looking out at the Piazzetta and the pink side of the Doge's Palace.

"What went wrong?"

"The Sultan had already stolen most of their trade routes and empire in the East; the Spanish and the Portuguese had already found a better route to India by sailing around Africa and had discovered the Americas; the Venetians couldn't fight the Ottoman Empire alone any longer and the rest of the Europeans were so busy fighting among themselves that they didn't come together against the Sultan until it was too late for Venice."

"But what about Lepanto?"

"It was a huge victory, but it was a last performance: a magnificent encore turn. The great engine—the merchant power of Venice—was failing. She survived another 200 years on her diplomatic wits, her high culture and her miracles. Western Civilization, of course, finally stopped Islam on the walls of Vienna. But it took almost another century to get around to it."

Chucky wandered the city streets. One by one he sought the exact places from where Venetians during 1500 years had drawn strength; miraculous events that formed and reinforced their being, their conduct, their history. His guide for the moment: a series, a *teleri,* of Renaissance paintings called the "Miracles of the Holy Cross" depicting miracles performed by a fragment of the Cross enshrined in an ornate gold reliquary. The Chancellor of the Kingdom of Cyprus and Jerusalem had donated the priceless relic in 1369 to one of the Venetian merchant confraternities, the Scuola Grande di San Giovanni Evangelista. The wealthy Scuola 140 years later commissioned the nine paintings of the *teleri* with six notable Venetian artists. Each of the eight surviving paintings depicted along with the miracles a location in Venice still easily recognizable.

"You do not have to be a Dominican scholar to understand these things," Father Mocenigo said. "You are a Catholic. That is enough. Maybe later we will make you a good Dominican.

"Don't I have to be a good Catholic first?"

"Not necessarily, but it would help."

Chucky entered the Piazza San Marco, looking toward the gleaming Basilica. This is where he would have been standing in 1444 to view the Procession on the Feast Day of the Holy Cross painted by

Gentile Bellini. The reliquary, carried under a red canopy by white-robed members of the confraternity, is passing. A merchant kneels before the relic and prays for the life of his dying son. The son recovers immediately.

Continuing his search, Chucky lost his way. After crossing two canals, he found himself in a narrow empty alley; high grimy house walls closed off much of the sky; ancient shutters blocked most windows. He backtracked; turned down another narrow street; turned again into another at random; at the end, a canal and a stone bridge. Then, as he crossed it, he saw what he was looking for: just up the canal was a second stone bridge. It was the bridge of San Lorenzo.

It may or may not have been the same bridge that Bellini painted and the water was no longer blue, but otherwise there was little change. From where Chucky stood, he could see the entire scene:. A procession with banners, taking the relic of the Holy Cross from the Scuola to the Church of San Lorenzo, is stopped on the bridge. The crowd presses in on the procession; the reliquary falls into the canal; but miraculously it floats. The Queen of Cyprus and other *nobili* stand at the edge of the canal. Many of the faithful dive into the water, but they fail to recover the precious relic. The gold reliquary clearly eludes them. Then the Grand Guardian of the Scuola enters the water. The elusive reliquary floats into his hands and is saved.

Chucky pressed on to the Rialto and its famous bridge over the Grand Canal; a bridge of stone with the Virgin on one end and the Angel Gabriel on the other. This is not the old wooden bridge of the miracle painted by Carpaccio. But otherwise the view is very similar: many of the same buildings crowd both banks of the canal; people jostle everywhere; gondolas jam the water. High on the left in a loggia of the patriarchal palace, the Patriarch of Grado uses the relic of the Holy Cross to heal a madman.

Ten minutes away in the spacious Campo Santa Maria Formosa, Chucky sat at a table outside a trattoria making notes and drinking a double espresso. It was mid-afternoon and he was only half way through his tour of sites of Holy Cross miracles. He would do the second half tomorrow. Across the campo, schoolboys on their way home shouted and pushed each other. Two attractive French women with packages from Gucci sat at the only other occupied table. A peddler of newly-minted crude Canalettos slept in a chair beside his cart. Chucky, recording his 16th Century explorations, was oblivious to his surroundings when he felt a sharp vibration in his jacket pocket and heard a low buzz. When he snapped on his cell phone and put it to his ear, the voice was unmistakable.

"Chucky! How goes the good fight?"

"Just fine, Bobby. Where are you?" he said warily, fearing Bobby was back in Venice, sitting at the bar at the Gritti, making dozens of phone calls, sending emails, holding court.

"In Washington, of course," Bobby said. "Just walked into the office. Haven't even had coffee and we already have one hell of a problem."

"Sounds like every morning."

"No, no, now listen to me, Chucky, I mean A PROBLEM. OUR CLIENT, no names, but you know whom I mean when I say OUR CLIENT: He needs a speech; probably be the most important speech in his life; probably the most important this decade; and only one guy I know can write it except myself, of course, and I'm already committed."

"Whom do you have in mind, Bobby?"

"Screw you, Chucky. You want me to kiss you, too. Listen, this is YOUR speech. And I know YOU can knock it out in a couple of days: take a week if you need it. Then you can take an extra month to work on your damn book. I tell you it's that important. It's BIG! OK? Now can I count on you, you rotten bastard? I know I can. Call me on the secure line at 2 PM my time and I'll fill you in."

He was gone. Four hours later, back in his apartment in Castello. Chucky was patched into the Executive Office Building on a secure conference call with Bert Montgomery, lead White House speech-writer, and Bobby Spoon. Montgomery explained with a heavy dose of condescension that OUR CLIENT needed a speech that would justify major military action; rally the electorate in a mounting patriotic fervor; clearly differentiate OUR CLIENT from his pusillanimous predecessors, and, as Bobby interjected, drive all political opponents back under their rocks. Several "first drafts" had already been written and rejected. Now Chucky was to write a new " first draft." Montgomery and Bobby, who apparently were the authors of the original "first drafts," would take it from there.

"What's wrong with what you have?" Chucky asked.

"Nothing," Montgomery said. "It says exactly what he wants to say. He just didn't like it."

"Bertie's right," Bobby said. "What we have is OK, but Our Client says it doesn't sound like Churchill. Frankly, I thought it was a good mix of Lincoln and Franklin Roosevelt, but we always give OUR CLIENT what he thinks the situation needs. As I told Bertie, you, Chucky, can give us Churchill."

An Air Force lieutenant colonel flown by chopper from the U.S. base at Aretino delivered the two "first drafts" to Chucky at his apartment shortly before midnight. The drafts, all on flashpaper, were in a secure box controlled by a continually changing code card. Any attempt to open the box without the code of the moment would result in immediate incineration of the contents.

Chucky read the drafts immediately, but after an hour of doodling on a computer screen with three bad starts, he quit and went to bed. He did little better the next morning and by 10 o'clock he went for a directionless walk that brought him to the Scuola Grande de San Giovanni Evangelista.

He stood a long time in the oratory before the altar looking at the 700-year old Reliquary of the Holy Cross. It was a magnificent piece of craftsmanship, a maze of twisted precious metal. In the crystal monstrance he could see the small piece of wood from the True Cross. Could not the power of such a relic help him? He found himself praying that it might.

Later that day he leaned on the rail of the San Lorenzo bridge. The water below was dark and empty. But maybe he saw something floating there in an erratic pattern; something that he could seize if he reached out in his mind; a precious vessel; a precious idea. And then, as he stood on the bridge, words and phrases came to him in orderly procession:

> *The founders of America said it was a City on a Hill that held up a beacon of liberty for all mankind. Today America is a mighty nation on a mountain that holds up even higher the same beacon against the evil dark.*
>
> *We have always had people amongst us who mocked God. And in recent years that mocking has been louder than usual. But, it has been truly said, God will not be mocked. America is a God-fearing country. Jehovah—Yahweh—is in our genes. He will guide us and forgive us. But ,in the end, if we disregard Him, if we fail, He will abandon us and try again with others as in the past.*
>
> *Many voices continue to chant the tired litany: we must parley, we must trim, we must compromise. Have they never heard of the long spoon required to sup with the Devil? I say there is no spoon long enough on earth today to make supping possible with the evil men who seek to return civilization to intellectual darkness, widespread ruin and early death.*

We Americans have not come so far and achieved so much to be mugged in the world's back alleys by ignorant vandals and garbage-can cut throats. We forget: Such are always with us, lurking on the shadowy periphery of civilization, waiting for a chance to loot the homes of the weak and the muddleheaded and the overly comfortable.

One of America's greatest warriors, General George Patton, rests in an endless military cemetery in a forest glade in Luxembourg. He lies under a simple white cross at the head of a vast army of the dead, American warriors who saved Europe from Nazi Germany. There, near the Rhine, they lie athwart one of Europe's ancient invasion routes. Today, as I think of that cemetery, I think of a poem called "Drake's Drum." It's about another great warrior, Sir Francis Drake, and the saving of England from invasion by the Spanish Armada. One verse says:

"Take my drum to England, hang it by the shore
Strike et when your powder's runnin' low;
If the Dons sight Devon, I'll quit the port 'o Heaven,
An' drum them up the Channel as we drumm'd
them long ago."

If, in our present mighty struggle, the armed might of America must move again to defend Western Civilization, I am sure that on that day someone will sound a drum and Georgie Patton will quit the Port of Heaven and be with us standing as always in a lead command car. And, as in the past, America will prevail.

"You say words came to you when you were on the Bridge of San Lorenzo," Father Mocenigo said. "You didn't have them; then you had them. Wonderful words, powerful words, great words, memorable words. Where did they come from? Was God thinking out loud and you overheard Him? Surely, that is not impossible."

"Probably not. But at one point, I thought I saw the flash of a sacred vessel moving through the water. That can't be true."

"Well, why not? The canals are so very ancient. Who is to say what has fallen into a canal in 1500 years?"

"I finished the speech yesterday. It was sent to Washington last night on the top secret line. I understand they like it. As soon as Bobby Spoon was certain of that, he called it 'pure Churchill'"

"What will you do now? Go back to work on your book, I would hope. You seem to be making excellent progress. I've thought that in a few more weeks I might start calling you Charles."

"No question that I want to continue. The book grows every day in my mind. But we could be involved in a new global war next week. I'm being told rather forcefully that I'm needed."

"And are you? "

"Maybe. Maybe. I may possibly be more able than others to help keep what you refer to as our sacred truths alive."

"Well, that could be correct. Certainly, it is very flattering. Will you go?"

"A good 12th Century Venetian would, wouldn't he?"

"A good 12th Century Venetian would have to go or be exiled and disgraced."

"Fortunately. those good Venetians didn't have to deal with Bobby Spoon."

"You are misled. Venice has always dealt with many Bobby Spoons. And often to its great profit."

"Then I suppose I have no choice. I would not want to be exiled and disgraced even if only in my own mind. But this may all blow over. I will be back in any case."

"Of course you will. You must. There is so much more instruction possible for you. With help from St. Mark and Our Lady, Venice will be here."

Father Mocenigo essayed one of his small, sardonic smiles. The gauzy afternoon light partially illuminated his thin face, the picture behind him of the Battle of Lepanto and its saints along with Chucky who was standing by the window looking into the enclosed garden.

"I would hope," Chucky said.

Cleansing the Sepulchre

In the beauty of the lilies Christ was born across the sea,
With a glory in His bosom that transfigures you and me:
As He died to make men holy, let us die to make men free,
While God is marching on...
    —Julia Ward Howe, *Battle Hymn of the Republic*

I shall...subdue the isles and countries of the West. I do not want to lay
down my arms until there is no longer a single infidel on earth.
    —Saladin, Muslim general, 12th Century Sultan
    of Damascus and Cairo,

For where God built a church, there the Devil would also build a chapel.
    Martin Luther, *Table Talk*

Kyrie, eléison
Christe, eléison...
        Order of Mass (Introductory Rite)

Adam Drake was old when he visited the Holy Land for the first time. It was not a pilgrimage. It was business.

Adam, who was 85, had fought in three wars; helped found a successful robotics firm; served as an occasional Pentagon consultant under four Presidents. He was well-thought of or feared, sometimes both, by those he encountered as he bustled about the world. He exuded a palpable certainty based primarily on belief in three things: American destiny, Roman Catholicism and U.S. Marine Corps honor. Now, half-retired, he was still in demand in the development of the new so-called electronic battlefield. That was why he was in Jerusalem where war was never far away.

His first day, after a large buffet breakfast at the American Colony Hotel, he met under conspicuous security at the Knesset with four of its Members who carried military portfolios. The following morning at the American Colony he met with a military advisor to the so-called Quartet "peace process" group. The Quartet maintained headquarters there in shabby offices brightened by a silver-banded swagger stick belonging to the late General Edmund "Bull" Allenby, World War I imperial British liberator of Jerusalem and victor over the Ottoman army on the field of Armageddon. Later in the week Adam would travel into the Negev Desert to observe work at a highly secret Israeli Air Force installation east of the Dead Sea between Masada and Beersheba. But his afternoon schedule on his second day he kept open. He told his Israeli hosts that as "a somewhat flawed Christian" he wanted to visit the "the holy places."

Adam had a guidebook recommended by a Dominican friend and two maps of the Old City, one highly detailed, the other a highly abbreviated and inaccurate pocket version. Adam's military mind was very good with maps and guides. He studied the big map and the guidebook in his room at the American Colony after eating lunch alone in the hotel garden, developed a plan for the afternoon, committed it to memory and changed from his business suit into what he thought to be a more appropriate costume. He dressed as if he were going for a walk on the English moors. He wore a tweed jacket with leather patches on the sleeves and the left shoulder and carried a heavy Irish blackthorn stick. He stuffed the smaller of his maps one into a coat pocket for backup. He probably would never look at it. He had almost perfect recall. He also brought along for inspecting ill-lit ancient chapels a small high-beam Special Forces flashlight.

Leaving the conspicuously guarded hotel courtyard, he turned left and walked briskly down the old Nablus Road, only a century ago a country byway, now crowded on each side with buildings and walls. Behind one of the walls on his right was the Anglican Cathedral of St. George. Behind another wall on his left was the Dominican Basilica of St. Stephen the Martyr. Behind still another lay the Garden Tomb that Major General "Chinese" Gordon enroute to being butchered by natives in the Sudan in the 1880's insisted was the "true" site of Christ's crucifixion. Then directly ahead was the Old City wall and the Damascus Gate with its towers built on Roman ruins.

Adam did not go through the Damascus Gate. Instead, he turned to his left and walked along the wall about 1000 yards until he came to Herod's Gate. This was where Godfrey of Bouillon, Duke of Lower Lorraine, and his knights broke through into Jerusalem on the First Crusade. They pushed a huge siege tower against the wall, lowered a bridge and screaming "Deus vult!" stormed over it, cutting down the Muslims on the battlements. Adam settled for walking through the gate.

His next objective was to visit the site of the Crucifixion and Christ's Tomb in the Church of the Holy Sepulchre; then the Citadel, fortress palace of Jerusalem's successive military masters: the Herodians, the Romans, the Crusaders and the Caliphate. He knew by choosing to enter the Old City through Herod's Gate he was not on the most direct route. He would have to pass through the Muslim Quarter, a labyrinth of ancient narrow streets. Back at the hotel, he had plotted his way through that maze to the Via Dolorosa. Once there he could follow it much as Christ had while dragging a cross to Golgotha. But soon Adam was lost. A surging crowd jammed the dark medieval streets. Dubious one-room shops crammed with tourist shoddy lined both sides. Nothing looked like his pocket map. And as he shuffled forward in a viscous river of alien humanity he was an obvious target for Arab shopkeeper after shopkeeper who shouted at him in mutilated English: "Hello, hello...where are you come from?... see my shop...all good things...best prices...you like coffee?"

Then, just ahead, next to a shop with bins overflowing with miniature stuffed camels, ill-made olive wood Jerusalem crosses and baseball hats with stars of David, possible salvation appeared. There, inside a closed glass door, he saw a well-dressed Arab sitting in a low chair, smoking a thin cigarette. The man, surrounded by Orthodox icons and ivory-embedded tables and boxes, was reading a newspaper. Adam entered the shop and closed the door against the cacophony in the street. The man folded his newspaper and smiled a voiceless welcome.

"You speak English?" Adam asked.

"Of course," the man said with an Etonian accent that was clearly a product of the old British Mandate.

"I fear that I am lost," Adam said.

"So are we all, I am afraid," the man said. "Do sit down, dear boy. Possibly I can help."

"Thank you, but I have very little time," Adam said defensively and remained standing while leaning on his stick. "I am looking for the Church of the Holy Sepulchre."

"If that is what you are looking for, you are almost there. I can direct you. But first do sit down. Let me tell you about my icons."

"I can see them. Very nice. But I am not a collector."

"With these, you could become one. And possibly more. All of these are the very best, all 18th Century or older. Of excellent provenance. I buy them from poor Jews who bring them from Russia. I ask few questions. That is how I have such attractive prices."

"Possibly another day," Adam said. "If you could tell me the way to the Church of the Holy Sepulchre..."

"Of course," the man said. "I will give you a shortcut. Turn right outside my shop, go back up the street to the first very narrow alley on your left. Be careful: it is easy to overlook. Simply follow it to the Via Dolorosa and then look sharply for the signs of the Stations of the Cross. They, too, are easy to overlook if you do not know what to look for."

"Thank you," Adam said, started for the door and then turned back. "Your icons do appear to be very fine."

"Yes," the man said, "I have an undoubted Saint John the Baptist from the Sinai. But another time, perhaps. Come back. I will be here. I will look for you."

Outside in the street Adam moved slowly with the pack for a few minutes; then on his left he saw what looked like a dark forbidding slit between two buildings. But when he reached it, he could see that it was about two shoulder widths wide and that there was daylight at the far end of a dim passage. Instinctively gripping his stick in one hand as a weapon and his blinding flashlight in the other, Adam carefully made his way down the alley. Twice he flattened himself against the grimy brick walls: first to allow two fat Arab women with covered faces coming the other way to pass; then, a tall Orthodox priest with a great beard.

Emerging from the other end, he again entered the slowly moving pack of shoppers, tourists, pickpockets, layabouts and groups of pilgrims that seemed even thicker. Again Arab merchants on both sides of the street shouted at him. Smells of cooking and unwashed bodies, old dust and heat filled the street. But at least now he knew he has moving in the right direction. Just ahead he saw a small sign in Arabic, Hebrew and English identifying the location as *Ecce Homo*, the First Station on the Via Dolorosa at the site of Herod the Great's Antonia Fortress.

For the next half hour Adam moved step by step firmly imprisoned within the crowd, reassured only twice when he saw a sign at the Third Station where Christ fell for the first time and at the Fifth where Simon the Cyrenean was recruited to help Christ carry the cross. The afternoon turned unpleasantly warm. The general noise level in the tight street increased. Daylight diminished. At the end of the street near an ancient pillar he saw a sign marking the Seventh Station where Christ fell the second time. Here, at the time of the Crucifixion, was the Gate of Judgment that led outside through the Herodian city wall to Golgotha. But now the street moved to the right over the buried rubble of the gate and the wall to the entrance of the seething, overcrowded courtyard of the Church of the Holy Sepulchre.

What Adam was looking at was still the much-repaired Crusader church. Originally in 70 AD the Tomb and Golgotha were buried under the ruins of Jerusalem when the Roman X Legion at the conclusion of the Jewish Revolt leveled the Second Temple, the walls and most of the city and then encamped there. Subsequently, 65 years later the Emperor Hadrian rebuilt Jerusalem as a Roman city called Aelia Capitolina and covered the site of the Tomb and the Crucifixion with a magnificent pagan Temple to Venus. That was torn down by Constantine the Great when in the 4th Century he converted to Christianity and replaced the pagan temple with the Church of the Resurrection, the first Church of the Holy Sepulchre. That, in turn, was burned in the 7th Century by the Persians; restored by the Byzantines; thoroughly wrecked in 1009 by the Muslim Caliphate; restored again only in part by the Byzantines; greatly rebuilt and expanded by the Crusaders in the 12th and 13th Centuries; and repeatedly repaired over the next 800 years after various desecrations, fires and an earthquake. Beneath this ancient layered pile of a basilica lay the holiest shrine in Christendom.

To reach it Adam faced a churning sea of people through which he must pass. Milling about him were knots of priests and friars: Greek Orthodox, Franciscans, Abyssinians, Copts, Armenians; dozens of Israeli soldiers, both men and women, Uzzi automatic weapons casually slung on their shoulders; groups of tourists wearing red, green and yellow baseball caps; singing pilgrims; Arab vendors peddling crosses and crudely decorated scarves; armed Israeli security guards lounging against the walls.

Finally reaching the church door, he found the interior even more crowded, noisy, chaotic. Most disturbing of all, it was almost filled with a darkness that was deep, supernatural, stygian, aphotic to the point of being almost palpable. Slowly, as his eyes adjusted, he was alarmed to see through the murk men and women on his left crawling on the stone floor and pushing past each other to kiss and touch the rectangular Stone of the Anointing. A hundred yards farther on in the gloom, he could make out the ugly little temple, the ercule, covering the Tomb itself. Low hanging, dully-glowing lamps of Eastern Orthodoxy all but blocked its entry. A press of people six deep surrounded it, waiting for admission. Many carried lighted candles; many others, digital cameras. Doubling back past the Stone of Unction, Adam sought to go up a flight of stairs to the Greek Chapel of the Crucifixion and the Latin Chapel of the Deposition. But he failed. A large group of Orientals wearing orange waterproof jackets emblazoned with Jerusalem crosses completely blocked the stairwell. Their leader held a large red paper flower in the air to mark her position. Digital cameras flashed in the darkness. Adam fled to the courtyard. He was appalled. This was desecration. This was blasphemy. Where was sanctity? Where was piety? Where in this of all places was respect for others? Hieronymus Bosch would have loved it.

Outside in the sudden sunlight the crowd was still an inchoate mass. Adam slowly pushed his way back toward the street. Halfway there he found himself shoved together with two young Franciscan friars talking in English.

"Is it always like this?" he asked.

"Unfortunately most of the time," the shorter of the friars said.

"Late in the day is usually better," the taller advised.

"Or try 4:30 in the morning for our early Mass," the first said and both laughed.

Adam clenched his mouth in annoyance but, by the time he reached the street, he had made a new plan. He would proceed to the Citadel, but return to the Church of the Holy Sepulchre late in the day.

The route to the Citadel was only slightly easier than the route to the Church of the Holy Sepulchre. The heavy flow of people moved toward him; he moved against the flow by walking on the side of the street while seeking to ignore the persistent commercial pleas of the shopkeepers. His progress was slow, but in a half-hour the gantlet ended. He emerged in the square in front of the Citadel and the remains of the Jaffa Gate.

Adam climbed to the top of the Citadel's great 2000-year old tower. From here, he looked directly across the city at Temple Mount and the Dome of the Rock. Two-thousand years ago this tower was new and he would have been looking at the grandeur and the glory of the Second Temple. He could easily have heard the trumpets announcing the sacrifices. At the heart of the Second Temple and, since the Muslim conquest in 650 AD, at the heart of the Dome of the Rock rose the exposed peak of Mt. Moriah: there Yahweh had stopped Abraham from sacrificing his son, Isaac, and a rectangular empty indentation in the bare stone indicates where the Ark of the Covenant once rested in the Holy of Holies.

Adam slowly descended the tower stairs to a parapet overlooking the many layered archeological excavation at the center of the Citadel. On his left behind him on a wall stood a standard of the X Legion. Below him, amid the jumble of walls and ruins, he envisaged the palpable presence of Herod, of Pompey, of Godfrey and the Crusader kings, of Omar and Saladin. And the risen Christ walked among them looking amused.

Back on the street, he stopped at a lunch counter near the Jaffa Gate and drank a glass of newly squeezed orange and pomegranate juice. The gate was actually an open passage; in the early years of the last century the Ottoman Empire, eager to curry favor with Germany, removed the wall through which the gate once passed so that the German Emperor, Wilhelm II, could enter the Old City on horseback during an official visit. General Allenby entered the Old City through the same enlarged gateway after the Ottomans surrendered in 1917.

Adam looked at his wristwatch. It was already 4 o'clock. Time to go back. The Church of the Holy Sepulchre closed at 7:00. He found the return to the church somewhat easier. The crowds moving through the narrow streets had lessened and now most people were moving towards him and the Jaffa Gate. But the shops were still open and the Arab shopkeepers appeared desperate to make end-of-day sales.

"Cheaper now!" they shouted. "Best prices it's true...my customers always happy...come honor my shop."

Shortly before 5:00 he reentered the courtyard in front of the half-blocked main door to the church. The courtyard was only partly filled. As he crossed it, he was temporarily blocked by Russian tourists whose leader, an elderly fat man holding a red umbrella in the air, was trying to organize them . Dodging around the Russians, he was sucked into a group of Ukrainians in purple jackets taking pictures of each other. Beyond them a dozen armed soldiers lounged near the outside stairs that lead to the Golgotha shrines. Three tall bearded Orthodox priests in high black hats argued near the main door as Adam entered.

The church was even darker, even more stygian than it had been on his first visit. But as his eyes adjusted he was pleased to find that the crowds to a large extent were gone. Only two women, their heads covered with voluminous scarves, and an Orthodox eastern Rite priest were prostrated at the Stone of Unction. A short line waited at the Tomb. Ambient noise and the dank odor of an unwashed mob had greatly diminished. He no longer felt that he was moving through a cloud of grime.

He walked past the row of huge Crusader columns in the nave and at its apse came to the stairs that led down to the highly ornate Armenian Chapel of St. Helen and its crypt where St. Helen, Constantine's mother, found the three crosses of the Crucifixion. Except for an Armenian priest who was trimming large candles in the chapel's great sanctuary, the chapel was empty.

Adam sat on a marble bench in the sanctuary and watched the priest silently move from great candle to great candle. Finally, finishing his task, the priest genuflected toward the altar, crossed himself backwards in the Eastern style and departed. Adam, now alone, felt for the first time that he was in a holy place.

He sat in the choir for a long time, mesmerized by the silence and his surroundings. When he rose from his seat, he saw the ancient stairway that lead to the crypt. The stairway was dark. He used his flashlight to edge down its stone steps into what actually had been a royal Jewish quarry dating back to 700 BC. Great limestone blocks were taken from here for the first Temple. It was under rubble from such blocks that the crosses used to crucify Christ and the two thieves had been discarded.

The small low-ceilinged room was surprisingly illuminated by several modern floodlights. There were two altars, one Latin, the other Greek. A life-size black statue of Helen holding the Cross stood over the first. The second was an ironwork railing surrounding a floor mosaic where a half dozen vigil candles fluttered. A red sanctuary lamp hung from the ceiling. A folding chair was the only furniture.

Adam sat in the chair, bowed his head and prayed for the first time since he had arrived in Jerusalem. When he started to get to his feet, he changed his mind and remained seated. He felt totally exhausted from his afternoon of struggling through crowds. He would rest awhile. In minutes his head nodded down and he slept.

The crypt became cold and he dreamed that he was in Korea again on the Yalu River. The Red Chinese had come into the war. It was winter and he led a Marine company in constant combat back down the Korean peninsula to Seoul. At the end of the long retreat, they marched into camp carrying their dead and wounded, turned around and helped fight the Chinese to a stalemate. Just before he awoke, he was shouting something about air support and "gooks in the trees." The only light in the crypt came from the red sanctuary lamp and two vigil candles. He felt rested but realized with alarm that he must have slept for some time. He looked at his watch. It was almost midnight; the church had been closed for hours.

Using his flashlight, Adam now began a cautious retreat up the stairs from the crypt, through the Armenian Chapel where only a garish sanctuary light burned in the darkness and up the stairs to the ghostly darkness of the main church under its great domes. No one was there. The darkness except for the red sanctuary lights near various altars was complete. Nothing stirred. The air was cold and close. Silence packed the chamber.

He walked past the Tomb and the Stone of Unction to the main door. It was bolted and locked. There was no bell to ring for help. There was no alternative exit in sight. He doubled back into the church.

He was rewarded. Standing alone in the darkness and silence of the rotunda not far from the Tomb he could feel at last what he had come to feel. There, not 20 feet away, Christ had risen from the dead on a spring day just outside the city walls. Here in this rotunda kings and captains had kneeled. And suddenly he could visualize what he had only read about: Godfrey of Bouillon, Robert Duke of Normandy, Raymond Count of Toulouse and the other surviving leaders of the First Crusade coming from the smoky, bloody streets through the great doors, tears in their eyes, the *Te Deum* echoing around them.

On his right, his flashlight picked out the door to the Latin Chapel of the Franciscans and he walked there. Inside, he found a sizeable chamber lit only by a simple sanctuary lamp near the altar. There were many benches in front of the altar and high on the far wall hung a row of relatively modern Stations of the Cross. Adam sat down on a bench while deciding whether he would try again to find an unlocked door to the church or simply wait until it reopened in a few hours. It was at that moment that he realized that he was not alone. A man wearing a broad-brimmed hat was sitting nearby in the dark.

"Good morning," the man said in precise, foreign-sounding English. "You are here early."

"Not by choice. I'm locked in," Adam said.

"Apparently you didn't hear the bells," the man said. "Our Greek brethren always ring little bells. "

"Apparently very little. I was in St. Helen's quarry. Now I find the main door bolted, but, unless you're also locked in, you must know another way out."

"Ah, well, I can come and go; unfortunately there is no way out for you. But the church will reopen in a few hours for early Mass. Meantime, you can stay here and we can chat. My name is Eusebius Hieronymus Sophronius. Call me Jerome."

The man moved closer on the bench and adjusted his robe. He did not proffer his hand.

"Adam Drake," Adam said, looking at his watch and resigning himself to three more hours before he could leave. "I assume you work here."

"Only part time," Jerome said. "I used to engage in a lot of scholarship near here. Translations. And then translations of translations.

But now after a lot of years I am more of a general consultant and troubleshooter."

"I sympathize. My situation today is much the same."

"You are a scholar?"

"No, no. I am a U.S. Marine and a technologist, but now I, too, am a consultant, a so-called troubleshooter."

"Then you must be helping our Jewish brethren in their many troubles. Tell me what you think: Will they ever solve them?"

"I think they can," Adam said. "Based on the strength of the Israeli Army and Air Force, I think they may be near a solution if their leaders don't waffle."

"Yes, perhaps. But it all depends on God's Plan, doesn't it? And He doesn't tell us, does He?"

Jerome laughed sarcastically, leaned over and patted Adam's hand to emphasize what he apparently thought was a tremendous joke. For a moment, Adam could see him more clearly. His hat and robe were red and his face looked familiar but Adam couldn't place him.

"You probably have been here many times," Hieronymus said.

"No. this is my first visit. A few days here in Jerusalem."

"Then you should take the time to see more of the Holy Land while you're here. At least a trip through the desert."

"I will tomorrow. I'm going to Beersheba."

"Perfect. I assume you go to the IAF base at Navatim. Give yourself time to see nearby where Abraham planted the tamarisk tree and invoked the name of the Everlasting God. Later Jacob in a dream there saw the Stairway to Heaven and God repeated to him the promise of the Covenant.

"I doubt that the latter are on my schedule."

"A pity. But at least you have been to some of the holy places here in Jerusalem. How do you find them?"

"Frankly pretty awful. I can't get over the crowds and how they behave, particularly here in this church. It's a scandal. It's an offense. This is not supposed to be Disneyland. The exhibitionism is outrageous.

Jerome nodded and sighed. "Many of the faithful would agree. Particularly the faithful from the West. But don't be too hard on our attractions here. This very place, as I'm sure you know, was only open rubble when our Lord was crucified and rose here. You would have liked the first Basilica of the Resurrection when the Emperor Constantine built it here in the 330's. Constantine built great basilicas. But only a few parts of that church survive after many unfortunate vicissitudes. The Tomb and the Stone of Unction have been replaced a number of times. The ones we have today are only 200 years old. For some this place absolutely bare would be enough; others need artifacts. And just what those are and how they should be presented is heavily burdened I fear with ecclesiastical politics. Of course, from the beginning politics have intruded here. And, in the greater scheme of things that we hope for, what does a little bureaucratic desecration and chaos matter? Our Lord, who knew chaos from the beginning, died here for man's sins. Our Lord rose here. But his Kingdom, the Kingdom we seek, is elsewhere."

Jerome smiled fleetingly. "Besides, by being locked in, you are blessed. You will be here at the best time. Very soon the Franciscans, the Custodians of the Holy Land, celebrate early Mass in this chapel. Only a few of the faithful will attend at that hour and, I assure you, they will behave properly. Moreover, this chapel is really the most important and sacred place. It was here, you know, that our Lord first appeared to Mary Magdalene making manifest His resurrection."

As the man talked on, always with a sardonic edge, Adam recalled where he had last seen his face. It was in a portrait of St. Jerome at the Frick Mansion in New York; an El Greco over the mantle in the mansion's Living Hall. In the painting, St. Jerome appeared not as he often did: an aging, holy scholar sitting in a library in a cave or monk's cell with a lion at his feet. El Greco painted St. Jerome as a wily, red-robed Cardinal, a counselor of Fourth Century Popes and Bishops.

"I can see from your expression that you think you may have recognized me," Jerome said, apparently quite delighted by the idea of discovery.

"You do seem to have an amazing resemblance to a famous portrait by El Greco," Adam said.

"Which one? There are several."

"The one in the Frick in New York."

"Ah, very flattering, very authoritative, not very pious, but you have a good eye. Usually, unless I look as if I'm half dead and have a lion at my feet, no one recognizes me. Most times, that's preferable. Best you keep that in mind."

"I shall," Adam said. "Who would believe me?"

"Certainly not your Jewish clients. As I remember, I share the wall at the Frick with some interesting company: Holbein's portraits of two of Henry VIII's Lord Chancellors, Thomas More and Thomas Cromwell. Both beheaded. More is a saint now. Cromwell most certainly is not."

"El Greco painted you to look something like a Lord Chancellor yourself."

"Not exactly. El Greco probably was thinking of my role as confidential secretary and librarian to Pope Damasus the First and of the counsel I often gave to his successors. But he also has me holding the *Vulgate*, my translation of the Bible into Latin from Greek and Hebrew. That was much more important than my counsel which I admittedly gave freely and which was not always welcomed. I could never be a Lord Chancellor anyway. What they do most of the time really isn't very important. The same goes for most princes, presidents, prime ministers and dictators."

"That isn't an opinion generally held."

"Well, I exaggerate for effect. Always have. Lord Chancellors have free will, of course, and that's important for the whole human race. But what snares mankind is its marriage of convenience with the world. It's all Caesar stuff. However, God's Plan is still God's Plan. Sometimes you might call them, to paraphrase that arch devil Lenin, God's useful idiots. What all these puffed up Lord Chancellors do is make choices that push events one way or another within the much bigger program."

"Events like the Second World War or the Spanish Armada or the rise of Islam or...?"

"Come, come! All events that could have gone one way or another," Jerome said, waving a hand in dismissal. "They affected millions of people's lives positively or adversely, but the important thing is how those people and their descendents conducted themselves. That is the game that is always afoot. That is God's game."

"So whatever happens, no matter how brutish, how evil, how destructive, is OK?"

"Evil is never, as you say, OK. But evil is always with us and evil has its uses. Evil serves as heaven's catalyst for behavior and development of virtue. The test is what you do before or after that really matters. In my day, Alaric sacked Rome! Rome! Unthinkable! The end of the world! Here in my monastery in Bethlehem I did what I could to help refugees fleeing the mayhem. They came here beaten, penniless. But that did not mean I didn't recognize that Alaric and his barbarian looters and rapists were only an inevitable event and that we, the Romans, had failed. We loved the things of the world too much and too long; our leaders corrupt; our generals, weak fools; our legions, foreigners brave only on parade and then only for cash."

Jerome smiled again, this time bitterly, and struck his chest with his fist, one of his favorite gestures. He said: "I wrote very clearly about all of this to my old friend Heliodorus, the Bishop of Altinum. Possibly you have read some of my letters. Even in English translation, the warning is unmistakable. I told Heliodorus that I had long felt that God was angry yet we did nothing to appease Him and that I shuddered when I thought of the folly and catastrophes of our time. For the last 20 years of the Fourth Century Roman blood was shed daily throughout the Empire, our great cities and lands pillaged and plundered by barbarians: Goths and Huns, Vandals and Marchmen; our matrons and virgins, virtuous and noble ladies made the sport of brutes; bishops made captive; priests slain; graves of martyrs despoiled; horses stalled at Christ's altars. By 410 there was nothing to stop Alaric. Triumphant Evil swept Rome away. So sad."

Jerome glared for a moment, and then he laughed. "Now the good news. It really wasn't the end of the world. When more promising players emerge from the ruins, God always tries again. And He did."

"Is that why ruins can seem so attractive?" Adam interjected.

"Yes. Of course. Anyone with a good mind is attracted to ruins. Go to Egypt...go to Rome...go to Berlin...go to rotting castles in Europe and seedy mansions in America. Human triumph and failure are palpable in such places. Signs of sin and redemption are stamped on the broken stones and tattered silk. Our mouths taste sour and sweet. Ruins remind us that we are mortal; that the glitter of the world passes away. At the same time, they buoy our spirits: the once grand occupants of the ruins somehow failed and are gone. Makes one feel good. We are still here. Pride bubbles beautifully through our being. And pride is a terrible sin, a sin I know well."

"I have always thought of you as a humble hermit in the desert."

"You have been taken in by Renaissance rogue artists. They loved, as I said before, to depict me as an anchorite, a humble scholar living in a cave. Sometimes I'm a desiccated and half-nude old man pounding my chest with a rock. Sometimes I'm looking a bit better in a torn cardinal's robe and I share my cave with a few books and a tame lion. All partly true if a bit colorful. "Actually, I was born rich. I could afford to study with the greatest scholars and I did. I became one of the most learned Christians in the Empire, an Empire where Christianity was now the official religion. I was consumed with intellectual arrogance and pride. Then guilt ate at my soul. So I fled to the desert outside Antioch where for three years among scorpions and wild animals I fasted and prayed and fought off visions of dancing Roman maidens. But I also continued to study and was taught Hebrew by a learned monk who had converted from Judaism and finally I returned to the world."

"Is that when you went back to Rome?"

"I went to Constantinople first, that's where the Imperial power now ran the world. Then I went to Rome to serve the Pope as his secretary and librarian. Heady, heady! He was my patron and started me on what became the great project of my life: the translation of the Bible from corrupted Greek and better Hebrew into the Latin *Vul-*

gate, essentially the official Bible for more than 1500 years; not, you'll agree, a shabby run. Also, I was indeed the Pope's counselor, and, dare I say it even today, I thought I might be his successor. Me: Vicar of Christ! Pride and arrogance! It sweeps you to great heights and hurls you down. I have always had a sharp tongue. My success and my pride and arrogance in Rome made it sharper. I made many enemies among high churchmen whose main anxiety centered on their fancy clothes and noble ladies whom I characterized as painted voluptuaries. When the Pope died, those enemies made my presence in Rome untenable. I fled again to the East, to this holy land."

"To Jerusalem?"

"No, nearby to our Lord's birthplace in Bethlehem. I founded a monastery near the original Basilica of the Nativity. Later my blessed friend, Paula, and her daughter, Eustochium, followed me from Rome and founded a convent and a guest house. We lived very simply there, but I always remained in contact with the world. I carried on a wide correspondence, completed the *Vulgate* and many other works, continued my studies and always prayed. And from Bethlehem, I watched the Empire drown in sloth and folly. God, indeed, was angry."

"Forgive my 21st Century cynicism. Where did you get the money to do this?"

"Oh, I always had money. There was my inheritance. And Paula, who came from some of the best and oldest Roman families, was a rich widow."

"Money it seems always easies the way to piety."

"I quite disagree. Your cynicism, for which you definitely would be wise to seek absolution, is a protective palliative in a world that you believe is devoid of virtue. However, the truth is that comfort and riches do not make achievement of piety easier. On the contrary, piety is easier when you give up nothing because you have nothing to give up. However, having nothing material can indeed be a goad to acquiring much. And much comfort and riches tend over time to become powerful enablers of overt and covert sin often disguised as virtue. In effect, instruments of Satan, providing catalytic encouragement to our sinful hearts."

Adam raised his eyebrows. "In reality," he asked," with the usual obvious exceptions, how sinful would you say those hearts are on average?"

Jerome returned the facial expression. "Very," he said somberly. "They all are. Do not forget the condition of all men at birth since the time of your namesake. Five thousand years ago in Sumer, one of their great hero- gods explained much of the world's problems in three words: 'Man behaves badly.' Nothing has changed. St. Paul and my contemporary, Augustine of Hippo, are quite clear on this point."

"I'm not sure how much credence the bulk of mankind these days gives to the idea of original sin."

"Exactly. But that does not negate its reality. There is a deep central fault today in the mind of modern man: The comforting but totally fallacious and deadly philosophy that what one says makes it so. A fatal idea! At first there was indeed the Word, but the Word, as you might recall, was not Man."

"And, therefore..."

"All of us are born in sin. Some employ free will to seek virtue and salvation with the help of God's grace. Many give up. Some never try. God is always hopeful. But God is a realist. The world is always crowded with sin and evil. You will be close to both when you visit your clients."

"You think the Israeli Air Force is infected with sin and evil?"

"I think Israel is surrounded by great evil. The Muslims, the children of Ishmael, indiscriminately launch rockets into civilian homes and schools and hospitals. They strap bombs on their own sons and daughters and send them to blow up the innocent. They have made a specialty of beheading their own people and their prisoners. They brutalize and murder women. They lie, steal, and plunder. Their minds rot with hate and envy. They are Alaric and his horde come again to the gates of Rome."

"How does that make Israel sinful and evil?"

"Israel must muster all of its power and courage and virtue if it is to triumph and then survive. As its successes to date have shown, the attributes of power triumphant include pride and arrogance and eventually sloth. Those attributes, all instruments of the Devil, are great sins and, if unchecked by will and grace, virtue is destroyed and only death remains. Great Rome, Venice, the Hapsburgs, France, the British Empire, all succumbed; America staggers crazily but still struggles on. Surely you, an American warrior, recognize this danger. "

Adam started to speak, but Jerome interrupted him.

"Enough. It is time to go. The Franciscans are approaching for the first Mass."

Jerome rose and Adam began to hear deep chanting that echoed somewhere in the nave of the basilica. Jerome said: "Good luck on your mission in the desert. Do not be fooled by confidence among the Chosen People. They have been chosen many times and have often failed. But their Covenant still holds. And, more than many, they do understand much about sin and evil."

He raised his hand toward Adam and made a large cross in the air.

"Watch yourself. The Devil likes the world of comfort, but he adapts easily to the desert as well."

A long line of Franciscan friars in brown cassocks belted with white cords triple knotted to remind them always of poverty, chastity and obedience began to process two by two into the chapel. Each friar carried a long lighted candle. Adam watched fixedly as they filed into the choir seats. When he turned to make a comment to Jerome he found himself alone except for three early communicants in the far shadows: an elderly harridan with a large sack sitting down front; a smartly dressed young woman accompanied by a small boy in a blue school blazer sitting near the last row.

A single silver bell rang. The Franciscan celebrant, a heavy blonde man with a short beard, entered from the side led by a friar with a crucifix and a second friar swinging a smoking censer. The sweet smell of frankincense drifted through the chapel. Adam and his three fellow communicants stood along with the friars in the choir. The celebrant kissed the altar, took his position at the back of the sanctuary and began intoning in Jerome's native tongue: *In nominee Patris...et Fili...et Spiritus Sancti...*

An hour later, Adam was again on the Nablus Road, walking swiftly toward the American Colony Hotel. Back in his room, he showered, dressed for a day in the desert and went to the diningroom for a large buffet breakfast including an omelet and four non-kosher sausages. His military driver and an armed Israeli Air Force captain waited for him outside the front door in an armored Land Rover Defender emblazoned with a regimental marking that looked like an apotropaic eye.

The day was still mildly cool and clear as they headed on the highway into the Judean Desert. The highway ran east through tan sandy cliffs dotted here and there with the long black boxes that the Bedouins used for housing. On one cliff, two Bedouins and four camels stood out against the pale sky. At the Jericho turn, the armored-car would drive south past the Dead Sea scroll caves and the Ahava cosmetics factory to the ruins of Masada, then west into the Negev toward Beersheba.

"I've called ahead. sir, and told IAF that we will be running about 20 minutes late because of a minor incident on the Jericho road," the Captain said in perfect Oxbridge. "As you know, they've arranged a full day for you but they have room to adjust."

"Good, good," Adam said, breathed in the slowly warming desert air and wondered whether his full day included a meeting with the Devil in one form or another and, if so, would he recognize him.